Thirty, Flirty and FOREVER ALONE

OTHER BOOKS BY CHRISTINE RICCIO

Again, but Better

Better Together

Attached at the Hip

CHRISTINE RICCIO

This is a work of fiction. Names, characters, organizations, places, events, and incidents are either products of the author's imagination or are used fictitiously. Otherwise, any resemblance to actual persons, living or dead, is purely coincidental.

Published by Montlake, Seattle
www.apub.com

EU product safety contact:
Amazon Media EU S. à r.l.
38, avenue John F. Kennedy, L-1855 Luxembourg
amazonpublishing-gpsr@amazon.com

ISBN-13: 9781662532153 (paperback)
ISBN-13: 9781662532146 (digital)

Cover design by Caroline Johnson
Cover image: © Lilia_Ulizko, © Peter Dazeley / Shutterstock; © Leontura, © Heorhii Aryshtevych / Getty

Printed in the United States of America

For all the ladies out there post twenty-
nine, persistently braving the anxiety-ridden,
conversationally stunted dating-app minefield to
find their person. *blasts "Don't Stop Believin'"*

PROLOGUE

I was supposed to bring a date.

Maybe if I'd been able to wrangle one, this wouldn't be happening.

A date would have kept me calm and distracted.

Maybe I wouldn't have had to panic-pee four minutes before I was scheduled to speak in front of 150 people.

Maybe I wouldn't have been attempting to break some sort of speed-stripping record as I ripped the zipper down the side of this satin dress.

I'm wearing shapewear that goes up to my boobs, so using the restroom was no easy feat. It required unzipping, followed by a series of careful, painstaking, strategic spandex maneuvers.

I've now peed. I've reassembled the spandex. *But dear god, I can't get the dress back on.* Sweat beads along my brow as I tug at the silver sliver of metal dangling at my hip.

Sweet mother of Christ, move.

It doesn't budge. *I don't have time for this.* I didn't have time to pee. I absolutely do not have time for a wardrobe malfunction.

I squeeze my eyes shut and count to five before glancing down at my delicate silver watch. My aunt started her four-minute speech—four minutes ago.

I heave the zipper upward again with everything I've got. My sweaty fingers slip off the metal, and my knuckles slam right into my forehead. I stagger back a few steps. "Fucking fuck!"

I trudge up to the sink, livid. My champagne-colored dress hangs like an unwrapped flour tortilla draped around my torso as I bend to wash my hands, boobs swinging in the wind. I'm not even wearing a bra—it's built into the outfit.

I glare at myself in the mirror.

This is karma for checking the guest box on the invitation.

I knew it was risky, but I did it anyway because we sent out those invites six months ago. One of my staple goals has always been to be with *my person* by my thirtieth birthday, and I've been hurtling toward that landmark. Checking that guest box was manifesting! *If you visualize your goal and project what you're looking for hard enough out at the universe, it will come to be.*

I quite literally made this goal a part-time job. We're at the end of July. I've been on thirteen first dates and entangled in six approximately one-month-long relationships since January.

I'm losing faith in humanity.

I just want a healthy, loving, supportive relationship based on a foundation of shared passions, understanding, humor, open-mindedness, mutual respect, support, and trust! Apparently that's too much to ask!

I might as well have spent the last six months in a circle of candles with my eyes closed, holding a piece of paper with an in-depth description of my perfect person clamped between my teeth, hoping really hard he'd come to life.

My cousin paid for me to bring a *plus-one* to her wedding, and I failed to conjure even the semblance of a romantic relationship.

Hence, *karma*.

People who were happily coupled off early in life might not be aware of this, but there comes an age where, all of a sudden, it's socially unacceptable to come to a wedding alone. That age is me. It is now. It's twenty-nine.

The shift happens without warning, like waking up from a coma to find yourself in an abandoned hospital amid a zombie apocalypse. One wedding you're singing and dancing with a million single friends—the next wedding they've all evaporated. A love ballad is playing, and you're standing alone, on the edge of the dance floor, catatonically drifting backward, internally reliving each and every time a teacher instructed the class to find a partner and you were left the undesirable loner that had to either do the project alone or be assigned as a pity third-wheel member to a partnership of two people who clearly don't want anything to do with you.

I catch my exhausted gray eyes in the mirror, bright with panic amongst my smoky eye makeup. My hair's been curled and swept into a high pony on the crown of my head à la Whitney's orders. I look like a high school cheerleader from 2009 if she tripped and fell into a dark makeup palette. With a groan I chuck my hand towel in the trash, press the dress into place against my chest, and throw myself from the restroom.

A polite spattering of applause rises from the guests as I creep my way back to the rustic reception hall. Whitney picked this aesthetic, open, barnlike venue in Palm Springs, with a stunning view of the desert hills. I found it for her online back in December. They have a 40 percent–off discount during their offseason, hence this date in the dregs of summer. The ceremony kicked off after sunset so we wouldn't all die of heatstroke.

"And now"—the wedding singer booms into the mic—"we have some special words from our maid of honor, Rikki Romona!"

And that's my cue.

There's no actual spotlight that falls over my position at the back of the room, but the figurative one feels just as harrowing. One by one, family members twist in their seats to track my progress toward the microphone. I keep my head down as I power walk in the general direction of my seat, right palm pressed tight against my chest, and left forearm flush against my shoulder blades to hold up the broken dress.

I need to grab the notes I carefully curated onto ten different color-coded index cards for optimal reading efficiency before I jet over to the mic. My best friend, Jordyn, considerate goddess among mortals, is perched at the edge of her chair, palm outstretched, holding said cards out for me to snatch. Ten more steps. Five.

"Do you need help?" she squawks as I close in. Her amber eyes bug out of her olive skin as I drop the back flap of my dress to take the cards.

"Are you Rikki?" a man's voice lurches through the speakers. My head snaps up and the wedding singer snags eye contact. *Great,* he's speaking to me over the microphone, for the entire room to hear.

I drop him a curt nod as Jordyn begins to grapple at my side with the zipper, yanking me back and forth as she tries to force it closed.

"Can you come up?" the singer continues. "We're on a schedule here."

I almost snort. *We're on a schedule*—I made the schedule. "Yes, I'm Rikki! Give me two seconds!"

I glance at Jordyn. She's hunched over in her navy-blue dress, grumbling as she troubleshoots, jerking up and down, left and right.

People are watching.

Everyone's watching. I can hear myself breathing.

Sixteen excruciatingly silent seconds pass before Jordyn's husband, Micah, hops up from the table to join us.

I cringe, tilting my face to the ceiling.

Hey, Universe, apparently we got off on the wrong foot with the whole manifesting a life-partner thing, but if you could let us get this zipper up so I can do my speech without flashing my family, I'd super-duper appreciate it.

"Rick, take a deep breath. You're sweating bullets," Jordyn whispers.

"The maid of honor's zipper appears to be stuck!" the singer belts into the mic.

Gasps erupt around the room.

Does this really warrant gasps?

"There have been two people working on her for the past three minutes, and they still haven't cracked it!" he continues.

"Did you try pulling it down and then pulling it up?" says a random two tables over.

"You gotta hold the top fabric closed with two hands!"

"Why is she naked underneath?"

"Is this real life, or am I having a very vivid nightmare?" I sing-talk through a pained smile.

"This thing is welded down," Micah laments.

"Okay," the singer announces. "We're gonna improv here and bring up the best man! Matt Highsmith. And we'll circle back to you, Rikki!"

"Cool!" I throw two encouraging thumbs up. Across the dance floor, Glenn's best man makes his way to the mic.

Purple movement grabs my attention a few tables up. My mother. She stands and hustles toward me in her whimsical lavender gown, hunched forward like that'll make her invisible to the naked eye. She's quickly followed by my Aunt Teresa. And they're both followed by my mother's partner, Layla.

"Honey! What happened!" my mother yelps as she joins our sad, sweaty huddle.

"I don't know, it zipped earlier."

"What happened to your face?" My posse steps aside as she reaches for my zipper.

"Nothing's wrong with my face," I whisper as she begins to fight with my dress. "We need to be quiet—the best man is talking."

"There's a big red mark right in the middle of your forehead." She laughs, bunny hopping in place to coerce the zipper into movement.

"Rikki, Whitney told me you were bringing a date?" My aunt has replaced my mother. I emit a sad, noncommittal noise of agreement as she tugs me to the right. "You've been out with so many guys this year. It's hard to believe now that you refused to even speak to the male species till the age of sixteen."

Or, Universe, if it's easier for you to just teleport me the hell out of here, that would be grand.

My aunt yields the zipper to my mom's girlfriend, Layla. And Layla proceeds to cede the duty to Cousin Fran. Fran steps aside for our Uncle Bob to try. And Uncle Bob relinquishes the task to Fran's boyfriend, Buck, who "works out." Buck, in a flustered state of failure, cedes control to Fran's seven-year-old, who comes over whining that she, quote, "wants to play."

A crowd—no, a line—has literally formed.

Throughout the entirety of the best man's eight-minute speech, a rotating group of my relatives—and then strangers—arrive at my (naked) side to test their strength. Like my zipper is the goddamn sword stuck in the fucking stone.

1 | BAGGAGE

My longest relationship only lasted five months. Does that count? Can I say I've been in a long-term relationship? I've *almost* been in a long-term relationship.

When I was in that short long-term relationship, I had a clear vision of my future, of our future *together*. I could see a path with clear milestones I wanted to walk.

Now single, feat. my unstable gaping black hole of a love life, when I try to picture myself in five years—I can't. My future's woefully out of focus. An indistinguishable blob of maybes and what-ifs. Trying to visualize it in my mind's eye is akin to shaking one of those stupid magic eight balls and seeing the words *Try Again Later* float to the surface every fucking time.

My future never used to be a blur. I'm a planner. I've always had hard-set goals ahead, grounding me in purpose. Guiding my choices. Each one a stepping stone en route to a successful life. I'm ambitious, resourceful, and pretty feisty. I've yet to come up short on one of those babies. Until today, obviously. I missed my love deadline.

The lack of control I have over this facet of life is infuriating. When is the universe going to meet me halfway? I don't think anyone's ever been this persistent on Hinge for such an extensive length of time. Six straight months? They should give awards for that.

My various jobs have cumulatively proven to repel men.

Each of the six, one-month relationship-ish things I dove headfirst into this year—crashed and burned once I started opening up about what I do. Don't ask me how many times I've been ghosted in a Hinge chat after sharing that I write the relationship column for *The New York Minute*.

(Eleven. Eleven times.)

The fact that I write under a pseudonym doesn't seem to move the needle on the lack of enthusiasm. No one wants to date the woman publicly dissecting her romantic endeavors for the second-largest paper on the Eastern Seaboard.

Also, I'm cursed.

My name, Rikki, is old Norse for "forever alone."

I'm not kidding.

Richard and Kelli didn't bother doing research on the atrocity they were concocting between their two names. *Rikki.* They thought they were being cute, smashing their consonants together.

I discovered the meaning via the internet for a school project in second grade.

Not a fun day. When I presented it to the class, my then-crush yelled out *finally something accurate*, and I had to excuse myself so I could go to the bathroom and cry.

So began the Rikki curse. And so it continues today.

Recent highlights include:

(a) Ted, the aforementioned five monther. He works in my officc, so I still have to see his face regularly.

(b) Sal, a firefighter I dated back in February. He was suddenly "needed for a fire" on our way to the restaurant for our fifth date. He dropped me back at my apartment, and I never heard from him again.

(c) Neil, the hot scientist I was banking on bringing to Whitney's wedding. Post date five, he was poached by the government for a classified project and relocated to DC.

I could keep going. The Rikki curse is ever present and relishes the number five.

"What part are you at?"

I blink away from the darkness outside my window.

"Huh?" I turn to Jordyn. Her makeup still looks great. It's 1:30 a.m. I have to get the name of her primer. My "smoky eyes" have smeared up my forehead via careless, stress-induced face touching. I jolted at my reflection in the plane bathroom mirror twenty minutes ago. I look like the Pattinson Batman when he takes off the mask.

"Where are you in *Heir of Fire*?" Jordyn clarifies. We host a biweekly witch-themed book club. As always, Jordyn's ahead of me in the reading.

I glance down at the large green book on my drop-down table. "I finally got to the part with the witches, but they were such assholes, I put it down."

We've been reading *Throne of Glass*. One of our four members insisted there were witches in this series, despite there being no mention of them in the book-one synopsis. We're a *witch-book* book club, and we've spent our last two meetings chatting about *assassins* and *fae*. It's been a very off-brand summer.

"Keep going! I have things I need to chat about."

I flick the book. It hurts my nail. "I'm kind of too bummed out to read."

Jordyn sighs. "Rikki, no one noticed you didn't have a plus-one. They were too busy laughing about your dress." The bride had to stand next to me, physically holding it closed while I delivered my six-minute toast.

"Jordyn. I was wandering the perimeter of the room, like the ghost of dead spinsters past, during every slow song."

Jordyn laughs. "Yeah, well, we were dancing, so we didn't notice. And now you get to find a way to write about it. Your angst won't go to waste."

I roll my eyes. That room was full of family. They all know what I do for a living. They all noticed, and they all asked. Jordyn repositions herself to see me better, and I catch a quick glimpse of Micah snoring in the aisle seat on her left.

"Rick, you organized a gorgeous wedding. Your cousin was on cloud nine. I know today was hard, but it's done. You killed it. Tomorrow will be better. You don't have to play wedding planner. You're not the maid of honor. You won't have to juggle family. You can let go—celebrate your birthday! Celebrate freedom from Whitney's weaponized incompetence! It's gonna be fun."

We have another wedding tomorrow. On the East Coast. Another wedding where I checked yes on the plus-one card (I *know*).

I twist toward the window, closing my eyes as the sluggish tug of failure saturates my bloodstream.

The soulmate search takes up so much mental capital. Looking for the one is a contrarian mission. It requires an almost-comical level of optimism packed snug and warm under an equally thick blanket of cynicism. That's the only way you make it through the slew of duds, dickheads, and misfires you encounter along the way.

Give everyone the benefit of the doubt, but laugh it off when they let you down.

Trust no one, but keep looking for someone to trust.

Take everything with a grain of salt, but keep taking it.

Everyone's an asshole, but eventually someone won't be!

◆ ◆ ◆

Six hours later, my luggage and I push into my new box-laden one-bedroom apartment.

I invested in new bags before this trip because my second round of Marshalls discount luggage self-destructed during my last flight. A-plus decision on my part because it made spotting my shit at baggage claim a breeze. I can't help grinning as I lower it to the floor to unpack. It's one of those Away bags everyone raves about. A *limited edition* turquoise-green Sunrise Away bag the exact color of the default WordArt gradient I used to use in school back in the early 2000s.

Between the ages of nine and eleven, I spent an extensive amount of time typing up "articles" reporting on the "relationship" drama going on in my classes, using Microsoft Word. I printed them out with big WordArt headlines, slid them into plastic paper protectors, and stored them in a neon-green three-ring binder. A three-ring binder I proudly carried everywhere, touting to anyone who'd listen that it contained my "work samples." When I look at this bag, I think of that ambitious nine-year-old girlie, and it makes me happy.

My brow furrows as I flop the suitcase open. My curling iron isn't in the zipper compartment. My meticulously curated neon-green packing cubes are nowhere to be found. My retainer is not in the little pouch I so carefully stashed on the left-hand side.

This bag is full of someone else's shit.

The Sunday Minute

LOVE TODAY

HOW MANY DATES DOES IT TAKE TO FALL IN LOVE?

By Rose Thyme

You'd be surprised how often this question comes up: How many dates *should it take* to fall in love? I wish there was a straight-up answer. Guidelines would make the wildly abstract concept of love feel way less intimidating. We love an instruction manual in this house. But according to my vast, extensive polling research with readers across the country, one cannot exactly *math* love. It's nuanced and elusive, and every couple is unique. The responses I got spanned from first sight to five years into a friendship.

But.

While we can't scientifically organize our fall into love, *we can* objectively construct and utilize a set of dating rules for ourselves in the effort to lessen the unbearable *Is this going anywhere?* anxiety that perpetually plagues our weary single souls.

We can mark milestones that can help us decide if a relationship has the potential to lead anywhere long term.

If you're a regular here, you know, I jumped headfirst into the dating world this year. One month into that adventure, I implemented a foolproof rule that I now live and breathe by: *The Phoebe Decree*.

Did I make it up? Yes. Does it hold water? Also yes.

What does it mean? It's a flashy name for *five dates*. If things are going well-ish with a love prospect, I give said person and myself up to five dates. If we aren't mutually wanting to be exclusive by date five—*we're done*. If we've spent *five dates* worth of time together, and that person doesn't like me enough to commit to exclusivity—we're looking for different things.

What exactly constitutes a date, you ask? In this context, the meaning's a little amorphous. It might make sense to think of *the Phoebe Decree* in terms of encounters so we can avoid any confusion.

Five encounters. If an encounter with your prospect lasts more than twenty minutes—it's viable. If you've spent five full encounters worth of time with this person, and you don't like them enough to commit to exclusivity—if monogamous love is what you're looking for—that person doesn't have the physical or emotional capability of providing it for you. You're setting yourself up for disappointment, and you deserve better.

FIRST ENCOUNTER

2 | BABE'S WEDDING

Coming as Rapunzel was an error.

I counted five other Rapunzels from my aisle seat in the eighth row during the ceremony. They were all accompanied by Flynns (Rapunzel's sexy, scruffy love interest). I should have picked a costume that doesn't involve a love interest. The dragon from *Mulan*. Or a mop from that creepy old Disney movie with no words.

Babe Lozenge, neighbor, book club member, and friend, is now officially married to her partner, Willem. Her wedding is Disney themed, hence my Rapunzel getup. Every guest was required to come as a Disney character. I'm wearing a billowy long-sleeve sheer blouse under a satin, lavender corset with a full purple skirt, and I have a tiny stuffed iguana hot glued to my shoulder. I had an atrociously long blond wig, but it was giving me a headache before I even left the house, so I threw on a pink and purple flower crown and called it a day.

It's incredibly cute in here. Each table in the reception hall is themed after a different Disney movie, complete with props and a wide array of colorful flowers to complement each film's color palette. Fan art pieces from Disney classics sit on easels lining the ballroom walls, alongside an assortment of photos of Babe and her new husband.

The bride is breathtaking, clad in a gold princess gown. Her hair is done up, and her dark skin is glowing in the amber light. Her husband's wearing long elaborate blue lapels with gold buttons. Everyone has gathered around the perimeter of the hardwood floor at the front of the ballroom to watch their first dance.

Everyone except me.

I've retreated to the shadows like the villain in a teen movie. I'm leaning against the chilly mirror-paneled walls, nursing a gin and tonic.

To recap: It's (practically) my birthday, I lost my luggage, and I'm alone at a Disney-themed wedding, dressed as Rapunzel with an empty seat next to mine at the Aladdin table for my second consecutive nonexistent plus-one.

Babe and her Prince Charming are floating across the floor to an instrumental from the classic Disney cartoon we've all been subjected to at one time or another: *Beauty and the Beast*. I could never get into that one. The Beast *kidnaps* Belle's dad. Then he kidnaps Belle, and then she *falls in love with him*.

"I've never understood the love for *Beauty and the Beast*."

I startle—some of my barely touched drink sloshes over onto my hand as I whip my head to the right. There's a Flynn standing next to me. Why is someone's attractive husband standing so close to my elbow?

"How long have you been here?" I blurt.

"Long enough to catch you eye judging their first dance." He's a broad-chested, pale, Scottish-looking guy, probably in his early thirties, with a face full of sharp angles and thick, wavy, deep red-brown hair buzzed into a sort of military-esque cut: shaved on the sides and longer on the top.

"I was not 'eye judging' their first dance."

His lips tug up. "Okay."

"I wasn't," I insist.

"All right." He raises an open palm in surrender. "Long day?" He leans against the mirror next to me, clutching a whiskey, looking out at the bride and groom.

"Who are you?"

"Who am I?" he repeats, glancing down at his Flynn costume in amusement.

"Not your costume."

He meets my eyes for a hot second. His are a bright turquoise blue. Scary blue. Sharp like his features. They match his Flynn vest. I wonder if that's why his wife chose this costume.

"How do you know the bride and groom?" I ask.

"I went to high school with the groom," he explains. "We were two of only five dudes in the drama club. That bonds you for life." His warm tone completely contradicts the intensity of his face—it's like witnessing the statue of a war hero come to life and do stand-up. The guy's a living, breathing oxymoron.

I smile into my glass. "I didn't know Willem was a theater kid. Babe was a theater gal, so this is all making sense."

"So you know Babe," he confirms confidently.

I nod. "We met a few years back. Babe is in, my, uh, book club."

His eyes flash. "A book club, eh? What kind of books you read?"

Over on the dance floor Willem is twirling Babe. He catches her in a dramatic dip. The crowd applauds as their first dance ends. The music immediately shifts into a punk rock cover of "Be Our Guest." Inventive.

"Who do you belong to?" I gesture toward the crowd with my drink.

Flynn snorts, a boyish grin cracking his statuesque face. "What do you mean by that?" It's fascinating how much his aura shifts as he speaks. He's so animated.

"I mean, there's a million Rapunzels out there. Which one is yours?"

Flynn shakes his head like he's sharing an inside joke with himself. "I don't have one. I came alone."

My eyes cut back to his. "You came to a wedding alone?"

He nods.

"Dressed as Flynn?" I ask skeptically.

"Borrowed it from Willem."

"Hmm." Babe does have a Rapunzel getup. I squint at him. "People don't come to weddings alone."

"Are you here with someone?"

I glance out at everyone dancing. "No. But I planned to bring a date. Filled in the plus-one card, the whole enchilada."

"The whole enchilada, huh," he says, pale-red brows dancing across his forehead. "What happened?"

I take a hefty swig of gin and tonic. "I couldn't find someone worthy of bringing."

"Ah, the lady has standards." He sips his whiskey. Out on the floor the wedding guests link hands, cheering and skipping in a circle around the married couple.

"So who are you?" I prod suspiciously.

"I'm Reed."

"What do you do, Reed?"

"I write."

My lips press into a line. "Your name is Reed, and you write."

"Unfortunately. Among other things."

"Books?" I ask.

"I have, yeah."

"Mystery, thriller, historical, dark academia, literary fiction, horror, romance, sci-fi, self-help, or fantasy?"

"Wow, you know *all* the categories," he says dryly.

I look at him sidelong. "Which is it, Flynn?"

"It's Reed."

"Is that a pen name?"

"What's your name?" he asks instead.

"Are you single?" I ask.

"Yes," he says plainly. "I think we've established we're both single."

I snort, staring out at the floor as I process this.

This man can't be single. It goes against the laws of singleness. There are usually approximately zero to two single people of the opposite sex at a wedding. They are creepy, drunk, very young, or a combination of the three. They're not handsome. Or quick witted. Or cute. Or age appropriate.

"Why are you single?" I ask.

"Why are you?"

"I'm a lot," I tell him.

"I'm also a lot."

"I'm cursed."

"You're cursed?" he repeats dubiously.

"My name is Nordic for 'forever alone.'"

A hearty laugh falls out of this sharp redheaded war-hero statue man. "What is it?"

"And dating is terrible," I add.

He arcs a brow. "Dating is fun."

I scoff, rotating, to lean my shoulder against the mirror so I can study him straight on. This man's only a hair taller than me in my heels. Maybe five foot ten. The white shirt he's wearing under Flynn's classic blue vest is pulled taut over his shoulders. He turns to mimic my posture and hits me with the full force of his topaz-blue eyes.

My heart does an involuntary 360 twist in my chest.

Shit. They're like laser beams. My arms fold protectively across my torso. "Reed, dating is the most stressful thing on my to-do list."

His mouth twists up the side of his cheek. "Then I don't think you're doing it right."

I cock my head. "I'm sorry, are you about to mansplain dating?"

He laughs, folding his arms. They're shapely arms. I mean . . . chiseled. Hot. He has hot arms. "What's your name?" he asks again.

I find that the more shapely/hot/chiseled a guy is, the harder it is to trust anything he says. This has only been cemented by my months of intensive dating-app escapades.

"It's Rikki. My name."

"Rikki, are you not having fun right now?"

I quirk a brow. "Reed, this isn't a date."

"So that's a yes?"

"It's not a no."

He takes another sip of whiskey. "This conversation is getting weirder by the second."

"All right, folks." We snap to attention as the Disney DJ comes over the speakers. "First course is about to be served! If guests could all head to their tables, that would be fantastic." The upbeat show tune playing morphs into a calm instrumental as the masses disperse from the dance floor.

I take a step toward my seat. "I'm this way."

"All right." Reed grins, heading in the opposite direction.

I turn and collide directly into an adorably dressed Jordyn. She and Micah came as the Boy Scout and dog from *Up*. She loops her arm through mine, clutching my elbow as we make our way to the table. "Who was that?"

"An attractive guy who *claims* he's single." I carefully reposition my party favor before taking a seat. We've all been gifted a yellow hoodie that says *We Made It to Happily Ever After* in a circle of multicolored Mickey outlines and *Babe & Willem Forever* on the back in Disney font.

Jordyn laughs. "Why do you say it like that?"

A waiter skillfully swoops over our heads, placing plates of Caesar salad before us. "Because he's too idyllic to be real."

"What's too idyllic to be real?" Micah says as he plops down next to Jordyn with drinks.

"I don't think you're using *idyllic* correctly," Jordyn interjects.

"A guy dressed as Flynn just, kind of, hit on me."

"Flynn, the love interest from *Tangled*?" Micah asks.

"That's the one."

"Dang, there's like seven of them floating around here," Micah comments as he stuffs a forkful of salad into his mouth.

"Rikki," Jordyn says dramatically. "It's the *Disney gods*! They're blessing you on your thirtieth birthday."

I stab a crouton.

"Do you want us to run interference?" Micah offers. "Which one is he?"

"Which one is who?" a voice says behind me. My neck snaps around as Reed pulls out the empty chair next to me and sits in it.

I blink at him.

We're all silent for a moment. Micah's brown eyes dart from me to Reed. After a beat Jordyn sticks her hand across my plate.

Reed takes it.

"I don't believe we've met," she says. "I'm Rikki's best friend, Jordyn." She flicks one of her fake dog ears away from her face. "And this is my husband, Micah." She gestures to Micah, who's casually sitting in his Boy Scout costume with a bouquet of balloons next to his chair.

"*Up.*" Reed nods approvingly as he shakes Jordyn's hand and reaches to shake Micah's. "Love it. I'm Reed, Rikki's wedding date."

3 | MAKESHIFT DATE

"Oh wow." Jordyn beams, not even attempting to conceal her amusement. "When did you two meet?"

"Today." Reed smiles broadly. "We hit it off."

"What's happening," I mumble.

"Do you have a job?" Micah asks across the table in the most nonthreatening, happy-go-lucky voice of all time.

Reed nods. "I do."

"Are you in the military?" Jordyn asks.

He chuckles. "I'm not."

"Where are you from?" Micah asks.

"Secaucus! Went to high school with Willem."

"Ah, a Jersey boy, how cute," Jordyn coos. "Micah's a Jersey guy."

"Really, where from?" Reed asks eagerly.

"Point Pleasant!" Micah smiles.

My lips have shrunk into a ball. What do I do with this? Also, what is his job? Stay on task, Micah.

"Ah nice! Jersey Mike's!" Reed cheers.

"Hell yeah, Jersey Mike's!" Micah cheers back.

"So what do you do, Reed?" Jordyn asks. *Thank you, Jordyn.*

"Among other things, I run a podcast production company with my brother."

Color me intrigued.

Jordyn's brows fly up. "Podcasts, huh? Interesting."

"Name some that you produce," Micah prompts.

Reed's mouth twitches with amusement. "Have you heard of *Attached at the Hip*?"

I've heard of that. I quickly chew the heap of Caesar salad I just stuffed into my mouth. That's the new reality show that's like *Survivor* meets dating. It's on my to-watch list. Jordyn's been—

Jordyn slams a hand down on the table, rattling our plates. "*Yes!* I'm obsessed with it! I can't wait for season two!"

He nods. "Yeah, we produce the official weekly deep-dive recap podcast. They're casting the second season right now."

"You produce the official *AATH* pod with Jamie and Dawn?" she screeches.

"Dude, we listen to that podcast." Micah smiles. "It's hilarious. Rikki, you gotta watch that show."

I stab another crouton. So he's a writer of books (maybe, no proof yet) and runs what might be a successful podcast production company. He sounds pretty employed (30 percent of the men I come across on Hinge are "funemployed").

"You know what Rikki does, right?" Jordyn prods.

I shake my head. "Oh, let's not—"

"No, actually, we hadn't gotten there yet," Reed clarifies.

"She's a columnist," Micah volunteers. "For *The New York Minute*!"

Reed's faint brows rise as his attention slides back to me. "*The New York Minute*? Damn."

"She's the columnist for Love Today at *The New York Minute*!" Jordyn corrects.

"Jordyn." I shoot her a death glare.

Micah nods. "She used to be a staff book reviewer, but she was promoted last year—"

"Okay! That's enough," I warn.

"*And* she's an LMFT," Jordyn continues, completely ignoring me.

Fear gurgles up my throat like acid reflux. "Seriously?"

"And"—Micah keeps talking—"she runs a greeting card shop on Etsy—"

"Micah!" I nervously glance over at Reed.

I'm surprised to find him happily soaking this all in like none of it has horrified him. He's grinning like pretending to be my wedding date is his new favorite pastime. Maybe he doesn't know what LMFT stands for. I find it's never great to lead with "Hi, I'm Rikki, licensed relationship therapist" either.

"And she runs our biweekly book club: Which Witch United!"

"Jordyn," I protest. *"Please."* Dear god.

"Plusshecohosts*TheMinute*'s*LoveToday*podcast—" She spits the words at light speed just as the DJ's voice comes over the mic.

"All right, crew!" he booms. "Time to get things moving again! Come out onto the dance floor for this one if you know it."

"And that's my cue." I stand and push back my chair, itching to escape this info dump about my life as soon as humanly possible. I shoot Reed an apologetic look. "I think I'm gonna take a lap—"

The opening beat of "I Just Can't Wait to Be King" blares from the speakers, cutting me off. Jordyn gasps (she loves this song) and lunges for the dance floor. Micah's fork clangs onto his plate as he follows her out. The strangers at our table abandon ship as well, scurrying away to scream-sing with the mob of guests converging around the DJ.

A lot of Babe's friends are Disney enthusiasts.

Reed's eyes slide up to mine. "I like your friends."

I suck in a slow breath and nod. "They're more like family. Jordyn and I grew up together, went to college together. We've been inseparable since kindergarten."

"Wow, and Micah?"

"Yeah, he came out of the woodwork during our senior year of college. He's pretty great too."

He tips his head in the direction I was about to flee. "You want to take that lap?"

A healthy dose of skepticism snakes through me as I trail Reed to the edge of the gilded event room. I guess he's still interested post job reveal. *Brave.*

The dance floor's in full swing. Lights soar across the hardwood. A spotlight floats around, landing periodically in a bright circle around the bride, and a disco ball sends scattered diamonds over the guests. The rest of the room is fairly dark. Small candles scatter the tables, and tiny colored bulbs sit in sconces along the walls.

I like it. The darkness offers the illusion of privacy.

The two of us come to a stop next to the closed double doors that lead back out to the lobby of this New Jersey country club.

Reed's expression renders back to serious handsome-man war-hero chic as he juts out the crook of his elbow. "A promenade?"

Wow, he knows the word *promenade*. I cut him an amused look and slip my arm through his.

"You're confident," I say flatly as we start toward the back of the room. This man just sat his ass down at our table and pronounced himself my date.

"I think you like it," he says immediately.

A grin snaps onto my face.

"So you write the Love Today column for *The New York Minute*?" he asks. "And you started there as a book critic, and you're a therapist?"

Damn, he does know what LMFT means.

I cut my eyes to his. "So you're a podcast producer and an author?"

He dips his head to the right. "I haven't published a book in seven years, so it's a loose interpretation of the word *author*."

The statement isn't funny, but the irreverent way he delivers it is. "Why haven't you published a book in seven years?"

Reed purses his lips. "So you write the Love Today column for *The New York Minute*?"

I shoot him a delighted grin. I've recently encountered way too many dudes who can barely hold a conversation, let alone play in one. "That Love Today stuff is top secret info, Reed. My friends were not authorized to release that data, and later I will have to kill them."

He laughs. It's a hearty rumble that sends warmth skidding across my collarbone.

I smile harder. "I write under a pen name for a reason—no one wants to date the girl who does the Love Today column. The *Love Today* podcast is a totally different beast. We bring on people in various relationship situations and interview them about *their* story, but the column can get personal. So . . ." I throw my hand up and let it fall.

"So, am I gonna read about this evening in the Sunday paper?"

"*Pffi*, you don't get the fucking paper."

The edge of his mouth lifts. "No, Rikki, but I do have the internet."

I huff a nervous laugh. "No, Reed, I don't post journal entries of my personal life as weekly column pieces in *The Minute*. But—"

"But—" he repeats enthusiastically.

Another laugh huffs out of me. "Every so often my personal life will inspire a piece, and then sometimes bits of my life become vaguely public, but only in the surface-level sense. No one gets named. It's all shrouded in mystery and—" I glance over to gauge his reaction. "Am I freaking you out? You don't have to worry, I'm not going to write about this"—I do air quotes—"*date* in my column this week."

Another hearty rumble from his chest. "You're not freaking me out. I'm an"—he throws up air quotes—"*author*."

My head kicks forward in a laugh.

"I know how writing works," he continues. "Your life slips into your work. It's why your work *works*. It's why writing works. It's part of the job. It's amazing that you have a weekly column for *The Minute*."

Wow. That's a new reaction.

I'm beaming like he's presented me with a Pulitzer. I attempt to recalibrate my face. "Well, don't tell anyone, Reed."

"If word gets out, you have full permission to murder me."

Damnit, I'm beaming again. "No one's ever given me that before."

"Please don't use it."

Laughter fizzles out of me as we reach the back of the hall. There's a long table against the wall, covered in wedding doodads, a guest book, and more framed pictures of the happy couple over the years. A large Mickey-shaped poster of their engagement photo in front of the Buzz Lightyear ride in Orlando sits on an easel, along with various colored markers for us to sign it with.

Reed picks up a black Sharpie to scribble his name and a congratulations note. "So how did you end up at *The Minute*? How did you find yourself as a staff critic for Books Today? They do so much for new authors! They're a big reason why my first novel did so well. Their pull quote is printed on the cover."

"Oh shit!" I lean forward to pen my own congratulations note. "That's amazing. You gonna tell me what it's called?"

"Mmm, not yet," he says behind me.

Curiosity pounds against my chest. "Wow, really giving me nothing here, Reed." I replace the marker on the easel.

He offers me his elbow again. "I'm not quite ready to be judged based on my novel, by a once-professional book critic."

I scoff, sliding my arm back through his. "I am *not* going to *judge you*. I love books! I took that job because I love shining a light on amazing stories and helping them find an audience. Not shitting on things. You said your book got a great review."

"Tell me how you got started there." He tugs me back into a slow stroll.

"I got an internship during college. They took a chance on me as a staff critic for a YA book, liked my review, and things unfolded from there."

"What book was it, the first review?"

I slit my eyes at him. "I'm not fucking telling until you stop being so dodgy."

His lip quirks up. "What can I say, Rikki? I have trust issues."

"Join the club."

"Is Which Witch United taking new members?"

A laugh explodes out of me. "You wouldn't want to join Which Witch United. It's a coven book club. We only read books about witches."

"Only books about smart, powerful, innovative, cutthroat women? You're right, who would want to be a part of that?"

I suck in a disjointed breath, blinking at him. *Who is this man?* "We make everyone come in witch slash wizard attire," I say as coolly as I can manage in this moment of overwhelming lust for Reed the pro-witch book club air quotes author.

He raises his brows. "Like witch hats?"

"I wear a black corset, skirt, and an old-fashioned red riding cape, and we put the book we're reading in the center of our circle in a cute little cauldron. It's a whole over-the-top campy event. Jordyn and I host it every other Sunday. It's my favorite."

He stops walking to stare at me for a moment before closing his eyes and nodding twice. "That's incredible. Seriously, do I have to audition? Is there a link somewhere?"

A blush burns up my neck as we restart forward, curling around the back-left corner of the hall. "I'll mail you a QR code."

"I look forward to it." He gives my elbow a squeeze via the crook of his own, and it sends a gush of heat up my arm.

This guy is too good to be true.

What's going to happen when I google him? He's probably a murderer. Or a robber. Or a con artist. Or like a fish that got changed into a human for a day but will revert back at midnight.

The assortment of easels with fan art from famous Disney scenes are scattered along this wall leading back up toward the dance floor. We move even slower now, weaving among the frames.

"So," Reed continues, "how did you go from Books Today to Love Today? And how are you also a therapist?"

I shake my head. "Nope. Your turn to share your life, mystery boy. How'd you get into podcast producing?"

I watch the decision to concede trickle through his features—his gaze softens and his lips follow, settling into a small close-mouthed grin. "Well, I listened to a bunch of baseball podcasts back in high school and loved the community feel of it. Then, freshman year of college, my brother and I started our own podcast, *Books & Baseball*."

Amusement dances through me. "Not a classic combo."

He chuckles. "Yep. It was super niche, but we launched it back in like 2010."

"And how did it turn into a production company?"

"Well, we put out a tight, thoughtful show. My brother majored in audio engineering, so we had great sound quality. We started going to podcast conferences on our college breaks, met a lot of people in that world, and started getting requests to edit other shows, help friends start their own podcasts . . . We eventually decided it'd probably be a good idea to turn it into an official business. So we opened our LLC. It snowballed from there. Now we have an indie podcasting company with five other editors on board and a social team. We produce twenty-five podcasts."

"Dang, congratulations, that's a huge accomplishment." I reach over and lightly squeeze his forearm. It's muscly. Ropy. I tamp an urge to lift it up and inspect it.

"Can you really call the company that makes the *Attached at the Hip* official podcast indie? I feel like you've gone mainstream."

He tilts his head left and right, weighing his response. "We were hipster underdogs for so long. We only got that gig because I know the *Attached at the Hip* host, and she brought us in."

"You know the host?"

"We were in an improv group together back in the day."

I blink at him, aghast. "You did improv?"

He smiles. "Drama kid, remember?"

"Damn, slipped my mind between author and producer. You do a lot of different things." I glance at him sidelong.

"And you *also* run an Etsy shop?" Reed continues.

"Did you take notes when Jordyn and Micah were spewing my life story?"

A goofy smile splits his face as he taps his head with his index finger. "Always taking notes up here."

We stop for a moment to appreciate a framed stained-glass-style piece of Cinderella and her fairy godmother as we pass its easel.

"So, what do you make?" Reed asks, peering at me curiously.

"Nothing like this." I gesture to the art around the room, because I can tell his mind is wandering in that direction. "I'm not an artist. I make silly personalized greeting cards."

"People still use those?" he asks, sounding genuinely surprised.

"Yes!" I skip forward a step, dragging him along as my enthusiasm gets the better of me. "Mostly couples place orders for birthdays or anniversaries. I do these silly doodles of things like inside jokes or scenes from a moment in their lives, and I'll write jokes or funny poems for them if they request it. They give me some information about what they want, and I make it into a greeting card."

Reed presses his lips together as we mosey our way through the shadows on the outskirts of the dance floor.

"I know it's kinda random," I continue quickly. "But doodling's my anti-anxiety, and I love knowing I helped someone tell another person they love them."

He turns to meet my eyes. "That's ridiculously sweet. You . . ."

He trails off, staring at me. "You're really fucking cool." *The hot man thinks my greeting card doodles make me* cool*?*

A tingling sensation dusts over my skin, stalling my ability to respond. *Giddiness.* I'm *giddy*. Shit. I reach into the mental void for my blanket of cynicism. Cynics are refined, sexy. They don't internally explode into giddy pieces when people they're attracted to pay them a compliment. They feed on the praise, absorbing it into their life force like a power-up in a video game. *Keep calm and sexy on.* "You smell really fucking good," I offer in return. He laughs like I'm joking. But he smells like a freshly sanded cedar bookshelf sitting under the sun at the beach. We're almost back around to where we started this walk. I'm not ready for this semiprivate microcosm of a date to end.

Along the final wall we're tracing is a door. I stop outside it, bringing Reed to a halt beside me. We're directly behind the DJ's setup, on a thick strip of deep-blue carpet that runs parallel to the dance floor. I drop a hand to the knob and twist, glancing up at him in question. "Shall we?"

"Be my guest."

4 | OUTLAWS

We are most definitely not allowed to be in here.

This room is a fire hazard. Candelabras: antique, elaborate, *Beauty and the Beast*–esque *candelabras* litter the floor. Every candle is lit, and a variety of lavish red sofas have been artfully arranged among the fixtures.

"Wow." Reed whistles. A caterer looks up as she sets a bowl on a table twenty feet away.

I cringe, braced for a scolding. But a moment later, she skitters wordlessly from the room through a silver door on the far wall.

I unclench. We're in a dessert area. The offerings are being arranged in an artful arch, framing an elaborate chocolate fountain in the heart of the space. Curtains of milk chocolate waterfall aesthetically through four different tiers. All the fixings for fondue are lined up on a long curved table along the wall: cellophane-covered bowls of strawberries, chopped bananas, blueberries, raspberries, sliced kiwi, balled watermelon, pretzels, and marshmallows.

Another caterer comes in. I freeze again, but they just set down a plate of cookies and zip back out.

Two much grander doors sit at the center of the wall we entered from. Those will presumably be opened to the guests later.

I follow behind Reed as he pulls two thin wooden skewers from a bucket on the fondue table. He hands one to me. "You allergic to any fruit?"

"No, but Reed, I don't think we're allowed—"

I stop breathing as the first caterer walks in with a tub of ice cream. She sets it down without making eye contact and whooshes out.

Reed takes my hand and places a skewer in it. "Live a little, Rikki."

A contentious huff slips out of me. "Live a little?" I point the skewer in his direction. "I'm the one who snuck us in here. I am living."

"You opened a door, and we walked through. If that's sneaking, I sneak everywhere, all the time."

Laughter buzzes from my throat as he removes the cellophane from the strawberries. I wander over next to him. "Time to tell me why you haven't written something in seven years."

He skewers a strawberry. "I've been preoccupied with other projects."

I stab my own strawberry. "Dig a little deeper for me, Reed."

Reed chuckles, closing the few steps back to the fountain. He pops the strawberry under the chocolate waterfall. "I guess I haven't been inspired enough. You need to really believe in the story you're writing for it to flourish into something worthwhile, and I haven't felt that way since my first book."

I reluctantly stuff my strawberry into the liquid chocolate. "How many books do you have out in the wild?"

"Two . . . I was young, and I signed a two-book deal, despite not having actually planned to make the story a duology. The publishers thought the first book would do really well and asked if I'd write a sequel. I told them I would. Then the first book did do really well . . . the second one . . . not so much.

"My heart wasn't in it. I deluded myself into thinking it would do well anyway, and people saw right through it." He belatedly removes his strawberry. It's dripping everywhere as he pulls it off the skewer and eats the entire berry in one bite, somehow managing to escape without a drop of chocolate on his outfit or face.

He watches me watch him chew, amusement flaring in his gaze. He swallows. "What?"

"Were you like some, quote, youth-prodigy author?"

He closes his eyes and nods. "Twenty-three."

"You published two YA books?"

He closes his eyes and solemnly nods again.

"Reed, why don't I know your name? I was in college back then, I read all those big titles. How old are you? Thirty-one?"

"Recently thirty-two."

I stare at him a beat longer before pulling my drenched piece of fruit from the fountain. I take a careful bite before meeting his eyes again. "No matter how long you go without publishing, you still put out two books. You're still an author. No air quotes."

His mouth relaxes into a small smile. "Thank you."

"I'm going to figure out your book."

"I don't doubt it." He watches as I finish off my strawberry.

"Have you been actively trying to write another one?"

"I've started maybe seven books over the years, and I've yet to make it past Act 1. My confidence really took a hit back when the second one didn't come together. There was this one negative review that really hit home. My brain always shoves it in my face when I'm having a shitty time in a Word document."

I twist the empty skewer between my fingers as my brain rifles through old YA titles. "Did that one review mess with your head so hard that you won't let yourself even attempt to finish another project?"

He crosses his arms and eyes me thoughtfully, leaning against the marble table. "It's complicated."

I cock a brow. "I'm sure it is."

He peers at me harder, those laser beam eyes of his melting through my protective outer shell to liquefy my organs.

I take a lazy step away. "All right, let's circle back to another mystery. Why are you actually single?" I saunter backward toward one of the blood-red sofas (I hope I'm sauntering).

He grins down at his tan lace-up Timberland boots. "It's a variety of things."

"Is one of them the tendency to shove an entire piece of fruit in your mouth and swallow it whole?"

He snorts, and I decide it would be sexy to throw my arms out dramatically and sit on a red sofa while I await his response.

I know the sofa's behind me because I can feel it against the back of my calves, so I go for it. I throw out my arms as I collapse backward. My right hand cuts smoothly through the air, but my left knuckle slams into something hot.

And said something—goes flying.

Reed's head jerks up, eyes following the projectile I just sent slow-motion soaring through the air via pure stupidity, as my ass flops down against the curved edge of the couch. It hasn't even hit the ground, but I can already see the police report. *Thirty-year-old woman without a plus-one dressed as cartoon character accidentally burns down wedding.*

The candle thumps against the floor and immediately starts searing the carpet. A larger flame flares to life. *That's gonna need to be smothered.*

In one fluid motion, I rip off my lavender skirt, hop up, and chuck it toward the flames. But Reed's there next to the fire—he catches the skirt, tosses it away, and stomps out the flames with his boot.

Shit.

The two of us stare at the smoldering new black circle in the red carpet, catching our breath. Reed looks up at me wide eyed, hair flopped out of place.

My legs are bent, and my arms are thrown out like I'm going to catch something in my black lace thong and heels, wearing a princess blouse, purple corset, stuffed iguana, and a flower crown.

My stomach dips into my ass as another caterer punches through the doors with a stack of bowls. He stops short, gaping before dropping the stack on the nearest table and bolting back out.

Reed catches my eye and starts to laugh. And once he starts to laugh, I start to laugh. And we cackle at each other cackling, until we're both bent over in hysterics, unable to breathe. I point to the charred circle, unable to articulate words. He points behind us at my skirt, the bottom of which is—now in the damn chocolate fountain. *That's definitely not hygienically sound.*

I stumble over, yank it out, squeegee the bottom, and drunkenly laugh my way back to Reed, who catches me by the arms. There's chocolate all over my hands. I smear it off on some napkins from the fruit table.

"We have to get out of here," he hisses.

I nod in assent. *We really do.*

Reed inhales, steadying himself. "And as great as that thong is, I think you should put the skirt back on before we stealth back into the party, or you're gonna draw some unwanted attention."

I push him with all the strength of a feather because I can't stop laughing and my limbs have turned to rubber. I bumble into the skirt and straighten it into place. Our heads drop at the same moment to assess the chocolate damage.

"Reed. It looks like I walked through a puddle of shit."

Air hisses out of his mouth as Reed takes my hand and pulls me toward the door.

My heart pounds as we slip back into the ballroom. The DJ provides a decent amount of cover, shielding us from the eyes of all the guests currently jamming to a classic rock song on the dance floor. (They mixed up the Disney playlist. *Good for them.*)

Reed power walks the perimeter until we reach the door to the lobby. He shoves it open.

We breeze past a table full of lavender wedding goody bags, across a brightly lit empty marble-tiled foyer, and down a polished hallway. Unisex bathroom signs are stamped on two doors at the end of the corridor. We fumble into one and slam the door behind us like we're on the run from the wedding-fire-dessert police.

It's a single stall room. Very shiny. White. Clean. We're heavy breathing, watching each other stupidly when there's a knock at the door. I startle away from it.

Dessert police?

"Rikki?"

Jordyn. A distressed Jordyn. I exchange a look with Reed. His face is lit up, mouth in an open grin. Hair mussed.

"What's up?" I squeak.

"I've been looking all over for you! Babe's asking me where you are. She wants you for the next wedding thing she has planned. I was about to go *CSI* on that Reed guy's ass. All your crap is still at the table, so I jumped to the most likely conclusion: He kidnapped or murdered you."

"Don't worry, I'm fine. I just need a second."

"Are you going to be in there a while? You okay?"

Reed starts to laugh. I swat his arm with the back of my palm. "I'm fine! Just stomach . . . troubles. I'll be out in ten minutes."

"Okay . . . you're okay, right?" she asks one more time. "Patty pebbles?"

"Pineapple crepes!"

"All right." She hits the door twice and retreats.

Reed arches a brow. "Patty pebbles?"

"Code for 'all good' in case we're ever being held at gunpoint and being told to pretend we're okay."

"Ah, of course. Discreet."

"Women have to plan for these things." We smile at each other for another moment before I remember my chocolate-soaked skirt. "Shit, I have to wash this, and we have to get back out there."

"Right. Okay." He fiddles with his pockets for a moment as we both realize I'll have to get undressed again. "Meet you in the ballroom?"

5 | WANTED (FOR WEDDING STUFF)

"Oh my god. Did you take a shit on the floor and then walk through it?" Jordyn yells over the music.

I sigh. There's only so much water, hand soap, and hand dryer can do. "No! It's chocolate. There was a fire—it's a whole thing."

Jordyn's eyes bulge. "We're going to circle back to this." She drags me by the biceps around the edge of the floor to where Babe is dancing to Kesha's "Your Love Is My Drug."

"Babe!" Jordyn shouts. "She's here!"

Babe disengages from the group she's with. "Ah! Rikki! Perfect! I couldn't do this without you! And I've always wanted to do it!"

"What is *it*?" I shout back.

Babe waves to the DJ and gives him a thumbs-up before pulling me to the head table, where she picks up her bouquet. Then I'm dragged back to the dance floor. The DJ picks up his mic.

I start to scan the crowd for Reed, but I'm cut off as my retinas are burned out via spotlight. I whip up a hand to protect my eyes.

"All right! Single ladies!" the DJ spouts. "It's time to make your way out to the dance floor."

Single—oh god.

Beyoncé bursts from the speakers.

"Our bride is ready to toss the bouquet!"

I attempt to pull away from Babe and melt back into the ether, but she holds fast to my arm. "Rikki, come on, it's my wedding!" she gripes.

I meet her pleading gaze and slump in concession. A triumphant smile spreads across her cheeks as she places me in the center of the dance floor. The rest of the guests huddle around the perimeter.

"Why am I the only one out here?" I hiss as Babe steps up onto the DJ's little platform.

"Single ladies! Please, don't be shy, come out to the dance floor!" the DJ announces again. I rotate in place, looking for someone else who might be making their way to join me. The rest of the guests stare back as I eye beg them to step out onto the floor.

You've got to be fucking kidding.

I catch Jordyn's eye: She's directly in front of me along the edge of the wood. I glare at her in her stupid dog costume. She grins back and motions for me to smile like a dance mom hover-parenting from the stage wings.

"The bride has just informed me that there's only one single lady present here tonight!" the DJ announces.

Kill me. Kill me now.

"Let's give her and the bride a clap." A crowd-wide clap on beat with "Single Ladies" comes to life. The light of the videographer's camera falls on my face.

Oh joy, I'll be able to relive this for years to come.

"Okay!" Babe's amplified voice rings over the speakers. "Let's do this, Rikki! Happy thirtieth, girl, your time is coming."

Not the birthday.

She hands the mic to the DJ and turns her back on myself and the guests.

What is she doing? I'm the only one out here—just hand it to me!

"Let's count her in, y'all. Five!" the DJ yells. "Four!" The crowd joins him for "Three! Two!"

Babe tosses the bouquet over her head. I watch as it arcs through the air. The flowers land at my feet with a loud disappointed *oohhhhhhhhh* from the audience.

Babe turns, clocks them on the ground, and scowls. The DJ hands her the mic again.

"Woman, you have to catch them," she demands.

I shoot her an exhausted look.

"Don't look at me like that. Reset!" she scolds. A wave of chuckles echoes through the crowd. Her blond maid of honor (Sleeping Beauty in the pink dress) runs out, snatches the bouquet, and hands it back to Babe.

"You have to work for it, or the magic of this tradition won't work!" Babe lectures.

I shake out my arms. "All right, all right! Throw it."

"You heard her, folks, one more time," the DJ yells. There's an abrupt change in the music. The running guitar of AC/DC's "Thunderstruck" blares over the speakers. "Give her a clap, folks!"

The clapping starts again. Babe comes over the mic. "Catch it, Rikki, or we're doing this again."

I lean forward, hands braced in front of me, playing along.

"Let's count 'em down folks. Five, four!" The crowd joins in, gleefully clapping and counting. When they reach one, Babe chucks the bouquet at a hard left away from me.

Goddamnit, Babe. I take three giant strides and dive for it in a skirt and heels. My elbows scrape the floor as the flower mound hits my palms. The guests erupt in cheers. I gather myself from the floor and hold it over my head like a good sport as I catch the bride's gaze. Her eyes sparkle as she claps at me with her arms stretched straight out in front of her like the Joker in *The Dark Knight*.

"Okay, hold on to that, Rikki!" the DJ yells. "Can we get a chair for the bride?"

The maid of honor sprints into the center of the dance floor with a dinner chair. Willem helps Babe off the stage and leads her over to it. I hustle off the wood to stand next to Jordyn, clutching the bouquet limply at my side like an old-fashioned suitcase. Micah comes up behind us and hands me a glass of wine.

"Thank you," I breathe, taking it from him and gulping down half the contents.

"You did good, Rick." He pats me on the shoulder.

Babe sits on the newly appointed chair, and Willem kneels before her.

"Are people really still doing this tradition?" I mumble as "Walk This Way" comes over the speakers. "Isn't it like, problematic?"

Babe kicks her leg out from under her elaborate wedding dress, and slowly, Willem starts working his way under the layers of fabric and up her calf. She lifts her leg higher, letting the opulent gown gather around her thigh, giggling as a lacey scrunchie-like white garter is revealed on the top portion of her leg. Willem lunges forward and grabs it with his teeth to a load of hoots and whistles from the guests.

Jordyn nudges me with her shoulder. "If you don't want to do it, just tell whoever catches the garter to put it on your wrist. Babe thinks it's super fun and hardcore believes in the, quote, magic of it all, because she met Willem after catching the bouquet at her aunt's wedding. She thinks she's giving you a gift."

The crowd erupts with cheers as Willem navigates it over her knee, calf, ankle, and finally her foot, heel, and all. He stands with the garter dangling from his mouth and their friends go wild. Babe tosses her hands in the air, whooping as Willem twirls the garter around his finger.

A smile breaks through my carefully cynical expression. Babe's enthusiasm is contagious.

"Ladies and gentlemen, Mr. and Mrs. LaRue!" The DJ cheers. "All right, folks, can we get all the single guys out on the floor?"

Sleeping Beauty dashes out and removes the lone chair. (How many Red Bulls has that woman had today?) "Whip It" blasts over the speakers as a gray-haired man in his sixties dressed as Prince Eric, a for-sure teenage boy dressed as Woody, and Reed as Flynn step out onto the dance floor. Adrenaline spikes through me as Reed meets my eyes, mouth rolled up his cheek in an amused pout.

I forgot what this was like. Flirting with someone *in the wild* that you're attracted to, that you might actually like, and who might actually like you back. Someone you're genuinely connecting with.

I feel like somebody plugged me in. Like all this time my skin's been a collection of a thousand grievously neglected blazing lights. I'm hyperaware of my limbs as I hold his gaze.

I casually mouth, "You better catch this." A demand. Like I've known him for years rather than the growing compilation of minutes we've spent together thus far.

Reed glances at the two other single candidates and smiles. He's positioned himself directly in front of me, at the center of the three. Willem climbs onto the DJ stand and turns his back.

Jordyn bumps my shoulder. "Wait, are you smitten?"

I cross my arms, tucking the bouquet under my armpit. "No comment."

The DJ's gaze slices to me. "Oh snap, look at that, there's a Flynn on the board. Did he come with you, Rapunzel?"

I shake my head.

"Shit, he didn't come with her! Flynn, did you come with someone?" the DJ prods.

Reed smiles to himself and shakes his head.

"Well hot damn!" The DJ throws his hand up. "The Disney gods are working overtime at this wedding."

"What is with everyone and the fucking Disney gods?" I mumble.

"Accept it and move on, Rikki," Jordyn says. "You have been blessed."

Willem slings the garter backward toward the men. I suck in a sharp breath as it soars toward teenage Woody's head. But then Reed's behind him. He moves fast, jumps, and snatches the thing out of the air. The crowd cheers—to my surprise, I'm whooping right along with them.

"And we have our duo, folks," the DJ announces. "Uninvolved *Rapunzel and Flynn*!"

Babe sidles up next to me. "You okay to do the garter thing?"

I glance over at Reed. He's still in the middle of the dance floor, lips pursed, eyes locked on me. He quirks a brow. The rest of the room falls away.

What's happening?

The rest of the room has fallen away? I glance up at the ceiling suspiciously.

I nod belatedly to Babe. "Yeah, I'm good, Babe. Thanks for asking."

Sleeping Beauty darts out with the chair again and sets it in the middle of the floor next to Reed. She gestures for me to take a seat.

The DJ picks up his mic. "All right, folks, legend has it the couple who catches the garter and the bouquet are blessed with romantic luck for the next year if they complete the loop. Rikki and . . ." Willem calls out Reed's name. The DJ nods. "Reed, is it? You up for the challenge?"

I chug the rest of my wine, hand Jordyn the glass, and walk toward the lone chair with my thumb up in the air. Reed throws his thumb up as well and we meet face-to-face at the center of the floor.

"Are you comfortable with this?" he says.

"I'm comfortable."

"Rated G, or a show?" He smiles.

I bite my lip, debating this for half a second. "Give me the show, drama kid."

His eyes light. "You sure?"

I nod, thrilled that I actually am. I'm more than comfortable with a show if it's Reed putting it on. I want a show if it's Reed kneeling in front of me. If it's Reed's hands on my leg. Just conversing with this man is pumping glitter through an IV straight into my veins.

The music switches again as I sit: from "Whip It" to "Bad to the Bone."

The guests chuckle along with me as Reed, a man I just met, backs up and dramatically lowers onto one knee in his Flynn costume to the beat of "Bad to the Bone." He proceeds to extend his bent leg out and pull himself forward across the floor, three times to the damn music, performing all the way. I drop my neck back, beaming at the ceiling to expel the emotional overload bombarding my system. Shaken-up champagne-bottle levels of giddiness are taking up all the space in my chest.

My plan was to hold on to a cooler-than-thou smirk, but I am smiling about as hard as my face can physically manage.

When Reed's close enough, he reaches for my right foot. He takes my ankle and lifts it toward him. His touch sends chills running up my leg. My floor-length skirt glides up my calf. With his other hand, Reed slips his fingers under the strap of my silver heel and slowly slides it off, brushing the bottom of my foot with the pads of his fingers.

He tosses my shoe to the side. Guests whoop and holler. Someone wolf-whistles. I grab the seat with my hands and grip it for dear life because he hasn't broken eye contact this entire time, and my muscles are losing purchase as his eyeballs cook me from the inside out.

His hand tightens around my ankle, and he tugs me closer. I cackle, as myself and the chair slide into him. My raised foot brushes his chest. He *smirks* at me as he slips the garter from his wrist and slides it over my toes and up my ankle to the beat.

How can he hold a smirk *at a time like this*? *Why don't I have that skill?* It's taking all my willpower to dull my raging smile to a faint beam.

His hands slip under my long skirt. I suck in a breath as all five of his fingers caress the side of my calf in a slow, repetitive, circular motion, inching the garter up. Each cycle sends a flurry of sparks shooting up into my center.

Oh. My god.

I maneuver the skirt up, over my knees, and tuck it strategically under my left leg, to prevent any potential flashing.

When he reaches my knee, I lift my leg an inch higher so he can get under my thigh. He takes my ankle and secures it over his shoulder.

Good lord.

I must visibly react without realizing it, because a smile finally splits his smirk. He tilts his chin and presses his lips to the inside of my ankle. My breath hitches as his fingers move the garter up three more inches. I think people are screaming. Whistling, clapping. Lights flash. Everything blurs as three more lingering circles of sparkling, all-consuming, magical-Disney-gods-level fire rage through me.

He takes my leg off his shoulder to a roar of applause. Slips my shoe back on. My skin pulses under his touch. He stands, takes my hands, pulls me up against him, and spins us. My hand is in his hand. His other hand is on my back.

Dancing: He's leading me in a dance. I blacked out for a second, but I'm back. "Bad to the Bone" is still playing.

"So you dance too," I breathe over his shoulder. The rest of the guests converge, taking to the floor around us.

"Theater kid. Trained in waltz, tap, swing, and Lindy Hop, thank you very much."

"Overachiever."

"Calling the kettle black."

"Kettles can be other colors."

He snorts. "You dance, too, I see."

"Yeah, well, I trained in ballet, tap, and jazz until senior year of high school, was on the dance team all through college and taught it all through undergrad, so I should hope so." I follow his steps as we whirl around each other in tight, quick circles.

He pulls back from my shoulder to look me in the eyes. "Was that too much?"

I cock my head curiously as we fly around the floor. "Are you a Leo, Reed?"

He smiles. "Aries, but I don't know much about it."

"Aries is another fire sign," I tell him.

"Interesting. So you're a fire sign?" He grins.

"Why?"

"You're full of fire." He pulls me closer against his chest. Our noses touch. "I see it in your eyes. I hear it in your voice."

I roll my eyes. "And *you* are full of bullshit."

"That's the god's honest truth, Rikki. Take a harder look in the mirror. I don't know how you're missing it."

I scoff. "Shut up."

We're so close I can feel his intake of breath as his smile widens. "Learn how to take a compliment."

I bite down on my smile as a galaxy of stars bursts from my heart.

I barely know anything about this man. I haven't asked any of my important first-date questions. I've yet to check on the murderer / con artist / fish status.

But I feel something tangible. I can feel the raw possibility. The potential of an *us*.

And I want it.

What you forget when you're not in a relationship is how high you can feel when you *are* in a relationship. There comes a point, post your latest breakup or dating experience, where you've reached *happy*. You're feeling good—you're great! You're perfectly *content*.

But then you meet someone you like, and you remember *this*.

This is a different level of happy. A different kind of happy. The *effortlessly vibing with another human, ascending to a higher plane* kind of happy. And it reminds me why I wanted a partner in the first place. I forgot how potent real connection can be. I forgot how intoxicating it is to exchange cheesy nonsense with a beautiful human.

"You didn't mention it was your thirtieth birthday."

"It will be at midnight," I say quietly.

"Can I interest you in a celebratory drink?"

6 | WE LOVE A NATURE

Armed with fresh drinks, we spill into the muggy summer night.

A large set of glass doors at the back of the room has been propped open to an expansive stone balcony. There are a few Disney-themed guests milling about outside, mingling, resting against the balustrade. I wander up to it and lean against the cool stone. It seeps into my skin, sobering me a bit. A lake sits in the distance, surrounded by hills of soft green grass. Fireflies flicker among the bushes and trees. It's majestic. Straight out of a fairy tale. Which is obviously why Babe chose this venue.

Reed sidles up next to me. He takes a sip of his old-fashioned. "Why are *you* single?"

I glance over at him. "You never did get to why you're single."

He spins the liquid in his glass. "I'm going to rewind us back to our earlier discussion: trust issues."

"Same. But probably in a different way. My trust issues stem from the fact that for the first chunk of my life, I was the human manifestation of the song 'Don't Stop Believin'.'"

Reed drops his head with a rumbly laugh that wraps around me like a fresh sweatshirt. "Explain."

I catch his gaze. "The voice in my head . . . the internal monologue we all have and listen to on the daily: Mine used to be the optimist of all optimists. And just like the song, you listen to her too many times—she'll drive you insane. For so long I believed that *people* would be true to their word and do better. And then they would screw me over. They'd apologize, promise to do better. And I'd believe them.

"And then they'd screw me over. And apologize. Promise to do better. And I'd believe them." I purse my lips, glancing down at my drink as I hurtle involuntarily through my archives, careening through over a decade's worth of disappointing snapshots across a three-second span. I exhale a measured breath before turning my gaze back to the relative stranger a foot away. "I have trouble filtering toxicity out of my life. So I do this thing where I try to filter it on the way in instead. Does that make sense?"

Reed closes his eyes and nods. "It does."

I take another sip of my mojito, a masochistic grin tugging at my lips as I look out at the view. "No matter how many times people have shown me who they are, my instinct is to keep hoping they'll evolve. And sometimes that works out, but sometimes your dad's just an asshole, and no matter how many chances you dole out, they never fucking change."

We're quiet for a moment.

I'm a little tipsier than I thought.

I slide my eyes back to Reed.

He eyes me thoughtfully. "Daddy issues?"

I smile. "You familiar?"

He swigs the rest of his drink. "Very."

I raise my glass in acknowledgment. "They plague the best of us, Reed. Someone had to mess us up along the way to adulthood. It might as well have been our parents. More predictable. Easier to treat through therapy."

He barks a sharp laugh, and we both sigh.

I drop my chin onto my hand. "It's so picturesque out there by the lake."

"It really is. They should have a path leading down there from here." He glances around. "Why is this a closed-off balcony? We're only like six feet off the ground."

I look down over the railing. "You're right. Maybe we should jump it."

"Jump it?" He eyes me skeptically. "You want to jump down into the grass and wander around in your heels?"

I've done enough random shit tonight—might as well add this to the list. I don't see anyone around to yell at us. I swipe off my heels and place them on the ground with my drink.

He cocks a brow. "What if you get hurt?"

"What if *you* get hurt? I'm turning thirty, not a hundred." I throw my leg over the balustrade.

"Whoa, okay, wasn't expecting—should I go first to catch you?"

I maneuver myself over like Jack on the back of the *Titanic*, shimmy down into a squat, hold on to the bars of the balcony, and lower my body toward the ground, one foot at a time.

I drop barefoot into the grass, my skirt getting caught under my feet. The thing's a little long without the heels, but it's already screwed from the chocolate, so I'm not worried about grass stains.

"Coast is clear," I say up to him.

Four seconds later, he drops down next to me. "Is this in character for you?"

"Definitely not." I smile. "But I'm having some sort of last-day-of-my-twenties existential crisis: knocking over candles, eating dessert early. I'm just gonna lean in—tonight I'm an outlaw, Reed."

He laughs as we fall into step toward the pretty, probably artificial lake. "Thirty's not so bad."

I watch him, studying his sharp features again. "So, how do your trust issues manifest?"

He snorts. "Rikki, you don't want to know how my trust issues manifest. That shit's for my therapist." His eyes bulge. "Shit, I momentarily forgot you're also a therapist."

We hike the grassy hill surrounding the water. "Double majored in psych and creative writing at Columbia for undergrad."

"Kudos." Reed points to himself. "NYU, acting."

"No way. Wow, not just drama kid—drama man! That's why you're trained in fifty styles of dance! A drama man writing YA contemporary during his free time as he perhaps processes the trauma and loss of his first breakup?"

Reed stops in his tracks, narrowing his eyes at me. "What the fuck, Rikki?"

I stop a few feet ahead of him, smiling. "Am I close?"

He shakes his head, blinking at me in disbelief. "Why would you guess that?"

I gnaw at my lip, focusing on a spot in the distant trees. "Well, you wrote it while you were in college. You're single due to trust issues. You're super guarded. We put up those walls because we've been hurt. And since you're putting them up on a first date, maybe you've experienced some sort of romantic betrayal. We're not that old, and like that song says, the first cut is the deepest. A lot of times that happens in college. With a significant other from your hometown, you go to two different schools, something happens, you break up. That's painful. It'll make its way into a book one way or another for sure if you're experiencing it for the first time, and you're writing. I mean, cutting out that sort of relationship gives you *the* time to want to write a book in the first place so . . ." My gaze shifts back to Reed, whose jaw is hanging open. "Educated guess."

He closes his eyes for a moment.

". . . And I've freaked you out."

Reed shakes his head, looking at my feet instead of my face. "No, that's—no. I just didn't think I was that easy to read."

"You're not *easy to read*. I'm just paying attention."

He takes a beat. Pulls on a small smile. "Sorry! We can keep going."

We start forward again, continuing to crest the hill by the lake.

"You don't have to apologize."

He huffs a self-deprecating laugh. "Yes I do. You being good at your job threw me into a baby panic, and that was uncalled for."

"To be clear . . . I don't actually have clients at the moment, but being a licensed LMFT is what qualifies me to helm Love Today."

Reed peers at me. "Was that your plan all along? Get the masters so you can write a relationship column?"

I shake my head, laughing. "No, I thought I'd write in some way, shape, or form, part time alongside being a therapist. But it turned out, the work brought me a lot of ubiquitous anxiety that I didn't pick up on for a while. I really wanted to help people. I didn't anticipate the side effects it'd have on my own mental health."

It was the little things that started to add up two years ago when I worked at the clinic. Losing belongings on the train. Dropping my phone ten times a day. Forgetting plans. Running into door jambs, table corners. Waking up every three hours in the night. Making Jordyn repeat herself constantly because I'd lose the thread of all our conversations.

I clear my throat. "So when there was a perfect full-time gig available at *The Minute* with the LMFT prerequisite, I jumped on it. Now I like to think I help people in a different way. Less direct, but still valuable, hopefully."

"I can see that," he says gently. "Taking on everyone's most intimate, intense issues hour to hour, daily. That's a lot."

I nod, growing increasingly uncomfortable with how vulnerable I've made myself, eager to shift the focus back to Reed.

Who is this author I'm haphazardly spilling my trauma on?

He wrote a contemporary book that was big nine years ago. Probably a college-age-ish protagonist.

Derek Roosevelt's *Broken and Bruised* was huge around that time. That was my first assignment at Books Today. I read an ARC before it came out—my pull quote *is on the cover*. He only ever released one other book, which was also assigned to me, and I was so disappointed with it.

I can't visualize an author photo of Derek Roosevelt. Was there one? All I can picture is the book cover. Stark-black background, neon-blue outline of a broken heart. I thought it was going to be cheesy and melodramatic, but the characters were endearing, funny, and deeply relatable. The metaphors had a way of striking hard in that completely unexpected, stunning way that leaves you feeling extremely seen and understood.

The lead had a whole thing he was going through, with his dad not being his actual dad. He gets the chance to rewind and do the twenty-four hours of the breakup with his high school girlfriend who he was engaged to, over and over, whenever he wants. But he can never save the relationship. It always ends. He does mend the relationship with the father he grew up with. And there's a new love interest by the time the last chapter rolls around. He learns that *yes,* relationships can end and cause you pain, but it doesn't mean they're a waste of time or memories or effort. The protagonist comes to terms with the fact that he's changed for the better from the heartbreak he went through.

That really moved me as a twenty-one-year-old. It was the first sad-ish book I didn't hate. My rave review in *The Minute* is sitting at home, framed, in a box of art and photos I haven't unpacked. It's hung on the wall in my room ever since that issue went to print.

Am I on an air quotes date with Derek Roosevelt?

Reed smiles thoughtfully up at the sky as we reach the top of the grassy knoll. The moon is full: A stark bright hole punched through the deep-indigo night.

Guilt clangs through me. Did I write the review that's stanched his ability to finish a book for the past seven years?

He looks over and catches my eye. "You're gorgeous. And super intuitive and smart, and I'm really enjoying this impromptu birthday-crisis date." He says this casually, but the words hit me like a hot flash, burning over my skin. My brain spins, trying to process the book dots I've connected in the last thirty seconds.

"What's wrong?" he asks, tone shifting.

I shake my head. "Nothing." My mouth is dry. I rearrange my features, letting my flushed smile rise to the surface. "Thank you."

He steps closer, studying me. "You really have trouble with compliments."

"I don't have trouble with them, I just don't know how to respond because my first thought isn't that you're being truthful, it's 'Are you blowing smoke up my ass to manipulate me for one reason or another.' Especially when it's coming from a hot dude."

A grin breaks across his face. "So are you calling me a hot dude, or are you blowing smoke up my ass for one reason or another?"

I hold his gaze, pursing my lips harder than I've ever pursed in my life as I try to maintain some semblance of a chill smirk. *Hold. Stay cynical.*

He tilts his head toward the lake. "Shall we?"

I nod, conceding to put a pin in this possible author revelation. "We shall."

I break eye contact to look down at the water. The other side of this hill is considerably steeper. There's a thin strip of sand hugging some areas of the lake, but the majority of its edges are grass. I take a step down.

I make it four steps before my foot gets caught on my skirt. Five before I'm airborne.

Reed yells my name in a panic as I instinctively throw out my arms and tuck my chin to my chest. Something tears. A groan rips out of me as I tumble into the grass palms first and proceed to roll horizontally downhill at a speed yet unknown to man. *Goddamnit.*

My forehead slams into my biceps as I attempt to reposition my limbs to better grapple with the ground flashing by my eyes. I grit my teeth and press my fingers into the earth, thrusting my nails into the cold dirt. My body yanks to a hard vertical stop just as my legs and ass splash into the lake.

A slow-motion millisecond passes before I see Reed, rolling at top speed straight for me.

A "fuck!" flies out of him as I rip my nails from the ground and lunge out of the way. My feet squish into the lake's muddy bottom as he goes soaring in beside me.

I gape at the spot where he disappeared into the water. *What the actual fuck.*

Reed surfaces with a frantic gasp, ten feet away, sopping wet, hair flopped forward across his left eye like an emo kid from 2010. "Rikki—this wedding is trying to kill us. Are you okay?" He yanks on his wet vest, shaking it out.

A laugh explodes out of me. My upper body flops forward with the force of it as giggles fizzle through my teeth.

Reed shakes his head, a grin breaking through his distressed expression. "Glad you're finding this just as hysterical as the fire."

"I'm—a slut—for an adventure," I hiss back, my voice escaping in delighted, jolting bursts.

He lowers into the water, submerging himself to his collarbone. "Yeah. I mean, same."

That sends me into a fresh cackle.

"Steer for the deep waters only," he says fondly.

I sink down, letting the water swallow my torso, so I can match his eyeline. "Did you just quote *Walt Whitman*? After I said *I'm a slut* for adventure?"

His eyelids droop as he rolls his pupils upward. "It basically means the same thing."

"I can't believe you just quoted poetry. How unexpectedly pretentious."

"Astute," he corrects.

"Obnoxious."

He grins at me across the two-foot span of water between us. "I like literature. Sue me."

That takes me out for a second. I study him, treading water. He studies me back, turquoise eyes searching mine.

"So, are you okay?" he asks.

I nod, a chill skittering through me as my body finally registers the water temperature. It's *cold*. "Yeah, I think I tripped on my skirt."

His lips twitch. *"You think?"*

"How did you end up down here with me?"

He clenches his teeth. "I made a dive for you and caught your skirt."

"Ooooh noo."

He bites his lip, nodding. "Note to self: Don't dive after someone on a steep incline. It will not end well."

I snort as he slinks underwater.

He emerges, inches away, directly in front of me, hair slicked back. Droplets stick to his light reddish-brown lashes. Roll down the straight edge of his nose.

"Note to self," I say quietly. "Trotting down an incline in an oversize skirt may lead to death."

"Note to self: Rikki makes a shitty outlaw."

My mouth falls open, feigning annoyance as his knee parts my thighs under the water. Heat twirls up my center. "Excuse me, it was your idea to go down to the lake."

"You're forgetting you wanted to jump the balcony."

I shift the slightest bit, and my chest brushes against his. "You're forgetting you wanted to stroll around this grassy park. I was making that happen for you, podcast boy."

His crystalline eyes slide to my lips.

They hover there, static crackling in the space between us. Tickling my skin. Want blooms, expansive and insistent, in my chest. I raise my arms in the water, just enough to drape them over his sturdy shoulders, and lock my hands around his neck. I can feel his strength radiating under my forearms. It sets my heart running. He tilts his forehead into mine. Our noses touch at the tips as his warm hands slide against my lower back. I let my legs drift through the water and secure them around his torso, pressing into the heat of his abdomen. I feel each individual muscle tense against me as he sucks in a breath. The moment hovers like a bead of water on the edge of a knife. The static builds, penetrates my skin, rises to a roar in my ears.

"Have you murdered anyone?" I whisper.

Reed's laugh is soft against my cheek. "Negative. Have you?"

His left hand tightens on my waist. His right slides up my spine to the nape of my neck.

The pressure in my chest is overpowering. I can barely breathe. "No."

"Great."

We collide. It's a match setting off a series of small explosions down my torso, sending an iridescent wave of euphoric energy jetting through my nervous system, eviscerating any lingering semblance of rational thought. The kiss is hot, wet, frantic, intense, debilitating.

We shift, tongues flirting. Exploring. He catches my lip between his teeth and tugs. I gasp into his mouth as my nails dig into his shoulder blades. When he pushes me up against the damp earth wall that lines the lake, truly deepening the kiss, the desire roaring through me solidifies into a need. An ache. My thighs grip harder, plastering his body against mine as I spear my fingers up into his hair.

I don't give a shit that we're trespassing on what might be a golf course during someone's wedding, and we're in a random artificial lake wearing matching Disney costumes. We're out of sight, hidden by the hill. I will have this man now. Happy thirtieth birthday to me.

My hands travel down his back, fingers skimming along the edges of his pants, brushing against the searing hot strip of skin at the bottom of his taut, sturdy torso. The pad of my thumb lands on the button of his brown pants. I'm a millisecond away from stripping him down, when a shriek echoes out from the venue.

7 | YOU ARE AT A WEDDING

I break away from Reed as the frantic voice slices through the night.

"Rikkiiiiii?"

Reed and I gaze at each other for one short, dazed moment, before I scramble into action. "Fuck!" My lady parts scream in protest as I spin toward the edge of the lake and hoist myself out of the pit.

Jesus Christ. You're at a wedding! You haven't even stalked his LinkedIn.

"Jordyn!" I yell, fumbling up the grass on a diagonal, stumbling to all fours three separate times as I race to the top.

"Rikki?" she screams again.

I crest the hill on my hands and knees and heave myself to my feet. My skirt has taken on five pounds of lake water. Jordyn is leaning over the balustrade with my shoes dangling from her hand, expression rapt with fear. I wave, flailing my arms like a castaway trying to flag down a helicopter.

She throws a hand over her chest. "Woman, I legit thought you had been murdered!"

"I'm so sorry! We fell into the lake!"

"We?"

Reed appears next to me and waves as well.

"Please bring your phone with you the next time you consensually disappear into the night with a random hot man!"

Reed and I take refuge under the stone balcony to change out of our wet clothes. My top got ruined during the hellfire mud-wall kiss that's still ricocheting through me. My iguana's gone. Flower crown is missing. My torn skirt is in a heap on the grass. I steal a peek at Reed. My eyes bounce from his muscular thighs to his fitted purple boxers. He's pulling on his yellow hoodie. I glance away. Jordyn brought us our party favor sweatshirts. She tossed them down, and I gave her the go-ahead to rejoin the party, promising to fill her in later.

Now I'm stuck in my freezing, mud-covered corset. I didn't think this quick-change idea through before I suggested it. *Corsets aren't a quick-change attire.* They are an intricate, slow-moving ordeal. Jordyn had to tie me into it earlier.

"Hey Reed," I call out. "Can you help me with this corset? It's like a whole thing."

"Oh, sure . . . uh."

I glance over my shoulder and find him looking at my ass and then up at the sky as he approaches. Then he looks back down at my ass.

"Reed, we almost died together via small grassy knoll, it's okay—you have permission to look at my ass."

He coughs. "Nice work. It's really something."

I snort as he runs his hands over my shoulders and down to the strings hanging along the back of the corset.

"So? Is it like unlacing a shoe?"

"Pretty much. Just untie the knot and work your way up, gradually loosening it all, and eventually I'll be able to shimmy out of it."

Reed begins to work out the knot, tugging and sliding the laces around. The moon is so bright that I hadn't noticed before—the stars are out. It would have been a nice night to sit by a lake had we made it down without tumbling into oblivion.

"Do you collect things, Reed?" I ask the night air in front of me.

He laughs. "Where did that come from?"

"It's one of my first-date questions." If you collect something, you care about it an enormous amount, and caring about things enormous amounts is a green flag I look for in a partner. And if they collect toenail clippings, dead animals, or packets of sugar, it's nice to know that sort of thing up front so I can immediately run the other way.

"You have a collection of first-date questions?" I can hear the satisfied smile in his voice.

The side of my mouth kicks up. "You don't?"

"I mean, yes, I do, but I haven't ever discussed it out loud with another . . . person."

"All right, Reed, what do you collect? Other than first-date questions."

"Obviously books." He tugs at a string and slides something free. "I do this thing where anytime I go into a bookstore in a new place, or a new area, I scout out a book I want to read, and on the inside flap I write the date I bought it, where I got it, what I thought of the bookstore, and what was generally going on in my life that day. How I was feeling." He pauses, tugging gently at a new spot. "It's transformed my bookshelf into a scrapbook of sorts, of different moments and places I've been throughout my life."

My lips smush together, emotion welling at the thought of this shelf. "That's really beautiful."

More gentle tugging. "I've got one," he says after a moment. "What's your most irrational, long-shot, endgame life goal that you tell yourself will never happen, but in your heart of hearts you're still holding out hope for?"

"This is a first-date question?" I ask. "Or an SAT writing prompt?"

Laughter rumbles through him.

I exhale a slow breath, gathering my thoughts. "I mean, I think one is to write a book with someone someday. The other more irrational one is, I guess, maybe to, like . . . have an afternoon talk show like Kelly Clarkson. I don't know why, and I don't have any, like, experience in that realm, and I'm pretty sure you have to be independently famous pre–talk show, but it would give me such a big platform to talk about relationships and books, and I love talking to different kinds of people and helping them share their stories. I love talking in general . . . yeah."

"I love that," he says, fingers moving at a glacial pace. "I think those big random reach-for-the-stars dreams are so important. They keep us striving to learn and evolve and be curious about the world. You have to be a little deluded to push yourself. Can I ask, do you not want to write a book yourself, or does that just not feel grand enough for this particular list?"

I shrug. "I already spend so much time alone writing and planning for the weekly column, I think it'd be fun to try writing with a partner, less isolating."

I've never articulated any of this out loud. I'm as surprised as anyone to hear these things coming out of my mouth. *A talk show like Kelly Clarkson?* No one's ever asked me this question. "What are yours?" I ask back.

"The pie-in-the-sky goal has always been acting. Successfully, though. I've done some commercials and stuff over the years, but the dream is to be a part of the storytelling journey in that living, breathing way you only get when you're fully inhabiting another person's whole being. I love living different lives through books, but living them, like actually slipping into the physicality of what makes a person, and bringing them to life, is magic for me."

I smile to myself. "You really undersold your passion out the gate by offhandedly calling yourself a theater kid."

We reenter the ballroom in our matching yellow *We Made It to Happily Ever After* sweatshirts, clutching our wet clothes in bunched-up balls like children who shit their pants on the class trip.

Lucky for us, the dessert room seems to have recently opened up and is providing a very well-timed distraction. The majority of the guests miss our walk of shame in favor of the red fire-hazard room and its four-tier chocolate fountain.

The entire Aladdin table is MIA. Reed and I sheepishly take a seat for the first time since the Caesar salad. There's a predelegated slice of wedding cake at each place setting. I grab a fork and dig into mine, mind whirring as "Can You Feel the Love Tonight" plays gently over the speakers.

The wedding is drawing to a close. I *feel* it like you *feel* a hardcover straining to shut as you desperately try to soak up every last word in the final ten pages.

Fifteen minutes ago I was about to have frantic sex in a golf course lake during my friend's wedding. *What in the hell was that?* Reed could have a million STIs. He could be simultaneously dating five other women. He could be an escaped convict who stole the real Reed's identity, or a cult leader, or an . . . alien spy from a foreign planet.

"Rikki?" Reed says next to me. I swallow the cake in my mouth, swiveling in my seat to face him rather than the table.

Am I going to invite him back to my place after one date? I don't do that.

Before sex, I've had borderline lecture-style discussions about getting checked for STIs with all of my partners. I haven't done *it* with anyone until they've come back to me with a verified clean bill of health.

But also I have condoms at home.

Reed smiles. "What's happening in there?" He's been holding my eyes for a solid fifteen seconds of silence.

Or has he been silent? Did he say something?

I clear my throat. "Is this date thing we're doing something you'd like to do again, or was this a *you were here, I was here*, carpe diem sort of thing? And I just decided that I'm not going to sleep with you tonight, no matter what the answer is, so don't let that sway you."

He drops his eyes, grinning. "I would love to do this again."

"Yeah?"

"Maybe not this exact series of events, but yeah. I would very much like to see you again."

A thrill crackles down my spine. *We're going to do this again.* I found a handsome, smart, employed, thoughtful, funny, age-appropriate, *probably not a felon*, ambitious man in the wild, and *we're going to do this again*?

Reed holds out his phone, mouth quirked in a bashful smile. "Speaking of which, can I get your number?"

I pluck the phone from his palm, tap my number in, and call myself before handing it back. As I do, he catches his lip with his teeth, a knowing glint in his eye.

"What?" I ask.

"I have to tell you something."

I have to tell him something too. "Okay," I say playfully.

"I saw you boarding my flight last night."

I tilt my head. "What do you mean?"

"We were on the same flight," Reed says. "Last night. You were on my flight. You were wearing a black Columbia sweatshirt and tan UGGs."

I blink. I *was* wearing a Columbia sweatshirt and tan UGGs.

Reed's seen my UGGs?

I squint at him, confusion fogging my thoughts. "Wha . . . You were on the red-eye out of LAX?"

"I was."

"You *flew in from LA*?"

He nods. "Yeah."

"We were on the same flight?" I repeat numbly.

Reed smiles. "Yeah, are you based out there? You have an LA number, and you flew here, but you work at *The New York Minute*. Trying to pinpoint your home base has been a roller coaster."

"What?" I close my eyes. "You're not based in Secaucus."

"Are you . . ." He takes a breath. "Do you live in New York?"

Disappointment hits my windpipe like a boot to the neck. "You live in LA?"

He nods. "Moved out there with my brother five years ago."

Of course he did.

"To follow your dream. To be an actor."

He nods again, the light dimming in his eyes. "I take it you live here?"

I bob my head solemnly as the molten ball of relationship potential floating between us explodes in my face, splattering my skin like hot wax. *Fucking hell.*

"I live in Hoboken," I say slowly. "My family's in the Valley and Pasadena. I grew up in LA. Moved out here for college twelve years ago." I stare out at the dance floor. "When do you fly back?"

He runs a hand down his face. "Tomorrow morning."

We're silent for a long, depressing moment.

"Well, actually I'm not sure anymore," he mumbles absently. "They lost my luggage, and the airline hasn't managed to track it down yet."

My eyes dart back to his. "What?"

"What?" he repeats.

"I lost *my* luggage—I took the wrong one. I bought the most niche suitcase that's ever lived so I would never have to question which bag was mine again, and my first time flying with it, I lost it."

Reed's brow furrows. "You don't mean . . . the limited edition Sunrise Away bag?"

I frown, peering at him. "Why do you know about that bag?"

He arches a brow. "I have that bag."

I level my gaze on him, annoyance pulsing through me. "Fuck off. You do not own a limited edition Sunrise Away bag."

A smirk slowly finds its way back onto his face. "I do, and apparently you stole it."

8 | HOSTAGE EXCHANGE

"Why in the hell do you have a Sunrise Away bag?"

Reed and I sit at opposite ends of the bench in the back seat of an Uber, dressed in our yellow sweatshirts, clutching lavender *Babe & Willem* goody bags, en route to his hotel.

The bubbly outlaw vibe has all but evaporated. My social battery instantaneously depleted upon learning that this man lives three thousand miles away. I've tripped headfirst into a Rikki-curse spiral. *Of course he doesn't live here.* Stupid curse. Stupid fucking name. Stupid giant-ass country. I should have asked about this earlier.

I have no right to be angry. But here we are. "That was supposed to be my signature bag!"

Reed's mouth has been stuck in a subtle side smirk for the past fifteen minutes. "You do know the company made more than one Sunrise Away bag . . ."

"It's limited edition," I snap.

"Not *that* limited."

I cross my legs and uncross them again ten seconds later. "*Limited* apparently means nothing anymore," I grumble.

"Are you gonna be okay?" Reed asks, bemused.

Am I? I blow out a long breath, glaring at the back of the passenger seat in front of me. "Yes. It's just been a really long day."

"I don't think I've ever gone to a wedding this elaborate," Reed says, cheerfully changing the subject. "Sweatshirts and a goody bag. They went all out."

I huff out a muffled laugh. "Babe's been thinking about this her entire life, so I'm not surprised. Her personality's very 'go big or go home.'"

Reed lifts his bag with a wry grin. "Should we do an unboxing?"

We dump our bags onto the seat between us. A load of cute little souvenirs pour out.

A QR code to a Babe & Willem Wedding Playlist.

A Babe & Willem chocolate cigar.

A deck of Babe & Willem playing cards.

Babe & Willem matches.

A bag of kettle corn. A bottle of water. Electrolytes. Two Advil.

And an old-timey brown leather journal with a white garter around it—a replica of the one currently outfitting my thigh.

Wow. Expensive gifts.

No journal fell out of Reed's bag. I pick mine up, running my finger down the spine. It's real leather. The binding feels worn, soft, old.

"Wow." Reed whistles through his teeth, watching me admire it. "That's nice. I wonder if that's like an every-fifth-bag-gets-one gift." He points at the back. "Your name is on it!"

"What?" I smile, turning it over in my hand. My name *is* on it. Rikki Romona is carved into the leather along the back cover in small cursive font. I gape at it. "Wow. Yeah, this is quality." It almost feels warm. Cozy. Like laundry fresh from the dryer. I slide the garter off and onto my wrist. There's a snap closure underneath it. "I love a good journal. It's been a while since I used a notebook for anything other than work."

Reed grins. "It's a sign. The universe reminding you to write for fun."

I sneak a glance up at the car ceiling. "The universe and I have such a *will they, won't they?* relationship."

Reed laughs. "Do you believe in the universe?"

I tilt my head. "Do you?"

We peer at each other for an extensive, static moment, in our damp oversize sweatshirts and underwear. The reverberating sense of *seen-ness* I've felt echoing through my bones since our promenade thrums in the silence. The sex goblin that hijacked my ability to rationally exist while we were intertwined in the lake rouses in my gut.

"The universe is made of stories," Reed says finally. "Not atoms. And I sure as fuck believe in those."

"*What*?" I squint at him. "Did you just quote . . . Muriel Rukeyser?"

He drags a hand down his face, a blush climbing his pale neck. "Why do you know that?"

"I took a feminist poetry class in college. Why do you?"

Reed purses away a smile, staring down at his palms. "I'm a poetry enthusiast. The 'Speed of Darkness' is wild!"

"Why do you keep quoting poetry to me?"

"Because it's in my brain, and it seemed appropriate in the moment!"

"So do you?" I prompt.

"Do I what?"

"Believe in the universe!"

He mashes his lips together, hesitating for a beat. "If you asked me this any other day, I'd say no."

I wait for Reed in the car while he runs up to get my suitcase from his hotel room.

I couldn't go up with him. I like him too much. And I don't know him well enough. And I don't trust the sex goblin.

He returns five minutes later, loads my bag into the trunk, and slides back into the car. Five more minutes pass before the Uber pulls up to my apartment building. I make Reed wait in the car while I go up, drop off my goody bag, and grab his suitcase. I sneak another look at the luggage tag in the elevator. *R. Tyler.*

Reed Tyler.

When the doors ding open, he's there. Waiting for me in the lobby. The war-hero look is back. All hard angles. But his mouth is tipped up just slightly at the edges. A small, sad smile. I mirror the expression as we stare at each other for another beat, clutching each other's luggage.

"Time for the hostage exchange?" he quips.

We swap suitcases.

I meet his cyber-blue eyes one more time. "Well. Thanks for being my date. Have a safe trip home."

He smiles. "Yeah. Thanks for the adventure, Rikki."

We hug. As I pull back, he plants a soft kiss on my jaw. It throws me completely off-kilter. A tingling heat spreads from the spot on my face, racing down and across my collarbone.

I need to get out of this lobby.

I will not invite him upstairs. I can't form a doomed romantic attachment with Reed Tyler. Absolutely not. I grab my luggage and spin toward the elevator.

Reed snags my gaze as I throw one last confused glance over my shoulder. "Night, Rikki Romona."

"Goodbye, R. Tyler."

He drops a curt nod, pushes open the front door, and disappears into the darkness.

9 | THAT'S MY LIFE

What the fuck was that?

It's 1:00 a.m. when I lock the door to my new place and lay my actual Sunrise Away bag down on an open patch of floor among the box towers cluttering my living room.

I need to unpack. My phone pings as I kneel down next to my suitcase.

> Dad: Out late celebrating tonight? Almost your birthday here. Happy 30th, sweetheart. Love you.

I frown at the message. Out late?

I glance toward the door, a pit yawning open in my stomach. I hadn't consciously clocked the fact that there's a Ring doorbell on this place, but there definitely is. I've never had one before. I squeeze my eyes shut.

Until last week I lived in a two bedroom down the hall, with Jordyn and Micah. Jordyn and I lived there first. Micah moved in with us when he was still in law school. The three of us lived there together through their engagement and wedding because rent near the city is absurdly expensive. But Jordyn found out she was pregnant a month ago, and for the first time in my years of knowing them as a couple, I started to feel like a third wheel.

It was time.

Me: Thanks, Dad! Hope you're having a good night. Love u, see me on the Ring?
Dad: Yeah, interesting outfit choice for a night on the town.

I glance down at the Babe & Willem sweatshirt I momentarily forgot I was wearing.

Me: Ha. Ha. It's a party favor from the wedding I was at. Do you think you could transfer over the access to that Ring account to me for the time being, until I move out?
Dad: Rikki, that apartment is my investment. I need to be able to keep an eye on it while I'm not there and workers are in and out during the remodel.

Shame curdles uncomfortably in my gut.

Single. Poor, despite working three jobs. And living in your unstable father's new investment. Welcome to thirty.

I pull up my thread with Jordyn, who insisted I text her once I made it home alive.

Me: Made it home, sent boy away
Jordyn: I'm sorry he doesn't live here. <3 I'm coming over
Me: what? you're pregnant. it's past your bed time

There's a knock at my door. I pull it open to find Jordyn holding a pink cupcake with a lit candle stuck inside it. "Happy Birthday!"

A begrudging smile slips up my cheek. "Aw, thank you."

I blow out the candle, and we collapse on my father's brown couch.

She waggles her shoulders. "So, how does it feel to be thirty, flirty, and thriving?"

I snort derisively.

"If you could use your words, that'd be great." Jordyn rips the cupcake into halves and hands me one. It's pink in the middle as well. Strawberry.

"How are *you* feeling?" I ask, accepting the offering.

"I'm fine, Rick, I've been thirty for three months now. How *are you feeling*?" she repeats firmly.

I shrug, slumping down into the couch. "I feel like the universe is fucking with me, and"—I gesture to my boxed-up mess of a living room—"also like a hypocritical piece of shit."

She pulls her legs into a pretzel on the couch and bites into her half of the cupcake. "Your dad text you?"

"Yes, the second I entered the premises. I answered immediately, and politely, like an AI bot. He has a Ring camera on the door that he won't transfer over."

Jordyn presses her lips together. "I'm sorry."

"It's not your fault."

"My unborn child is the reason you moved out."

"I wanted to give you space."

"Yeah, well, I wish you told me that meant moving into an apartment your dad is flipping before you actually moved. I would have told you to say no."

"That's why I *didn't* tell you." I pull my legs to my chest and tuck my chin against my knees.

Jordyn studies me with her big brown doe eyes and naturally perfect eyelashes. "I know what it's like for you with him, Rick. You could have stayed with us until your contract renegotiation. You're gonna get the raise."

I should hope so. I stuff the cupcake into my mouth and smile at her through it. "Fanks for da cupcape."

She snorts. "Rikki."

I swallow and sit up straighter on the couch. "I'm okay, Jord. Thanks for popping over. I'm just tired. I'm gonna unpack and go to bed."

Jordyn purses her lips. "All right. But at dinner tomorrow, I want every detail of what happened with that man tonight. Play-by-play. Micah's excited too."

She leaves, and I flop onto the floor next to my Sunrise Away bag, unzip, and toss it open. The top half lands with a thump on the gold throw rug coating the hardwood floor.

Relief cascades through me at the sight of my neon-green packing cubes. At least I got my suitcase back. I'm reaching for my turquoise toiletries bag when I clock the old-fashioned leather journal with the white garter wrapped around it, lying atop my pristinely organized belongings along the bottom of the suitcase.

I still, blinking at it.

The purple goody bag with my journal in it is sitting on the kitchen table.

I lean forward to inspect this one. Pick it up.

Rikki Romona is carved into the leather on the back.

I drop it back onto the packing cubes and stand, skittering over to the kitchen table. I pick up the purple goody bag and dump it. The contents fall unceremoniously across the wooden tabletop.

The journal's not here.

I glance between the mess of Babe & Willem products and my open suitcase on the floor. A seed of fear prickles up my spine. Am I drunk? Did I somehow put it in the suitcase?

But when? I just got this back.

I snatch up the journal, bring it to the bedroom, and shove it in the top drawer of my nightstand.

An hour later I've unpacked the bag and stuffed my luggage away in the bedroom closet. I collapse on the couch and stare at the ceiling. Silent tears are streaking their way down my cheeks at 2:30 a.m. when my phone dings again.

Reed: Happy Birthday Rikki. You're smart and cool and gorgeous [no smoke] and I had the best time putting out fires with you tonight.

I stare at the message for a long time.

I know what happens now if we start to text: It goes on for a few days before he ghosts, and I'm left feeling shitty about myself, holding a pointless grudge against a guy who doesn't live here, who I hands down just had the best first date of my life with, for the rest of time. I don't want that. Nobody wants that.

I heart his message and write out a quick reply.

Me: I had the best time with you too R. Tyler. Say hi to your Sunrise Away bag for me.

That's it.

We're not texting.

I'm half asleep when I slink into the bedroom at 4:00 a.m. with a giant glass of water. I plop it on my nightstand next to the journal, turn off the light, and collapse into bed.

Reed [4:11 a.m.]: Away bag says he's gonna need therapy from the trauma you put him through

Reed [8:00 a.m.]: I need a book for the flight back. I require the expertise of a professional. What's the best thing you've read lately?

Me [9:01 a.m.]: Elizabeth Ross Falls for Ryan was spectacular. And there's a Hulu adaptation coming soon!

Me [9:04 a.m.]: It's about this woman who's doing research on vets coming back into society after World War I and with a drop of magic, she ends up back in the 20's post war, talking to this guy Ryan who's trying to find his footing back in his regular life. It's profound and moving and she gets stuck back in time living with Ryan and his best friend. Ryan starts super rough around the edges, and closed off from the world and Elizabeth has spent most of her life working and has never formed a real romantic connection. They learn so much from each other. It's beautiful.

Reed [9:04 a.m.]: I've already read that one. I feel the exact same. New favorite.

Me [9:05 a.m.]: You've read it? I keep telling people about it, and no one's heard of it yet! I can't make the WWU read it because there aren't any witches.

Reed [9:06 a.m.]: so to confirm, you had fun last night?

Me [9:07 a.m.]: Yes, Reed.

Reed [9:08 a.m.]: I told you dating is fun.

Me [9:09 a.m.]: *****OCCASIONALLY FUN

Reed [10:27 p.m.]: Can I get your email?

Me [10:29 p.m.]: . . . because that's your preferred mode of communication?

Reed [10:31 p.m.]: because I'm going to send you an email

Me [10:32 p.m.]: because you're in need of a tenth person to fulfill your quota for a threatening fwd chain?

Reed [10:33 p.m.]: 😊😊😊😊😊😊😊😊😊😊 can I get your email?

Me [10:45 p.m.]: rikkirolling28@gmail.com

10 | EMAIL

We haven't spoken for six days when I get the email.

I'm vaguely annoyed. I knew I would be. I feel ghosted. It's ridiculous. Technology is obnoxious.

I've unpacked my boxes. I've hung up some photos and art. I took down a picture of me and my father from when I was a child, which was hanging in the bathroom. I organized my bookshelf and closet, color coordinating the clothes and novels that I had shoved quickly into their appropriate areas earlier in the week. And I thought about Reed. About how when you google him, his podcast company Oh Brother Audio comes up, and his personal Instagram, which is private. Not his books. Not any acting.

When I google Derek Roosevelt, an outdated author website comes up, but it has no pictures. This man compartmentalizes his life in such a fascinating, unconventional, bad-for-branding way. He must act under another, completely different, name.

I'm making dinner alone in the kitchen when my phone pings.

I have broccoli in the oven and pasta on the stove.

I swipe my cell from the counter.

—

SUBJECT: Been feeling inspired. Had some fun.

Reed Tyler <RTYLER48@gmail.com> August 3

LINK

—

What in the fuck.

There's nothing in the email but a link that says *link*. He couldn't name it something else to make it look less suspicious? Is this *spam*?

It can't be. He asked for my email. *This* is the email. I glare down at the link, anticipation mounting in my gut.

Well, I have to know what it is. I can't not click the link. And I can't text him to ask about the link because then he'll know I'm clicking the link mere seconds after it arrived in my inbox.

My thumb juts out to tap it.

Google Drive opens on my phone.

I wait for the doc to load.

TYLER-ROMONA | MESSAGE IN A BOTTLE

CHAPTER 1 | FIRST DATE

Reed

She was wearing UGGs, she had my suitcase, and she was making a run for it.

I throw my phone across the kitchen counter onto the couch. It bounces off and clatters onto the carpet.

"Oh my god."

I gape at the phone lying on the floor halfway across the room for fifteen seconds before I run over, snatch it up, and reopen the doc. Without reading, I thumb through. Page, after page, after page—*there are thirty pages.*

The last one reads:

CHAPTER 2 | THEN

Rikki (Renee?)

My stomach folds up and slides down my colon. I thumb up to the end of chapter one.

> Her attention is all-consuming, she has a certain je ne sais quoi. That kind you look for when you're casting the lead in a film. She has the power to hold you rapt, no matter what the topic is.

I throw the phone down on the counter. *This man is blowing smoke up my ass via a book retelling of our date.*

I stare at my lock screen for ten seconds before I open it up again.

> I can't not see her again. I can't stop feeling the heat of her pressed against me in the water. Can't stop replaying the way she read me out by the lake like I was an open book when I thought I was a goddamn fortress. I can't stop wondering, thinking back to those two book reviews in *The New York Minute* that saw right through me. Saw the good and the bad so clearly, it scared the shit out of me all those years ago.
>
> I can't stop wondering if I'm sitting next to Renee Granger.

My eyes flit to my first published review, now hanging proudly among my photos over the couch in the living room. My heart is pounding. My breaths feel stifled.

Something hisses and pops behind me. *Shit.* The pasta's overflowing. I lunge to switch off the stove. While I'm at it, I turn off the oven.

Phone in hand, I sprint for the door. Throw it open. Run down the hall and pound on Jordyn's apartment. She and Micah have a date night scheduled, but it's five and their reservation isn't till eight.

Jordyn throws the door open. "What! What's wrong? Is someone in trouble? Are you okay? Did you set something else on fire?"

I'm heaving in breaths like a dying woman who just climbed a hundred flights of stairs. Fuck. *Calm down.*

I can't. I can't calm down. The guy I've been obsessing over all week sent me the opening chapter of a romance novel retelling of our one spectacular during-someone-else's-wedding *date*, left the second chapter open for me, and he somehow knows I'm the one who reviewed his books in *The Minute* despite never having gotten around to telling him.

"Email," I gasp to Jordyn. I bend over, bracing an arm against my thigh. Suck in a breath, counting to four. Blow it out, counting to four.

"Email? Are you joking. This is a reaction to an email? I thought you were legitimately dying, Rikki."

"I am *figuratively dying*." I stumble in past Jordyn, who's in sweats and a T-shirt, and fall onto her champagne-colored sectional, holding out my phone. "He. Emailed. Read it."

"It only took him six days." Jordyn walks over and sits next to me.

"I need you to read it and tell me about it, please!"

Jordyn puts a hand on my shoulder and rubs it up and down. "Do you want a weed gummy?"

"I'm fine! I'm calming!" I concentrate on inhaling and blowing out another slow breath. She still hasn't taken the phone. "He wrote a chapter."

"A chapter?"

"He wrote a chapter about the other night!" I belt it out in one breath, and Jordyn rips the phone out of my hand.

I fall forward, hanging my head between my legs.

"*Renee*?" she yelps. "He knows?"

"Please read it from the beginning and play-by-play anything important as you go!"

11 | THE CHAPTER

"There's a whole flashback segment about how seen he felt by your review. Well, Renee's review, of *Broken and Bruised*."

I hold my hands over my ears. "Oh my god."

Jordyn brings my phone back to her face. "How it fulfilled some deep-seated need for validation he had never gotten from an authority in writing." She scrolls. "It literally changed his life because it put his book on the road to being a bestseller. And! He talks about how Granger's review of *Harrowed and Used* cut exceedingly deep because of how accurately it mirrored his own fears about the book. He knew it didn't have the substance it needed to hit the way he wanted. He knew it wasn't based on anything he'd ever experienced, and he couldn't tap into the emotions he needed to really make it work. But he thought he disguised it with enough sparkle and flash. Threw enough plot twists in here and there for it to still resonate in some way, shape, or form. To still make a splash."

She takes a second to skim a paragraph before continuing. "'Renee's review sliced through all my bullshit. She articulated all the concerns and anxieties I had about my fledgling writing career in one concise paragraph.'" Jordyn blows out a loaded breath. "And he's been second-guessing everything he's plotted since."

She's quiet for an agonizingly long fifteen minutes while I pace an infinity-shaped hole in the floor of their living room, racking my brain for what my next move should be in this situation.

Jordyn finally puts down the phone. "Rikki, I know you think the Disney gods fucked you over . . . but this man seems extremely into you. This review-connection stuff, that *doesn't happen*." She pauses, thumbing through the pages again.

The phone dings, and Jordyn pulls it back to her face.

"Your dad. He says, 'What's going on? You okay?' How does he know something's going on?"

I take the phone from her. "He's watching me come in and out on the fucking Ring camera. He's been doing it all week."

Me: I'm fine, just ran over to ask Jordyn something.

"Jesus, Rikki. You're a thirty-year-old woman. That's so creepy. Can you disconnect it?"

Dad: Please don't cause a ruckus in the hallway, I don't want to get complaints.

"I can't risk upsetting him while I'm living for free in his apartment." I fall back onto her couch.

"What's he gonna do all the way in California if you disconnect it?"

I cut her a weary look. "I don't know. I don't want to know."

Jordyn blows out a deep, flustered sigh but drops the topic.

I jam my hands into my hair. "So what should I do? What do you think?"

"About what?"

"The opening romance novel chapter I just received in my inbox!"

She shrugs. "I think you write the next chapter. I want to know what happens after this Renee cliffhanger."

"Jordyn, you know what happens."

"No, what happens in the fictional version of the night. This is romantic shit. Write the ideal next scene."

"The ideal next scene is him coming back up with me for sex, Jordyn. That's what should have happened. I got sad and in my head about a potential relationship dying before it could begin after six months of failure—but we had so much chemistry! What a goddamn waste. Why did I just say goodbye? *What is wrong with me?*"

She waggles her brows. "I think you should write it. Look at the reaction this PG-13 chapter had on you. If this is going nowhere . . . what's the harm in giving him something to think about? He gave you a full-on lust meltdown, and you read like, two extremely tame sentences."

"Three."

"What do you have to lose?"

"I'm not a romance writer."

"Who cares? Just have fun. Write it for you."

"But he's going to read it."

"Again, what do you have to lose?"

We're never going to see each other again. He's in LA, regularly interacting with celebrities. He'll be distracted within the week.

If I don't respond, it's going to be impossible to move past this. Writing the alternate ending to that night could be cathartic.

12 | NOTHING TO LOSE

I write it.

I sit in front of the computer, pull up Word, and I don't get up for four hours that pass like ten minutes. When my eyes finally slide to the clock, it's midnight.

That was—fun.

I'm all mischievous smiles as I save the PDF of the first raunchy(-ish) scene I've ever written. Fiction Reed confronts Fiction Rikki about the review of his novel mid-sex, and she screams out *I'm Renee*, and he yells *I'm Derek*, right as they're climaxing.

It's both hot and hilarious, and I'm very happy with it.

Before I have time to second-guess any of the nonsense I just put on the page, I attach it to an email. My reasons for not using Google Docs are twofold.

1) Google Docs will show you when someone else is in the doc, and I cannot know when he is reading this, or I will die.

[RIKKI ROMONA: Single woman past thirty, and professional RELATIONSHIP COLUMNIST for The Minute *dies, with no prospects, of simultaneous combustion upon realizing three thousand miles away the guy she wrote a short piece of mild erotica about was reading said erotica. Still single. Used Hinge.]*

And 2) I will go in within the hour and delete my chapter if I put it in something as accessible as a Google doc.

I don't even let myself stare at it. I just press send.

—

SUBJECT: RE: Been feeling inspired. Had some fun.
Rikki Romona <rikkirolling28@gmail.com> August 4
SEE ATTACHMENT

—

I slam the laptop shut, plop on the couch, and flip on the TV, my stomach suddenly in knots.

"Holy shit," I mumble.

What if he's reading it?

I squeeze my eyes shut. *I shouldn't have sent it.* I had them slam into so many walls. They scream *I'm Renee* and *I'm Derek* like, five times.

I stuff my face into a pillow. My opening line was *I still know next to nothing about this man, but his synopsis has me hook, line, and sinker: I want to open him up and devour all the small print.*

Help. *Help.* What have I done? Help.

I should have sent it to Jordyn! I should have had her screen it first! I sent him a first draft! I lunge toward my laptop—

My phone dings.

13 | CRAP

Whitney: Rikki are you awake I need you

That's the text I got from my cousin last night. The same cousin I maid-of-honored for last week in Palm Springs. Not at all what I was expecting when I practically flew across the room to my cellular device.

I haven't heard a peep from Reed Tyler.

Glenn is missing. Whitney's husband of exactly seven days is MIA, and she's inconsolable. Jordyn's driving me to the airport so I can catch a noon flight to LA.

Apparently, Whitney and Glenn had a big blowout yesterday when they were packing to leave for their honeymoon. He let it slip that he had been married once before: a secret he's kept through their entire relationship and went out of his way to conceal when they got their marriage license. He left the apartment after their tiff to "surf it off" and never came back.

Glenn's car is still parked at the beach. His phone goes straight to voicemail. She can't get into his credit card history because they just got married and haven't shared all that yet. Her mother, my Aunt Teresa, reported that there'd been weird tension between them all week as they moved into their new place.

Last night when I called Whitney, Aunt Teresa had to come on the line to help articulate the situation, because beyond *I need you Rikki.*

Come home. Please, I need you, she could barely string three words together without hysterically sobbing.

Whitney really needs her cous-sister right now.

Aunt Teresa calls us cous-sisters. We've kindly asked her to stop. The word *cous-sister* burns. I physically shudder every time it's said aloud.

It's been a weird eleven months for Whitney and me. Other than helping coordinate and plan every minute detail of her wedding, we haven't spoken. We've been almost exclusively communicating about wedding shit since she and Glenn got engaged last November. She had only met him three months prior at a Harry Styles concert. Before that, we would talk on the phone every afternoon as I walked from work to the train, or my apartment to the coffee shop I like to write in.

I miss nonwedding Whitney. Of course I booked a flight.

Jordyn reaches out and turns down the radio. "So, have you told him about Whitney?"

I pull my eyes from the monotony of the black tar highway. I've been in a sort of trance, tracing the white dotted lines along the road with my eyes. Between the erotica email and Whitney's distress call, I didn't get much sleep last night.

I frown. "Him who?"

"*Reed*," Jordyn says loudly as she changes into the fast lane.

My stomach dips. "Why would I tell him about Whitney?"

"Not about Whitney, just that you're going to be in LA for a few days! You're going to be in the area! You have to see him again."

"Jordyn, I'm going to LA for Whitney."

She blows out the sigh equivalent of an eye roll. "I'm sure you can find a few hours to see the *best* first date of your life again. Send him a text."

"Jordyn. Last night I sent that man homemade porn. He hasn't responded. I am not about to casually text him that I'm now coincidentally *going to be in the area*. That will not come off casual. It will come off *serial killer*." My voice is squawking higher by the second as I imagine this scenario from his point of view. "We don't know each other well enough for that chapter. I shouldn't have sent it. We don't even follow each other on Instagram."

My phone dings. I glance down. From Instagram: @R.TYLER followed you. A scream flies out of me as I throw the phone at the windshield.

Jordyn screams right along with me. "What is it?" She swerves across the right lanes and pulls over to the shoulder. Several cars blare their horns at us. I brace against the door as she throws the car into park and turns to glare at me.

"Sorry!" I bleat, dropping my head into my hands.

"What happened!"

"He just followed me on Instagram."

Jordyn blinks. "Right after you said you didn't follow each other on Instagram?"

"Don't say Disney gods—"

"Rikki, this is the Disney gods!"

I drag a palm across my face in shame. "I'm sorry I just almost got us killed for Instagram."

Jordyn turns the hazards on and shifts in her seat toward me. "Rikki. If you don't see him while you're out there, you're going to regret it. You met him through an actual meet-cute! You know him through an actual friend! That *never happens.* He comes preapproved through mutuals! And you already really like him."

I stare down at the notification in my hands. "There's no point in entertaining this! To what end? He doesn't live here!"

Jordyn shifts the car into gear and pulls back out onto the road.

"I don't think you should worry about how it might end." She maneuvers us back into the fast lane. "I think you should just let it start and see where it goes."

"Glenn could be in serious trouble," I mumble. "I can't go gallivanting around with a new random guy I have a crush on while I'm there."

Jordyn throws her hands up and lets them land on the steering wheel. "Glenn could be fine. Life is complicated. Sometimes you have to juggle two situations at once." She pauses. "I don't think I've ever seen you like you were at that wedding."

"Like how?"

"You were incandescent. Like somebody plugged you in."

I scratch at my arm nervously. *I thought that exact same thing.* Jordyn and I have always been in sync like this. Our brains weave the world together in very similar ways. We have epiphanies at the same time. We get good news at our separate jobs around the same time. We get sick at the same time. It's part of what makes our soul-sistership so powerful. She's correct. I was radiating joy at that wedding.

"Reaching out now gives him *so much* power."

Jordyn sighs. "You're not giving him power—you're seizing yours. If you don't reach out, nothing happens."

I've been leaning forward without realizing it. I flop back into the seat.

"How did your chapter end?" she says suddenly.

"It ends with a quick conversation of how epic the sex was, and then the topic of trust comes up and things get vaguely deep before realizing they only have a few hours left together before his flight home. He dubiously suggests that they meet at the golf course lake one year from their first date and do it all again, and Fiction Rikki shoots that down with an abrupt no before he even gets the full thought out. He says *all right, all right*, and then she says *so what now?*"

Jordyn nods, as we turn off the exit toward Newark Airport. "Nice throw to his court."

"If I text him now, I *will* come off like a psychotic stalker."

"Rick, he just followed you on Instagram. That's not nothing. You have an in to open up communication. Use it."

14 | WHAT AM I DOING

I've been hunched over at the airport gate, staring at the *request to follow* sign on Reed's private Instagram page for thirty-seven minutes. His profile picture appears to be a candid shot of him in a pair of sunglasses with a palm tree backdrop. What is he thinking, hiding those eyeballs of his in a profile picture?

He definitely read the chapter. Why else request to follow me? Why not text me? Why not email? *Why is this so weird?*

I drop the phone into my jacket pocket. I need a distraction. I should read. Part of me was relieved I had to cancel book club tonight because I'm still fifty pages shy of the end of *Heir of Fire*. I packed the giant hardcover.

I lay my carry-on edition of the Sunrise Away bag collection on the ground and unzip it as discreetly as possible. I hate opening hardtop carry-ons in public. It feels like such an invasion of privacy. Everyone can see the contents of your entire bag in one fell swoop.

Carefully I lift the top portion of the bag. But where I thought I placed *Heir of Fire*, sitting atop my clothes is the old-timey journal from Babe's wedding. *Goddamnit.* I groan, drop the bag closed, and zip it back up. I was in such a rush to pack last night after talking to my aunt, and they were both on my nightstand. I must have grabbed the wrong one.

"Now boarding groups one and two to Los Angeles!"

Great. I have nothing to read on the plane. I pull my phone back out and send Whitney a quick *boarding the plane, see you soon* text before jumping back over to Instagram and reopening Reed's page.

I'm not giving him power. I'm seizing mine.

I *request to follow* and immediately flip to Airplane Mode.

I will not spend the five-hour flight having one giant anxiety hot flash as I await the moment he potentially accepts my request.

Instead, I spend it drafting a one-sentence message to *maybe* send at *some* point when I feel that it's appropriate.

Hey Reed, I'm actually unexpectedly in LA, you want to grab a drink?

My cousin/best friend is in crisis so I'm in LA unexpectedly this week. Let me know if you want to grab a drink before I head back.

Hey I'm in LA by accident. WHATTT'S UP.

Hey Reed, I just tripped over a curb and ended up outside your door, ready for date number two?

Can I get your home address? I want to google map exactly how many steps it is from my house.

HEY REED. IT'S ME RENEE. I FLED ACROSS THE COUNTRY AFTER OUR ONE GOOD DATE AND I'M HERE TO START OUR OFFICIAL LONG TERM RELATIONSHIP. DON'T FREAK OUT I'M A CHILL PERSON.

Free Tuesday for a second date? 7 p.m. Barney's in Studio City at the bar. Eat beforehand. Wear clothes.

The Sunday Minute

LOVE TODAY

DEBUNKING THE STIGMA OF INSTALOVE:
WE CAN FALL FAST AND LOVE LONG.

By Rose Thyme

Hast thou happened upon the phenomenon of instalove? We've all read or watched some rendition of *Romeo and Juliet*. At the very least you've heard the lyrics to Taylor Swift's 2008 triumph "Love Story."

Perhaps you're just not familiar with the term *instalove*—it's possible you missed the great internet instalove protest of the late 2000s.

The youths of the time (millennials & zillennials) were devouring every young adult novel being cranked out in the wake of *Twilight*, and a large faction of them were up in arms about the idea of love at first sight. The majority of our favorite paranormal romance books narrated tales of young women falling, almost instantly, for the vampire/angel/shapeshifter men that walked into their lives, usually via AP bio.

In their humble opinions: Edward Cullen had no right to instantaneously be in love with Bella Swan. The two of them needed to spend a certain undisclosed amount of time together for their love to become legitimate. More dialogue had to be exchanged for it to feel "real." Videos and posts ranting about how ridiculously quickly these emotionally charged teens were falling in love with their ancient men counterparts were inescapable at the time.

The kicker of it all was—these complaints were coming (mostly) from the youth, the majority of whom hadn't ever been in love themselves. And most of whom fell irrevocably in love with Edward Cullen right alongside Bella Swan. So who were we, really, to say that instalove was a sham?

Who is anyone, who hasn't experienced the phenomenon that is *love at first sight*, to denounce its legitimacy? As adults I think we've all realized there's no viable way to actually measure how fast the scientific process of "falling in love" doth take. Because love isn't technical. It's not logical. It's inexplicable and irrational. If instant love wasn't naturally occurring between any humans in our world, I don't think we would be sitting here talking about it. And after consuming many a season of *Love Is Blind*, I think it's fair to say that people can indeed fall in love very, very quickly. Whether love is *enough* to support a successful long-term relationship is an entirely different can of worms.

My twenty-eight-year-old cousin has recently fallen at light speed for a man she met eleven months ago in the parking lot of a Harry Styles concert. They're about to get married, and thus, I have embarked upon this week's instalove deep dive in her honor.

Over the past six months, various members of the family have pummeled her with doubts, condescending questions, and cutting comments on her romantic choices.

So I sent out the Bat-Signal here at *The Minute* for couples in long-term relationships who met under whirlwind circumstances: who fell in love, fast and hard, and fostered that love long term.

[continued on page 4]

15 | HERE FOR WHITNEY

Breaking: Reed accepted the request. He only has obscure photos of random crap on his feed—no humans. *He's one of those.*

"So any word from Glenn?" I ask carefully as Aunt Teresa merges onto the 405. We've spent our first fifteen minutes together catching up on the mundane aspects of life. Aunt Teresa's a doctor in the emergency wing of the local hospital. She was a single mom throughout my entire childhood, but—big news—she's currently dating another, very attractive, doctor. There was a lot to dig into there.

"No, no word. His phone is still off. Whitney's still in the fetal position," she says.

Whitney is one of those people who can't be alone. She wilts away like spinach on a stove. And Aunt Teresa works a lot; hence, the deep-seated need for me to be present during this missing persons situation.

"What do you think happened? You know him better than I do."

"Honestly, I don't know." My aunt sighs. "I don't feel like I know him that well either. He's always so polite and reserved, you know, in that English way. It'll be forty-eight hours soon. She'll be able to file an official missing persons report."

Aunt Teresa drops me at her house and heads back to the hospital she works at. Inside I find Whitney curled up on the bed in her old room.

Whitney's always been tiny. These days she's five foot one with beautiful dark eyes, thick brows, long gray-blond hair, and heart-shaped lips. Her gold skin is perpetually sun kissed, and her personality's a ten. The woman's magnetic. Today her skin's pale. Her eyes are red. Her face is swollen and puffy. Her under eyes are a sad shade of blue.

I change out of my jeans to match her vibe: sweatpants, baggy T-shirt, messy bun.

I spend the afternoon giving her hugs and back rubs on her mother's couch.

Aunt Teresa's living room is the definition of cozy. She's got a big bright-blue sectional, burnt-yellow walls, and a gold-framed flat-screen TV surrounded by bookshelves, cluttered to perfection with a combination of knickknacks, DVDs, pictures, and tomes. When I manage to get my own place someday, I want to recreate this vibe in my own living room.

I listen as Whitney laments the moving process she's been through this past week—how it tugged and pushed on the easy-loving rapport she typically shares with Glenn. The small secrets she stumbled into as she helped unpack his things—the most troubling being the woman he apparently married six years ago after a four-month stint in Hawaii. He ghosted her when his father fell ill and he had to return to the UK on short notice. They eventually got divorced, but it was a long-winded drama because he avoided it for so long.

I like Glenn less and less as the evening wears on. Whitney's utterly convinced he's been attacked by a shark or pulled out by a riptide and is currently lost with his surfboard at sea.

I'm skeptical. I tell her I think Glenn is going to be fine. That he probably needed some space, and he might have trauma around confrontation. She's not sold.

We order Thai food and call Glenn several times (straight to voicemail). We keep *Friends* running on the TV so it never gets too quiet.

My mom and Layla barge into the house around seven with dessert. They set two large cups of cookie-butter ice cream in front of us from our favorite shop, Afters, and we all settle in at the table to catch up.

I find myself zoning out as Mom jumps into her third back-to-back tale about a silly dog she's been babysitting. My mother, Kelli, is the charming, chaotic lady wearing a Stevie Nicks sweater, who never quite makes it through one story before she gets distracted and starts another.

We weren't allowed to have a dog, growing up, because Dad had no patience for animals. Post divorce, Mom rescued my boi, Udon Noodle, who has since passed, and when I moved out to New York for college, she started a dog-sitting business. She's twelve years in now, and it's thriving. Her house is always overrun with adorable pups. There are a minimum of six doggos there at all times, and while I, too, love dogs, I prefer a house with a little less canine activity. A little less activity in general. When I visit now, I tend to stay with Aunt Teresa.

We're about an hour into casual chitchat, mostly directed at Whitney, when my mother turns to me and says, "How are things going in Dad's apartment?"

I stiffen. I haven't told her about moving into my father's apartment. Whitney doesn't even know. Which means . . . my father must have told her.

"You talked to Dad?"

"We got coffee the other day, yes."

I hate when they get coffee. I hate it with the kind of burning, all-consuming passion that eats away at your internal organs. It started about five years back. These sporadic in-person catch-ups.

I clear my throat. "To discuss me?"

"To catch up." She smiles. "And yes, we discussed you. You're our kid. You're typically our main topic of discussion. You're not exactly an open book, Rikki. We cross-reference our intel about your life."

I inhale, shoving my rising tide of emotions into a filing cabinet for later examination. "We've talked about this, Mom. There's a reason I restrict the amount of information I share with that man about my life."

My mother sighs. "That *man* is your father. He's family."

She's said this to me about ten times in the past five years. Every time I hear it, I want to throw myself through a window.

I feel like "family" privilege should be revoked once a restraining order has entered the chat.

"I'm glad he's helping you out," she finishes.

I glance at Whitney and Layla, both of whom are averting their eyes, looking incredibly uncomfortable. I let the topic drop, shifting my focus to the bookcase behind my mother's head and letting my mind wander as she easily breezes onto another subject.

"Rikki, baby?"

I snap back into myself ten dissociative minutes later. "Yeah?"

"Before we leave, we wanted to tell you something." My mom glances over at Layla. "Well, I wanted to ask you something. While you're here, on the West Coast, in person."

They smile brightly at each other and then at me.

I raise my brow. "What's up?"

"Well"—my mom dances in her seat, bouncing her knees like a little kid—"I asked Layla to marry me on Friday!"

"And I said yes, of course!" Layla says. She holds out a hand with a silver ring featuring a cluster of amethysts that make up a delicate floral design.

The angst winding through my system melts on sight. A smile burns into my cheeks. It's enchanting. And unique. Just like her.

"We're getting a matching one made for your mom," Layla adds.

"It's perfect. Congratulations!" I beam at them. "I'm so happy for you two."

"And sweetie." Mom reaches across the table, grabbing my hand. "Would you—it would mean everything to me if you'd be my maid of honor. Will you?"

I suck in a sharp breath, smile wilting just the slightest bit as my insides twist in consternation. *Another wedding.* "Yes, Mom, of course."

◆ ◆ ◆

"So what about you?" Whitney blurts.

It's been about an hour since Mom and Layla left. Whitney and I retreated to the couch. We've been sprawled out in the nest of pillows on the sectional. *Friends* is on. I've been silently running through a slew of grounding exercises to regulate the wedding-planner anxiety shivering in my chest.

I blink out of my happy place and come back to reality on the couch, shifting to look at Whitney. "What?"

"What about you?" she says again.

"What about me?"

The two of us have gone six hours without her asking a single question about me, and it's been a welcome relief to be out of my own head.

Whitney sits up straighter. Her giant messy bun flops backward away from her face as she studies me with her currently bloodshot brown eyes. "How are you doing?"

I cringe as an image of Reed reading my erotic chapter comes hurtling back into my mind. "I'm okay."

"What's going on with your dad?"

I wave her off. "Nothing new."

"You're living in his apartment?" She hugs a pillow to her chest. "I thought you were trying no contact again after the last bout of fuckery."

I sigh. His last "bout of fuckery" was inviting me to a resort in Mexico with him and his girlfriend last year post my big five-month relationship breakup. I flew to Mexico City and took a car to the resort only to receive an email from my father explaining that he had to cancel last minute. I tried to check into his room, but they *couldn't find* his reservation. I tried to get ahold of him through every possible venue and failed to get him on the line. I turned around and flew home to Newark. I was so mad, I managed to hold on to no contact for five months before finally accepting one of his various apology texts, calls, emails, and messages relayed through my mother.

"He's not living in the apartment," I answer curtly. "It's one he's flipping."

"Why are yo—"

"It's temporary. I'm due for a raise at work. I'll be out of there as soon as it comes through."

"Okay. . . What's the latest on the dating scene? How'd it go this week? You set your dates on Fridays right? And Saturdays? Tell me things."

When I stay quiet, she takes my hand in between both of hers and shakes it. "Pleassssee. Rikki. Distract me."

16 | DISTRACTIONS

"Text him." Whitney sits up, rallied by my Reed saga.

"Your husband is missing, and you want me to text some guy to potentially spend time away from you while you're here, fretting all alone?"

"*Yes.* Then I can fret over you for a second instead of the five thousand horrific explanations of what's happened to Glenn that I've cooked up in my head. Help me tune out Catastrophizing Whitney and live in a romance bubble with my cous-sister for a second."

I cut her a serious look. "I thought we agreed never to use that word."

"Mom says it a lot. It's rubbing off on me." She holds out her hand. "Let me see what you came up with on the plane."

I reluctantly hand over my iPhone, watching nervously as she scrolls through the list of text drafts.

She taps one. "This."

I peer over her shoulder.

Free Tuesday for a second date? 7 p.m. Barney's in Studio City at the bar. Eat beforehand. Wear clothes.

"That?"

Whitney makes some edits: switching out Tuesday for tomorrow (Monday). She changes 7:00 p.m. to 9:00 p.m. and flips the phone around to show it to me.

"This isn't a text—it's a demand. This draft was a joke! Most of these drafts were a joke."

She shoots me an impassive glare. "How many people have you casually dated?"

". . . Zero," I mutter.

"Exactly. And how many people have I casually dated?"

I hunch forward with the weight of her expertise. "Everyone ever until you met Glenn."

"And did I seduce them successfully and make them come to me wanting a relationship?"

"Yes, many times," I mumble.

Whitney can date multiple people at the same time. Honestly that's some sort of superpower. How does a person even have time to *think* about multiple people romantically, let alone date them?

She taps my phone again. "Send him this text."

"That text has absolutely no context about what I'm doing here at all."

"That's the point, Rick."

"It acknowledges nothing that's gone on in the email realm of this situation."

"Again. That's the point."

I pull a blanket over my head and yank it tight under my chin. "It doesn't sound like something I would say."

"I thought you wanted this text to be casual."

"Yeah."

"So that. Is. The point." Whitney comes alive for the first time since I got here. She grabs my arm, shaking it, eyes flashing. "You need to gauge how much you actually like him. That way you'll know if pursuing him further, in any fashion, is worth it.

"Think of it as a research date. How much of the wedding-date chemistry was you being swept up in the moment, and how much of it was cold, hard, irresistible sexual magnetism? Do you legitimately have an emotional connection or was that just a one-night passing feeling?

You'll only find out if you see him *again*." She pauses, mushing her lips together in thought. "You know what, I'm going to give you an official assignment because I know how much you fucking love your homework."

I guffaw. "I don't 'fucking love' homework. I enjoy taking a task and accomplishing it on time to my fullest ability—"

"You do, too, fucking love homework. All your jobs are adult homework." She squeezes my arm. "I want you to come back to me having evaluated both your emotional and physical connection on a scale from one to a hundred. Here." She yanks a notebook from under the coffee table glass and rips out a page with a breakdown of physical and emotional categories to grade him on, including but not limited to: physical attraction, kissing, casual touch, emotional intelligence, comedic compatibility, and "other."

I stare at it for a minute, committing the categories to memory.

The woman's right—having this tiny shift in perspective makes me feel less vulnerable. It shifts the power dynamic just the slightest amount in my direction. Now this isn't necessarily a date, it's a research project, and I can rock a research project.

Me [11:01 p.m.]: Free tomorrow for a second date? 9pm Barney's in Studio City at the bar. Eat beforehand. Wear clothes.
Reed [11:30 p.m.]: 👀 Okay Renee.

SECOND ENCOUNTER

17 | RESEARCH PROJECT

I'm wearing one of Whitney's scoop-neck "hot girl" (her words, not mine) white sundresses, with platform sandals and a leather jacket. She insisted on curling my hair into some loose waves, which I allowed, but her play to switch out my leather jacket for a jean one, was swiftly denied. One doesn't waltz into a battle without armor, and I don't go on first or second dates without my leather jacket. *What's the difference, Rick?* The difference is stark and yet almost subconscious to the casual observer. A jean jacket says *come talk to me*, the leather jacket: *don't fuck with me.*

I get to the bar ten minutes early to stake out a spot. I picked this pub because it's never too crowded. They play fun Irish rock music at the perfect volume, and the walls and ceiling are draped with colored Christmas lights all year long. There's a consistent backdrop of cheerful chattering, but it never gets so loud that you can't hear yourself speak. It's cozy and unintimidating, and during high school I used to come here for dinner with Whitney and Jordyn on Friday and Saturday nights all the time.

I choose a stool at the center of the bar and order a glass of red wine. Then I spend seven minutes swirling it into a maelstrom, thinking *this is what my stomach looks like right now.*

What's he going to say about the chapter? also runs through my brain about fifty thousand times.

Maybe he won't show. Maybe he lied. Maybe the combination of *chapter* and *random-ass text* were lethal, and he's figuratively died and become a ghost.

He's going to think I flew out here to have sex with him. Literally. That's what he has to be thinking. *It's what I would be thinking.* I can't believe I sent that stupid idiotic chapter—

"Rikki?"

My head snaps up so suddenly that some of my wine sloshes over and plops onto the floor. Reed casually swipes some napkins off the bar and lunges down to clean it. Heat floods my center.

Why is this hot? Does it count as *other*? *Mental note to award an* A.

He rises from the ground a beat later, lips twisted in that amused knot from the wedding. His neon eyes snag mine like two searchlights piercing the night, throwing my heart into that same 360 twist it did the first time he spoke to me.

"Hey," he says cheerfully. He tosses the wine napkins on the bar and grabs a stool.

"Hey," I parrot. Tonight Reed's in dark jeans, a white button-up, and a *leather jacket*. I clear my throat. "Nice outfit."

The edge of his lip twitches up. "Likewise. The text said to wear clothes, and I really took that to heart."

I choke on a laugh as the bartender swings by to take his order.

"I'mnothereforsex," explodes out of me the moment the server's out of earshot.

Reed cocks a brow, eyes glinting. "Come again?"

"I'm. I'm not *here* for you," I clarify louder, articulating each word with hand gestures.

His lips spread into a grin. "Well, I *am*, *in fact*, here for you. Did I misread the text? I believe I was invited on a date?"

My heart wiggles up into my windpipe. "Yeah. This is *a date*. I just mean I'm not here in California *for you*," I explain. "I was in the area. And I thought I might as well invite you to stop by, to join me, while I stopped by . . . at this bar."

His smile widens. "Well, I'm glad you invited me to stop by, to join you stopping by."

I swirl my wine. "Well, I'm glad you stopped by, to join me stopping by, this time that I stopped by."

Reed scoots forward an inch so our knees interlock. Without breaking eye contact, he takes a sip of the beer that's appeared in front of him. I press my lips together as a flurry of sensation floods my thighs. *Casual touch, A.* He lowers the drink. "So what are you doing here, Rikki?"

I take a sip of wine. "Whitney lost Glenn."

"Is that the title of a play, or are those people you know?"

"Whitney's my twenty-eight-year-old cousin, and Glenn's her thirty-year-old husband."

He drops an elbow onto the bar. "Her thirty-year-old husband died?"

I shake my head vehemently. "No, they got married last week. It's why I was flying back from LA before Babe's wedding. They moved in together *this* week, had a fight, and now Glenn's been missing for about seventy-two hours with his phone turned off."

Reed's mouth falls open.

I wave him off. "The police aren't very concerned, but his absence is obviously deeply upsetting to Whitney."

"Shit," Reed says softly. "Where have you looked so far? Where was he last seen?"

I tuck my hair behind my ear. "He was last seen at Ridgerock Beach, where he likes to surf, and his car is still there. And, I mean we haven't *looked* anywhere since I got here . . . Whitney's been so distraught. She's staying at my aunt's right now. She checked the beach three days ago—that's when she found his car. She thinks something horrible happened to him in the water."

I notice a faint spattering of red-brown freckles across Reed's nose and cheeks as he studies me. "What do you think?" he says.

"I think there's a high probability that he's staying with friends and avoiding confrontation."

Reed finishes up his beer and throws down a twenty. "All right."

"Are you . . . leaving?" I ask.

He stands. "Let's go look for Glenn."

"What? We just—" I squint at him. "You want to look for Glenn with me?"

"Rikki, I want to do anything with you."

I scoff, sliding off my stool. "You want to do *anything* with me?"

He nods, waiting for me to grab my purse. "That's what I said."

I glare at him as I pull my crossbody over my head. "Don't blow smoke up my—"

"I'm not blowing smoke up your ass." He pivots toward the door.

I stare at his back for a moment before hustling after him.

The two of us emerge onto the well-lit Studio City sidewalk. People mill about in cute outfits, wandering in and out of the restaurants and bars. I follow Reed, mind spinning as I weave through passersby, and stop short as he circles around to the driver's side of a blue Mercedes sedan parked on the street.

I gawk at him across the hood. "What is this?"

"This is called a car." He opens the door and steps into the driver's seat.

Reed drives a Mercedes? What is he, like . . . a financially stable millennial adult? I don't know if I've ever dated one of those.

He rolls down the passenger side window and leans over to catch my eye. "Do you know about doors?"

My brow furrows. "Doors?"

"Have you operated them?"

I give him the finger, yank open the door, and shove myself inside, hastily buckling the seat belt.

"Okay." He twists toward me. "What do we know about Glenn?"

"His birthday is in November, and he likes Harry Styles," I reply automatically.

Reed's mouth presses into a thin line. "What *helpful* information do we know about Glenn?"

I swallow, grappling with that for a moment. "He likes to drink and play pool with his buddies, I think. He likes to surf. He smokes cigars. It's disgusting."

"You two seem close."

I slap the dashboard. "I think I've heard Whitney say he goes to that billiards bar down in Sherman Oaks."

"There we go." Reed pulls out into the street. When the light in front of us turns green, he hangs a U-turn, sending us back in the opposite direction on Ventura Boulevard.

The radio's set to a classic rock station. Pink Floyd plays faintly over the speakers. We're quiet as the car glides past a slew of familiar landmarks I haven't seen in a while. It's only been seven months, but so much has changed since the last time I drove around out here. It's bizarre how the seemingly permanent landscape of your hometown shifts like sand on a beach the second you move away.

"Maybe I should have driven," I mumble quietly.

"You should have driven my car?"

"I've given you the power to kidnap me."

He purses his lips. "Ah, and you'd prefer to hold the kidnapping power."

"Of course."

"Do you want me to let you out?"

"No," I say quickly.

"Okay." Reed sounds amused. He shoots me a smile. "Can I ask another first-date question?"

"You may."

"What's your fatal dating flaw?"

I blow out a harsh laugh. "Reed. Your first-date questions are not questions. They're essay prompts."

His toothy grin catches the light.

I turn toward the window, watching the reflection of the streetlights float across the glass. "Welp. It's probably—needing to control everything . . . but also not wanting to have to control it at the same time?

I want a copilot, not a passenger. And men I've dated see me taking charge of things, and either become intimidated by it all, or sit back, relax, and let me do all the work in the relationship. And . . . it takes me a while to realize it's even happening because I can so easily become an out-of-control control freak."

Reed chuckles gently from the driver's seat. "Hmm . . ."

"*Hmm?*" I repeat.

His lip curves up his cheek. "Hm, sounds like you've dated some lazy assholes."

I bark a laugh, studying his sharp profile for a beat as he gazes confidently out at the road. "How did you know?"

"About the assholes?"

"No."

He pauses. "That you wrote the reviews?"

A chill wisps through me. "Yeah."

"Educated guess." He offers me a shy smile. "The timing lined up. You lined up. It wasn't that big of a leap after talking to you all night. You have a distinct voice." He pauses, tapping his finger against the steering wheel. "Honestly, after how that day went, I would have been more surprised if you weren't Renee. That was . . . kismet like I've never experienced before.

"I meant everything I wrote about that review."

I watch the lights change as we drive past the Ralphs on Hazeltine. "That I ruined your writing career when I didn't like *Harrowed and Used?*"

He shakes his head, shooting me a smirk. "Noooo, that you gave me the career with the *Broken and Bruised* review. You legitimized it for me. I have that thing framed on my wall, Rikki."

My eyelids snap up as I cough-laugh in shock. "No, *you don't.*"

"I do."

"I do too."

18 | MAN HUNT

"What's Glenn look like?" Reed asks as we power walk toward the billiards bar.

"British."

"British?" He repeats the word back like it means nothing.

"Yeah, like you look Scottish, he looks British."

"Scottish is British."

"English!"

"English?" he repeats dryly. "Come on, Rikki, you're a writer. Do better than that."

I *pfft* and cut him off, grabbing the bar door first and hauling it open. "He's white with brown, voluminous hair and a lean physique. He looks like every other classically handsome English white boy I know."

Reed follows me into the building. "So he looks like Harry Styles?"

"He wishes he looked like Harry Styles," I correct.

"Really painting a vivid picture for me."

Country music hums low over the speakers. There's a haze of smoke fogging up the air. Cigars droop from mouths in every direction, and pool tables stretch as far as the eye can see.

"Wow, it's gross in here. Isn't this illegal?" I mutter, frantically swatting the area around us with my palm.

Reed steps up next to me. "Keep doing that with your hand. I think it's working."

"Reed Tyler. I'm in detective mode. Do not sass me."

I spot a large wooden crate up against the wall, step up onto it, and scan the room. The place is loaded with men clutching pool sticks and alcohol. After a good three minutes, I hop down, shaking my head. "He's not here."

Reed steps onto the crate I just hopped off.

I glance up at him. "What are you doing?"

"Has anyone seen Glenn?" Reed's projected voice booms across the bar.

I freeze as the place goes comically silent. Slowly, every head spins in our direction. I close my eyes, fidgeting under the weight of the unexpected secondhand attention.

"Yeah!" says a voice in the back right.

"Yeah?" I blurt excitedly.

The guy nods. "Yep, he was here last night! Drunk off his ass, lost fifty bucks to me."

My heart leapfrogs around my chest. "Do you happen to know where he's staying?" I yelp over the music. "We're family, and we've come from out of town to visit."

"No clue. He comes in here a bunch. We drink, we bet, we play pool."

Reed puts a hand on my back and rubs the spot between my shoulder blades with his thumb. "All right, thank you for your time!"

I jog down the steps of the bar and spin around, hands held aloft for a double high five. "He's alive!"

A new high-octane, close-lipped smile I have yet to be exposed to overtakes Reed's face, highlighting—dimples? *A* dimple. In his left cheek. He meets my high ten, weaves our fingers together, and steps closer as he shines our arms down by our sides.

Wow. The way this man maneuvers his body is so effortless.

"It's a good lead. I think we should go check out that beach he likes, take a look around."

I nano-nod, admiring him. "All right."

"All right." He dips in for a quick peck to the right of my lips before tugging me in the direction of his car.

The roads get darker as we approach the coast.

This date is confusing. It doesn't feel like a second date. It feels like a weird hybrid of a first date and a twentieth one. A casual, intimate, to-the-right-of-my-lips peck? Like we've been together for years? What was that? Why did it ping around my chest like a metal disc in a pinball machine.

"I'm really curious," Reed starts, breaking me from my trance. "About what your dad did."

A sad laugh falls out of me as I turn away from the window. "To give me the issues?"

"Yeah." Reed gnaws at his lip self-consciously as he makes a left.

"Are you gonna tell me what your dad did in return?"

He's quiet for a minute. The streetlights run over his sharp profile every fifty feet. "Yeah, okay."

"How 'bout," I propose, "we hold the backstories for the postmortem. Keep date two from getting too dark."

He smiles. "Okay, I'm gonna hold you to that. I'm a sucker for good character flashback."

I snort as snapshots of *Broken and Bruised* come to mind. "Yeah, that rings a bell. So tell me, how much of Derek's story was autobiographical? Was there a girl who broke your heart?"

His mouth scrunches into an adorable pout. "Yes. Of course."

"Were you engaged right out of high school?"

He grips the steering wheel harder. "Yep." The word is dripping with the self-deprecating humor that comes with time and self-awareness. "It fucked me up. I was an angst monster for years. I wore all black, *through the rest of college.*"

I chuckle. "Awww."

"I had a trench coat, Rikki. A black trench coat."

I snicker. "Oh nooo."

"I called it my writing trench. I bought it when I started *Broken and Bruised.* I would wear it every day to class, and I would wear it inside at my desk, typing, convinced I looked like the coolest person that ever lived."

"Tell me there are pictures from this era."

He smiles out at the night.

I sit up excitedly. "*There are!* Reed, I am going to need to see those, stat. Please blow one up for me and sign it. I'll hang it on the wall next to your review."

A laugh bursts out of him.

"Tell me you didn't walk in on her cheating while you were visiting on Halloween."

"I diiiid," he says solemnly.

"Reeeed." I chuckle. "I'm so sorry you had to live the plot of the sad, cliché teenage post–high school love story."

Reed parks the car in the small lot along Glenn's favorite beach, turns off the engine, and looks at me, eyes alight. "So what's your relationship damage, Rikki Romona?"

I shake my head and unbuckle my seat belt. "Nah, it's not as fun as yours." I swing my door open and climb out of the car.

Glenn's white Ford Explorer is parked in the far corner of the lot. I start toward it, and Reed catches up, quickly falling into lockstep.

"You're not gonna tell me?" he says, stricken.

I shoot him a small smile. "Reed, my answers to these essay questions are quite sad." The wind off the water barrels into us, tossing my hair around my face.

He nods, empathy flushing the disappointment from his eyes. "Yeah, I get it. I've had nine years and a book to process mine."

I chuckle. "I'm only on year two, so it's still working its way through."

And it was only a five-month-long relationship. And maybe the breakup shouldn't have affected me so dramatically.

He cocks an evil brow. "You know what might help you through it faster?"

I arch one right back. "A trench coat?"

His face cracks into a full grin. "Buy yourself a motherfucking trench coat, Rikki. It's gonna change your life."

I snort as we come to a hard stop next to Glenn's car. We flip on our iPhone flashlights, and slowly, the two of us circle the Explorer, peering in through the windows. There are clothes scattered all over the trunk. The back bench is folded down to accommodate a surfboard running vertically through the length of the car.

This fucking bastard.

I knock my finger into the window twice, pointing to it. "That wasn't there when Whitney found the car. She thought he was lost in the ocean with it."

Reed takes a few steps toward the beach, glancing around for any signs of life. "You want to take a walk down there, see if he's around?"

I carry my sandals as we mosey down the dark, empty beach. The sand is grainy and cold against my bare feet. It's cooler here near the water. We walk on a slight angle, my sundress flying up against my legs, our accidentally matching leather jackets tucked closed, hunched against the wind.

A pale-blue wooden lifeguard tower sits unoccupied down the shoreline, closer to the water: That's our heading. Reed turns to smile at me, and his auburn hair blows up vertically over his head. "What's on the docket for this week's Love Today?"

I purse my lips, a little embarrassed to share any of my recent topics given our present circumstances. "Um." I kick up a spritz of sand. "Well, my latest went out yesterday. It's been in the works for a bit. It was inspired by, well, Whitney, and her wedding. Her and Glenn's love story." I scuff more sand out toward the water.

Reed's shoulder brushes up against mine, and I bump his back. The close proximity has my skin buzzing. "What's the angle?"

I stare out at the water as a series of small, dark waves crash against the shore. "It's called 'Debunking the Stigma of Instalove: We Can Fall Fast and Love Long.' Basically, I pontificated on five different love stories from couples across different generations who spoke to me about their whirlwind romances that spawned successful marriages of ten-plus years. I wove together the similarities between their stories and theorized how and why each relationship was a long-term success."

Reed raises his brow, cynicism in the slant of his grin, the set of his eyes. "And what was their secret?"

An anxious laugh rattles out of me. "The classics. Empathy, communication, love. Basically, love is transcendent. Almost supernatural." I shrug. "It's not hard to believe in magic when your job includes sifting through the stories of thousands of happy couples across the country."

Reed bumps my shoulder again. "That sounds . . . so wholesome and uplifting."

I nudge him back. "Your expression says otherwise."

He rolls his eyes, mouth falling open. "I mean." He sighs and takes a few steps backward toward the car. "I don't know if I can do this conversation without my trench."

I snort.

He shrugs, laughing at himself. "Yeah, like I said, that college incident burned. It's not that I don't believe in love—I've been in it—it's more like I don't quite trust it. If people that love you can hurt you so hard, do they truly love you?" He twists his lips together for a pensive beat. "Love has too many different meanings . . . If you and your partner's definitions don't line up, the relationship is autodestined to fail, and someone's going to get wrecked in the process."

I eye him thoughtfully. "So what's love to you?"

He looks at me, mouth screwed back up into the knot. "That's a deep cut, Rikki."

"Says the guy doling out memoir prompts."

A grumbled laugh. "All right. Can I get back to you on that?"

I nod, a knowing smile on my face. "It's a tough one."

"Do you have an answer?"

"What's love to me?" I huff a laugh. "Not a complete one."

"Give me the incomplete."

I focus on the sky. Tiny pinpoints of light dust the smoggy onyx abyss. "It's . . . knowing that when you call them at 1:00 a.m., they're going to pick up," I say quietly. "Flying home and knowing someone's going to be there for you, waiting at the airport. Knowing when something's heavy, there's someone who's going to carry it with you. Hard truths, warm comments, tight hugs, follow-through." I shiver, wistfulness slinking through me. "Love's a team sport. It's the urge to recalibrate your entire life to line up with someone else's so you can get from point A to point B in lockstep, even if it means taking a longer route."

I glance over at Reed as we reach the base of the lifeguard tower. His eyes are glassy.

"Are you okay?" I ask softly.

He coughs, looking out at the ocean. "Yeah, I'm fine."

We stand there for a long moment while he studies the horizon, and I study him.

"Has she ever apologized?" I say quietly. "Was anything that happened in the second book real?"

In his second novel, his cheating fiancée has a redemption arc. They end up trying their relationship over from scratch, and, in the end, they're together. Unfortunately, the emotional arcs didn't feel realistic or genuine. The relationship moments were half baked. You could tell the author didn't believe in their own story.

Reed shakes his head, mouth pressed in a tight line.

"Did she at least reach out after the second book was released?"

He shakes his head again. There's more to it that he's not saying. I see him holding it in the set of his jaw.

I take his hand and give his palm a squeeze. "I'm sorry. I can't imagine what that was like. But I know how it feels to be hurt by someone you love and have the situation get brushed over, without acknowledgment.

"You have to forgive them to move on, but it's so hard to move on without validation that your pain was real. That what happened, *happened.* It wasn't the nothing that they're making it out to be."

Reed sucks in a shaky breath and turns away from the ocean to peer at me. His features look soft, sanded down. His eyes have melted to the clear blue of a watercolor sky.

He's somehow more attractive than he was two minutes ago.

"I don't do this," he breathes.

I motion to the ramp. "Investigate lifeguard towers?"

A laugh slips out of him as I tug his wrist, leading him up the six-foot ramp.

"I don't talk about the story behind those books—I've had that whole era locked up in a neat metaphorical box since they came out."

I smile over my shoulder as we reach the top of the platform. "Proud of you for opening it. When you keep your emotions in a box, you never know when it'll burst open and fuck up your life."

He eyes me cheekily as his chin cuts forty-five degrees to the left. I waggle my brows and spin away, turning to take stock of the tower. A flimsy-looking wooden fence lines a two-foot walkway that circles a small roofed . . . hut? Hutch? Not sure of the technical term. The tiny indoor area's closed up for the night. The windows and doors are padlocked shut. I do a quick lap, scanning for Glenn.

No one's around. Reed waits with his hands in his pockets at the top of the ramp, watching me with his lips quirked to the side like he's hoarding a secret.

Probably thinking about the sex chapter. We still haven't addressed it.

I plop down on the wooden porch and stretch my legs out in front of me, leaning against the hutch. Reed lowers himself to my right so our sides are flush, my bare leg against his jeans. We watch the waves crash for a few quiet moments.

"I—" we both start at the same time. We go quiet, smiling at each other. I shift, rotating to put my shoulder against the wood so I can see him better.

"What were you gonna say?" I ask.

"You go first," he says, watching me carefully.

I lean my head against the wood, searching his eyes. "Sorry about the chapter."

His lips turn up. "I'm not."

I guffaw. "I'm so embarrassed. I've died of shame seventy-five thousand times since I sent it."

Reed laughs. "Rikki, I just got *choked up* on a second date. *I'm so* embarrassed."

"Men are allowed to have feelings!"

His warm, rumbly laugh bubbles up. "I lost my fucking mind, reading that chapter. I opened it at a business dinner. I had to excuse myself from the table. I read it in the hallway next to the bathroom. And then I had to go home and take a cold shower."

I cough out a laugh, covering my face. "Noooo. I'm so sorry! Did I mess up the dinner?"

"No! It was fine. My brother was there to pick up the slack. It was great."

I continue to hide under my hand.

Reed gently tugs my wrist, removing my palm from my face. He leans his head against the wood, inches away from mine, bright eyes beaming straight to my damn soul.

Reed Tyler is a master in the art of eye contact. He could convince anyone to do anything with those babies.

I watch his lips twitch up.

"What?" I ask.

His eyelids drop to half mast as his gaze skates down my neck. I feel it like a flame held inches from my skin as it teases over my chest.

"R. Tyler, what kind of smoke are you about to blow up my ass?"

His mouth kicks up one side of his face, eyes glittering as they slice back to mine. "Get over yourself, Rikki."

I smile as those words lurch through me like an adrenaline shot. "*Fuck off*, Derek."

His mouth captures mine. His hand comes to grip my neck, securing me in place as his chin shifts, stubble brushing my cheek. I twist closer without breaking the kiss—sliding over him until my knees bracket the outside of his thighs. My palms glide under his leather jacket and across the firm expanse of his chest as I settle into his lap. His hands close over my hips, and he tugs me tight against his abdomen, sending a symphony of sparks spiraling out from my center. This kiss is long, languid, shimmery, and wonderful.

When it finally breaks, Reed pulls back slowly, assessing me with those eyes. "Being a control freak is a cop-out flaw."

"Bullshit—being a control freak is a universally acknowledged flaw."

"It's the flaw you tell the CEO interviewing you for a management job."

My lip quirks. "Still a flaw."

His hands skim up from my knees. "I'm a control freak. Does that bother you?"

A cone of shimmering light flips on in my chest as he playfully searches my gaze.

No, I instantly like him more. He must have charts and planners and a color-coded calendar. Labels. Organized bookshelves. Multiple sets of clean sheets. I shake my head slowly.

Something unclenches inside me at the thought of being able to relinquish control to someone who *knows what to do with it*. "No, it doesn't. It's actually kind of a turn-on."

His hands close around my thighs, and I tilt forward, catching his mouth for another fathomless, heart-pounding kiss that billows through me. My hips roll against him, a bouquet of starbursts blooming in my stomach. He groans against my lips.

This man is getting straight As.

I break away, pressing into his forehead as my heart rackets against my rib cage. Last weekend wasn't a fluke.

Sex has always been a crapshoot for me. Sometimes it's good. Mostly okay. On the very rare occasion, great. You can tell when great is coming. You can feel it in the foreword. You can gauge it in each touch. Greatness builds out of dazzling kisses, witty exchanges, and sparkling caresses. It just comes to a crescendo in the sex.

The potential here is off the charts.

But we need to talk. I need to know what we're doing. What the rules are. Because if we don't communicate the complicated nature of whatever this is or isn't, things are going to be that much more confusing when I leave the state and return to my normal Reed-less, unplugged life.

I exhale a steadying breath. "I actually think we should figure out—what we're doing here."

His arms disappear under my jacket. Two strong hands slide up my rib cage. Heat floods my center. "Looking for Glenn?"

"I think we need to have a weird chat." I close my eyes as he dips under my chin, pressing his lips to the hollow behind my ear, along my neck. Electricity sings through my bloodstream. "We need rules."

I feel him nod. "You're right." He straightens, gaze resting on my lips, hands on my waist. "I like you. A lot." He says it softly. Like he's talking to himself rather than to me.

"Easy to say as I straddle you on a beach."

Reed's mouth tips up into his closed-lip smile, dimple shining. "I'll say it again later then."

I sit back an inch, putting some space between us. "Are you talking to a hundred other women right now?"

He shakes his head, a lock of hair falling out of place. "I'm not talking to anyone else right now."

"Am I going to see you again after tonight?"

Reed's fingers tighten over my waist. "Rikki, if we lived in the same place, this would be date eight."

I tip my head back in an eye roll scoff. "Reed, we've only known each other exists for nine days."

"Exactly my point."

"But we don't live in the same place," I point out. "And I like you too."

He sighs, head falling back against the hutch. "If teleportation was a thing, I'd be all over this. But we can't start something . . . real, with our lives so out of alignment. It'll just crash and burn."

I nod. "So what does that mean? Should we be friends? Do we talk after this? Cut off communication?"

He squeezes his eyes shut like he's preemptively bracing for a jab. "May I propose a dubious experimental idea?"

I cock my head. "You may."

His eyes crack open again. "I would love to keep dating you."

I would love to keep dating you too.

"Might we perhaps be friends when we're not in the same place, and more when we are?"

I raise my brow, lips pursed skeptically. "That sounds like a recipe for disaster."

Trouble flashes in his eyes. "But think of the fun."

A smile creeps up my face. *It would be fun.* To have someone wonderful to look forward to seeing every so often. To adventure with when I'm here or when he's on the East Coast.

"All right," I say slowly.

"All right?"

I nod. "Accepting the proposed rule, if we add a clause."

"Hit me with it."

"Friends when we're not in the same place, more when we are, but no sex unless we do mutually decide to start"—I throw up air quotes—"*something real.*"

Reed tilts his head a few degrees to the right, lips curling into a wicked smile. "Interesting addendum, Romona."

"Less messy, R. Tyler."

His hands sweep under my jacket, up to my shoulders, and drift down my back, caressing the skin with his nails through the thin fabric of this dress. I shudder as they brush over my ass, a flush of gold dust sweeping up my torso. Reed's pupils dilate, eating away at the hypnotic neon blue.

"Doth thou accept the clause?" My voice is quiet.

He nods. "Thou accepts the clause."

I reach up, placing my thumb over the middle of his wide mouth, pressing into his lips. Want pulses under my skin, like a shock. "So if we're in the same place, and one of us has started seeing someone else, we're friends?" I pull my thumb down to his chin.

"And if we start seeing someone else we actually like, we let the other know?" He tugs me closer again, so our stomachs are flush. "That's what friends do."

I chuckle, dropping my hand from his face. "Slow-mo short-distance dating, long-distance chill."

Reed grins, touching his nose to mine. "Are you going to tell me every time you're in the area?"

"If you want me to. I don't want to be weird about it."

He squeezes my legs. It sends corkscrews of shivering light bounding up my thighs. "Tell me. And I'll tell you—let's make that a rule so there's less chance of miscommunication. Even if we don't have time to see each other. Let's just inform anyway."

My brain whirs through the lust fog, testing for cracks in the boundaries we're setting up. "All right. Should we make an escape clause?"

His fingers come up to trace my temple, down the sides of my face, and tuck my hair behind my ears. "Should we?" he says skeptically.

I bob my chin. "I think it's the smart thing to do. How 'bout if we want to pull the plug on this whole ordeal at any time, we can say . . . 'The Sunrise Away bag is lost.'"

He frowns. "What then? We're just friends in person and away?"

I nod. "Yeah, and if we need a complete break with no contact, maybe, 'The Sunrise Away bag is lost for good.' That way we don't have to ever get weird about it. We can be adults. No ghosting. Just healthy moving on."

"Okay," he says quietly, the hint of a smile returning to his eyes. "Organized, thorough. I like it. Can we also have a code phrase that means the opposite? Something stealth for 'the game is fucking on—I'm having an amazing time.' It feels like bad karma to not balance that out."

A toothy smile breaks across my face. "Okay." I slide off him, settling back onto the blue wood of the lifeguard tower, against his right side where there's no danger of me violating the sex rule I just instated. "What'll it be?"

He peers out at the ocean for a beat. I watch as it comes to him—something softens in his jaw. He quirks a brow. "I'll see you at the airport?"

I close my eyes, smile burning deeper into my cheeks. "That's perfect."

I relax my head against the hutch. Lean into the heat of Reed's side. We sink into the quiet, listening to the waves break and recede. I don't know how long we've been like that when he breaks the silence.

"For me, love is . . . feeling safe," Reed says pensively toward the water. "Honesty. Loyalty. Leading with kindness. Being gentle with your hard truths.

"*Yes and-ing* during an argument instead of making excuses and throwing up walls. Everyday things. Respecting each other's quirks. Picking up the slack when you know your partner's struggling, and knowing they would do the same. Going out of your way to sync up your schedules so you can climb into bed at the same time." He swallows. "Yeah."

My heart's wiggled its way back up into my throat. I blink at the uncalled-for emotional response building behind my eyes. A faint noise breaks the silence of the night, and we both startle, scrambling to our feet. A car crunching over gravel. A door slamming shut. A hundred yards down the beach, a car just dropped a man off in the parking lot.

He lumbers toward the Ford Explorer.

I hit the sand at a sprint, rage flaring to life in my chest. My legs are screaming after thirty seconds. I open my phone camera and hit record as I'm rounding Glenn's car. His trunk is open, and he's sitting, hunched forward, legs dangling, holding an empty bottle of rum like a drunken pirate.

I step out in front of him, heaving in gusty, dramatic breaths and clutching a cramp on my right side. "Get out of the car, Glenn."

Glenn glares at me, frustration shining in his eyes for a brief moment before he deflates and hangs his head. "Sorry."

19 | MAN FOUND

Reed and I sit in the dark, parked on the street outside my aunt's house.

We drove home with Glenn in the back seat. I punched my aunt's address into Reed's GPS. He drove while I scoured the internet for the next flight to Newark. I booked one for 8:30 a.m. tomorrow.

LA to NJ is a long day when you factor in the three-hour time change. I can write and brainstorm from wherever tomorrow, but I need to be back in New York for the monthly pitch meeting Wednesday morning.

I sent Whitney the video I took of Glenn with his rum bottle as we were pulling out of the beach parking lot so she'd be mentally prepared when I rang the doorbell with him, like a policeman who'd found a stray, twenty minutes later. Glenn apologized to me as we made the short trek from Reed's car to my aunt's house. My theory checked out: He has trauma wrapped up in confrontation. He was scared Whitney would want to leave him after she found out about his previous marriage, so he left *to prevent her from being able to do so*. I told him to find a therapist.

Whitney mouthed an emotional thank-you to me on the front steps as Glenn hobbled drunkenly into the house. I nodded and retreated back to the blue Mercedes parked along the curb.

And here we are. A slow sadness is oozing through me from the top down. I really like this man. So much so that *I've agreed to a dating pact*. Now it's going to be weeks, months, ages before *I maybe* see him again. At any given moment I can receive a text that says *The Sunrise*

Away bag is lost, and for no apparent reason, this will just be over. I've never entered into something like this before. It feels like playing the slots. The chances of him actually following up with me when he's on the East Coast, despite the rules we agreed on tonight, are probably like 5 percent. No amount of kismet and physical connection can make up for living three thousand miles apart.

"So when do you go back?" Reed asks.

"I have an 8:30 a.m. flight tomorrow."

His brow shoots up. "Will you need a ride to the airport?"

I eye him skeptically. Locals despise driving to LAX. Some people don't even drive their spouses. It's a running joke out here. "Where do you live?"

"I have a place with my brother right in Sherman Oaks."

That lands like a swift kick to the ass. He's ten minutes from my mom's house. It's like I forgot to update my home address with the universe before I asked for a match.

"Where?" I ask again.

He rattles off an address on Greenly Street, right off Beverly Glenn Boulevard. I know the exact neighborhood. Jordyn's dad rented an apartment in that area back in high school.

This is a second date. He's not allowed to drive me to the airport.

"It's all right. My aunt gets up early for work tomorrow. She'll take me. You don't have to put yourself through driving to LAX."

He tilts his forehead toward me. "I'd be happy to."

"That's bullshit."

"I wouldn't offer if it were bullshit."

I wave him off. "I'm good, it's already 1:00 a.m. Go home, get some sleep."

He juts out his bottom lip, eyeing me carefully. "There's a good chance I'll be out in New York in about two months for work. See you then?"

Two months. *That's a century in dating years.*

I bob my chin, icy disappointment spilling through my veins. "Yeah."

"Text me when you get home safe?"

"Yeah," I say again.

He leans over the center console, and I shift to meet him in a wholesome, quick goodbye kiss. It's still too good.

"Wait—" I blurt.

Reed grins, settling back into his seat. "What?"

I huff a bland laugh. "Um, I just had a thought—for the pact. I don't think we should text when we're not in the same state."

Surprise flits across his face.

"I just think with a two-month gap, this could get really messy before we even got the chance to hang out again. You know? I don't want that to happen. It'll be cleaner, I think. With texting off the table." Safer.

He purses his lips, pensive for a moment before he nods once. "Okay."

"Cool. You know, unless we're ever in a place where we're going to make this something real. I think this is the way to go."

He closes his eyes, schooling his serious war-hero expression back into place. "All right, throw it on the constitution."

"All right."

Reed leans forward and kisses me again, but this time he grabs my chin, pulling me to him across the console. His mouth parts my lips hungrily, sending my insides spinning. When it breaks, he studies my eyes. I get lost in his for a moment before I hastily stumble out.

The window *zmmms* down as I shut the passenger door. "See you at the airport, Renee."

I turn to blink at him, confused for a moment before the meaning hits.

The anti–Away bag is lost.

I snort. "TTYL, Derek."

Reed [7:50 a.m.]: Still in California?
Me [7:51 a.m.]: Yep at my gate, should be boarding soon!
Reed [7:52 a.m.]: Have a safe flight! <3

Whitney [7:55 a.m.]: Can you do some couples therapy sessions with Glenn and I like over zoom or something?
Me [7:56 a.m.]: I'm not actually supposed to take on family members as couple's clients
Whitney [7:57 a.m.]: What if you don't charge us? Just like four sessions or so? We're postponing the honeymoon while we work on our communication skills and conflict resolution
Me [8:00 a.m.]: Sure
Whitney [8:01 a.m.]: Thank you thank you! What'd Reed get on his report card?
Me [8:01 a.m.]: 98%
Whitney [8:01 a.m.]: holy gods marry him

Dad [8:15 a.m.]: Next time I need to know when you're going to be out of state, Rikki. I was scheduling painters to come in and do the apartment.
Me [8:17 a.m.]: Okay! Could you please let me know when they're coming?

20 | THE HEART EMOTICON

Reed sent a heart emoticon. He said, *Have a safe flight, HEART.*

I've been hyperfixated on that goddamn less-than-three for *seven hours.*

The sheer audacity.

Here I am gaslighting myself into thinking this pact is a good idea, and *he sends a heart emoticon*. We've hung out twice! We just drew up a very *casual* contract. *Heart emoticons are the anti-casual.* Why would he do that? Is it a manipulation tactic? What's his angle?

I exhale a flustered breath as I rehash this mentally for the fiftieth time before stuffing my key into my door and pushing into the apartment. A few things register at once as the door swings open—the one that sends fear sprinting through my nervous system is the TV. It's on.

I slam myself back into the hall.

The lights were also on. And it smelled like paint.

Did my father send a minion to let painters in?

I swallow, glancing up and down the hall, positioning my keys between my knuckles before slowly opening the door again and peeking in. The living room, which used to be a bland white, now gleams a soft blue. Some HBO show is playing on the TV.

"There you are."

I trip sideways into the door, fumbling with my Away bag. My father is sitting on the brown couch in suit pants and a white button-up that he's undone around the collar.

What in the actual—

"I've been waiting for you to get home, kid. Thought we could grab some dinner. I've got a meeting with a big potential client tomorrow in the city. Figured I'd head out here early when I realized you weren't going to be around to let the painters in."

Fuck.

"They left maybe four hours ago, after they finished up the main bedroom."

Every window is open. There are fans I've never seen before running in various areas of the room. The photos and framed art I put up last week have all been taken down and set on the ground.

I focus on my exterior. Appearing calm. I move slowly, pushing the front door shut, locking it. Recovering from the shock. "Hi, Dad, I—I can't go to dinner. I have work to do. I have a pitch meeting tomorrow. I'm sorry—I need to prep."

"Then we'll get takeout. Let's do Italian."

I press my lips together for a moment. "Okay? Is it safe to be in here with the paint fumes?"

"I have two air purifiers running. We're fine." He taps the remote and mutes the TV. "What were you thinking with that bookcase in the bedroom? Nothing's in alphabetical order. It's like *The Wild Wild West* in there."

I cough. "It's by color."

"But all your series are separated. That's ridiculous."

"I guess so."

"What are you reading right now? Any recommendations?"

This is always his first conversation stop with me nowadays. I get my love of books from my father. It's a smart, distracting topic to hit, and he knows it.

I shrug, trying to act normal, pulling my suitcase into the bedroom. "You might like *Ninth House* by Leigh Bardugo." The windows are open in here as well. The walls have been painted a goldish brown. I do a double take at the sight of the leather journal with the garter on it, sitting on my nightstand. I frown, sliding my eyes back to my unopened carry-on. It was in there, right?

"Oh yeah, I think I remember seeing Stephen King blurbed that," my father says from the next room. He loves Stephen King. "Can I borrow it?"

I pull *Ninth House* off the shelf, bring it into the living room, and drop it in his open palm.

"Thanks, sweetheart."

I walk into the kitchen to wash my hands as my mind winds back to the text exchange with him about this apartment.

What do you mean you don't want me to pay rent? Is there something you want me to be doing for you in that place?

I only want to know that you're safe and cared for out there, and I want you to talk to me honey. Pick up my calls, text me back. Bring me into your life. You're my only daughter. I've been in therapy now with a new guy, he's great. I'm on new medication. I'm feeling so zen. I want to be here for you. Let me be your dad. Let me help you.

"Why the long face?" my father says from his perch on the sofa.

I shake my head. "I just wish you gave me a heads-up that you were coming by."

"This is my apartment, Rikki," he says, putting his feet up on the coffee table as a pit the size of Rhode Island stretches open in my gut. "I'll sleep on the couch tonight and be out of here tomorrow. I have an afternoon flight back to LA after my meeting."

He's sleeping here?

I dry my hands with the bookish dish towels I have draped over the oven handle.

"Okay," I say with as normal a tone as I can manage. "What do you want from the Italian place I order from? I'll go pick it up."

Five minutes later I burst out the lobby doors, gasping for breath.

I inhale deeply as I stride down the street. Swipe at the two tears that managed to escape. *Toughen the fuck up. You did this to yourself.*

It's 11:47 p.m. when I flop into bed with my door safely locked.

I never texted Reed back. To be fair, the phrase "have a safe flight" alone doesn't necessarily warrant a response; but the heart emoticon at the end changes things. I maybe should have said thank you. Or at the very least dropped a positive emoji. It didn't have to be a heart. I could have sent something less intense, but still upbeat like . . . a star, or a pretzel, or that monkey with its hands over its eyes.

Texting back now would break protocol and give him the power to ghost me without consequence. I'm already struggling to keep the part of me looking for a serious relationship locked and gagged in a closet.

I lock my phone screen. I have to stop thinking about this, or I'm going to lose my fucking mind. *We're casual.* We have a fun pact. I don't have to send anything back. If Reed's ever in the area, he'll contact me, and *that's* that.

I glance over at the nightstand where the leather journal still sits.

When I unpacked my carry-on earlier—the journal wasn't in it, but *Heir of Fire* was.

I'm already losing my mind.

I'm losing my mind, or the journal is . . . moving.

Which is insane and would bring us back to option A: I'm losing my mind.

21 | INFECTED

It's been three weeks.

I'm still thinking about the stupid fucking heart emoticon.

He's a virus. This man is in my dreams. He's in the subtext of my articles, and he's wormed his way into all my relationship-related thoughts. He's lingering like a hacking cough after a cold.

I absentmindedly doodled him a stupid apology card last Thursday after I finished my Etsy batch.

Sorry if that heart was genuine.

I thought I was getting conned again.

I hope you don't feel ghosted.

That would suck the most-ed.

I can't stop thinking about your stupid face.

Fuck you.

I haven't been on a date since we made the pact.

I haven't even been able to bring myself to open Hinge.

I'm fucked.

I feel ghosted, but I'm the one who made the rule not to text. I'm the one who didn't respond to the heart emoticon. I cut *him* off.

I blame Jordyn. And Whitney.

I knew I shouldn't have seen him again. I could feel it in my bones. The man's a Rikki magnet. And now here I am, almost a month later, clinging to whatever the hell it is we are for dear life, like Mufasa dangling over the edge of that goddamn cliff.

"I really loved that too! She's such a badass!" Babe's voice yanks me from my thoughts.

I blink, guilt gathering in my gut as I try to catch the thread of the discussion. Babe's excitedly gushing about *Queen of Shadows* from her spot across the coffee table in a new witchy black dress and blood-red riding cape that matches mine, clutching a hardcover copy against her chest. My own copy is in a little cauldron at the center of our circle.

The WWU has convened this week on a Wednesday evening because Jordyn was pregnancy-ill on Sunday. I have no idea what the group is talking about. I loved the book, but my life has been slowly slipping off its axis, and I've been finding it increasingly hard to concentrate. Dealing with my father's random drop-ins, the creepy journal, and perpetually pining over Reed, on top of juggling the podcast, writing Love Today, planning my mom's wedding, counseling Whitney and Glenn, and running the Etsy shop is taking a hefty mental toll. My brain's melting, and I'm not quite sure what the best course of action to remedy the situation is.

Micah, Jordyn, and I have a couch chat scheduled after book club. It's time for me to get their thoughts on my growing list of woes. I haven't wanted to burden them with my nonsense because they've been overloaded as well. They've thrown themselves into nesting. They've been going to birth-prep classes during the week. Jordyn's been enduring a few excruciating weeks of morning sickness. Micah's prepping for a big case where he'll be traveling back and forth from Texas in the weeks ahead.

Shit, I stopped listening again. I tune back into the conversation. We should be wrapping up about now, but Jordyn and Babe are bickering about love interests.

"But I'm so happy for Rowan!" Babe gushes.

"He can't be endgame. It has to be Celorian."

"Rikki, you're so quiet. Who do you ship as endgame?" Babe prods.

I blink at her. "I guess I'm shipping Manon and Do—"

We all tense as a phone dings. Our quietest member, Adrienne, sighs.

"Who didn't put their phone on silent?" Jordyn scolds.

The sound came from my cape pocket. "Sorry!" Shame paints my cheeks as I reach down and pull it out. I glance at the notification as I switch the phone to silent. An email.

Before I can think better of it, I swipe down and audibly gasp.

"What's wrong?" Jordyn asks.

My heart rages against my chest. I tear my eyes from the screen. *Shit.* "Nothing."

"Nothing?" Jordyn repeats dryly.

Babe sits back in her chair. "Rikki, you gasped. We can see your face. It's not nothing."

"Just an email," I say too quickly as the beat of my elevated pulse fills my ears. I glance at my watch. "It's nine, y'all. I think it's time to wrap this up."

Adrienne picks her bag up from the floor.

Jordyn's brow arches. "Is it from him?"

"Him? Him who?" Babe asks.

The last thing I need is Babe reporting back to Willem, who could report back to Reed that I'm having a mild giddy meltdown over his possibly completely benign-nothing email.

"No one. It's fine. Thank you for coming. This was lovely. I'm actually having a stomach thing happening at the moment, so I'm going to run to the bathroom. I ship Manorian, and I'll see you all in two weeks for the first half of *Kingdom of Ash*."

I rise from the circle and swish toward the bathroom. My cape gets caught in the door as I lock myself in. I'm full-on sweating as I struggle to yank it out and fail. I have to reopen the door, tug it in, and lock it again.

I drop the phone as I try to bring it to my face. It clatters against the white tile.

Jesus Christ. Stop freaking out.

I plop onto the ceramic edge of my shower-tub combo. Pick up the phone, exhale a slow breath, counting to five, and tap open the email.

—

re: RE: RE: SUBJECT: Been feeling inspired. Had some fun.

Reed Tyler <RTYLER48@gmail.com> August 27

LINK

—

I tap the link.

TYLER-ROMONA | MESSAGE IN A BOTTLE

CHAPTER 3 | PACT

Derek

I miss her. I don't remember the last time I legitimately missed someone. Let alone someone I've known for a week.

A week?

I suck in another counted breath, concentrating on slowing my heart rate, and exhale, realizing belatedly that he's picking up the story where I left off: post sex chapter. It ended with Renee and Derek in bed. Derek was about to leave for his flight and Renee asked *what now?*

Sounds like Fiction Reed left their sex-capade with no plan.

That was the best first date I've ever had. Not just because it ended in the most fateful, erotic night of my life. But because I liked her.

[RIKKI ROMONA: Single, past society-allotted prime, found dead in bathroom upon reading that man with whom she has only been on two dates called their fictional sex-capade the most fateful erotic night of his life. Wearing witch costume for no apparent reason.]

But because I liked her.

A lot. I liked the way she smiled. Constantly. She tried to hide it, but it just traveled to other areas of her face. Her stormy gray eyes sparkled with it. I like how she talked. How delightfully honest she was about the deepest shit humans deal with on the daily. I love her insightful questions. I love how *me* I felt like I could be in her presence.

Renee's a bulldog in a princess dress.

I don't think I've ever had that thought before about a human being. Let alone a gorgeous one. It's the most endearing quality I've ever had the honor to stumble across. I want to be in her orbit.

So the question now is—how the hell do I keep her in my life?

We parted ways the morning after the wedding. I woke up that day feeling like I was in a movie, and I was finally playing the main character.

The fall back into reality was devastating. She lives three thousand miles away.

I used to be the Hopeless Romantic Guy. The one who believed love could conquer any obstacle. The dude who would do *anything* for the person they were dating.

That guy was naive. The girl he was in love with back in high school took that worldview, held it in her palm, and crushed it with her delicate manicured fingertips.

He was proceeded by Sad Emo Breakup Guy, from which I eventually graduated to Commitment Issue Asshole Academy. I've been that guy for nine years.

I date casually. And I let go.

It's never bothered me. I never feel connected enough for it to bother me. I hold people at arm's length, and they let me. I've mastered the art of getting through a date without sharing a single shred of information about my own life.

I had my arms out that night at the wedding, but Renee shoved them out of her way. Cuffed them behind my back. Exposed my chest. Without even trying.

My god, it was (forgive my crudeness) hot.

It's been six days since we woke up in that bed together. I'm afraid to text her. She already has such a foothold on my mental state.

If I reach out, and she doesn't answer, I'll feel like shit. If I reach out and say something wild that she doesn't reciprocate, I'll feel like shit. If I reach out and we end up doing something stupid like long-distance dating and whatever's left of my broken duct-taped heart shatters into slivers too small for even the most meticulous therapist to puzzle back together, I'll feel like a steaming pile of shit.

It's at this precise moment of angst that my iPhone lights with a text.

Renee: Free tomorrow for a second date? 9pm Barney's in Studio City at the bar. Eat beforehand. Wear clothes.

Someone knocks on the bathroom door, and I startle, dropping the phone.

"Rikki?" Jordyn asks.

"Yeah, I'm so sorry. Can you give me ten minutes?"

"Is it from him?"

"Is everyone gone?"

"Yes."

". . . Yes."

She claps her hands on the other side of the wood. "Okay, Micah's waiting in our living room with tea on the stove for our chat, so come over when you're done."

"Thank you." I listen as her footsteps retreat, and pick up the phone again.

Chills skitter through my nervous system as the chapter moves into our second date through Reed's eyes. It's so earnest and incredibly funny to hear his inner monologue as compared with my own. He's so confident. And complimentary. And occasionally nervous around Renee, and it's the most endearing shit I've ever read.

Ten minutes later I come to the final page of the doc.

> I don't know exactly when I'll see her again, and it's messing me up. I spent two hours at the gym today rather than my usual one, trying to burn up the ravine of anxiety in my chest.
>
> How do people deal with this . . . yearning? What is she doing right now? I want to talk to her. Learn more about her. See her. Touch her again. Take her to all the best places in LA.
>
> Looking down the barrel of forty-five days feels like a lifetime.

Jordyn's already on the couch with a mug of English breakfast tea when Micah lets me into the apartment. This was a little tradition when we all lived together. We'd sit down before heading off to do our separate night things and catch up on our days over tea.

I miss it.

Jordyn waggles her brows. "What'd he say?"

I suck a breath through my teeth. "I think I need to start with the other thing I wanted to get your thoughts on before I lose my nerve."

Micah hands me a mug on his way to the couch. "Go for it, Rick, what's up?"

I take it and settle in next to Jordyn. "Thank you." Micah plops down at the other end of the sectional.

"What is it, Rick? You're making me nervous," Jordyn demands.

I press the mug against my chin. "Okay . . ."

Jordyn motions with her hands for me to continue.

"Um . . . here goes." I clear my throat. "I think I'm being haunted."

Micah sets his mug on their glass coffee table. "Haunted?"

Jordyn squints at me. "Is this metaphorical?"

I sigh. "No, bear with me."

"We're bearing," Micah says calmly.

I take a small sip of tea and clear my throat. "You know those nice old-timey leather journals Babe had in the goody bags from her wedding?"

"No, I didn't get a journal," Jordyn says.

Micah shakes his head. "I didn't get one either."

My brow furrows. "I don't know, Reed also didn't get one. Maybe like every tenth person got one—they're nice. It has my name carved into the leather on the back. Anyway, the night of the wedding when I got up to the apartment after trading suitcases with Reed, that journal *was in the suitcase* when I opened it, even though I hadn't moved it from the goody bag."

"The same one with your name on it?" Micah asks.

"Yes."

Micah tilts his head. Jordyn narrows her eyes.

"Then, when I flew out to see Whitney, I'm like, 80 percent sure now that I didn't pack it, but it was there in my carry-on when I opened it at the airport. And then when I got home, before I had unpacked *that same carry-on*, it was out sitting on my nightstand. At the time I tried to write it off, like, I'm tired, and I'm seeing things.

"But, I've been putting it away in the top drawer of my nightstand every night. And I keep coming home from work to find it *on top* of my nightstand. And for a short while I told myself maybe my dad was coming in and taking it out, to read it, because he does show up randomly for renovation stuff now. But that doesn't make any sense because it's happening consistently, and I've never written in it. Like, there's no way he'd be coming into my apartment every day just to move a notebook onto the nightstand."

They blink at me in silence for a good long fifteen seconds.

"You got back from seeing Whitney like, three weeks ago," Jordyn says.

"Yeah."

Jordyn sucks a tooth and repositions herself. "I'm sorry. So you're saying the journal is moving itself from the drawer to the nightstand *every* day of your life?"

I drop my chin in the barest nod. "It's happening when I'm at work. And I've been moving it around to different hiding spots this week, just in case I was like, night moving it in my sleep—which doesn't make sense since it's moving after I leave the apartment. It always manages to end up back on my nightstand by evening."

Jordyn gapes. "Why in the hell haven't you mentioned this? Three weeks, Rikki? It could have murdered you in your sleep by now!"

"Because this is legit batshit! I didn't think anyone would believe me!"

"Why wouldn't we believe you? We're your best friends!" Jordyn cries.

"Because I barely believe me!"

Jordyn slams her mug down on the coffee table. "Woman, if you told me you turned into a turtle every night, I would believe you. I love you."

I snort.

Micah sighs. "To clarify, you still haven't opened the journal or written in it?"

"No."

"Why not?" Jordyn exclaims.

"Because I'm, like. . . scared of it now. It feels like a demon's living in it or something."

Jordyn picks her tea back up. "Jeezus Christ, Rikki."

"Have you touched it since last night when you put it away?" Micah asks.

"No."

"And you put it back in the drawer last night?"

"Yes—I can't sleep with it there next to my face."

Micah stands up and rolls his neck. "All right, both of you get up, let's go get a look at this thing."

"So wait, you haven't spoken to Reed this entire time?" Micah asks as I lead them down the hallway. "Have you been talking to other guys?"

"No."

"Don't you have a friendship with benefits pact? If you're not getting any physical benefits and you ghosted, what is the point of the pact? You're not friends, and there are no benefits."

"I didn't ghost him! We have a rule to avoid ghosting! There's no texting allowed unless we're in the same state." I stick my key into the door.

"Yeah, but he texted a heart, and you didn't even drop a heart on the text. If that were me, I would have died," Jordyn says. "If that were you, *you would have died.*"

"I wouldn't have dropped a heart after a second date! It's sus!"

"Or he's just expressing that he likes you, and you're pushing him away five seconds into knowing him."

"I didn't do any pushing. I just let it be!" I catch Jordyn and Micah exchanging a look over my shoulder. "What?" I demand.

"Nothing," Jordyn says as I push my apartment door open.

"The no-texting thing was the smartest way to move through a two-months-of-not-seeing-each-other gap without someone feeling hurt!" I spout, despite my extremely hypocritical secret feelings on the matter.

I move aside so Jordyn and Micah can walk past me into the living room.

"You always assume the worst when it comes to the guys you're dating," Jordyn mutters. "You never give them the benefit of the doubt. You give them *the* absolute *doubt*."

I glance at Micah, who's hovering near my coffee table. "You do tend to jump pretty quickly to the doubt."

I push the door shut and lock it. "I've met too many assholes to always give *the benefit* of the doubt."

"But you treat everyone you date as if automatically they're going to be an asshole. You don't give people the space to be good. And if you don't give them the space, how will you ever know?" Jordyn lectures.

I squint at her. "Is this a roundabout way of telling me *I'm* an asshole?"

"No," Micah says at the same time as Jordyn says, "Only sometimes."

I cross my arms, leaning against the door. "He sent a new chapter in the email."

Jordyn holds out her hand. I tap open the Google doc and hand it to her. She falls on the couch reading.

"Rikki, the notebook?" Micah asks.

I stride to the bedroom and gesture through the doorway toward my nightstand. It's sitting there. As predicted.

Jordyn looks up from the couch. "Wait, Rikki." She widens her eyes at me. "This is so good."

I sigh guiltily. "I know."

"He says *he's yearning for you*! You have to email back."

"It could just be for the drama of a chapter," I say quietly. "To get me to think he's yearning, so he has the upper hand to turn the tables on me if I were to reciprocate."

"Come *on*, Rikki."

I throw a hand up and let it drop to my side. "I'm trying to sort out what to say."

Micah eyes us wearily. "Are we here to inspect the journal or . . . ?"

"Yes," Jordyn hops up from the couch. The three of us file into my room. We come to a standstill, gathered around the nightstand like doctors at an operating table.

After a few seconds Jordyn nudges me. "Pick it up, Rick."

I do as directed and take a seat along the edge of the bed. Jordyn and Micah situate themselves on my left and right respectively.

"Open it," Jordyn says.

Micah nods. "Might as well do it with us here in case an evil overlord leaps out from the pages."

"I feel silly."

"Just do it!" Jordyn demands.

I slide the garter onto my wrist and unsnap the closure. The journal flops open easily. Like it's been worn in. Micah and Jordyn crane forward to inspect the blank first page.

"Write something," they say in unison.

We all laugh.

I pull a pen from my nightstand drawer, click it on, and hover over the page.

Hi, I'm Rikki. What's up?

22 | THE JOURNAL

The ink doesn't disappear into the page.

Words don't appear underneath it.

Jordyn raises her head. "Huh, I really thought that would trigger something."

Micah frowns. "Maybe it just wants you to vent about your day."

"Or." Jordyn hops her butt sideways on the bed in excitement. "You could draft out what you're going to say back to Reed."

"I think it'll stop haunting you if you just start journaling," Micah says.

Jordyn taps the page impatiently. "Try journaling."

I flop the notebook shut. "Not with you two hovering. I'll try it later."

"Fine." Jordyn grabs Micah's arm and drags him from my room. "We'll leave right now so you can try journaling." I follow her and Micah back to the living room. "And then email something back to Reed!" she says.

"Okay," I concede.

"And also forward me that chapter because I'm only on the first page."

I nod, my lips curving into a small smile. "All right."

"And report back."

"I'll report back!"

"And stop giving your cousin free couples therapy!"

"Jordyn."

Showered and ready for bed, I slide under the blankets and pluck the journal from its spot on the nightstand.

The wedding garter's back around it. I never put it back on—so that's great.

Reed's words from the Uber post Babe's wedding swing back around in my head: *It's a sign. The universe reminding you to write for fun.*

I glance up at the ceiling. *Universe? This you?*

I slip off the garter again and tug open the snap closer again.

My stomach drops as I blink at the first page.

It's . . . covered in text. The three words I put down on a blank canvas earlier are nowhere to be found.

> Finally. Congratulations! You have met the following qualifications to gain access to this rare teleportation device.

I slam it shut and throw it across the room. It hits the corner of the TV on the wall and drops to the floor.

Shit.

I hustle out of the covers and pick it up again, pulse hammering behind my forehead. *It's okay. It wasn't aggressive. This is fine. It said congratulations. You're an adult, be normal.*

I get back into bed with the thing. Heave in a deep breath and open it again.

> Finally. Congratulations! You have met the following qualifications to gain access to this rare teleportation device.
>
> 1) 30+ years of age
>
> 2) Lives alone

3) Single
4) Searching for love
5) Does not commit murder
6) Has a profile on a dating app
7) Knows people who don't live within a 50 mile radius
8) Has at least one rocky parental relationship

What in the fuck.

Congratulations again on qualifying. If you wish to proceed, turn the page.

I turn the page.

Chapter 1: Teleportation Might Be the Answer to Your Problems

Teleportation is an extremely useful tool that can become dangerous if placed in the wrong hands. Please proceed with caution.

As you may or may not know, teleportation requires two mechanisms. A hyperconductor and a base. In tandem you may utilize these to complete a successful vault.

Your hyperconductor can be found hooked into the loop sewn into the cover of this journal in the form of a pen. This journal itself is your base.

When you wish to vault, remove your hyperconductor from the loop. **It is a twist pen, not a click.** Twist to release the ballpoint. A click, once the base is charged, will initiate your vault.

Step one: Release your **ballpoint**

Step two: Flip to a **destination request** page

Step three: Print the address of your destination **upon**

the provided line

Step four: Turn the page for your **vault task**

Step five: Complete **vault task**

Step six: **Apply thumb** to the head of your hyperconductor

Step seven: **Click**

* This base will provide you with **13 vaults**, be cognizant.

* Tasks must be completed without assistance or will not result in a charge.

* When the vault task is complete, the head of your hyperconductor will appear green.

* A valid address complete with a five-digit zip code is required to vault.

* In event of emergency, if you cannot complete the allotted task, destroying the base (this journal) will allow you a final vault.

* Only those who qualify are capable of operating this gift.

So far, so good?

I flip the page.

I'm going to take your silence as a yes.

I flip to the next page.

Rules:

One: By utilizing this gift, you enter into a mandatory nondisclosure agreement. Teleportation is a dangerous ability that, when shared with others, can lead to perilous consequences and an immense disruption of our world.

A gag order will be implemented upon commencement of use.

—Off-limit descriptors/verbs/nouns will include but are

not limited to:

teleport, teleportation, teleporting, telly, port, space-time, space-jump, jumper, continuum, superpower, wand, journal, notebook, pen, hyperconductor, base, vault.

—You may not describe your base book as magic.

—You may not describe your hyperconductor as magic.

Two: To protect the nondisclosure of rule one, vaults must initiate in a private space.

That is all.

Have fun.

I flip to the next page.

1) Where would you like to go

X ____________________

I flip to the next page.

It's empty. Every page from this one forward is empty. My heart's racing. The directions said there would be a vault task?

I flip to the end of the journal and find a thin writing utensil hooked on a brown cloth loop sewn into the leather binding: a black-and-red click pen.

I pick it up and twist the body, as instructed. A ballpoint pops out.

I stare at the blank line. This journal says it's a teleportation device.

That's obviously ridiculous.

But obviously I'm going to write down an address.

If someone tells you blowing out a candle on your birthday gives you a free wish, you're gonna shoot your shot. If someone casually mentions you've been given the ability to fly and to initiate said flight, you have to go fart in a closet, you're gonna fart in the closet. This journal is telling me it's going to let me teleport if I write down an address? I'm going to give it an address.

The first that comes to mind is Reed's: 1889 Greenly. It's been burned into my psyche since the end of that second date.

I feel like a ten-year-old with a crush as I scribble it down on the empty line in black ink. I do a quick google for the zip, finish it off, and turn the page.

23 | TASK

Submerge yourself in a tub full of 2 percent milk. Take a sip. x

That is all.
Have fun.

I'm heavy breathing as I tug on my UGGs and rip the grocery cart out from the back of the closet.

Maybe the talking notebook is fucking with me. Maybe at the end of this I'll just be some idiot who went out and purchased thirty gallons of milk. But I'm gonna get the fucking milk.

I sprint (as fast as one can in UGGs, dragging a portable grocery cart) down the two blocks to the nearest twenty-four-hour ACME. It's 10:20 p.m. as I roll on through their automatic doors. Once I've located the proper section, I dump an entire column of 2 percent milks from their massive refrigerator into the cart.

I dump three more columns, jumping between brands because I'm clearing out the 2 percent. When the cart's overflowing, I maneuver to the checkout and start lining them up on the grocery belt. A teenager is working. She eyes me like the unhinged milk woman I currently am.

"That's a lot of milk," she says flatly.

I focus on the conveyor belt as she scans, too embarrassed to look her in the eye. "Yeah. I'm having a party."

Scan. Scan. Scan. "A milk . . . party?"

I hesitantly meet her gaze. "I'm making desserts with them."

Her nose scrunches. "What dessert needs twenty gallons of 2 percent milk?"

"Are there only twenty gallons?" I bleat.

I filled the cart! Google says bathtubs take between forty and seventy gallons of water.

"*Only* twenty?" the teenager says, aghast.

"I have to use the milk for . . ."

She peers at me expectantly.

"Decorations."

She cringes. "Ew."

"It's like this new thing on TikTok."

"Eww."

"It's for my friend's birthday."

"Stop, ewwww."

I frown deeply at my sad, unfilled milk tub.

I have to go out again. Twenty gallons is not enough. It's 10:50 p.m.

I drag myself back to the twenty-four-hour ACME.

I deplete them of their entire stock of 2 percent milk and head back to the front register, shame flooding every niche of my sad little soul.

It's still just that one girl working.

I'm watching her from afar when she glances up from her phone and makes eye contact. Her gaze dips to my cart before slowly making its way back to my face.

I push into her aisle, focusing on the jugs as I plop them one by one on the belt. The thick silence is penetrated only by the rhythmic beeping of the grocery scanner. When I dare to look up, she's glaring at me in judgmental silence. I frown back, racking my brain for some, any, nongross excuse. "I have a baby."

Her lips part in a grimace.

"And a cat."

Her silence is deafening.

It's 11:32 when I dump the final milk into my stopped-up tub. I have the journal open to the task page on my closed toilet, with the pen/hyperconductor lying on top of the page.

Forty milks later. I just spent $160 on a milk bath at 11:00 p.m. on a Wednesday.

I strip out of my clothes, fold them in a neat little pile on my sink, and dip a foot in the tub. *It's freezing.*

Correction: I spent $160 on a milk cold plunge.

What if I get hypothermia and die in this tub?

[Thirty-something, unmarried, single, dies alone in bathtub full of milk (2 percent), convinced it would teleport her to California in an effort to see some guy she was obsessed with after two dates. President of witch-themed book club. Delulu.]

I slide in.

The temperature is offensive. Devitalizing.

I hold my nose, dip under, soaking my hair, pop back up, open my mouth, and sip.

Oof. I forgot how cow milk tastes—like it's just hovering on the verge of sour. I gag down the liquid and aggressively stand, grabbing the bright-yellow towel I have thrown over the shower rod.

I'm shivering violently as I dry off and squeeze out my hair. I tie the towel around my chest and step out of the tub onto my soft blue throw rug. My eyes jump to the pen I left on the open journal.

It's green.

The pen *turned green.* I grab it off the toilet and click.

I'm not prepared for the bloodcurdling scream that rips up my throat. Fifteen agonizing seconds pass where I feel like I'm being burned alive. Then everything goes black.

24 | THE STREET

It's dark.

Quiet as the heat recedes. I gulp down a lungful of cool air. For a second there, I couldn't breathe. Now I'm . . . sweating?

Am I sweating, or am I still covered in a sheen of milk?

I'm on my hands and knees. I must have blacked out. I lift a hand and find tiny black rocks stuck to my slick palm. The ground under me is cold and hard. And black.

I raise my head, groggy as I blink at my surroundings. There's a streetlight thirty feet away.

I scramble to my feet.

I am not in my bathroom. I am in the street. I clamp a stone-littered hand over my mouth.

My toe catches a book—the journal. The journal is in the street with me. With the garter back around it.

I'm leaning over to pick it up when I realize I'm naked.

I am naked in the middle of the street.

A street that could be Reed's.

My gut falls through the world and out the other side.

Oh my god.

Why didn't I put on clothes? *Where the hell is my towel?*

I snatch up the journal and position it over my vag, fumbling out of the road and onto the sidewalk with my other arm across my boobs, squinting at the street sign on the corner.

I gasp in a breath that feels like a thousand little cotton balls being forcibly shoved down my windpipe as the words come into focus, confirming my location.

BEVERLY GLENN BLVD. & GREENLY ST.

My cheeks collapse into each other, lips puckering like the cartoon on a Warhead candy wrapper.

My body is having a visceral reaction as I bumble backward, away from Beverly Glenn, a main road with lots of traffic, toward where I originally appeared, eyes bulging, shuffling sideways so my bare ass faces away from the street.

I clock the house numbers via their mailboxes. 1885, 1887—

I come to a halt outside 1889 and crouch against some bushes like an awkward, naked sorority girl posing for a group photo. Hyperventilating, I shove the garter off the journal and throw open the snap. The pen has returned to its little loop. I slip it out.

The top is red again. The charge is gone. I flip to the destination page where I wrote down Reed's address. The ink shines silver in the streetlight. It changed color.

All signs seem to be pointing to—yes, that happened, Rikki—160 dollars' worth of milk well spent.

I'm in front of Reed's house.

An enormous hedge and an elaborate, six-foot, solid-black gate block off the driveway. The house itself looks like one you'd see in a movie that's set in California. Two stories. Spanish style? I've never looked into buying a home, so I don't know the official names of the styles. The roof is made of those squiggly burnt-orange shingles. Some sections of the house are white stucco, and there's a castle-looking column made of tan brick. It looks new. It looks *nice*. Nice enough that there's most definitely a camera embedded out here somewhere.

Probably a Ring. And . . . I am hunched, tucked into a ball at the edge of Reed's hedge, shivering in the wind.

I am . . . sweaty and naked, off a main road in California with no car, no wallet, no ID, and no phone, crouching in front of a guy's house. A guy I went on two dates with and haven't spoken to in three weeks.

He *cannot* find me here.

I twist open the teleport pen, shaking as I flip to a fresh page. The milk-vault task has gone silver as well. The page across from it now reads:

Feedback?

I need a new destination page. I flip again.

Feedback?

Another page.

Feedback?

A flustered groan slips out of me as I press the pen to the page.

There was nothing in those directions about appearing naked!!!

I turn the page.

Rikki, it's a metaphor.

My eyes bulge as I fumble the notebook, suppressing the urge to chuck it into the bushes.

You need the creepy journal.

I flip again.

2) Where would you like to go
X ______________________

I scribble down my current home address at record speed and squeeze my eyes shut, dreading whatever awaits me on the next page.

And turn.

25 | EFF

Take a picture with him on the Santa Monica Pier. x

That is all.
Have fun.

"No!" I slam the journal shut and crouch lower against Reed's hedge. *Take a picture with him on the Santa Monica Pier?*

I cannot do that—*like this.* Santa Monica's twenty-five minutes away! I have no car. I don't even have underwear!

I scan the area, heaving in desperate breath after desperate breath. I'm hyperventilating again. I inhale, count to four, and exhale.

I need to get the hell out of here.

I'm going to have to go up to a random stranger's house—inexplicably *naked*—ring the doorbell, and ask to use their phone. But I can't attempt to speak to a human until I at least find something to cover my vag and ass simultaneously.

I scour the rest of the block. There's a **For Sale** sign stuck in the grass three houses down. *That'll work.*

I'll have to walk past Reed's gate to get it. Should I pass the gate, ass to camera? Or head down, boobs and journal-covered vag to camera, ass to street?

I can't crawl and stay out of shot because it's a wide-angle lens. Reed would get a notification of a naked woman sleuthing on all fours across the driveway with her hair covering her face like The Grudge.

We're doing ass to camera. I side shuffle with my body facing the street, and chin to my chest, letting my hair fall forward as I move as fast as possible toward the **For Sale** house. Once I'm past his gate, I start running, journal over my lower region, arm flat across my chest to keep my boobs from flailing.

I make it across a second lawn, a third. Breathing hard, I launch myself behind the flimsy cardboard sign stuck into the grass of a dark, quaint, one-story home.

Adrenaline's thundering through me as I drop the journal, wrench the sign up from the ground, and hold it against my torso. I shiver as trails of cold dirt slip down my skin.

The sign's just long enough to cover both my nips and vag. I can use one hand to hold it in place and the other to hold the journal over my ass. It's awkward, but it's the best I've got.

This is going to be okay.

I maneuver to a small bush at the edge of this property and crouch next to it, sign pressed to my chest. I have to pick a house with a light on, bite the naked bullet, and ring their doorbell.

Best to keep moving in the direction *away* from Reed's home.

I skim the selection farther down the street. The majority of these houses have gates. Tall, elaborate gates. I can't stand naked outside a gate, and I can't climb a gate naked. I'll get arrested.

There's a cute gateless red house on the corner of the next cross street, three more houses down, with a light flipped on upstairs. Red houses feel kind of quirky. Maybe they'll be more accepting of a naked stranger in need of a phone?

Please, be accepting of a naked stranger who needs to use the phone.

I exhale a slow preparatory breath and launch into a waddle-run, grass tickling my feet. I am Bruce Willis in *Die Hard*. I am Tom Cruise in *Mission: Impossible*, I'm Cameron Diaz in the goddamn *Charlie's*

Angels movies. I am . . . one house into my dash when a car comes around the corner of the cross street I'm aiming for. The bravado blows out of me like smoke on the wind.

Momentarily blinded by the incoming headlights, I take a confused lunge-step forward, and then to the left, toward the house I'm in front of, before collapsing into a squat again behind the sign, body suddenly shaking like a leaf.

Eff. They could call the police. What happens to random naked people running through the LA suburbs? I've never seen one! Do they go to jail? *Will I have to go to jail naked? Will they let me make a pit stop at a Target?*

The car slows.

Oh, please no, don't slow. I hug myself into a tight ball, arms wrapped around my shins, struggling to condense myself to the point of invisibility. I can hear the wheels grinding to a halt across the tiny stones scattered over the pavement. Floodlights wash over me as it pulls to the curb in front of the dwelling I've collapsed in front of.

I cringe as the passenger side window *zmmms* down.

"Excuse me." A woman's voice. "Sweetheart, is everything all right?"

I peek my head up. An attractive older-middle-aged white woman with luscious long brown hair is leaning out the window. Slowly, I rise off the ground, clutching the sign, to my front, journal to my back.

I take a tentative step forward. "Um, I'm so sorry—I'm having a weird night." I'm about ten feet from her window. "By any chance can I perhaps borrow your phone?"

The driver leans forward, past the kind-looking woman in the passenger seat, and I die.

All systems down. Bye forever.

His mouth falls open. "Rikki?"

Reed.

I squeeze my eyes shut as the back window rolls down as well. There's another guy in the back. Another Reed. He gawks at me and back toward the front seat.

"You know the random naked woman running down our street?"

THIRD ENCOUNTER

26 | DEAD

Reed and his family shoot down to their house, leaving me shivering on their neighbor's lawn, feeling like one of Ursula's shriveled-up worm victims in *The Little Mermaid.* My fingers dig into the edges of my stolen **For Sale** sign, like if I will it hard enough, the thing will remold itself into a makeshift dress.

What now?

I've got nothing. Systems truly down.

Why? Why did he have to come around the corner? Why did I have to test this creepy fucking journal with his address? *Note to self: Test foreign magical teleportation object with a control address before attempting to leap through space across the country.*

I literally could have written down Jordyn's apartment! I could have gone fifty feet and walked right back to my door.

What the hell am I going to say? I never got to parse out my feelings via journal. And he's going to ask why I'm naked! This is bad. This is so bad.

Should I just stick to the plan? Run to the red house? Get the fuck out of here. Figure out an explanation later.

"Do you need us to call the police?"

I yelp, falling out of my crouch and onto my naked ass, clutching the sign against my front. *There's grass in my ass.*

"Oh no! You don't need to call anyone," I say, quickly scrambling to my feet. "I'm fine. This is just a silly miscommunication that got out of hand."

Reed's mom. She's back. I can see the resemblance now. She's fifteen feet away, under the nearest lamppost, with a large red-and-black plaid Sherpa blanket draped over her arm, approaching cautiously like I'm a rabid animal.

"Are you sure you don't need medical attention? Are you all right?" she says gently.

I nod adamantly. How do I say *I'm not hurt, I'm a naked teleporting stalker,* without ruining my potential relationship with her son? "Yes, I am so fine! I am all good. So good. Excellent. Thank you! I'm so sorry to interrupt your night," I squawk. "Thank you for your help."

She accepts this with a slow nod. "Can I wrap you up?"

"Yes, please, that would be wonderful."

His mom moves forward, spreading the blanket and expanding her arms for a second before engulfing me in it via bear hug. I drop the sign, but my hand clutching the journal ends up smashed up against my butt as Reed's mother burritos me tight and vigorously rubs my arms.

She holds my eyes, studying my face. Hers are a deeper blue than her son's but just as bright. Like the feathers of a blue jay.

"Seriously, I'm fine," I squeak. "Thank you."

Mrs. Tyler nods hesitantly one more time. "All right. Reed's waiting for me to give the okay that I've wrapped you up. I'll let you chat. If there's anything you'd feel more comfortable speaking to a woman about, my name's Michelle. I'll be right inside."

"Thank you—that's so kind. I'm fine, though." I move to raise my arm to give her a thumbs-up, but it's straitjacketed to my side.

The second she disappears behind the landscaping dividing the houses, I take off, waddling toward the red house. *Stick to the plan.*

I proceed to almost immediately fall to my death via the curb into the street. As luck would have it, I manage to extract an arm and stay upright via frantic flailing. *Keep moving.* I do my best to loosen my blanket restraints without letting the entire thing fall off my body.

I make it to the next lawn. One more to the red house.

"Rikki?" I hear Reed's voice behind me.

Shit.

I take off faster, causing the blanket to fan out behind me like a cape. *This is the stupidest thing that's ever happened to me.* I switch tactics, pulling the fabric up over my head like a cave troll.

Now you can't confirm I'm even Rikki!

"Rikki!" Reed yells. "Where are you going?"

I don't know. What's the new plan? I clearly can't stop at the red house now. He'll just catch up.

The intersection is looming.

I'll breeze by the red house and hang a left. *I'll lose him! If I do, maybe I can gaslight him into thinking he never saw me and I, too, have a twin? I could have a twin.*

I glance over my shoulder as I round the corner: rookie escape artist mistake. A millisecond later I'm falling over a bush and into the street.

My hand not clutching both journal and blanket lets go of its grip to break my fall against the pavement. I grimace as shards of gravel shove into my open palm. *Stupid fucking gravity.*

"Rikki! Shit!" Reed's voice. "Are you okay?"

I feel insane. "I'm fine!"

Before I can push to my feet, Reed's hands are on my torso, helping me from behind, pulling the blanket back up over my shoulders. I stand and hastily secure it under my chin. I don't even know where to begin processing what has just occurred.

Reed appears in front of me, wide eyed with concern, hands stretched out like he's going to touch me, but he must think better of it because he pulls his arms back and folds his hands behind his head, highlighting his biceps instead. They strain against the long sleeves of the black button-up he's wearing.

"Rikki, seriously, are you okay?" He says each word slowly. With feeling, like I've been in a car accident, and I've suffered a brain injury.

"Reed, I'm fine!" I blink at his arms, too chickenshit at the moment to look him in the eye. *What do I say? What's an uncrazy thing to say?*

Why am I naked? Why am I here? Don't you dare look at him until you have an idea!

"You don't seem fine," Reed says. "You're . . . nude."

Of course I'm nude! I couldn't magically teleport clothed like a normal person! That would be too easy.

I remain silent, pleading with my brain for a reasonable excuse. *You can do this. Think!*

"Rikki?"

I snap my gaze to his. "I was streaking." It comes out matter-of-factly and much more confident than I was expecting.

"You were . . . streaking?" he repeats.

I guess I'm a streaker now.

"Yes? It's a hobby. People do it. I just turned thirty. It's time to try new things before I die."

"You're making streaking your new hobby?" he asks pointedly.

"Yeah. I love naked-ing publicly."

"On my street?"

"Every street. I don't discriminate against streets."

He narrows his eyes. "Are you sure you're not in some kind of trouble?"

"Are you streak shaming me?"

Reed bites down a grin. "Do you need help? Are you hurt?"

"Nah, I'm all good. Just having a weird night."

That sentence comes out casual, like this is a normal thing that would normally happen to a normal person on any normal, weird night.

Reed blinks at me, utterly nonplussed. "Why did you run?"

Ah, great question. Working on that one myself. *I was going to try to lose you and pretend this never happened.*

Do I tell him the truth? I should try the truth.

I raise my hand, clutching the notebook. "Okay." I suck in a deep breath. "This is going to sound wild but hear me out, remember this j—"

I choke, keeling over as my windpipe squeezes shut. *Holy.* I glare at the journal as I wheeze like a dying man.

Once I can breathe, I straighten, hold it out, and try again. "This j—"

I have to brace myself against a fire hydrant as another painful bout of spasms racks though my lungs. *So that gag-order thing is real.*

"Jesus, Rikki. Are you all right?" A pleasant shiver runs through me as his hand lands on my shoulder.

I heave in a clear, blissful breath, and straighten, turning back to him. "Sorry, what were we talking about?"

He studies me for a beat before dropping his hand. "Why did you run after my mom gave you the blanket?"

I press my lips together for a moment. "Remember that heart you sent after the beach?"

"Yes?"

"I was not expecting that."

Reed closes his eyes. Presses his thumb and pointer finger into his forehead. "What?"

"I didn't text back at the time because it threw me after a second date. I got suspicious. Sus, if you will. You know how the kids say *sus*."

"We all say *sus*."

"I wasn't sure if it was like an *I actually like you a lot* heart emoticon or just like, an *I'm trying to get you to think that I like you a lot, but in actuality I want to break the pact and have sex with you then ghost* manipulative heart emoticon—nowadays you just never know with a heart emoticon. You know? Hearts. Emoticons. You get what I'm saying about the heart? What do you think? Was it a nice heart or like a diabolical heart? I've been really losing sleep over this heart."

Reed opens his mouth to say something, but nothing comes out. I'm babbling like a Chihuahua that's been gifted the power of speech, so I really can't blame him.

A breeze hits my chest a little too intimately, and I glance down to find that the blanket has slipped, and my right boob is out. "Shit." I reposition the blanket.

Reed throws his face toward the sky.

"Sorry, my boob was out. I didn't mean to—I'm not trying to be naked."

"I thought you were streaking."

"I was."

"Isn't that by definition trying to be naked?"

"That was before. Now the streaking is over."

His face is still tilted toward the sky.

"You can drop your face now."

He shakes his head, bemused as he meets my eyes. "I am so confused . . . Do you need clothes? Are you okay? Didn't you need a phone? Can I offer you shelter? Can we take this conversation inside? My house is right there." He points down the road. "You keep saying you're fine, but you don't . . . really seem it?"

I throw my shoulders back, gripping the notebook carefully as I knot the too-long blanket-dress over my chest. "Well, Reed, I really am fine. But yes, clothes might be helpful."

"That was not a manipulative heart."

I nod. "Good. You always gotta check. It's the only way."

Reed peers at me, confusion still etched into every aspect of his face as we start shuffling in the direction of his house. "So . . . you're in LA, and you didn't text."

"Yet," I clarify. "I didn't text yet. I was in the process of texting."

"You thought first you'd give streaking a go?"

"No . . ." I look up at him, face burning. "I lost a bet."

Reed tilts his head. "And what was the bet?"

What was the bet, Rikki? I swallow at the dryness coating my throat. "A bet with my cousin. The one whose husband we found back at the beginning of the month."

He nods. "Go on."

I focus on the sidewalk ahead of us, pulling together pieces of truth to forge a more well-rounded lie. "We were playing Ping-Pong in her garage, and she knew I was thinking about reaching out to you because I got your chapter, and she suggested—if she won I'd have to streak down your street. And if I won, I'd be done giving them couples therapy unless they wanted to start paying me."

Reed's mouth stretches into a disbelieving smile. "What?"

"I've been giving her and her husband, the one who went missing, free couples therapy sessions."

"Why was her bet so much more savage than yours?"

I shrug. "I have older-sister syndrome with her. I don't ever want her life to be difficult."

"Do you have your things hidden out here somewhere?"

"Things?"

"Your clothes and stuff?"

"Oh, no . . . I was dropped off with nothing . . . and she left."

Reed arches a single brow. "What kind of person is your cousin?"

I snort. "The kind that pushes you into traffic if you're afraid to cross the street."

A laugh barks out of him. "With nothing but a journal to document your experience? I can't believe you got out of the car. How un–control freak of you."

"Yeah." I hold up the journal and wave it guiltily. "What can I say? Always trying to work on my flaws."

His mouth resets into a smirk as we start moving toward the house again. "She casually shows up naked after three weeks of radio silence."

I fiddle with my fingers as a hard blush scorches up my torso. I sigh. "Yeah, well, I told you I was a lot."

A low laugh rumbles out of Reed, but he doesn't respond.

"We did agree to no texting, right?"

He dips his chin, grinning now. "Yeah, I just like talking to you. I regret not vetoing that rule."

"I like talking to you too. I just figured you'd probably ghost me before we could see each other again, and I, well, I was trying to prevent things from getting messy."

Reed nods diplomatically. "That's fair."

"But . . . this now feels messier than any sporadic texting could have ever been."

He snorts.

"You just found me . . . naked outside your house on a random Wednesday." I swallow nervously, before looking up at him. "So I understand if you want to end our pact."

Reed lifts a brow. "My neighbor's house."

"Oh, trust me, I was outside your house too."

"Oh, trust *me*, I know. We got the Ring notification."

My eyes widen as a full body flush burns up my torso.

Reed nods. "Yep. You're blowing up on Nextdoor."

Not just a flush, a hot flash. I'm having a hot flash. We've stopped moving again.

"No shit," I croak.

"They're calling you naked journaling girl."

I swallow. "Wow, I've always wanted a nickname."

"Well, you can check it off the bucket list."

A bead of sweat trickles down the small of my back as I hold his gaze. "Make sure they include it in my obituary."

Reed nods again, a somber expression smoothing out any crinkled lines of amusement in his face. "Rikki 'Naked Journaling Girl' Romona. Respected therapist. Columbia graduate. Relationship Columnist. Viral Nudes on Nextdoor."

I blow out a slow exhale, grateful as the hot flash ebbs. "I want those exact words. No edits."

He smiles, and a triumphant warmth washes across my chest. I snort, drop my head into my hands, and drag them down my face.

"Seriously, though," I say quietly, "I understand if this was a deal-breaker. It was creepy and weird. I shouldn't have agreed to Whitney's bet."

Reed studies me without comment.

Okaaaay. "Uh, yeah, so I'll make this easy." I squeeze my eyes shut. "I'm gonna count to fifteen, and if you're not here when I open my eyes, I totally get it. Text me the goodbye phrase. I'll have my phone back eventually . . ."

I give him a second to reply, but he stays quiet.

Okay, and here we go. Eyes closed, I clear my throat. "One, one thousand. Two, one thou—"

I pause as Reed's palms glide up both sides of my face. *I hope they're Reed's palms.* My eyes open.

Reed's ice-blue irises burn into mine with an intensity that roots me to the sidewalk. Swallows the embarrassment lingering in my veins. Swipes across my thoughts like Windex on a whiteboard. He's so close.

All I see. All I feel is him. The heat of his chest rising against me. His feverishly hot hands. His fingertips grazing my ears. The five o'clock shadow on his sharp jaw.

He peers at me until my heart is galloping against my chest.

Until my skin begins to hum.

Slowly, his thumb tips up my chin. His lips draw up at the corners. "Come inside with me, Renee."

27 | INSIDE?

Reed slides his hands from my face and steps back. My insides have dissolved into a collection of soap bubbles.

Whoa.

I would jump out of a plane with him after eye contact like that.

We needed a condom for that eye contact.

I could be pregnant.

Maybe I am.

We can't rule it out. Life finds a way.

Celibate thirty-year-old woman conceives human child via eye contact.

Maybe this is how Jesus happened.

I gave him an out to break up with me for naked stalking . . . and he responded with eye-sex.

Reed's palm moves down the ridges of my spine and settles in the curve right above my ass as he steers me the remainder of the way toward his home in charged silence. The heat of his hand sears through the Sherpa blanket. That incandescent feeling from the wedding is back, thrumming through my veins. The sex goblin from the lake has been roused.

This feeling is so foreign. I didn't have it with any of the five daters from earlier this year. It never used to happen with Ted. Or Maddox back in college. Or my high school boyfriend of three weeks and two days, Wendell. Those guys gave me *butterflies*.

But I never daydreamed about their weight on top of me, their hands pulling off my underwear, scruff scraping down my body, their teeth on my thighs. I never wrote smutty fan fiction about going home with any of them after the night we met. This is a new level of attraction that I've never mingled with. Reed's existence has kicked open the door to a whole new (sultry) room in my brain.

I stand firm on my assertion that this man is an oxymoron. Reed says he's overrun with trust issues, but he seems to trust me? He presents as guarded, but when I press him the slightest bit, he's vulnerable.

"This is it." Reed pulls me from my thoughts as he gestures to the house I crouched in front of fifteen minutes ago. I follow him into his open garage and shuffle around the Mercedes.

I startle as the garage door shudders closed behind us. Reed pulls open the door to his dark house, and I startle again as he flips on a hall light. Apparently, I'm currently one unexpected noise away from accidentally jumping out of my body.

If there is a next time that I see this man, then that next time I need to be chill as ice. Chill as detritus floating aloofly through space. Sexy, put together, wearing cute clothes—*wearing clothes, period.*

I step inside. A staircase leading to a second floor sits to my left, and a long hallway lined with art pieces looms straight ahead.

"So, how have you been, Rikki?" Reed says a few feet down the hall.

A quiet laugh whistles through my teeth. "Um, chaotic. You?"

Reed smiles over his shoulder. "Same."

"Is this your mom's house?"

"It's mine. Oliver and I moved in at the end of January. She's visiting from Jersey."

"You own *this house*?"

His smile stretches. "Should I be insulted by your flagrant disbelief?"

I bite back a grin. "No . . . question mark."

He laughs. "You rent?"

"Reed, I'm a writer-podcaster who lives directly outside of New York City. Of course I rent."

Reed laughs again, advancing down the hall. "We were renting, but we had a great business year, so we decided to take the leap and invest."

He seems incredibly relaxed now that we're in his home. I trail him, waddling in my blanket-dress, slowing to inspect the art pieces. They're all made of bottle caps?

There's a two-foot-tall portrait of a Yankees hat made entirely of bottle caps. A *Hamilton* the musical logo made of a mix of painted and organic bottle caps.

My jaw falls open when I reach an enormous, extreme close-up of Ed Sheeran's face, wearing thick, black-framed glasses made *entirely* of art-ed bottle caps.

I swing my gaze to Reed. He's ten feet down the hall, waiting in front of a door. "Reed, what is this?"

"That's Ed."

"Why is Ed here?"

"He's one of the greatest songwriters of our generation, Rikki. It would be weird if he wasn't here."

A smile rips across my face as he disappears into the room he was hovering in front of. I shuffle after him, coming to a halt in the doorframe.

His room.

It's spacious and full of warm wooden furniture. It smells like cedar, oakmoss, and musk. Like him. Reed's ducked into a walk-in closet off to the right.

I slink against the doorframe. "Where did you get a bottle-cap portrait of Ed Sheeran?"

"I made it," he calls from inside the closet. "I do bottle-cap art. It's a hobby. Not as edgy as streaking, but it helps with my anxiety."

He made it? That was like real art.

I gape at his back. He's in dark-blue straight leg jeans today with that black button-up. "I have so many questions, I don't even know where to start."

He glances at me over his shoulder. "I told you I was a lot."

I purse my lips as a giddy whorl gushes outward from my heart. It's typically women who get labeled *a lot*. Men are allowed to be eccentric, chatty, loud, and strange, and they're called *fun*. People will say they're hilarious—they're an *interesting character*. Women with the same traits: a lot.

I'm obsessed with him identifying as a lot.

I curl my toes into the plush navy-blue throw rug under my feet that matches the dark-blue lines shooting through the plaid red comforter on his bed. This room is cozy.

The bed is perpendicular to this wall, jutting out to divide the floor. On his nightstand, atop a small stack of novels is . . . a weathered, annotated, well-worn copy of the book I recommended to him the night after the wedding: *Elizabeth Ross Falls for Ryan*. My mouth splits into a smile. *He wasn't lying about it being a favorite.* Past his walk-in closet, a door is open to an en suite bathroom. There's a TV mounted on the wall across from the bed with a deep-cherry wooden dresser set underneath it. Gallery walls spatter the space on either side of the screen, and two overflowing wooden bookcases span the left wall of the room, flanking a window that faces the front of the house.

My eyes catch on *The Minute* review of *Broken and Bruised* hanging to the left of the TV. A flock of birds swirls around my heart and flutters down into my gut.

"For you."

I turn back to Reed. He's emerged from the closet, and he's executing a tiny bow as he extends a stack of folded clothes.

Ah yes, I momentarily forgot I'm a sweaty mess in a Sherpa blanket.

I lock myself in Reed's bathroom, toss the journal and clothes on the counter next to the sink, and stare into the mirror, inhaling deeply as a wave of repressed shock surfaces in my chest.

I'm in LA.

I appeared here.

My journal can . . . bend space?

To evaporate home, I need to take a picture with him at Santa Monica Pier?

Does this mean the universe has actually stepped in to assist me with my love life?

I glance at the journal again. The garter's back around it. I squint at the lacy white leg-scrunchie. Could this have been triggered by the . . . garter thing?

Did the universe step in the night of Babe's wedding, and I'm only just now realizing it 'cause I didn't open the damn journal for a month? Has this sort of shit been happening to women everywhere since the dawn of garter-tradition time? *Is catching the bouquet and having a random slide a garter up your thigh at a wedding some sort of mystical horny rain dance to herald in Aphrodite so she can help you secure a soulmate?*

There's a shower behind me in the mirror. It's one of those fancy-looking big rectangular glass ones with an elaborate showerhead. I pull open the door and flip on the water.

I fold Reed's Sherpa blanket, hop in, and let the hot water cascade right into my face.

Reed's mom is here.

I already forgot that I'm definitely intruding.

It's nine something Pacific time. Santa Monica Pier closes at eleven. I need to get us out of this house stat if I want to get home tonight. I have card orders to fill for the Etsy shop tomorrow, and I haven't done any prep because I spent my free time this evening collecting enough milk to support a Clifford-size cat.

All my shit is in Hoboken. I can't stay here in any capacity without a phone. My purse and ID and everything a human needs to live in society is *in Hoboken.*

We're twenty minutes from Santa Monica Pier. I just need to get Reed there, take a quick picture, and we can both go on our merry way. He can get back to family time. I can get home and spend the rest of the night parsing out what in the fuck this all means. Maybe Reed and I can plan an actual hang and spend time together sooner? How do I tell him I can now bend space and come back sometime this weekend or the next if that's preferable?

Aesop Coriander Seed Body Cleanser is arranged neatly among Aesop shampoo and conditioner on one of those metal hanging shelves. I take my time getting clean, deep breathing, reveling in the aromatic steam. It smells like man heaven: The soap is woodsy and irresistible.

When I'm done, I realize I didn't ask for a towel. I smear away the steam fogging up the glass shower walls and home in on the used navy-blue one hanging on the back of the bathroom door. I tug it from the hook and snuggle in. Reed's *if the forest took human form and sat in the sun on the beach for hours reading a book* scent is all over it.

I sift through the clothes he pulled for me. There's a pair of black boxers, an NYU T-shirt, NYU sweatpants, and folded underneath it all—a thin, well-worn, long black coat. I suck in a sharp breath as it flops open.

A trench coat.

I tug the loose gray T-shirt over my head. I twist the bottom of the shirt and knot it so it's more fitted, and I look at least a smidge cute. I roll the sweatpants a couple times so they fit better.

Reverently, I slide on the coat. The sleeves fall to my mid-palm, and the bottom brushes my calves. It smells like fresh laundry, it's surprisingly comfortable, and the journal fits easily into one of its enormous square pockets. I glance at my reflection. I look like a jock who traded jackets with the town flasher.

Steam rushes out behind me as I step back into Reed's room. He's sat on the corner of the bed, feet planted, turning his phone over in his hands.

His eyes slice up to mine, and the usual jolt shivers down my spine. His lips tip up. "The trench looks good on you."

I lean sideways against the doorframe. "Thanks, it's really helping with my trauma."

He smiles, offering up his phone. "Did you need to call someone? Do you want me to drive you somewhere?"

As I see it, I have two options here:

(1.) Pretend to call Whitney.

Or

(2.) Attempt to charades my way through explaining that I teleported here from the other side of the country using the magical normal-looking leather journal I got in my goody bag at Babe's wedding.

"Yeah, actually, is it okay if I make a quick call?"

Reed nods, unlocking his phone. "Of course."

"Thank you." I take his iPhone, wander back into the bathroom, and punch Whitney's cell into the keypad. I hit send and immediately hang up. Then I murmur into the phone awkwardly for thirty seconds before walking back into Reed's room and handing it back.

"All good?"

I nod. "Yeah . . . Do you think you could possibly give me a ride down to Santa Monica Pier? My cousin's down there for the night."

He blows out a low laugh. "She really left you here in the streets and drove all the way down to Santa Monica?"

I snort. "She's also a lot."

28 | CHURCH AND STATE

"So, Reed."

"So, where do you live, Rikki?"

I laugh. "Hoboken."

He smiles out the windshield. "I'm looking for exact parameters, floor, apartment number—you know mine. It's only fair."

My cheeks burn neon as I drop my forehead momentarily against the passenger side window. "Yeah, all right. I'm in Hoboken—fifth floor of this building along the Hudson." I rattle off the exacts of my address, and we lapse into silence as he pulls us onto the I-405. "Paradise by the Dashboard Light" by Meat Loaf plays lightly over the radio.

"So, Reed." I return playfully to my original unvoiced train of thought.

"Yes, Rikki?" He lobs the words back in a hot, professor-like murmur.

"Do you do your acting work under a whole other pseudonym?"

He grins out the windshield. "Been googling?"

"Oh, I googled you the second I got back from the wedding. Not much to find, which was obnoxious."

Reed laughs. "Yes, I act under another name."

"What is it?" I ask.

He glances over mischievously. "I don't think I'm ready to share."

I guffaw. "Reed. How can I ever truly know you if I can't go back and watch slash roast your backlog of commercial work?"

He smiles. "I have a bigger project coming up."

My brows jump to my hairline. "Go on."

"I've taken a step back from the podcast company for it 'cause, I mean, it's a *job* job. Oliver's been mostly running things at Oh Brother Audio himself for a while now."

"Wait, what? Congratulations!"

"I have to finally get an acting Instagram because the streamer wants me to be able to promote it on my nonexistent actor socials."

"Reed! That's amazing." I pause, studying his amused, guarded expression. "And what—you're not going to tell me what this project is?"

His mouth rolls into a decisive purse. "I feel like I should wait."

"Wait for what?"

"Wait for this to be a little more solid. It hasn't been announced."

"This being the movie or this you and me?"

He shoots me a playful smirk.

I guffaw again. "I can't believe you're about to keep this to yourself. Is it a Marvel movie? Is that house bought with Marvel money?"

He barks a laugh. "Are you going to tell me about the *us*-adjacent articles you're working on for Love Today before they go live?"

I squint at him. Has he read my last three pieces?

20 First-Date Questions to Keep in Your Notes App.

How Many Romantic IRL Meet-Cutes Does the Average Person Encounter in the Digital Age?

Can You Actually Meet Dateable Single People at a Wedding?

My stomach twists as the multiple failed five-date ventures I embarked on during the first half of the year come careening back to mind. Perhaps it would behoove me to keep that area of my life *separate* from the romantic one.

Reed meets my eyes for half a second and lifts his brow.

"I wonder if we should have a rule about work," I suggest.

He cocks his head. "Hit me."

"Should we separate church and state? Keep work details private from dating-life escapades? Can we keep that area of our lives out of our—conversations?"

"Interesting proposition. But what if you come by my work, or I run into one of your articles?"

I shrug. "I mean, then we're happy for each other, but we have a mutual understanding that our work is our work, and we don't need to let it affect whatever's going on between us?"

"So basically I keep acting under wraps and you keep Love Today separate? Like the pseudonyms doing those jobs *are actually* different people."

I grin. "Exactly. Maybe you promise not to read my articles or listen to the podcast for the span of this agreement."

Reed rolls that around in his mind for a long beat. "And are you going to watch the things I might appear in?"

I bite my lip. "Well—I guess I won't without your consent. But I'd love to watch the things you're in. I feel like they're probably not derived directly from your personal life."

He chuckles. "Maybe you avoid the press interviews. That's more equivocal to your podcast and column."

Press interviews? "Okaaayyyy." What the fuck is he going to be appearing in?

He grins. "All right. I agree to this amendment under the condition that we drop the texting law."

I smile out the window. "Okay."

"Okay?" he says. "We're allowed to casually speak between dates?"

"Okay," I say again.

"Can I call you?"

"On the phone?"

"Microwave."

I snort.

"Yes, the phone, Rikki."

I watch the white lines stretching and breaking along the black highway. *In no world will I be able to "remain" any semblance of "casual" about this situationship if Reed is calling me regularly.* "How about we can call each other, but only if we're both sitting on a bed? Like you have to be on your bed to call me."

"And if you're not on your bed when I call?"

"Then I can't pick up and vice versa."

He slits his eyes in my direction before looking back at the road. "Okay, Renee."

I smile. "Okay."

"All right, movement to replace no texting with separation of church and state approved. Calling while located on mattresses also approved. Add it to the constitution."

"Done."

He smiles at the windshield. "This all feels very *Mr. and Mrs. Smith*."

"I have another question," I prompt.

"I'm ready."

"You said in your chapter you've been Commitment Issues Guy for the last nine years? Let's dig into that."

"Wow, jumping right from zero to a hundred." Reed shakes his head, grinning.

"You said you were ready."

He takes a beat and sighs. "I haven't actually *dated* dated someone in a hot second. Just mostly one- to two-date flings here and there."

"How long is a hot second?"

Reed's eyes flick over to me and back to the road. "A while."

"Don't Edward Cullen me."

He blows out a hard breath. "Four . . ."

"Four years?" I ask.

"Fourteen," he says quickly.

"Fourteen?" I repeat, confused. "You're only thirty-two."

"Yeah."

I gawk at the green highway sign up ahead. "You haven't been in a relationship *since you walked in on your fiancée cheating on you?*"

Reed catches his tongue between his teeth, as we veer onto the I-10. "That kind of trust. That level of intimacy," he starts. "Being in a romantic partnership—it's big. It's different than physical intimacy."

He pauses, and I hold my breath, willing him to elaborate.

"It means openly trusting someone with every aspect of your life, and they're trusting you with theirs. You're willingly handing over the power to control your emotional well-being. It's—I mean, that's some scary shit."

We drive in silence for an interminable three minutes because I'm not sure what to say. I feel like I just dipped over the edge of a roller coaster.

He hasn't dated anyone since he was eighteen. And here I am, secretly hoping this long-distance nothing will at some point spontaneously evolve into "something real."

Bad news: I'm an idiot.

Good news: I am now an idiot *in possession of a teleportation journal.* It said thirteen jumps. I have twelve more. I could come out here once a week for at least six more weeks.

Bad news: I'm not some magical unicorn with the power to change his ways.

Four whole minutes later, when we're off the highway, sat at a red light, I finally work up the gall to speak. "So all these one-night, two-night casual dating stands you've been hitting these past fourteen years. What are they like? What do you do with these people you already know you don't want to see more than twice? How much smoke gets blown up each ass? Are you a serial ghost?"

He lets go of a breath as the light goes green. "I try never to blow smoke up any asses, Rikki. We usually do something fun and then go back to her place, and that's it."

"What do you talk about?"

"I don't usually talk much. They talk, I listen."

"You're telling me you're not a snarky 1860s statue come to life with every other woman you encounter in the wild?"

He snorts. "I'm sorry—1860s what?"

"Do you not engage in a playful back-and-forth with other suitors, Reed?"

"Maybe for a second, but then they have the floor."

"People ask questions back."

"I can easily spin a question."

I narrow my eyes, staring him down as we move through the numbered streets of Santa Monica.

"Do they know you don't do relationships when you embark on these dates?"

He microshakes his head. "No, not typically, but I've never lied if they asked."

"Why suggest a pact with me if you don't do relationships?" I ask, voice quiet but firm. "It's implying more than two encounters."

He pulls us into a spot and throws the car in to park. "What's your relationship thing, Rick?"

"What do you mean?"

He shifts to face me in his seat. "I mean on dates, what's your pattern when you decide you don't like the person? How do you escape?"

"I, well, um." I exhale a gust of nervous air. "I tell them I have a dog at home with separation anxiety. That it's crying and my neighbors are texting, so I have to get back."

"And then what?"

"What do you mean?"

"Then what happens? Do you text them after you leave?"

I open and close my mouth. "Um, well, no, because it was just a first date, and it was bad."

"Exactly."

"I mean yes, but that's only if they also don't text. So it's a mutual ghost."

He tilts his head. "Who's to say my dating experiences didn't end in mutual ghostings?"

"Okay." I cast my eyes toward the beach stretching out in front of us, adjacent to the pier. "You're right, after a *first* date it's not exactly ghosting. It's more of a taboo thing from the third date on, I guess."

"What happens when they text you after the first date, but you don't want to keep seeing them?"

I serve him a hard look. "I don't ghost. I have a text precrafted by Jordyn in my notes that says *I'm sorry I'm just not feeling the vibe here. It was great meeting you.*"

Reed nods, a small smile on his lips. "I like that. Nice of her to draft it out for you."

"Yeah, she understands that dating apps are modern-day vampires slowly sucking the life out of their users. They dangle the promise of love, and we open our veins to their fucking fangs." I bark out a laugh, remembering my first conversation with Reed at the wedding. "I see now why you called dating *fun*. You don't actually do it with the goal of a relationship. You go in, knowing you'll only see them once or twice!

"You don't have grand hopes of *finding your person* that you have to watch catch fire repetitively each time you find yourself across the table from some new brand of dick."

Reed huffs a laugh. "Rikki—"

I cut him off as another realization slaps me in the face. "Hold up . . . Does this mean you haven't been on a third date in fourteen years?"

Reed's mouth curves into a sad self-aware smile. "When you put it that way, I sound insane."

I widen my eyes at him. *"Reed."*

"It hasn't been fourteen whole years—I've just found that when you want to keep things casual, it's hard after three-plus dates. It starts to feel like something to the other party."

I slam a hand across my face. "You've been living with an actual two-date rule for a decade?"

Laughter rumbles through him. "Rikki! I've been full steam ahead with my career since I got out of college. I'm an efficient guy. I don't like to waste time.

"Remember how I was ready to get married out of high school? She said yes. I was a fiancé. I was getting married. I was a hundred percent ready to commit to someone forever. And don't get me wrong, I'm glad I didn't, because I didn't know who I was, and she didn't know who she was. But that doesn't mean I don't ever want to find someone I want to do that with again.

"I've put so much work into myself this past decade. I've done a shit ton of therapy.

"I'm not twenty-one anymore. It's not that I'm not looking, Rikki, I just know what I'm looking for."

He's quiet as his jet-fuel eyes find mine across the center console. My heart hammers as the implication reverberates in the silence.

I break eye contact and refocus on the dashboard. "I do enjoy efficiency."

His lips twitch. "I caught that. Do you feel like you're wasting your time?"

I should say yes. My brain says yes. It's been saying yes since I found out we don't live on the same coast. *You're dumb as shit to trust this guy. To risk putting your heart in this basket. To waste your time and mental space daydreaming about a future with this man.*

But the rest of me says no. The universe said no.

I meet his gaze. "No."

"Neither do I."

"Okay."

"Can I ask you something?" he says.

"You can always ask me things, Reed."

"Will you still be in California this weekend?"

I swallow hard. "Maybe."

"Any chance you're free Saturday?"

29 | SANTA MONICA PIER

I'm momentarily stunned into silence. "Are you only asking because I called you out?"

Reed shakes his head. "I like that you called me out, but I'm asking because I want to spend more time with you. I have a wedding on Saturday. I would love to take you."

I huff a laugh. "You're asking me to be your plus-one? Three days before?"

"My buddy's getting married. I texted him to ask if I could bring you while you were in the shower."

My brows pull together. "You did?"

"I did."

"And?"

"They've had a couple last-minute cancellations. He said yes."

"I . . ." I blink out at the darkness, trying to consider this logically. *I have twelve more jumps.* He cocks his head as I meet his eyes. "Can I think about it?"

The right side of Reed's mouth tips up. "Of course."

I nod, staring at my hands.

"Rikki. I don't want to be Commitment Issues Guy. I'm ready to shed that skin. That's why I suggested the pact. Because I like you. And I wanted to do something about it."

I swallow nervously. "What guy you shooting for now?"

I hear his hands slide down the steering wheel. "Enacting Intentional Change Guy? Making Intentional Dating Decisions Guy? Still working on the branding."

I look over at him, a smile teasing at my lips. He's staring at the dashboard.

"My therapist used to periodically ask this one 'would you rather?'" he says quietly. "Would you rather go on first dates with new people for the rest of your life or marry someone you've already been on a date with and stay with them for the rest of your time. From age twenty-four to twenty-nine, I instantly chose first dates. It's really depressing, thinking about that now."

"Yeah, the answer's obviously *marry*, dating's the absolute worst."

He snorts and glances over at me. "Dating you is not so bad."

I roll my eyes. "Shut up."

He grins. "No."

Take a picture with him on Santa Monica Pier.

The demand floats across my vision like I have my own personal built-in mental stock ticker.

He asked me to go to a wedding. Those are full of pictures. This shouldn't be weird. It's not a big deal.

Well, it is a big deal. But by inviting me to a wedding he's saying he's cool with the deal.

Reed threads our fingers together as we cross the parking lot.

"We're holding hands?" I ask.

His brow furrows. "Does this count as sex?"

I laugh. "No."

"Then yes, we're holding hands."

The sandals I've borrowed from Reed's mom flap against the ground as we make our way toward the old wooden staircase that leads up to the pier.

Once we reach the top we hang a left, approaching the SoCal landmark in all its nostalgic nighttime glory: the lights, the rides, the dumb carnival games. Foot traffic is light, being that it's 10:30 p.m. on a weekday. Teenagers and young couples line the railings that trace the perimeter, gazing out at the dark expanse of ocean surrounding the oversize dock.

I tug Reed along until I find a gap in the crowd under a curved lamppost and pull us over.

"All right," I say. "This is my stop."

"Here?" He grins. "We're not going to go hunt down your cousin?"

"No, I don't need you to linger around with me. You need to get back to your mom while she's there. I'm pretty sure I heard something that sounded a lot like *Catching Fire* upstairs as we were leaving. You should join movie night. I know how hard it is to find quality time with the fam when they live on the other side of the country."

Reed's face softens. "Are you sure you're gonna be okay?"

I let go of his hand and hold out my palm expectantly. "Give me your phone."

"Is this a mugging situation?"

I snicker as he unsheathes it from his pocket and hands it over.

"Pass is 8844," he says.

"Don't give your mugger your password, Reed!"

Reed's mouth rolls up his cheek into the knot. "Just trying to work on my flaws."

I glare up at him playfully before tapping open his iPhone camera. I set it to 0.5x, flip on the flash, and position it in front of us, angling it above our heads. The screen's facing away so I can't see the framing, but I'm confident we're both in the shot. I cut him a serious look. "Don't *smile*."

He chuckles, and I snap the picture.

Relief barrels through me.

"Want me to take it?" A random reaches for the phone from my hand.

"Yeah, why not?" Reed answers before I have the wherewithal to protest.

Reed shoots me a wry grin as he plucks the phone from my hand, transfers it to a random tourist guy, and poses next to me. The flash goes off.

I'm a deer in the headlights as I turn back to him.

"Got it, now kiss."

I chortle, about to lecture this random on decorum, when Reed catches my hip and effortlessly twists me in his direction so we're face-to-face. He catches a spot under my chin and tilts my mouth to his.

A glimmering wave of energy ripples through me as our mouths meet again. The sensation validates every irritating moment I've spent pining for this man over the past three weeks. *See, this just isn't a typical body response to a—* His hands snake under the trench, pressing into my lower back. His hot tongue flicks against my lips, and I give in to this new, ever-growing craving for him. For his mouth. His touch. His left hand runs down my left thigh, latches behind my knee. I gasp against his lips as he hitches the leg up over his hip, pulling me flush against his pelvis. My fingers tangle in the collar of his shirt to stay upright as the kiss expands. Heat races up my spine. His hand tightens around my calf, tugging me harder against his center—

"Fuck yeaaaah!"

Our photographer's voice snaps against my skull like a weaponized rubber band.

I resurface shakily, pulling away from Reed, dropping my leg—disoriented. Intellectually obliterated as Reed thanks the man and reclaims his phone.

When he turns back to me, I'm gawking through a dumbstruck open smile. "What the hell was that?"

He points his phone at me and snaps a picture, the flash making colors explode behind my eyes.

"Reed! I wasn't even doing anything!" I rack my brain for some sort of cute sexy pose and draw a complete blank before panic popping my hip and biting my pinkie finger between my teeth as the flash snaps again. "Oh god, wait, I don't know what I just did with myself."

He lowers the phone, grinning as he walks backward toward the steps we entered from. "See you at the airport, Renee."

I laugh. "Reed, wait! Your trench."

"Hold on to it. I'll text you the details for this weekend."

"I haven't said I'll come yet!"

"Do you want to come?" he says from the top of the steps.

I throw my hands up and let them fall. "Yes, I want to come! Do you want me to come?"

His smile widens. "Renee, I sent you a heart emoticon."

We're just yelling across twenty feet of dead air now. "Yeah but—"

"You're wearing my trench!"

"But—"

He cups his hands around his mouth and shouts, "I have a giant fucking crush on you."

I laugh as another gush of iridescence hurtles through me. "Okay!"

He beams. "Okay!"

"I have a giant crush on you too!"

He salutes me before spinning around and heading down the steps.

30 | BUFFERING

Must I always land on all fours like a drunk college student who just vomited in the street?

I'm on the sidewalk. And I'm sweating. I'm slick with it. Slicker than before. My freshly washed hair is stuck to my temples.

An unexpected wave of nausea roils through me, and it happens—I throw up on the concrete.

A wave of dizziness assaults my senses as I push myself to stand.

The journal's on my right.

I am still wearing the trench, shirt, and sweatpants. *Hallelujah!*

I was so worried I was going to lose Reed's clothes. Prejump I maneuvered into a slightly hunched position so I could clutch a section of each item in my fists, determined to hold on to them through the jump for dear life. It seems to have worked.

But I feel . . . sickly. My lips are cracked. And I'm outside my building, without a key.

I slip the journal into the trench coat pocket and stagger to the call box to buzz Jordyn and Micah.

"Hello?" Micah's groggy, confused voice crackles from the speaker.

"Hi," I croak. My throat feels like it hasn't seen water for days. "Micah, it's me, sorry I know it's late. I got stuck outside without my purse. Can you buzz me in? And can I swing by for my spare key?"

◆ ◆ ◆

I almost collapse in the stretch of hallway from Micah's door to my own apartment.

Once I'm safely inside my (dad's) place, I chug a Pedialyte and inhale two eggs over easy on toast. Then I drain the milk lake sitting in the tub and draw myself an actual bath. I slap my wooden bath table across the ceramic edge, toss the journal on it, and slide into the water.

Okay. *I'm going to a wedding with Reed in three days.*

I have to sort out the quirks of this journal before then.

Apparently two cross-country jumps in a two-hour window is killer. What would happen if I attempted a third jump right now? *Would I die?* If I was clutching my Away bag, would it jump with me?

I sit up, sloshing the water as I open the leather journal on the wooden table.

The print dictating the Santa Monica Pier task has gone silver, and the page across from it now reads:

Feedback?

I pull the pen from the loop in the back, twist out the ballpoint, and hover over the page.

A thread of trepidation tugs in my chest. Without the fear of (naked) discovery lancing through me or the ignorance of my blatant disbelief, writing in this is mildly scary. Interacting with any sort of sentient book was highly discouraged by the fantasy novels of my youth.

Oh well.

> *Thank you for choosing me! I'm excited about being granted this device, but kinda panicked about all the aspects I don't completely understand yet. How do you come up with the tasks? That was low-key mortifying.*
>
> *Can I ask, why does teleporting feel like being burned alive? Is there science behind that?*
>
> *You mentioned the jump takes a heavy energy*

toll—would I die if I jumped again right now?

How did I qualify for this exactly? Are you from the wedding? Was it the garter thing?

Can I tell Jordyn about you if I do it via charades? Is that against the rules?

Am I correct in assuming if I'm clutching an object, it will join me on the jump as well?

I reread my entry and nod. Okay. That should give me a good foundation of information. It's upbeat, grateful, inquisitive.

I swallow hard and flip the page.

Mortifying? You seemed to enjoy yourself.

I tip the notebook forward, frowning. *What.* I flip the page again, harder this time, praying there's a more thorough response pending.

Maybe don't dangle a teleportation device over open water, Rikki.

An offended noise slips from my mouth. I flip the page again.

3) Where would you like to go

X ______________________

I slap the thing shut and toss it away from the tub. My phone buzzes on the tile. I lean over the ceramic edge and snatch it up.

Reed: glad I found you naked on the side of the road today. Hope you got to your cousin's place safe. <3

I snort at the heart.

Reed: So it's a musical-themed wedding on Saturday. We're supposed to go as our favorite musical characters from the selection of musicals displayed on the invite. (I'm not kidding. My friends loves a theme.) I was thinking of doing Grease. You up for Sandy?

Reed: The reception starts at seven. It's down in San Diego so I thought we'd leave around 12:30, grab some food, check into the hotel.

Reed: Are you okay staying in the same hotel room together?

My eyes bulge as a photo comes through.

It's me. In his clothes, lit up by the iPhone flash against a dark background. No makeup, trench open, hip popped, smiling and biting my pinkie finger.

"Oh god."

The phone buzzes again, and my jaw unhinges. Another picture.

Us. Intertwined. My fingers are twisted in the front of his shirt, tugging it forward. Our mouths are mid-shift, so there's a sliver of space between our lips. I'm tilted back, supported by his one arm, and his other hand is behind my knee, hitching my sweatpants-clad leg up over his hip. The trench is blown back slightly like there's a wind machine on us. It looks like we were caught making out during a . . . tango.

Reed: This is some book-cover shit

I respond to Reed and proceed to spend an excessive amount of time staring at that photo. I will be thinking about that photo for the rest of time. It has its own room in my mind palace now, roped off behind glass like the *Mona Lisa*, to be visited mentally whenever I see fit.

I turn in bed and grab my phone again, too amped up to sleep.

@OliverTylerAudio has followed me on Instagram. I open the profile. *Reed's brother.* The grid's full of set pictures. He's a boom operator, it seems. And then there's a bunch of photos of him with . . . other podcasts they must produce. Smiling with the hosts. They're definitely identical, but he's thinner than Reed. More slight, like he doesn't spend as much time at the gym. Same eyes, though. Same hair, different cut. Different smile, more over the top. Less cool guy. There's a picture of him and Reed together in front of a sign on a wall for **Oh Brother Audio**. They're both wearing thick, black-rimmed glasses like the ones Ed Sheeran's wearing in the bottle-cap portrait in Reed's hallway. I'm beaming like a creep in the dark, a victorious feeling threading across my chest as I scroll my way down through Oliver's profile. A portal into Reed's life I wasn't aware existed! *Photos that include people's faces!*

I follow Oliver back.

A DM pops up in my notifications almost instantly.

Oliver: Hey, I didn't get to introduce myself formally because uh, extenuating circumstances, don't worry I heard you lost a bet and you're not a serial streaker. I'm Reed's brother Oliver.
Me: Hi! Nice to officially meet you! So sorry for the awkward pseudo-intro.
Oliver: you like him, right?
Me: of course
Oliver: Okay. I haven't seen him this excited about anyone in a long time.
Oliver: Don't hurt him.

◆ ◆ ◆

Thursday, August 28—TO DO

- Fulfill Etsy card orders
- Answer emails

- Laundry (clean Reed's clothes)
- Clean house
- Pack for the wedding weekend
- Prep next week's Love Today article
- Prep next week's podcast discussion
- Text Whitney about a Sandy outfit
- Don't forget Reed thinks you're still on the West Coast
- Write the next chapter for *Message in a Bottle*—it's only fair
- Test notebook prewedding. Can one jump feat. suitcase?
- Text Aunt Teresa; make sure you can stay there Friday night

Dad [9:30 a.m.]: What happened to you last night? What's with the two grocery store trips? Are you planning a party? Is everything okay? Did you get drunk? You were stumbling.
Me [9:33 a.m.]: I just wasn't feeling well.
Dad [9:34 a.m.]: Feel better. No parties in the apartment.

SUBJECT: Friday Morning Meeting
Maya Leigh <mleigh@nyminute.com> August 28
Hi Rikki,
I have some news to share tomorrow morning. Please report to my office first thing at 9 a.m.
See you bright and early!
Maya Leigh
Lifestyle Senior Editor
New York Minute

Aunt Teresa [10:57 a.m.]: of course you can stay here! I'm working the night shift tomorrow but just use the garage code

Dad [11:34 a.m.]: You didn't respond. No parties in that apartment, Rikki. That was not part of the agreement.
Dad [11:34 a.m.]: I have someone coming in to re-tile the kitchen tomorrow
Me [11:35 a.m.]: Dad, I have an important work meeting in the morning and I'm going on a last-minute trip to California to help Mom look at wedding venues this weekend. I was just about to text you about it.
Dad [11:35 a.m.]: Fine, I'll reschedule tiling for Monday at 8 a.m.
Me [11:36 a.m.]: Okay . . . I have a Love Today podcast recording I have to be at by 9:30 in the city on Monday. Can I leave them in the apartment?
Dad [11:36 a.m.]: Yes, be there to let them in.

Mom [1:03 p.m.]: Layla and I decided we want a dog themed wedding! It's going to be the cutest! Can we hop on a FaceTime with you to talk decor? I was hoping you'd be able to organize florals and drink specials!
Me [1:05 p.m.]: Did you land on a date? I thought you hadn't even chosen a venue. Did you look at the list of places I sent?
Mom [1:06 p.m.]: The park you found has an opening on New Year's Eve due to a cancellation! I BOOKED IT! WOOOO!
Me [1:06 p.m.]: Oh my god, that's so soon, Mom
Mom [1:07 p.m.]: That's why we need to FaceTime asap! We're so excited.

Me [1:08 p.m.]: we can talk while I'm cooking dinner later, I'll FaceTime you around 7.

At 5:30, armed with electrolytes, I venture to Coney Island with a carry-on, fifty bucks in cash, and an old purse to test the journal. I take a seat with all my crap on a bench and plug in my home address.

> Eat a piece of lined notebook paper. The whole piece.
> That is all.
> Have fun.

I eat a piece of paper via ripping it into strips and dunking it in water, and eventually make it back to the apartment.

Conclusions were fourfold:

(1.) I can bring things as long as I'm holding them in my hands.

(1.) Those things can be in a suitcase. As long as the suitcase is held, they will come.

(2.) I will always land on all fours and sweaty (unpleasant).

(3.) No one noticed me pop out of nowhere, and I was in broad daylight. I think it cloaks me for about thirty seconds post jump.

Whitney [8:37 p.m.]: Hey Rick, just confirming we still have a session during your lunch hour tomorrow right?

Me [8:38 p.m.]: Yeah—I have a busy day though so we might have to do 30 minutes. I'm heading out west this weekend for a wedding.

Whitney [8:39 p.m.]: WHAT? Whose wedding?

Me [8:39 p.m.]: Reed invited me to plus-one for him. I was going to see if I could borrow that Sandy dance outfit? It's a musical-themed wedding! Reed wants to do Grease, which is actually perfect because it's your favorite, right? You have like all her outfits from Halloweens past?

Whitney [8:40 p.m.]: Are you KIDDING? 98% INVITED YOU TO WEDDING WITH HIM? Yes I have the PERFECT EXACT WHITE DRESS!!!! CAN YOU WEAR WHITE THOUGH? SHOULD I DYE IT PINK? MAYBE I'LL DYE IT LIGHT PINK! When do you get in? I also have Cha-cha's dress! AND THE TIGHT BLACK OUTFIT FROM THE END! I'LL JUST BRING YOU ALL OF THEM.

Me [8:41 p.m.]: lol okay thank you! I'll hopefully be at your mom's by 9pm tomorrow night.

Whitney [8:41 p.m.]: I'LL BE THERE.

Once I've tackled almost everything on the to-do list, I curl up in bed with my laptop and have a marvelous time reliving yesterday's Reed adventure as I retell the experience in chapter form. As if no magic were involved. As if I would ever agree to a streaking bet. It takes me three hours, but I finally reach the end of our night.

Do people in situationships go to weddings together?

Do they take pictures on boardwalks, kissing?

Do they send heart emoticons?

I feel like we're doing it wrong.

Situationships are supposed to stay away from the high dive.

We're dancing on the edge of a cliff.

31 | FRIDAY

Feedback?

I stare down at the question as the 8:30 a.m. train jolts into motion.

Nerves bop around my chest. I have a mystery meeting with my boss awaiting me at work. And a mystery task awaiting me in these pages, pre-teleporting to LA. What if it asks me to bungee jump? Or steal? Or slap someone on the street? Do I do it, or am I going to have to drop a wad of cash I should be saving to grab a flight last minute?

I twist on the pen.

> *Eat paper? Aren't you paper? Is there a method to your madness?*

I flip the page.

> The task correlates directly to the severity of the jump. I'm not paper. I communicate through it for your convenience, Rikki.

I scribble a note down under the print.

> *What are you?*

Flip.

A teleportation device. We've been through this.

I loose a withering sigh and flip.

4) Where would you like to go
X ______________________

I pen down Aunt Teresa's address.

32 | TED

Confront the ex you've been avoiding.

That is all.
Have fun.

You've got to be fucking kidding me.

This teleportation device is trolling me. *The universe is fucking trolling me.*

Ted, of five-month-long-relationship fame, covers soccer in the sports section of *The Minute* and is regrettably the very last person I want to interact with right now.

I met him at an office party when I was working for Books Today, and the piece I wrote on our breakup seventeen months ago is what got me the position at Love Today. The man's office is one hundred feet away from mine: a quick weave through the no-man's-land of cubicles in the middle of the floor, right next to the restrooms.

Post breakup we've behaved as if our five-month stint as boyfriend and girlfriend never happened. Occasionally, I'm forced to engage in small talk with him when we make eye contact in the break room, but we've never discussed *the end*. We haven't spoken about *us* since the morning we broke up. I slam the journal shut.

Reed [8:45 a.m.]: that was delightful =P

The corner of my mouth flips up. He read the new chapter.

Reed: to be honest though—I'M ON THE EDGE OF MY SEAT FOR THE DARKNESS. you still haven't dropped your dad backstory.

I snort, weaving through commuters to Starbucks.

Me: Why the hell are you up at 5 a.m.?
Reed: I'm on my morning run.
Me: wow you can run and text at the same time?
Reed: it's an art.
Me: Americas got talent!!
Reed: we're getting off topic
Me: BACKSTORY IS A MOOD KILLER
Reed: I enjoy puzzling together how you became your wildly successful kind, delightfully suspicious, insightful self. Backstory is required.

I bite back a smile as I place my coffee order. It's a triple espresso kind of day.

Reed: Don't fret, I'm a gentleman—I'll start
Me: are you about to text me a backstory essay about your father while running?
Reed: Yes please hold.

It's 8:53 when the barista yells *Ribby* and presents my drink. I grab it and run. I have three blocks and an elevator to ride to the office, and my meeting is at nine o'clock.

I've conjured the loose outline of a plan: Meet with Maya—hopefully it's just a quick face-to-face in prep for my pending contract renegotiation and imminent pay bump. Then, casually stop by Ted's office. Tell him how the end of the relationship was shitty and assert a request for an apology.

I can do that. A Ted conversation is overdue. The journal's right: I have a bad habit of avoiding dealing with past relationships. Once they break, we never speak again. I just write about it and share with the general public. It'll be healthy to . . . tie things up so we're on good terms. (Good's a strong word. Neutral. *Neutral* terms.)

My phone buzzes as I'm sprinting across the second block.

Reed: My dad passed in a car accident when I was 18. Forced me and my brother to grow up pretty fast.

Me: oh my god Reed, I'm so sorry.

Reed: Thanks.

Reed: our relationship was pretty tumultuous toward the end and he passed before I could apologize for being a dick and make things right.

Me: That's horrible. I'm so, so sorry. What triggered the turmoil? [Running into a meeting apologies in advance for my delayed response]

I chug my iced triple-espresso latte in the elevator. I feel like an asshole, leaving this conversation right as Reed's opening up, but I have one minute to get to my meeting.

I put my phone on silent, drop it in my bag, and stride through the door of Maya's office at 9:00 a.m. sharp, sucking down the dregs of my drink.

Maya looks up from her computer as I pull out the bright-orange chair next to her desk and take a seat. "Good morning, Rikki!"

I smile warmly at my boss, a sharp-witted late-fifty-something Asian woman who dresses to the nines every day. "Morning, Maya. Hope you're well."

Maya nods. "I am!" She laughs, shuffling some papers into a pile and putting them off to the side. "Did you . . . run here?"

Yes. "Power walked!" I chuckle awkwardly. "Why do you ask?"

"You look sweatier than usual."

"Do I usually look sweaty?"

"No, hence the *than usual* bit of that sentence."

"I was running a little behind, and I didn't want to be late for our meeting."

"You need a second to grab some water? Your cheeks are flushed."

I wave her off. "No, I'm all good, we can start. I'm excited to hear what's going on."

She folds her hands on the desk and smiles. "Okay! Well, for starters I wanted to tell you the column's doing great—record highs on clicks thanks to the podcast."

"That's fantastic!" I beam.

"Your contract renewal is coming up for the podcast," Maya continues.

Well aware. My smile falters as a cramp pierces my abdomen.

"I can't tell you how much glowing feedback we've been receiving from your show these past six months. You know you're pulling in over half a million views per episode now."

I nod. *Yes, I do know. I've been waiting for y'all to acknowledge it.*

"It's hovering right above the amount of people we have subscribed via print. You should be very proud—you've spread *The Minute* to a whole new demographic."

My stomach seizes as a bolt of pain spikes through me.

"With the column and the pod's success, we've infiltrated the peak millennial and zillennial age bracket."

I keep nodding, inhaling and exhaling until the ache recedes. "Thank you, ma'am. Yes, I'm really proud of how it's all been doing. I've been giving it my all."

"And it shows! Listenership has been growing steadily now for months."

I try to smile again. "Yes, I know." I close my eyes as a higher caliber of pain rakes through me. *Fuck.*

She eyes me with concern. "Are you all right?"

I heave out a slow breath. Hold on for a few more minutes. Let her get to the point. "Yep, I'm fine! Please continue." *A raise. Mention a raise, Maya.*

"Well, I'm not the only one who's noticed the great work you're doing." She pauses.

I raise my brow expectantly. Good. *Spit it out, please.* "Oh?" I prompt.

"Yes, are you ready for this?" She waggles her brows at me.

I press my lips out into an exaggerated duck face to mask the cramping in my gut. "Ready as I'll ever be!"

"A producer from Netflix has been in contact with us over the past week."

I suck in a sharp breath, 50 percent excitement, 50 percent agony. "Oh my god!"

"She's extremely interested in turning the *Love Today* podcast into a show. She loves your voice. They want you to pitch creative for a series."

That's amazing! Too bad I'm about to die. I blink at her as a buzzing rises in my ears.

"That producer is going to be out here mid-September for another project. She's going to stop into the office during that time to hear your pitch. If you're interested, that is. She's looking for a pilot episode, a season-one outline, and a rough synopsis of where you would take the next two seasons. I think it's a fantastic opportunity not only for you, but for *The Minute* . . ."

I bolt from the chair as a fresh storm of pain thunders through me. "*Maya*, I am so sorry, can you hold that thought? Excuse me, for just a moment, I'll be right back!"

"Okay—"

I sprint from her office.

Muscles tensed, I power walk robotically across the no-man's-land cubicles to the far end of the floor. *Netflix wants to work with me? They want me to pitch creative? This is the most exciting thing that's ever happened! This is cooler than Kelly Clarkson!*

I'm ten feet out from the bathrooms. The waves are becoming unbearable. Coming closer and closer together. Fuck three shots of espresso. Fuck them straight to hell! Is this thirty? Not being able to handle pounding espresso? I smash into the first bathroom door with my palm on the handle, but it doesn't budge. My momentum causes the side of my cheek to bounce against the gender-neutral restroom sign. I glance down at the lock to find it flipped to occupied.

Oh no.

I fumble to the second door. It's also flipped to occupied.

No. No. No. No! I have to consciously decide not to bang on the doors like the victim in a horror movie because, dear god, that's the initial instinct. I pull my muscles taut as my body fights itself.

Fuck.

The door next to the bathroom is Ted's. It's ajar. It's *empty.*

I stumble in, slam the door shut, and flip the lock.

33 | RIP ME

[RIKKI ROMONA: Single woman past thirty dies with ass in small trash can after shitting self in ex's office. Failed to digest both her espresso and her shame. Couldn't afford her own apartment.]

My pants are around my ankles.

I need to strip. I need to burn this office down. Burn the trash can. Set everything on fire. Pull the alarm. Disappear in the chaos. Come back Monday and pretend this never happened. No one can ever know! *No one!*

Does Ted have spare pants in his office?

I'm going to need to get off his trash can to find out. And I can't get off this trash can. I'm stuck here. I think I've frozen over. Embarrassment has taken my joints and soldered them into place.

I startle as the door rattles.

Is this actually a fucking horror movie?

The lock is moving.

"Don't come in!" I screech.

Motor functions come back online, and I shimmy the best I can behind the desk on the trash can. I can't get off yet. I haven't cleaned up. I need time!

My eyes bulge as my blond, Justin Timberlake–haired, mustached ex appears in the doorway dressed in tan slacks and a white button-up.

"I said *don't come in!*"

Why did I ever decide it was okay to date a twenty-something with a mustache? Red flag.

"Rikki?" he croaks.

"Close the door!"

Ted slams the door behind him, craning his head to see me better. "Oh my god," he breathes.

"Ted, so help me god, get the fuck out of here and don't come back without toilet paper, Febreze, and a garbage bag."

He stares at me for an extensively mortifying moment. I scowl back.

This is not how I imagined our confrontation would start.

I heave in a breath, mentally flipping through the weeks of confidence-building exercises I went through with my therapist after our breakup. Don't shrink!

You are a strong, confident woman—they have body incidents just like everyone else!

"Ted," I repeat. "Toilet paper, Febreze, garbage bag. Run. Please, Ted."

He remains frozen. Ted was never good at following directions. I did everything in our relationship. "Ted. *Goooo!*"

He scrambles out of his office, door flopping closed behind him.

I jump into action, peeling off my pants. I toss them in the trash.

There are tissues on the desk that I utilize. And there's a decent-size hand sanitizer with a pump.

I bathe in it.

I tie up the clear mini garbage bag. Then I proceed to comb through all Ted's drawers, searching for anything helpful in this moment of crisis.

There's a can of Axe deodorant. I douse myself and spray the scene of the crime.

When Ted bursts back in, I'm naked from the waist down. I drop into a crouch behind his desk. He's clutching toilet paper and a bigger clear garbage bag half filled with trash.

Ted pushes the door shut behind him. "You found my emergency deodorant."

"Thank god, because you've returned Febreze-less."

He rolls his eyes. "I don't know where you thought I was just going to run into a thing of Febreze. What happened?"

"What do you think happened? I had an unplanned, out-of-control situation because the triple espresso I downed clearly made me ill, and I ran to the stupid bathrooms, and they were both occupied, and if I didn't want to shut down this entire floor with a biohazard, my only evacuation option was your desk trash!"

"Oh yes, that. Should have been obvious," he replies in monotone.

"You're hilarious, Ted. Do more sarcasm."

Ted drops his head. "I was in the bathroom."

"Of course you were. Do you have spare pants?"

"No."

"Give me your pants."

His brow furrows. "What do you mean?"

I hold his eyes for an extended beat. "I mean, give me your pants. I have to go back into an important meeting with Maya. She's already been waiting on me for eight minutes!"

"You're going to go back into Maya's office after this?"

"Of course I am."

"You're insane. How am I supposed to sterilize this area?"

"Open Amazon and buy a steamer. *Pants*, Ted."

He stiffens, his jaw set uncomfortably. "Pretty demanding for someone stranded naked in my office."

I level my eyes at him over the desk. "At the very least, Ted, you owe me the courtesy of your pants."

He gawks at me for a full ten seconds.

Welp, I guess we're doing this.

"Ted. You woke up one day, decided to throw a grenade into my self-esteem, and walked away as it exploded. You didn't even give me the space for a rebuttal."

He flinches.

"I don't want to be with someone who's so fucked up they don't even talk to their parents."

"Inaccurate, and you'd never even met my parents!"

"You were tired of 'defending my weird-ass coven shit' to your family and friends? I run a fucking witch-themed book club, Ted. Coven shit?

"And let's not forget the kill shot: 'You're too much of a hassle to love.'"

"Rick—"

"That shit was on a constant loop in the back of my head for months. It wasn't okay, and you've never uttered even the stirrings of an apology. I had to go back to weekly therapy for six months to believe I was capable of existing in a romantic partnership without ruining their life with my own weird quirks and baggage. Give me. Your goddamn pants."

Ted looks like he's about to cry. I watch as his eyes well up. He unbuckles his belt, unbuttons his pants, slides them off, and holds them out. "I'm sorry," he breathes without looking at me.

"Over here, please."

He stumbles forward in his white boxers. I pull the pants from his grip and slide them on. They get stuck around my thighs, below my butt. The man is a stick figure.

I suck in my ass, wiggle around, and manage to struggle them up to my waist. They're weirdly tight in the butt and loose around the calves, but they will do.

I glare at Ted as I zip up the fly.

"I'm sorry," he mumbles again.

I shake my head and snatch the larger garbage bag off the floor. I toss his entire office garbage can into it and power walk past him to the door.

"Sorry I took a shit in your office, Ted."

34 | DREAMS

The pen turned green.

I sprinted down four sets of steps to the dumpster, ran back up, gave myself a sponge bath in the restroom, and returned to Maya's office to finish the meeting. She knows I'm extremely interested and would love to do the pitch.

I collapse into my desk chair.

Netflix wants to do a *Love Today* TV show. *A show* curated around the topics and stories from my podcast.

This is a dream I didn't even realize was living in my brain, but I can feel it growing, expanding into the hidden niches of my heart by the second. I wouldn't have ever even conceived that this would be something I could be given the opportunity to do. I might have the chance to potentially be part of a writing team. To have more space to tell stories. Episodes' worth of space?

Euphoric energy compounds in my chest. Bubbles through my veins. I shit in my ex's office twenty minutes ago, but now, I could run through a wall with excitement. I want to dance!

The pitch is scheduled for September 16. I want to start immediately!

I dig my phone out of my bag, overjoyed at the idea of telling Reed.

I freeze before I get to unlock it. *Shit.* Telling him would violate separation of church and state.

I have a string of missed messages from him.

Reed [8:55 a.m.]: TLDR mom cheated on my dad a few years after they got married. They worked things out after, didn't divorce. But my mom got pregnant during that time.
Turned out we weren't our dad's kids—we were the other guy's. She never told us. We found out our senior year of high school when I did 23andMe for an AP bio project, and it gave me a match as the son of some guy in upstate New York we'd never heard of.
Our *dad*-dad always treated us like we were his. But Oliver and I handled the reveal pretty poorly. We were pissed at our mom for cheating and pissed at our dad for letting Mom cheat on him. Pissed at both of them for lying to us for years. Treated them like shit for a while. We were right in the thick of our most obnoxious teen years.
Reed [8:57 a.m.]: realizing mid-run, that was not TLDR.
Reed [8:59 a.m.]: rethinking this decision—that story was way too heavy for 5:55 a.m. Sorry! Should have held it for another time. You're probably working. Shit, you're definitely working, you said you were going into a meeting. Don't feel the need to respond.
Reed [9:02 a.m.]: Hope your morning is going well!
Reed [9:03 a.m.]: Jesus, I've now quadruple texted. This is the most uncool thread I've ever sent. Forget I was here. I'm going to sleep for another hour when I get home, I'm clearly delirious.
Reed [9:04 a.m.]: I swear I don't normally write essay texts.
Reed [9:05 a.m.]: I've made it so much worse. THIS NEVER HAPPENED. I was never here! *flails hands* *disappears*

I glance at the time: It's 9:47 a.m. He's had to sit on this for forty-two minutes.

Me: How can you be so hot, and simultaneously so adorable? It's against the laws of physics.

Reed: Quit blowing smoke up my ass.
Me: I'd imagine back when you found out about your bio dad you were also feeling bewildered and hurt that the other guy didn't try to be your dad. That sounds like such a confusing, complicated situation to deal with as a seventeen-year-old. And then to lose your father. I'm sorry you had to go through that.
Me: Thanks for telling me. I like puzzling together the pieces of your life that made you you too.
Reed: Your turn.

I hover my thumb over the call button.

But calling him would violate my fucking call rule because I'm not on a bed. *This is still casual, and calling during work hours to share exciting news decidedly is not.*

I put the phone down and stare at it.

Me: Mine's too long for a text. =P
Reed: Hit me up when you're on a mattress.
Me: I've got a crazy day ahead, I'll save it for the IRL
Reed: *waits with bated breath*

The Sunday Minute

LOVE TODAY

IS THIS GOING ANYWHERE?!
A CHECKLIST FOR ANXIOUS DATERS

By Rose Thyme

It is a truth universally acknowledged that dating checklists can both reduce anxiety and provide boundless entertainment. Y'all loved the Phoebe Decree a few weeks back. Here are ten landmarks to keep in mind on your quest for a long-term partner. If you can check all these boxes, I think you and your partner are on the same page. You might just be ready for a label. If you can check half, it sounds like you're on your way there. If you have fewer than half checked off, and you're looking for forever, maybe you and your person are due for a *where is this going?* talk. Let's jump right in, shall we?

Something's going right if:

(1) You like to talk—*to each other*. You're not just meeting up to tear each other's clothes off. You have things in common. Conversing is fun!

(2) You enjoy doing nothing together. If you can sit on a couch, watch TV, and have a good time.

(3) You're in communication daily, and you don't just text, you talk on the phone. Casual phone calls are a true sign of a long-term investment in another human being.

(4) You've met their family *on purpose*. Extra credit if they follow you on social media.

(5) You're not hiding your foibles! In their presence, you feel free to be your true unhinged self.

(6) They've gone out of their way to reschedule trips/meetings/friends' dinners/business things/other engagements to spend time with you.

(7) They've voluntarily binged your favorite show that ended ages ago, and/or have read your favorite book (no, movies don't count—that's too easy).

(8) Y'all regularly reference inside jokes in conversation. Don't underestimate the bonding power of an adorable inside joke.

(9) You've memorized each other's numbers. That's commitment in the twenty-first century.

(10) You've talked about a future where you're still together—you don't talk future with someone you don't want a future with.

FOURTH ENCOUNTER

35 | ROAD TRIP

When Reed pulls up to my aunt's, I'm waiting at the curb in black sweats and a stretchy pistachio-green crop top. Whitney's *Grease* costumes are safely tucked away in my carry-on. She made me try them all on when I arrived at the house last night, so I'm ready for anything.

Reed rolls down the window as he parks along the curb. He dips his chin, lips arranged in a subtle smirk. "Romona." He's got a brush of stubble today. It looks good.

I nod back, a smile itching at my lips. "Tyler."

He hops out in black jeans and a black T-shirt and swiftly grabs my things.

"Thank you," I chuckle as he loads them into the trunk and the back seat, respectively.

He walks back over, stands in front of me, and smiles. "Hi." I'm slightly taller than him from my perch on the curb as opposed to his position on the street.

"Hi."

"Wearing clothes today? That's new."

I retreat, lolling my head, but he steps up onto the grass, catches my hip, and tugs me to him, cradling my neck as he pulls me into a kiss that makes my heart bloom.

I feel like a flower in time lapse as he pulls back to catch my eyes. "They look good on you."

I cast my eyes skyward. "You explore the world of streaking *one* time."

"All right, who's getting married? I should know their names!"

Reed chuckles. Ed Sheeran's playing at a volume loud enough to warrant singing along as we pull onto the highway. He reaches out to turn it down. "My friend Matt and his fiancée, Marissa."

"Matt and Marissa. Got it. How do you know him?"

He grins, glancing at me sidelong. "Work."

"Ahhh, the ambiguous work. He plays a part in your secret Marvel movie?"

Reed snorts. "I guess you'll have to see."

"Waiting with bated breath."

He smiles out at the road. "So. I have a proposal for you."

"A proposal?" I repeat skeptically.

"That's what I said."

I laugh. "What are you proposing?"

Reed slides his palms down the sides of the steering wheel. "Hear me out."

I cock my head. "Ookaayy . . ."

"What if . . . we did make this something real?"

I blink.

He glances over, his smile slipping into a smirk.

My brows pull together. "What? Is this a joke? Are you kidding?"

He laughs. "I'm not kidding."

I purse my lips. "I don't believe you."

He gnaws at his lip as we whip past the Getty. "I've been thinking about it a lot these past forty-eight hours."

I drop my head against the passenger window. It's starting to drizzle. "You've been thinking about making this something real?"

"I have."

"Are you just suggesting this so you can get some tonight?"

A laugh barks out of him. He flips on the windshield wipers. "No, I'm saying it because I like you. During therapy this week, which was, by the way, the morning before I sent you that chapter, before the streaking—"

"I'm never living that down—"

"My therapist was like, if you like her so much, why aren't you 'something real'?"

I blow out a sigh. "And how did that make you feel?"

He smiles again. "Like running straight into a screen door."

"It made you want to run through a screen door?" I parrot dryly.

"Are you purposefully misunderstanding me?"

I cock a brow. "I mean the *running straight into a screen door* metaphor isn't your best."

He shakes his head. "I thought about you out dating other dudes a lot during our three weeks of not talking."

"And how did *that* make you feel?"

He drops a flustered laugh. "Very upset that I don't live on the East Coast."

I snort. "I feel like you're bullshitting me."

His smile widens. "I'm not."

I shift my body toward the center console. "To be clear, you're asking me to be exclusive with you? After we've been on two dates."

"Rikki, those were like super dates. I feel like they count as more than one each. Plus Streakergate."

A *pffft* wheezes out of me.

"That's three encounters," he says coyly.

"Did you read that article?" I bleat accusingly.

"Yes, Rikki, it was before church and state."

"Ugh!" I blink maniacally out at the highway. "Buh, I—you . . ." *What the fuck am I mad about?*

"All right there?"

I clear my throat, exhaling an irritated huff. "You?"

"Me?"

"*You!* The guy who's on his first third date in fourteen years wants this to be a real thing, *after two dates*?"

"Three encounters."

"Shut up."

He quirks a brow. "Your words, not mine."

The rain outside the car accelerates. "What about the pact?"

His broad shoulders shrug up and drop. "We built a something-real clause in. I'm just suggesting we enact it."

"Reed, you don't know me well enough to want to make this something real. We haven't spent enough time together for you to know if I annoy you or drive you insane and vice versa."

"Rikki, that's why people date exclusively, to spend more time together and get to know each other better."

"How am I supposed to believe that you're not lying to me for sex? This is the most suspicious timing of all time."

"Honest question," Reed says. "When would the timing *not* be suspicious?"

"I don't know . . ." I hesitate, glancing out at the road. "If we were like, going to your grandma's funeral."

"What if I wanted comfort sex after?"

"Fine, on a train."

"I can't want sex on a train?"

"Plane!"

Reed starts laughing.

"Stranded on a boat in the middle of the ocean, starving to death!"

"*End of the world* sex."

Laughter fizzles out of me. "Oh god! I don't know. Are you right?" I bury my face in my hands.

"Would you really rather I ask you to *go steady* on a plane ride to be less suspicious?"

A cackle escapes my lips. "Buy us two plane tickets, and let's fly to San Diego so this feels more legit."

We roll through a bout of hysteria, sobering slowly as the rain dulls back to a drizzle against the windshield.

Reed's still grinning confidently out the window. "I think you'll just have to trust that I mean it when I say I like you more than I want to have sex with you."

"*You know* I'm not good at that."

He laughs, and I shake out my arms, smiling as bright bouts of joyous light dare to ricochet through my chest.

"Reed."

"Rikki."

"You think you like me more than you want to have sex with me, but you don't know all my bad qualities and annoying tics. We've never even gone out to eat! Have you thought about that? You've never seen me eat!

"Our *let's be exclusive* stakes are way higher than your average Joe Shmoe couple, because of the distance. We'd need to push and prod the boundaries of what you can learn about someone in a short burst of time to ensure compatibility on a close-distance scale, rather than just a long-distance one, to even attempt to make up for that deficit.

"I've seen this with patients and listeners a million times. It's why only one in every eight long-distance relationships are ultimately successful. The couple doesn't see each other for more than like, three consecutive days at a time for an extended portion of the relationship, so they get really deep in without realizing they're not close-distance compatible because they haven't had the chance to pick up on the little things you learn about someone when you're seeing them consistently in your day-to-day life.

"They're convinced they're about to start their happily ever after together, after doing long distance for ages, and they move in together, which is a huge, life-changing ordeal because one or both of them have to move to make things work. And then, because they haven't done close-distance compatibility testing, their relationship implodes after one measly month in the same house because they realize they annoy the shit out of each other when they're living in close quarters, and they're not actually compatible at all. And it's incredibly sad and completely devastating. And—"

I trail off, glancing at our surroundings, as Reed puts the car into park at a random shopping center. When the hell did he get off the freeway?

I blink at him. "Where are we? Why are you still smiling?"

"You hungry?"

◆ ◆ ◆

He asked me if we could make this something real, and I gave him a lecture about the failure rate of long-distance relationships.

What is wrong with me?

Let's not open that door.

We've stopped at an In-N-Out.

I straighten as Reed slides into the opposite side of the booth and places a tray of food on the table. He pushes a burger, fries, a vanilla milkshake, and a cup of ketchup over. I didn't get to have lunch before we left, so I am actually hungry. "Thank you."

"Of course." His mouth rolls into the knot as he organizes his food. "All right, so I have another proposal."

I snort, unwrapping my burger. "Oh-kay, I'm listening."

"What if we use this two-hour-plus car ride for, how did you word it, close-distance compatibility testing?"

A laugh barks out of me. "And how do you suggest we do that?"

He catches me in his crystalline gaze, and my heart skitters. "You're the relationship expert, Renee. I was thinking some sort of intense probing via Q and A?"

I cock my head, glancing out the window next to us as I realize I've already been working on an article for a situation exactly like this one.

"Ah, she already has an idea," Reed says playfully.

I flick my eyes back to his. "I've actually been working on *thirty questions to compatibility* for *Love Today*, based on this famous guide that a husband-and-wife psychologist team, Arthur and Elaine Aron, put together in 1997, called '36 Questions That Lead to Love.' Mine is like a spin-off for new relationships . . . less intimidating to suggest doing on a date or something."

He arches a brow. "Interesting project, Romona. I wonder what inspired it."

I narrow my eyes at him.

He smirks. "What if we take turns asking each other these questions? And if by the time we hit San Diego, neither of us has run into a deal-breaker, we make this something real."

"Hmm . . ." I peer down at the table, mentally racing through what I remember from that list of questions. They're *a lot*. I pick up a fry and nervously roll it between my fingers.

"Scared, Romona?"

"Are you?" I throw back.

"Of rejection? Of course."

I roll my eyes.

"But I can take it," he finishes confidently.

"What if *you* reject me?"

He laughs. "I don't think that's gonna happen, Renee."

That sends a masochistic grin curling up the corner of my lips. "We'll see."

He tilts his head. "Indeed we will."

"No deflecting questions."

Reed nods. "Of course not."

"Answers have to be a thousand percent honest."

"Wouldn't have it any other way."

I push my burger to the side and open my notes app. "Fine. Ready?"

Reed puts down his drink. "Hit me."

36 | CLOSE-DISTANCE COMPATIBILITY TESTING

"Question one: What are your three reddest flags? Not the ones you look for in others. The ones that you yourself possess." I arch a brow, peering at Reed over my phone.

"Wow, you come right for the jugular."

"You asked for it."

He grins, tipping his chin in concession. "Well, we have the obvious one—I want to be an actor."

I put down the phone and fold my hands between us. "*Are* an actor," I correct.

"Yes, *I'm an actor*. There's a red flag in there somewhere." He throws up a peace sign with his right hand. "Two, another one we've already touched on. I haven't been on a third date in fourteen years."

I nod, beaming at the table between us. "Yes, valid, both valid."

"And three . . ." He presses his lips together, eyes darting to my hands for a moment before popping back up to my face. "Which Friend are you?"

"Excuse me?"

"I'm easing you into number three."

I pick up my milkshake and swirl it in its cardboard cup, attempting to appear chill at the mention of my favorite show of all time. "I guess Monica."

He shakes his head, smirking. "You can't have Monica—she's me."

I snort. "Why are you Monica?"

"I'm obnoxious regarding cleanliness. And germs."

I tilt my head curiously. "Go on."

He purses his lips, carefully considering his response. "Are you a morning-shower person or an evening-shower person?"

I shrug. "It varies."

Reed drops his head back, smiling. "Sorry, did I get too political? I'm going to need a more clear answer. Morning or night? Everyone's one or the other."

I sip my milkshake, unexpectedly amused by the turn this conversation is taking.

Reed laughs in disbelief. "She doesn't deign to answer the question?"

I set down the cup. "On the days I work out, I shower in the morning, and on weekends I'll shower before a date or something. And sometimes I'm craving a shower at night, so I shower at night."

"This is insanity! What kind of person doesn't know if they're a morning showerer or an evening showerer?"

I smirk at him. "Apparently me. What are you?"

He pops a fry in his mouth, and I laugh.

Slowly, Reed sits back and crosses his arms, mouth rendered down into the slightest smile. "I'm an evening showerer, Rikki."

I sit back and cross my own arms. "Oh, I'm excited to hear where this is going."

"I need to shower before getting into bed, and I really want anyone else that's coming into the bed to shower as well."

I arch a brow. "And what if your partner only showered in the morning?"

He runs a hand down his face, smiling bashfully. "Here comes the flag: When I was in my twenties, during the emo era, before I really started sticking to my two-date rule, I ended things with someone I was kinda seeing because she refused to shower before we got into my bed."

Laughter buzzes through my teeth.

"When I think about it now, I don't know if I actually cared that much, or if I was just too scared for things to get serious."

"And if I only showered in the morning?"

His eyes twinkle. "Well, now, a decade of therapy later—if you told me you didn't want to shower at night, I would tell you it makes me happy when my partner showers before we go to sleep because I'm a control freak, and things being a certain way makes me weirdly happy, but I'm a control freak who's done a lot of work on himself, and I would get over it."

A rush of affection storms my chest.

"I've never told someone that voluntarily." He looks away at the door and then back at me. Exhales another nervous breath, picks up the last bit of his burger, and tosses it down the hatch. "How are you feeling? You want to walk out the door, Uber back to Jersey?"

My smile cracks open. "No . . . I loved that."

"You loved that?" he says dryly.

I lift a casual shoulder and let it drop. "I love showering, and I'm happy to do it anywhere anytime. And the fact that me showering can make you happy makes me happy because I'd be happy to make you happy."

He goes silent for a beat, staring at me, lips quirked. "Wow, I'm so turned on right now."

I huff out a breathy laugh as a blush creeps up my neck.

Reed organizes his trash on our food tray, pushes it to the side, and leans forward across the table on his beautiful forearms. "Your turn, Renee."

I sigh. "Yours were so light and fun, and mine are so . . . dark and immovable."

Reed just grins. "Hit me."

I concentrate on the feel of the table under my fingers, trying to calm my nervous system.

"Um, well, there's the fact that I'm an LMFT, so you know, on top of the control freak thing, I'm a relationship know-it-all."

"I love that about you. Your reads are so intuitive, and your takes on life are so thought-provoking and reflective."

My brows pinch together as I fight a wave of hot pressure behind my eyes.

His smile grows. "I see you working up some way to deflect that statement. Just take it, Rikki. It's true."

I exhale slowly. "Thanks."

He bobs his chin, encouraging me to go on.

"Um, two, I, well, I'm not sure if I ever want to have kids."

"How is that a red flag?"

My voice gets unsteady. "I—I mean technically it's not, just like technically your actor thing isn't. But I've definitely lost a relationship because of it. Or at least they stated it as a reason they couldn't be with me. We talked about it during our first month of dating and then, when we were breaking up, he said he thought I was just in a mood when I said that, and that I'd get over it and change my mind." It was, of course, Ted.

"Asshole."

I nod. "Valid."

Reed presses his lips together, sympathy pooling in his eyes. "I have the same stance on kids."

I level my gaze. "Are you sure? Because I'm not just in a mood today."

He snorts.

"Why don't you want kids?" I ask carefully.

"It's never been something that I've yearned for. I wouldn't be against it, but it's not on my Christmas list." He pauses, studying me. "What about you?"

"I mean, lots of little reasons but . . ." I swallow. "I kind of weirdly feel like I've had them."

"In what way?"

My heart speeds up. "Well, I've been hypervigilant most of my life, worrying about my mom every day when I left for school. When I was sleeping. When she'd forget to pick me up from things." I heave a breath. "I was almost constantly wondering like, did she just forget again today, or is she hurt? Does she need me?"

"Why would she need you?"

I sigh. "My dad was sometimes violent with her. And I would try to like, fix their relationship. I'd lecture him about how to be *nice*. And how hitting people *is not nice*. And he'd promise to never do it again. And I thought I had fixed it. I'd believe him, because I was a kid, and I trusted everything he said."

Reed's forehead furrows.

"*Yeah*, um, and then when she left my dad, I worried about Whitney. She was eleven when we moved into my aunt's. I was thirteen. My mom was dealing with a lot, and my aunt was always working.

"So I was the one who made her food when she got home from school. Did her hair. I helped her with her homework. Quizzed her before tests. Babysat. I helped her pick out her first bra. Drove her places once I got my license. Sat by the toilet with her the first time she got drunk. I went with her to her first gynecologist appointment to get birth control when she was a freshman . . . I cowrote her college essay.

"I'm not like a hundred on it, but I don't know if I'll ever reach a place where I'm ready to go back to that precarious-eggshells mindset I was in for the first significant chunk of my life."

Reed's quiet for a beat, watching me. I can't hold his gaze for more than half a second at a time as I wait for him to respond.

"You're so impressive."

I exhale a gust of breath and roll my eyes.

"Rikki." He latches on to my gaze, serious war-hero face in place. "I'm serious. I'm sorry you had to go through all that."

"It's fine."

He rotates his drink. "It's all coming together now, Renee."

I snort. "What's coming together?"

The edge of his mouth quirks. "Well, obviously the daddy issues are becoming more clear. And you became an LMFT because you wanted to figure out how to heal the issues you dealt with in your childhood?"

I cast my eyes to the ceiling. "You have me all figured out now?"

He grins. "You had me figured out ninety minutes in. What's number three?"

I clear my throat. "Probably that I . . . currently live in my dad's apartment."

Reed's eyes widen.

I shake my head quickly. "He doesn't live there . . . I was rooming with my best friend and her husband. Jordyn and Micah—you met them. They got pregnant, and I had to get my own place. I wasn't being paid enough to get my own New York City–area place. Even though the podcast is doing amazing—I don't get to renegotiate my salary till next week."

I suck in a deep breath. "My father works in real estate, and he 'acquired' a one-bedroom apartment that he's flipping right down the hall from Micah and Jordyn. He told me I could live there for six months free of rent while he flips it. It was hard to say no."

He studies me for a beat. "But you wish you did?"

I nod. "Kinda. He has a Ring camera on the doorbell, and he sees me when I come and go. Texts me to ask where I'm going and what I'm doing. He shows up randomly without pretense, stays over. It's unsettling. I'm currently a thirty-year-old woman living under her father's rule. Which is most definitely a red flag." I run my hands down my face as anxiety nips at my gut. My hands are . . . shaking. I drop them into my lap before meeting Reed's eyes again. They're sharp, attentive, brimming with concern. "I know . . . it's weird that I even speak to him."

Reed shakes his head. "Family is complicated."

"He insists that he's different. He's repented. He's reformed. He's in therapy. He's on medication." I shrug. "I always want to believe him. I want him to be better. I want him to be the guy I used to think he was when I was a kid.

"Which, I know, I'm a therapist, it's impossible. He never was that guy, and he never will be. My father's a professional liar." I prop my arm on the table and rest my head in my hand. "But here I am. Living in his apartment. Giving him his millionth chance to prove me wrong."

"Rikki. I'm so sorry."

"It's fine." I shake out my arms. "Jeez. That was a lot. How are you feeling? Is this too much? You want to stop? Should I get an Uber?"

Reed studies me for a long moment, understanding swirling behind his eyes. "What else you got?"

37 | SAN DIEGO

The rain is an onslaught as we close in on our destination almost four hours later. We hit so much traffic that we missed the ceremony. Not that Reed had planned for us to go—he said it was going to be mostly family, and we'd probably skip it—but that's off the table now. We only have about an hour and a half before the reception. The clouds have been utterly assaulting the earth. I've never seen rain come down so hard on the West Coast. We spent the majority of the ride crawling down the highway among the horde of other vehicles braving the storm.

I've learned a lot.

Reed's biggest insecurity is being a bad novelist (I gave him a lengthy lecture detailing why he most definitely is not). Mine was not having a stable family life. (Reed went quiet. Leaned over, grabbed my knee, and squeezed it.)

His biggest body insecurity is his mouth—which I think is blasphemous. I told him so. Mine is how I apparently only present as cute and never hot (something Ted said to me once that still lingers in my psyche). Reed literally pulled us over among the virtual gridlock to discuss this.

"Who the fuck told you you're not hot?"

I shared my brief Ted story. Reed stared me down for thirty seconds (eye-sexed me) before pushing my hair back, leaning in over the shell of my ear and saying, "You present as hot, Rikki. I want to open you up and read all the small print."

The first line of the sex chapter. I proceeded to have a full-on lust meltdown as he put the car back into drive and pulled us back into traffic.

His most irrational fear is E.T. being real. Mine is a tie between the mere idea of bungee jumping and singing in front of people.

His most embarrassing moment is applying for *Survivor* for a fifth time and still not being cast, which is not embarrassing and should not count. Mine was, of course, being caught streaking. And just now he revealed that the thing he's most grateful for is his brother.

My heart.

"That's so sweet," I tell him. "He seems really protective of you."

Reed's brow scrunches up as we hang a right and our hotel comes into view. He cuts me a bemused look. "Why would you say that?"

"Well he messaged me on Instagram—"

Reed shifts in his seat. "Whoa, what? He *messaged* you on Instagram?"

"Don't worry, he didn't say anything bad. It was after the streaking night. He just asked if I liked you and told me not to hurt you."

Reed's body tenses, but he doesn't respond. He switches on his blinker, pulling us into the hotel roundabout under the protection of their overhang. Reed's fully frowning as the abrasive sound of the rain abruptly recedes.

I reach out to rest a hand on his forearm. "Sorry, did I get him in trouble? Are you okay?"

He nods, softening as two bellmen pull open the car doors and usher us into the hotel.

Reed booked us a double queen room. Brownie points for not presuming we'd be sleeping in the same bed.

But I do plan on sleeping in the same bed. He aced my questions. We didn't get to all thirty, but I'm about four times more in crush with him than I was when we started.

He took his time, sharing so much about his personal life. He went out of his way to be vulnerable. Thoughtful. Reflective. And he did it so easily. Answering the questions myself was like pulling my own teeth. Reed is good. And smart. And caring. And ambitious and driven. Motivated. Hardworking. He's everything I've been looking for. If anyone is worth giving long distance a shot, it's him.

I feel the same way he *says* he feels. I want to trust that he actually feels it.

Reed steps out of the bathroom in black pants, a tight black T-shirt, and a leather T-Birds jacket. His auburn hair is gelled up and forward to match Danny Zuko's classic look.

I'm still sitting in front of the full-length mirror, finishing my hair. I meet his eyes in our reflection as he sits down over my shoulder on one of the beds. I smile at him. "You look great."

He laughs. "I weirdly feel very New Jersey."

I unravel the final whorl of my hair from the curling iron. "Danny Zuko does give New Jersey."

Since he's wearing an end-of-movie look, I broke out Whitney's tight black Sandy outfit. I've done a red lip, and I've been fixing my hair into tight curls.

"You gonna hit me with number twenty-two?" He grins. We still have nine questions left.

"R. Tyler, I've heard enough."

He bulges his eyes in the mirror. "What does that mean?"

I unplug the curling iron. "It means . . ." I move to lean against the desk across from his perch on the bed, arms braced nervously on the tabletop. Reed's eyes drop to my heeled black sandals and ride back up my tight black satin pants and black bodysuit to my face.

"Holy shit." He clears his throat and grins up at me. "It means?" he prompts.

I laugh. "It means, yes. Let's do it. Let's try being something real."

38 | AUDITION

"Invitation?"

There's a bouncer outside the event hall.

"Wow, they have security?" I say into Reed's ear.

Reed doesn't respond. He pulls the invitation from his pocket and hands it to the large man in black outside the door. "She's my plus-one."

He checks an iPad. "You have your ID?"

Reed tugs his wallet from his back pocket, swipes out his ID, and hands it to the man. The guy inputs Reed's name. "All right, you're checked in. And plus-one Rikki Romona."

I raise my hand. "That's me."

"ID?"

Thank god I stuffed my ID and a credit card in the tiny, beaded sling purse I brought. I pull out my license.

The guy nods, returns my license, opens the door, and waves us on. We're shuffled into a small foyer-like room with a roped-off queue. We enter the line. There are only three people in front of us. Elphaba, Glinda, and Mary Poppins. We're all stood outside a wooden door. Not fifteen seconds have passed before someone emerges from it with a clipboard.

"Next!"

Mary Poppins gets escorted into the next room.

I cut Reed a baffled look. "I thought we were going to a wedding."

Reed cocks a brow. "Oh, we are."

"What is this line?"

My head snaps toward the wooden door as the unmistakable sound of "Supercalifragilisticexpialidocious" echoes from the next room. Is the woman who went in . . . singing?

"I think they're auditions," Reed says.

"Auditions?" I squeak into his ear. "You're joking, right?"

He chuckles. "They're not real auditions! It's just a shtick."

"If it still involves singing, what's the difference?" My muscles tense. "Reed, did you not *hear me* when I said karaoke is my biggest fear."

Reed huffs a quiet laugh and takes my hand, weaving our fingers together. "Most irrational fear," he corrects. "Not biggest."

"Semantics, Derek."

"Do we need to delve into this?"

"Do we need to go watch *E.T.*?"

He swivels to face me head on. "What's so scary about it, Romona?"

"I'm terrible at it."

His mouth tilts up. "So?"

I shake my head. "No, Reed, I hurt people via sound."

His grin deepens. "I promise, you're not going to hurt us via sound."

"No Reed, I have *no* vocal control. I'm a llama with the gift of speech."

"What does a llama even sound like?"

"Like me doing karaoke!"

He snorts, rubbing his thumb across the back of my hand. "Can I share a secret?"

I freeze as the wooden door opens, and Elphaba and Glinda are shuffled into the room together. Moments later "What Is This Feeling?" floats through the wall.

"Rikki?"

"Yeah." I stare nervously at the closed door. "Go for it. Share."

Reed's war-hero face shifts into my line of sight. His eyes are white hot, glowing with whatever he's about to say. "It feels really good to let go."

I peer at him, struggling to hold on to any of my various trains of thought. "Of what?"

"Control."

I blink, a smile flitting across my lips. "Come again?"

"You heard me." He twists me around, so my back is pressed tight against his chest, our arms crisscrossed over my torso.

His stubble brushes against my cheek. "It feels good to let go, Renee."

"What would you know about it, R. Tyler? I thought you had the same issue."

He presses his lips against the skin behind my ear. "It just takes practice."

I lean into him as my skin starts to hum. "Are you saying you've been *practicing* letting go of control?"

The vibration of his voice tickles the side of my face. "Actually, I have, smart-ass."

"Next!" Clipboard man appears back in the doorway to the singing room.

I dig my nails into Reed's forearm. He pulls me tighter against his chest. "It's gonna be fine." He guides us forward into the room.

Behind the door, someone dressed as King George from *Hamilton* is seated behind a wooden table. There's a TV set up on a low table in front of him and . . . two microphones. Two box lights are pointed in our direction, and a large camera is set up next to the mics, on a tripod.

Why? Why is there a camera?

"Good day," King George says from behind the table. "Thy king and queen of thy wedding demand an audition. Fee to enter is thirty seconds. A song of your choice from thy costume's musical. Don't worry, we'll play the actual track, so you'll be singing along rather than naked on thy karaoke version."

I raise my hand, looking at the king. "May I sit this out while my date performs? I'm just a plus-one."

King George stomps the scepter he's clutching in his right hand. "All guests must audition to enter."

Reed hands me a microphone with mock solemnity. "We'll get through this together."

"Reed, I can't do this. I'm going to die."

He wraps my fingers around the microphone. "I seem to remember you saying you were on a dance team all through college," he says pointedly.

"Yeah, dance team, not singing team!"

"We're on a schedule here, folks," Clipboard Guy calls from the wings.

"Throw on 'Summer Nights,' George," Reed instructs.

The king nods.

The dun, dun dun, dunt. Dunt. Dunt. Dunt opening of *Grease*'s "Summer Nights" starts, and I glare at Reed, with the scariest expression I can muster.

Reed's eyes twinkle with glee as he sings the opening lyrics with John Travolta.

I shake my head, missing Olivia Newton-John's line. "We should have come as the founding fathers from *Hamilton*. I can do the opening rap."

Reed sings the next iconic line, holding my gaze.

"Reed, you're going to look at me differently after hearing me llama!"

"I won't start the timer until you're both singing!" King George blurts as I glance nervously at the camera and miss the next Olivia line.

Reed holds firm, singing beautifully, about summer days and how they drift away, refusing to look away from me, using his stupid eyeball powers.

Fuck. They're working.

I pull the microphone to my mouth. Without warning the male part erupts out of me: I'm scream-singing *well-a well-a*s, an aggressive *UH*, and begging to be told more about how far he got.

Reed's eyes blow out with amusement.

I scream the next female part as well. And I black out after that.

I think I got into it. I think everyone in the room got into it, because I think it's utterly impossible to resist the sweet, sweet joy of scream-singing "Summer Nights" if you've ever enjoyed a musical.

I don't resurface till the king is reclaiming our mics, and Reed's taking me by the face, capturing my mouth in a swift, electric kiss that leaves me feeling legitimately weak in the knees. He takes my hand, pulling me along as King George leads us to the large set of double doors on the opposite side of the room.

"Enjoy the party, thespians."

He knocks twice, and they open outward in tandem.

39 | MUSICAL WEDDING

"Your friend is *Matthew Trent*?" The question explodes out of me as the bride and groom, dressed as the main characters from the film *La La Land*, execute an elaborate routine to the instrumental montage from the movie.

When they first emerged, dancing through the crowd, I was too charmed by the theme of it all to take in the guy's face.

This event space feels like a fever dream. I don't know what to call it. It's like a ballroom on steroids. It's laid out in circles. Like the inside of a tree. The center circle is the dance floor. In the very center of the dance floor is a raised circular dais. Outside the dance floor is a ring of tables, each themed, as expected, to a different popular musical.

Outside that ring are a whole string of what look like vendors? There's a *High School Musical*–themed photo op in like an adult-basketball-themed sandbox? A section of the floor is boxed off with like, fifteen basketballs and a mini basketball hoop. Wildcats jerseys are hung up along the backboard.

We just came from the *Sweeney Todd*–themed bar area. One bartender is dressed as Sweeney Todd, and the other is dressed as Helena Bonham Carter's character. There are several other stations—one is a Wonka-themed area full of colorful desserts and candy.

Like *they went hard.*

Standing adjacent to the door we entered from was a magazine stand full of *Playbill*-style booklets organized in alphabetical order by last name of each guest. Where it should say *Playbill* it says *Matt &*

Marissa. Then there's the musical poster correlating to one of the fifteen tables scattered around the third ring of the room, and under that, the guest's name.

Reed and I are at *Jersey Boys*. We haven't found our seats yet because before we could venture in that direction the festivities started. The lights dimmed as we were handed our Bloody Marys (elaborate ones featuring meat and olives, loaded onto a giant toothpick and a stick of celery) from fake Sweeney Todd. Rather than head toward our table, Reed and I made our way to the outskirts of the crowd gathering around the stage.

Moments later an instrumental from *La La Land* filled the hall and a spotlight fell on the newly married couple as they burst from the same brown doors we entered through not ten minutes ago. The two of them danced their way through the crowd, carving a path to the dais.

It wasn't till they actually stepped up onto the circular stage that I started to lose it. The guy, Matt, looked a lot like the kid I grew up watching in the adaptations of a children's book series I loved, The Lost Regent Prince of Yorlabala. And the woman, Marissa, looked kind of familiar as well, but I couldn't place her.

I glanced down at the Matt & Marissa *Playbill* in my hand, synapses firing at snail speed as I sucked down my Bloody Mary. The groom's name is Matt, and the actor's name in those adaptations was . . . *Matthew*. My jaw dropped in slow motion as the realization hit.

Reed is an actor.

Matthew is an actor.

Matt is Matthew.

That is Matthew Trent.

That is Matthew Trent, the actor.

Matthew is still very much in the zeitgeist. He's taken on various high-profile gigs over the past ten years, establishing himself as a versatile actor, not just the skinny, shy, fish-out-of-water *Regent* from the five Lost Prince of Yorlabala films he made in his tweens and early teens.

Then his wife clicked. Marissa. As in Marissa Gallucci, *Broadway prodigy*? She won a Tony when she was like, thirteen for her role in a revamp of *Annie* where she's adopted by a billionaire vampire family who really wanted a child. She's spent her twenties showing up in all sorts of random musical adjacent shows and films.

What in the hell.

"Matt is *Matthew Trent*?" I say abrasively.

Reed's lips twitch as he continues to watch the first dance. "That is his last name."

"We're at a *celebrity wedding*?"

"We're at my friend's wedding."

"You're friends with Regent Fallow, the Lost Prince of Yorlabala?"

"That's a fictional character."

My eyes bulge as the couple dance over to our side of the audience. "Reed, that's him."

"Rikki, that's the man who played him twenty years ago."

I tear my eyes away from their dance sequence to glare at Reed. He glances at me sidelong, mouth kicked to the right.

"How do you know him?"

He sips his drink. "We work together."

"Work? As in currently?"

"He's a colleague."

"And you didn't think to mention it?"

Reed arches a brow. "It's literally in the constitution not to mention it, Renee."

"We're at his wedding!"

"We're at his reception," he corrects cheekily.

"*Wedding* reception."

"I'm trying to watch their routine."

"Are we going to talk to Regent Fallow, the Lost Prince of Yorlabala?"

"We can if you don't call him that."

"Oh my god."

Reed's torso rumbles with a laugh.

"Did you not read those?" I accuse as I place my empty drink on a passing waiter's tray. I hold on to the giant toothpick full of garnishes because we haven't eaten since In-N-Out at noon, and I'm starving.

He smiles at me as I pop an olive in my mouth. "I read them. But I've known him for three years. If I was still freaking out, I don't think we'd be here right now."

"Is he doing a Marvel movie?"

"Rikki."

I sigh, sliding a piece of bacon from my stick. "Never mind. Church and state."

"You're at our table!" a beautiful Asian woman with long, wavy mermaid hair, dressed as Velma Kelly from *Chicago*, welcomes Reed as we finally sit down. There's bread at each of our place settings. I gratefully pick my roll up and start buttering it.

A stunning curvy blond woman dressed as Roxie Hart smiles at Reed as well. "Reed! The gang's all here."

A handsome Black man dressed in a suit sits down next to Roxie. He reaches out to shake Reed's hand. "So good to see you! And who's your date?" His eyes fall on me.

"Yeah, who's your date?" Velma and Roxie Hart exclaim together as I frantically chew the hunk of bread I just stuffed in my mouth.

Reed beams back at them all. "This is my girlfriend, Rikki."

40 | GAGGED

A chunk of bread goes flying down my windpipe.

"Rikki, so nice to meet you. I'm Will!"

"Hi Rikki! I'm Britt."

"Rikki, are you okay?" Velma Kelly asks.

My eyes bulge. Shit. I can't cough. Or breathe. *I'm choking.*

I grasp at my throat.

"Oh fuck." Reed jumps up. He slaps my upper back, and I watch as a piece of bread catapults from my esophagus into the red *Jersey Boys*–themed, rose-filled centerpiece.

"Holy god," Will yelps.

Girlfriend?

Reed's back in his seat with his fingers wrapped around my left forearm. His other hand is rubbing the slapped space between my shoulder blades as I wheeze for fifteen seconds straight.

Reed turns to his friends as I continue to sputter and cough. "She needs water, can someone go grab one from the bar?"

The Asian woman with the mermaid hair bolts for the bar. There's no water at the table, but there's white wine. I grab the glass in front of me.

"Oh dear, I wouldn't—" Will starts.

I choke down half the contents. "Don't worry, I'm tot-lly fine," I croak before I throw back the rest. "Bread tried to murder me. Happens all the time. I'm a famous bread assassin, and it senses danger when I'm near, you know."

His friends stare silently back at me.

I turn to Reed, who's trying very hard not to smile.

"Shut up," I mutter.

"I didn't say anything."

I turn back to his two friends. "So sorry." I clear my throat. "It's great to meet you both."

Velma Kelly appears at my side and hands me a glass of water. "Here!"

"Thank you so much! What was your name again?"

"Eliza!" She smiles. "No problem, are you okay?"

I throw back some water. "I'm excellent, so nice to meet you!" I smile wearily as she returns to her seat.

"The bread tried to murder her because she's a bread assassin," Roxie repeats somberly back to Eliza.

Reed pushes a chunk of my hair back. He leans in close, his lips brushing over my ear. "You sure you're okay?"

I nod as a river of chills spills down my spine. "Yes, I'm good." Also confused. My insides are burning. And not in the sexy way.

Am I his girlfriend? Is that what we agreed to? Reed's friends start to chat, and he slips easily into their conversation as my brain whirs.

If he wanted to throw around the word *girlfriend*, why didn't he discuss the word *girlfriend*? Was that the implication?

We said *something real*.

I rip off more of the bread and stuff it down my throat, careful not to die this time.

"I didn't know you had a girlfriend," Eliza says, smiling at me. "What do you do, Rikki?"

"Oh, I, uh." I glance quickly at Reed. Do I tell people here what I actually do? Reed nods encouragingly. Fuck it. *It's not like I'm trying to date them.* "I'm the Love Today columnist at *The New York Minute*."

"That's so cool! I've heard of that column," Eliza says.

Reed smiles. "And she's an LMFT, she runs the *Love Today* podcast, and she has an Etsy shop where she makes greeting cards to help people tell their significant others they love them in the perfect way for any special occasion."

"Wait, what? You're Rose Thyme?" Roxie Hart says slowly. "I listen to *Love Today* every Monday during my workout. I'm a huge fan!"

I grin at her.

"I didn't know greeting cards were still in circulation! That's fascinating," Will adds.

Reed nods. "The greeting card is a lost art. Rikki has this gift, to write something both incredibly heartwarming and funny at the same time. My heart grew three sizes scrolling through the samples and reading the reviews on her page."

What? He never told me that. I blink at him, adoration oozing out of me. Probably because my insides are melting from the fire. When did he read through my Etsy shop?

Am I drunk?

"If you ever need a specialty card for someone you have inside jokes with or something, she's your gal."

I only had two drinks. Albeit very quickly. With nothing in my stomach.

"Sounds like you're a woman of many talents, Rikki," Will comments.

"What's your Etsy shop called?" asks Eliza.

"Greetings, Love, Rikki," Reed answers.

I glance back over at Roxie Hart, realizing I didn't respond to her podcast comment. "Thank you so much for listening to the pod," I tell her, raising my water.

"Of course!" Roxie says. "So *Rose Thyme*? You work under a pseudonym just like Reed." She smiles at him. "I have to start calling you Rome so I don't fuck that up on the press tour."

Rome? I share a quick look with Reed. He meets my eyes bashfully before smiling down at the table. *Third name unearthed. Filed for later examination.*

"So you work for *The New York Minute*. Are you remote?" Will asks.

"No, I work in New York City."

"Oh wow," Roxie says. "How does that work with Reed in LA?"

"Well—"

"Wait, you're based in New York? You have to tell us how you two met!" Eliza urges.

"Are you two long distance?" Will asks.

My eyes dart between the three of them, unsure what to tackle first. Unsure I want to answer these things before talking to Reed in private about girlfriend-ship.

I vaguely register "City of Stars" starting to play.

Oh, I love this song.

"You know what?" Reed takes my hand and urges me to stand. "Rain check on those q's, we love to dance, and we can't miss this song."

I glance at Reed. *How does he know I love this song?*

"You just said it, Rick," he murmurs as he leads me to the dance circle.

What? How much of this have I said out loud?

A few guests are swaying out here on the dance floor alongside us as Reed pulls me into hold, slowly guiding me in a classic waltz.

His eyes rove across my face. "I feel like you're not okay."

"I'm . . . I'm confused."

"Are you panicking?"

"All right, thespians!"

We jolt as a voice booms over the speakers. King George swaggers onto the stage, wearing a Britney Spears headset and clutching a remote. He taps it, and "City of Stars" comes to an abrupt stop.

"That guy is on a power trip," I mumble.

Reed chuckles.

"We're gonna get thy party started with our first royal event, All American Bandstand! Peasants, it's time for some healthy competition. Get ready to dance! *Grease* style!"

Reed and I exchange a look as chatter rises among the guests. A wave of participants migrates over to join us on the floor as four camerapeople roll big old-fashioned-looking rigs on tripods in through the brown doors.

"Oh wow," I breathe.

"Prepare to *rock thy roll*," King George says stiffly. "Myself, our bride, and the groom will be watching and judging from our central perch. Here thee, here thee, be thy rules." He pulls a scroll from his pocket. It comically flops open, unraveling downward all the way off the stage.

"Rule one: Thy must be partnered up!" He looks around pompously. "Sorry, singles, you must mingle if you wish to participate.

"Two: You and your partner must be thy touching somewhere at all times. If you lose physical contact for more than two seconds, you will be eliminated.

"Rule three: If you stop moving for more than two seconds, *you will be eliminated*.

"Four: If you are not participating in this event, you must stay off the dance floor ring until thy competition concludes.

"And five: If you're on the floor participating, and you're tapped on the shoulder, you have indeed *been eliminated*. Evacuate the dance floor immediately.

"Winners, you're playing for glory! You're playing for these best-dancer sashes!" He holds up two Miss America–looking sashes. "And you're playing for two! Fifty dollar! AMEX! Gift cards! Let the movin' and groovin' *commence*!"

"Rock and Roll Is Here to Stay" blasts out from the speakers.

Reed spurs us back into movement, skipping to the beat, and I follow his lead. "All right, let's rewind. Are you okay?" he asks again.

I purse my lips.

He smiles gently, twirls me, and pulls us back into a loose hold. "You're freaking out."

"Sound of Music couple over there, already too long not touching. You're out!" George stomps his scepter on the stage.

"We need to clarify some things," I say as Reed and I fall into an easy rhythmic shuffle.

He nods. "Okay."

"So you're my boyfriend now?"

The corner of his lips flip into a grin. "I've submitted myself for the position. Waiting on approval."

I blow out an amused huff. "I thought we agreed to something real?"

"What exactly does something real mean to you?"

"*Something.* With . . . realness."

Laughter rumbles through Reed.

"Boyfriend-girlfriend comes with expectations," I continue. "How is that going to work when I go back to the East Coast? What are the rules? We haven't drafted any stipulations."

"Elphaba and Glinda, you stopped moving, out!"

Reed spins me once. Twice. He catches me by the hip—and quirks a knowing brow. "So this is another control freak panic?"

"And you've seen my Etsy shop?" I blurt accusingly.

His pout shifts into a smirk. "Did you think I wasn't going to google you?"

"Velma Kelly and Billy from *Chicago*, you're gonzo!" yells King George.

Reed lets go of one of my hands to execute some fifties' twist-like dance moves across from me, and I mirror him.

"*The Book of Mormon* over there, yes you! You're too stagnant, out!" George yells.

I frown, struggling to take stock of what's going on with my own emotions.

"Rikki. Talk to me. What's wrong?"

"I don't know?" I squeeze my eyes shut, forehead furrowing as he guides us back into hold. The song shifts, moving to something slower. "Those Magic Changes."

Reed adjusts our rhythm, rocking us smoothly from side to side. I inhale his ocean-forest scent, staring over his shoulder as I soul search. *Why am I so panicked about the word* girlfriend*?*

"Rikki, come on, you know," he says into my cheek.

"I *don't know*," I repeat.

Reed dips me over his arm and leans forward toward my lips. My heart skips a beat as he stills, a centimeter away from my mouth.

"I don't believe you."

"Fuck you," I breathe, as he whips me back up.

"Are you drunk?" He chuckles. "Already?"

"Maybe. I was so hungry."

He frowns. "I'm sorry, we should have grabbed another snack on the way here."

"It's fine. We didn't have time."

"Do you want to go eat some more?"

I set my jaw. "No, I want to win this!"

Reed snorts as "Born to Hand Jive," the track that backs the iconic Danny Cha-Cha dance scene, starts up. He whips us into a twirling frenzy, and I cackle maniacally as we fly across the floor.

"Something's definitely bothering you," Reed says, assessing me way too accurately. He tugs me harder against him and throws his right arm out and up on an angle. We swing around as one piece—chests flush. Fire, the good kind, roars at the contact. At the feel of him against my hips as I mimic his movements. I throw out my opposite arm, recognizing the action from years of obsessing over *Dancing with the Stars*.

His freakishly bright eyes pierce mine as we slow down. "Just tell me."

Just tell him, Rikki. Tell him things, instead of stewing in the suspicious explanations you've conjured up for his girlfriend announcement at the table.

Reed releases my back, catches my free hand, and ushers me back into a normal hold.

I blow out a flustered breath. "I guess I'm annoyed."

He spins me and catches my hand again. "Great, why?"

We fall back into a quick-but-consistent shuffle. "Because! You waited till we were at a public event in front of all your friends to mention a label. We've been in the car all day, and you didn't ever utter the word *girlfriend*. Your friends got to know I was your girlfriend before I did, and of course I have to wonder why. Why today? Why here? Why now? What's your angle? Is it a tactic to exploit me in some way?

"Am I fulfilling a fantasy you've had of actually bringing someone you enjoy hanging out with to a wedding after going to heaps of them alone? When I go home tomorrow are you still going to want to be something real? Are you still going to call me your girlfriend when I'm not around to physically touch, or will it expire at midnight like Cinderella? We haven't discussed it! Is it like the pact? Does it only work when we're together, or are you actually saying you want to be with me now—here and not here?

"Dropping that label in a public space leaves me subconsciously spinning, plotting out all the possible things you might be thinking that word means while we're supposed to be having fun at this grossly expensive, spectacular wedding for your extremely famous friend."

"Jump and straddle," Reed says.

"Excuse me?"

"Jump and straddle me. Now."

He drops a sharp nod as the music crescendos. I bend my knees and jump. He swings me and my hips up. My legs fly toward the ceiling like I'm made of helium, and he brings me back down into a straddle around his waist, my legs jutting out behind him. Then he swings me back out with the momentum and catches both my legs with one arm so he's holding me across his chest. I brace, recognizing this sequence and worrying he's going to try to swing me around his back without practicing—but he just spins in an arc before setting me back on the floor, sliding his hands down my arms, and pulling us back into hold.

"Jesus Christ, Reed. Are you also a part-time professional dancer?"

He tugs me close, keeping us moving, and presses his forehead into mine. "Rikki," he breathes. "I don't have an angle. You've got this image of me as a secret villain in your head. You're waiting for me to flip a switch that isn't there."

I pull back an inch to study Reed's eyes. Earnest, kind, open.

Jordyn's words reverberate in my head. *You never give them the benefit of the doubt. You give them* the *absolute* doubt.

Is that what I'm doing? Am I not being careful? Am I being distant?

"I'm not going to hurt you," Reed says. The words are backed with so much sincerity. It's impossible not to believe them.

I swallow as he spins me out and in. My back lands against his chest. "Men aren't this nice," I hiss over my shoulder.

His hands slide down my waist until his palms are pressed against my hips, urging mine to move with his, against him. My breath catches as desire flames through my core.

His lips hover over my ear. "I'm not nice, Rikki. I'm kind. There's a difference."

He lifts my hands up over my head and twists me back to face him, ensnaring me with his eyes as we gallop back into a shuffle to stay with the music.

"Reed," I breathe. "I don't think I've ever liked a person this much, and I'm pretty panicked about it."

The music shifts. Reed adjusts our tempo as "Super Trouper" fills the room. I can't help but smile as the voices of what sounds like every guest in this hall join in with ABBA to belt the opening lyrics.

"What about your exes?"

My lungs forget how to function as Reed's hands suddenly slide to my upper thighs. He squats, encouraging me with pressure to swing my hips from side to side as he makes his way back to standing and maneuvers us back into a close hold.

I'm going to be ashes by the time we finish this.

Amusement sparks in his eyes. He knows he has me flustered as hell.

What did he ask?

What about your exes?

"Through my twenties . . ." I start, out of breath now. "The bar I had was so low. Not on purpose, but in retrospect I can see that it was like, one foot off the ground. I was just looking for someone peaceful. Someone calm—I didn't know what I wanted in a partner. I just knew what I didn't want.

"I ended up with a lot of stagnant, passive-aggressive people that I never truly felt connected to. No one I could actually depend on to be there with me in whatever I tried to accomplish or do. No one could match . . ." I smile, glancing down at our feet for a millisecond.

"Your freak?" he finishes, grinning.

I blow out a slow breath. "Saying this out loud is making me feel like I'm on the edge of a panic attack."

"You're just facing more fears, Renee."

I roll my eyes for the millionth time today. "What do you know about my fears?"

"I know you do what I do," he says firmly. "You avoid opening up."

I cut him an obstinate look. "What?"

"To protect yourself. You're afraid of being known." He twists our arms into an infinity sign so we're side by side. We move forward in sync, shuffling from one foot to the other with the beat. "It's a classic defense mechanism. You would know."

I blink at him as the statement charges across my psyche, leaving a path of destruction in its wake. People are clapping around us. We have an audience now, standing along the edges of the circle, clapping to "Super Trouper" as it comes to its crux.

It's just us and two other couples left. When did that happen? Willy Wonka and a sexy blueberry girl, and another Sandy-Danny combo. On the stage, Matt Trent and Marissa are singing and dancing, watching us, now dressed in traditional bride-and-groom garb. Or maybe they're *Mamma Mia!* themed?

"The only place you speak completely freely is in your writing," Reed says against my neck. His breath sends renewed flames running over my already-charred skin.

"You only speak freely in *your* writing," I accuse.

"I'm gonna spin you while we walk. You ready to pirouette?"

"Yes."

He releases one of my hands and lightning fast whips the other up over our heads, twirling me. I spot his face, spinning like a top as we move forward to the final bridge.

The crowd is whooping, so we must be doing something right. Reed catches me in an abrupt stop against his torso. My free palm clutches at his biceps. He bends his legs. "Fall back," he breathes.

I drop my hands to his waist and let my torso fall back as he swings me in an arch, my hair tracing a parabola through the air as the audience explodes again.

I crunch back up and land with my hand against his pec.

"Once upon a time at the start of this, yes, I was only speaking freely in my writing," he says. "But—I realized I want you to know things about me. And since then they've started to just spill out.

"The things I've always wanted and worked for these past ten years . . . seem to finally be coming within reach." He shakes his head. "I'm stepping up to the plate and going to bat for all of it. And the biggest swing by far"—he sucks in a breath—"is you."

He twirls me twice and catches my hand as hot golden light floods my chest.

"I've spent fourteen years as an emotional recluse," Reed says simply. "I'm ready to stop being a fucking coward."

Pride swells in my chest. For his story. His openness. He's a living, breathing example of emotional growth. The inexplicable plugged-in feeling I always have around this man maxes out. I'm a human spotlight burning across the floor.

"I want you to know me too," I tell him.

"Super Trouper" ends and the intro to "Gimme! Gimme! Gimme!" rolls in. Reed pulls me back into a tight hold against his chest. We're nose to nose as the song ramps up. "Then let go." I feel his smile against my lips. "Step off the cliff with me."

I almost laugh.

Step off the cliff.

I tripped off weeks ago. At the end of our second date. Way too fast.

I had just published the piece about instalove. But I also knew that Whitney and Glenn had mad fucking issues. And as much as I wanted to make Whitney feel better by digging in and writing that article when our family tried everything to get her to postpone sealing her relationship with Glenn in marriage after a mere eleven months, I didn't believe it myself. I didn't believe in them. I didn't believe you could be so sure about someone so quickly.

But I've been counseling them for weeks now, and they're doing great. Glenn is showing so much potential and desire to grow. And he's taking initiative when I thought he would back down and feel ganged up on.

I misjudged him.

And now what? I'm going to push away the best guy who's ever walked into *my* life because I—what? Don't believe in fucking magical love stories?

I literally appeared here via magic journal from the Disney gods of the universe or some shit. Why am I pretending that isn't my reality? When did I become so fucking jaded? When did I decide to live in this bubble of bulletproof glass?

I tripped off the cliff weeks ago. And I shoved my knife into the cliffside. And I've been desperately clinging to it, trying to throw myself back up ever since.

But the more I spend time with this man, the harder it is to hold on.

It feels good to let go.

I peer into his ardent eyes as we continue to whirl across the floor.

A smile curls into my cheeks. "Reed, I already have."

Curiosity flashes across his face. "Wh—"

"We have our winners! End-of-movie Danny and Sandy, get on up here and claim your prize!"

Reed and I look up. King George is waving to us.

I'm floating outside my body as we stroll up to the bride and groom on stage. *Reed and I are official. Labels and pictures and introducing each other to people in our lives official. We're going to do long distance. He thinks I'm worth the trouble.*

I'm sweating and giddy and terrified, and Regent Fallow the Lost Prince of Yorlabala is here. King George drops sashes over our heads. Dancing queen and king, respectively.

"Reed!" Matthew Trent tugs Reed into a hug, and Marissa does the same. "So glad you could make it! Thanks for coming, man. You two were so great!"

"So happy to be here. Thank you for having us! This is my girlfriend, Rikki." Reed pulls me forward, and Matthew Trent hugs me as I tell him it's so nice to meet him.

Regent Fallow is hugging me.

"I didn't know this guy had a girlfriend. Good for him! You two looked great together out there!" He thinks we looked great together. The universe and Regent Fallow think we're great together.

"We should grab a picture," Reed suggests, pulling out his phone. King George takes it from him and grabs a shot of Reed and me next to Matthew Trent and Marissa.

One degree away from Regent Fallow of Yorlabala. What is my life? Or is it zero degrees? Am I zero degrees from Regent Fallow of Yorlabala? I need some air. I'm overheating. So much dance. So much new information.

King George hands us our AMEX gift cards and dismisses us from the stage before turning his mic back on to say more things to the guests.

I turn to Reed as he takes my hand. "Can we get some air?" The back of this airport-hangar-size room is all glass and opens up to a marina.

"I'd love to."

41 | AIR

Walking outside feels like breaking the surface after a high dive. I inhale deeply, bathing in the silence of the cool night, spinning on the wooden boardwalk with my arms out, before Reed catches up, grabs my hand, and pulls me close. The unpleasant burning is gone, usurped by a buzzing, underlying excitement. The mystical elation that comes with being seen, wanted, understood, and accepted. The sweet relief of validation when your feelings are reciprocated.

I catch his eye. "Bullshit you just took dance courses in college. That was insane."

Reed laughs as we start down a thin dock lit by scattered lampposts, littered with yachts and boats, all neatly tied up in their assigned slips. The faux wood planks glimmer with the remnants of this afternoon's downpour. "Hey, you were keeping up."

"Barely."

He lifts one shoulder and lets it fall. "I've had to get into West Coast swing for a project, so I went weekly for about six months."

I squeeze his hand. "Oh my god, I've always wanted to do that!"

He smiles. "I'd be happy to take you to a class. You'd love it."

I beam at the sky. Is this real?

"Should we sit?" Reed asks as we reach the edge of the dock. We're among an endless span of docks providing shelter for a small city's worth of boats. Every thirty feet or so to the right and left, another thin jet of faux wood shoots out, dividing the bay.

I plop down on the edge of the damp surface and tap the spot next to me. Reed lowers himself to my side. We let our legs dangle.

"So how are we going to do this, Reed?" I say out to the water. "Long distance with real labels?"

He grins, lifts one shoulder, and lets it drop. "I'm not worried. We're both resourceful, determined people. I think we just figure it out as we go."

I bump against his biceps. "If we're going to have a real label, I actually have a few more inquiries."

"Oh yeah? Twenty-one questions weren't enough for the boyfriend title?"

I huff out a breathy laugh. "Nope, my Reed questionnaire is endless."

"Yeah, I feel that. My Rikki one is too."

My mouth splits into a smile. "One for one?"

"Shoot."

"What's up with the bottle-cap art? How'd you get into that?"

He chuckles and fiddles with our intertwined fingers. "My dad collected bottle caps. He had bins and bins and bins of them—my mom would get annoyed sometimes with how much storage space they took up in their closet.

"I have them all now." Reed pauses, peering down at our feet. "He used to do it, make art out of them. Little pieces, all the time, when we were growing up. It was his big hobby, and I picked it up. We would make things with him from time to time. Doing it myself makes me feel like he's here with me. Like he's close."

I press my lips together. "I love that."

Reed nods. He glances out at the bay for a beat before turning to me. "My turn."

I bite my lip and nod. "Hit me."

He searches my eyes. "Is it safe? You living in your dad's apartment?"

I sigh toward the water, nervously swinging my feet. "I think it's safe. Healthy? That's a whole different question. But like I said, my contract is getting renewed at the end of September—as soon as that happens, I get the hell out of there."

He frowns. "That's still a month away."

I squeeze his hand. "I'll be okay. I dug myself into this hole with him, and I'm gonna get out."

"How often is he there?"

"He seems to show up every couple weeks for some random renovation project, and he'll stay however long he deems appropriate for whatever work-venture excuse he used to fly out to New York. I'm quiet. Really polite. I go along with whatever he asks. I stay on his good side."

"That doesn't sound like you."

I frown down at the water. "It's not me. But it's how I keep him under control. It's how I stay safe."

"What would you tell a patient who was in this situation?"

"I . . . well—oh fuck." There's a splash as my right sandal flops off into the bay.

"Oh shit," Reed mumbles. He slides himself off the edge of the wood, reaching for it. It's too far from our perch, and the current is moving fast. My shoe's already heading toward the dock adjacent to us.

"Eff." I start running down our dock in one heel so I can get to the other one before it passes.

"Rikki"—Reed sprints after me—"take off your other shoe before you trip and die!"

I hop up and down until I get it off, then I start down the dock next to us. Reed blows past the entrance of the second dock, heading for the third. "We're not gonna make that one!" he yells.

I pivot and run after him. He gets to the end of the third dock and throws himself on his stomach, reaching down as my shoe floats toward us. It must be low tide, because he's not quite reaching the water even when he hangs all the way to his hips.

"Trade with me!" I yelp as I reach the edge. "Hold my legs!"

He pops up, and I chuck myself down and off the edge of the dock, willing myself to focus as Reed's strong hands press into my thighs.

Before I'm low enough to even think about touching the water, my tiny beaded crossbody bag falls straight off my torso and splashes into the bay. A second later my Dancing Queen sash flutters onto the surface.

"Uh. Ohh." I watch helplessly as my purse sinks down under the surface without pause.

"What was that?" he asks.

"Umm," I say upside down, blood rushing to my head, hair hovering above the water. "My phone, a credit card, my fifty-dollar AMEX gift card, and ID."

"Oh. Fuck."

I skim the surface with my fingertips and hook the Dancing Queen sash as the sandal approaches. The shoe has floated a little off course, farther from the dock.

"Hold on, the sandal's coming. Lower me more!" I wiggle farther off the dock. My fingers can touch the water now. But the shoe is floating by three feet away. I swing myself out toward it.

"What are you doing? This isn't a trapeze!"

My finger skims the sandal—but it gets pushed farther out. I swing again and . . . it's way too far out. "Fuck me."

"Did you get it?"

"No," I mumble, feeling like an idiot. I am an idiot. I'm dangling by my knees off the dock, clutching a Dancing Queen sash. "I missed it. I don't know how to get up."

"I think I'm just gonna deadlift you by your calves until you can get your hands on the dock."

I stare at the water. "Yeah, okay. Please don't drop me."

I blink as the fairly calm surface starts to ripple. Tiny ripples erupt all around as Reed repositions himself to deadlift me.

"Fuck," Reed says as I slowly lift away from the water.

"Fuck what?"

"It's raining."

A laugh wheezes out of me as the dock comes into view again. I put out my arms, and Reed slowly lowers me onto the surface.

"Are you okay?" He drops to a seat next to me. I'm convulsing against the wood as laughter racks through me.

"Are you laughing, Romona?" Reed asks in astonishment.

I snicker, pushing up to a seat. "It's raining. And my shoe is gone, and my most important possessions are on the bottom of the bay."

A smile splits his face as I collapse against his chest. "You have the weirdest sense of humor." He takes my hand, a deep, hearty rumble vibrating through his chest as the rain starts to come down harder.

Giggles continue to slip from my mouth as he stands and helps me up. We glance up at the sky together. Rain falls in abrupt droplets across my face.

"Fuck it," Reed mumbles. He dips his gaze to mine for a second before letting go of my hands. He pulls off his shoes.

"Whoa—what are you doing? No! Don't—"

He jumps into the fucking ocean.

42 | WATER

"Reed!" I screech as he surfaces in the pitch-black water under the small pool of light provided by the one lamppost.

"Gimme a sec." He dives under.

"How are you going to get out?" I bleat.

I spin in a circle, scanning the area, desperate for a ladder as I'm pelted with thick sheets of fresh rain. *Goddamnit.* There's usually a ladder at the end of a dock. Did he even *look for one before throwing himself into the scary, black, dark night water*!

He pops up again. "Not that deep! Nine feet, maybe."

"Nine feet?"

He dives back down. My hair clings to the sides of my face as I squint into the rain-blurred darkness, wishing I had my phone flashlight. Stupid fucking Bloody Mary! What was in that thing? Never drinking one of those again—

I stop short, homing in on a skinny, rotting metal ladder hooked up along the edge of the wood next to a piling, outside the circle of light provided by the lamppost. It's folded up. I skitter over, shove the wet hair from my face, and yank on the bottom half. It's hooked on to the top half and needs to be released down into the water. The thing rattles and doesn't budge.

It's stuck.

Things that hate me:

Zippers

Ladders

"Got it!" I hear Reed yell triumphantly.

"There's a ladder over here!" I yelp.

I yank on the ladder again. It shifts about an inch.

The rain erupts off the water now. Leaping from the surface with its own momentum. Reed's outline appears six feet below me in the darkness. *Shit.*

"It's stuck! But I'm gonna get it!" I yell.

I shove my bare foot up against the piling for leverage. *Come on.* I grab it with both hands, bend my standing leg, and heave with everything I have. The thing flies upward, and I stumble back, relief flooding my nervous system. I stagger toward the water and push it out, away from the other half, into the bay. It bangs against the top piece and locks into place.

Thirty seconds later, Reed's climbing onto the dock, sopping to my soaking wet.

"What the fuck was that?" I screech as the rain whips up in the wind.

He smiles, pulls my crossbody off his torso, puts it on me. "Note to self," he yells over the rain. "Rikki cannot be trusted around large bodies of water."

I shake my head, ogling up at him, heart glowing in my chest. "You're insane."

His grin deepens. "I think you like it."

I grab his sharp jaw and wrench his lips to mine. Rain torrents down his face as our mouths fit together. The kiss is a roaring fire on a cold night. When we pull apart, a breathtaking, open smile lights his face.

I grin up at him, blinking water from my eyes as the sky ambushes us. "What do we do now?"

"Uber?"

We sprint hand in hand through the downpour, back toward the event building.

"Oh fuck," Reed blurts as we get close to the wedding.

"What?"

"I left my shoes."

"I also don't have shoes." I snort. "We should get your shoes." I pivot, tugging him back the way we came.

"And I did something stupid," he says as we jog back.

"Yeah, you jumped in the ocean in the dark outside your famous friend's musical wedding in a rainstorm for my purse."

"I jumped in with my phone in my pocket."

I bulge my eyes at him, a smile breaking across my face. "Oh no you did not."

Reed's mouth tips up. "This is not funny, Renee. We might have murdered two phones."

I keel over, his hand still clutched in mine, bringing us stumbling to a stop out of sheer hysteria as the rain pours down. It's totally not funny. It's tragic. I cannot afford to lose my phone. Or lose anything on it. But I can't be upset right now. I'm too happy.

He's beaming. "Are we going to go back inside like this?"

I'm dying. "At least you'll have shoes."

We huddle against each other in the Uber Eliza called for us. Reed's arm locks me against his side. His palm grips my elbow.

It's 9 p.m. We're something real, and we're going back to the hotel.

"Are we bad at weddings?" I ask from my spot, leaning against his shoulder.

"I think we're just super good at adventure."

I snort, pushing up off his shoulder, so I can see his face. He drags me onto his lap, and I settle over him, a knee on either side of his thighs, in the back seat. Under normal circumstances, I would never straddle a man in the back of an Uber. But these aren't normal circumstances. This is Reed, and I've never felt this particular brand of magnetism toward another member of the human race. It's enchanting, and utterly liberating in this moment, to give in to the ache.

If you asked me right now for a list of my favorite places, Reed Tyler's lap would be at the top. I take my time now, studying. Memorizing his beautiful angle-ridden face. His toned, *effortlessly lethal on the dance floor* body. Water still drips from his hair. It clings to his lashes as he gazes at me, his usual bravado stripped away as his eyes rove over me. I want to say things to him. Do things to him. *I want him.*

I comb my hand from his forehead into his wet hair and curl the front portion around my finger, dragging it forward again like his *Grease* counterpart. "Sluts for Adventure United."

A slow grin etches into his war-hero face as his hands glide up my thighs. "I'm a slut for you, Romona."

My heart pirouettes in my chest as that ridiculous-ass statement fills me up.

I slide my hands up the back of his neck, behind his ears, and meet his mouth again. His lips are cold as they brush against mine. Salty. I press in, and his tongue is blazing as it swipes over my lip, flicks against my own.

"I want you, so furiously." I whisper the words into his mouth. I barely recognize my own voice. "I've never wanted someone like I want you right now."

Reed pulls away slowly, eyes shining in the darkness. The edge of hunger in them liquefies me. He lifts his hand, fingers skimming my bare arm, over my shoulder and up the nape of my neck. They rake into my hair. I lean into the touch, chills tumbling down my spine. He pulls my mouth back to his.

"Rikki." He purrs the name into my mouth, and it does something visceral to my body. I suck in a sharp breath as heat pulses through my center. "You say another word, and I'm going to take you in the back of this fucking Uber."

I exhale a breathy laugh. "I dare you."

We both startle as the horn of our current car blares. "We are here," the driver blurts uncomfortably. "Kindly exit the vehicle. Please rate five stars. I'm never driving Saturday nights again, especially in the rain. Everyone is wet or horny or bot—"

Reed and I fumble out of the car and run for the hotel. I'm externally freezing, and internally on fire. I'm the human manifestation of Icy Hot as I sprint barefoot across the tiled lobby, gripping his hand as we race to the elevator.

It's a nice hotel. I was too distracted earlier, thinking about the questions, to appreciate it. Honestly, I'm kind of too distracted now as well. It's an indie fancy one I've never heard of, with a marbly Old Hollywood–looking aesthetic. Also Reed's shirt is soaked and clinging to every ridge of his muscular torso. *Dear god.*

He punches the up button with his knuckle. It dings immediately, the elevator sliding open to reveal an empty car. We stumble in, he jabs the floor 10 button, and we face forward, side by side.

I watch the doors close.

This is it. We're going to do the sex. Will it live up to—

"Was that chapter accurate to you, Rick?"

I turn my face to his and swallow as I admit the most vulnerable thing I've ever put on paper is true to life. "Yes."

Reed moves, his free hand closing over my hip as he pushes me against the cold mirror lining the wall of the elevator. His mouth finds mine again, hot and insistent, eager. I pour the raging gold river of lust pounding though me into the kiss, my hands skirting along the line where his shirt meets his pants and slipping under to trace the hard ridges of his pelvis.

The doors ding open, and his hands slide over the curve of my ass. He grips tight, securing me against him as we maneuver into the hallway without breaking the kiss. His hands slide up to grip my waist as the doors close behind us. He glances down at my chest. "Is this a bodysuit?"

"Yes."

"Jesus, I fucking love those things."

He pivots us around, swinging me into the striped wall opposite the elevator, and captures my mouth again, grinding against me in a graceful motion that feels like fucking heaven broke into my body and hijacked my nervous system. I gasp, my head falling against the wall as his mouth drags along the slope of my neck. Heat floods my core as he bites down lightly over my clavicle and traces over the bone with his tongue.

"Last chance to call this off." His voice is playful, husky against my skin. His eyes make their way back to mine.

I reach up, breathless, and run my thumbs up the sharp edge of his jaw. "Did you not hear me in the Uber?"

He slides his nose down mine, brushes my lips with his. "I heard you, Renee."

He takes my mouth again, and I secure him there, palms bracketing his cheeks. A moment later, those jacked forearms hook under my thighs and lift me off the ground, moving us toward the room as he continues to ravish my mouth.

"Did you want to call this off?" I murmur between kisses.

"Fuck no."

I gasp as my back hits a new wall. He rocks into me, sending a fresh burst of shimmering flame storming up my center, using the wall as leverage to take the kiss deeper. Desire is a windstorm hurling against my rib cage, tornadoing down to the hypersensitive point between my legs. I feel the kiss in my fingertips, my knees, in the pointed soles of my feet.

The door beeps open, and we're in the room, my legs still locked around his waist as the door slaps shut behind us. I pull back as I slide down his solid torso, dragging my hands down his chest. "Not having second thoughts about being a boyfriend, correct?" I arch a brow, feeling utterly feral as my fingers pause on the top button of his jeans, dipping behind the waist to tease the hot skin behind the metal.

Reed's searing blue eyes are locked on mine, the intensity of his desire radiating back at me as his lips curl into an amused grin. "Fuck no."

He's kissing me hard, hands back in my hair as I unbutton his sopping wet pants.

His fingers deftly undo the button on mine.

"Planning to ghost tomorrow?" I murmur as he slips down the length of my body.

He's on his knees now, working the pants off my legs. He looks up, his gaze piercing through me again. He tugs the second leg off and tosses the pants aside with a thwack.

"*Fuck* no."

That fuck ricochets through me. He runs his fingers up the back of my legs. "You're so unbelievably fucking gorgeous in every conceivable way." He presses his mouth into my inner thigh, and I almost collapse. I fist a hand of his hair to steady myself.

"I want to take fucking care of you." He gently clamps his teeth over a section of sensitive skin, and a breathy gasp wisps out of me.

I grab his shirt collar and tug him back up to standing. "I don't need to be taken care of."

He catches my mouth in an aggressive kiss. "Only makes me want to do it more."

My heart shivers as I shove at his pants. He maneuvers us, backing me into the bathroom, hands roaming, cupping my breasts, grabbing my ass. His finger finds the spot between my legs begging to be touched and strokes. I arch into the pressure, breaking from his lips to breathe, stumbling into the giant glass shower in this hotel bathroom. Reed moves with me, pressing my body into the glass, stroking, closing his lips over mine. Tongue and mouth moving in rhythm with his hand.

My breath hitches.

"Rikki, I want to make you things," he growls, voice deep, breath hot against my neck.

I gasp as pleasure jolts through me.

"I want to clean your fucking house."

"What the fuck." A moan rasps out of me.

He starts moving faster. Harder. "I want to worship you and all the fucking-too-much everything you have to offer."

I see stars as his fingers dive into me, as he grinds against my torso, hard in his underwear. Sparks blow out from my center. He catches my mouth, pinning me against the glass with his torso like a pressed flower as his fingers curl, work, stroke. I tremble around him, grinding against his hand, as an overpowering wave of bliss ripples through me.

I slide my eyes open, finding his locked on me, his hand still moving, coaxing out new tendrils of pleasure. "Fuck." I breathe hard. "You."

Reed smiles lazily, lifting his arm to brace against the glass. He bows forward, hovering his mouth over my ear. "You're so fucking hot."

I am molten as I push off the glass and shove open the door to a shower the size of the kitchen in my apartment. There's a bench, handholds, a second nozzle. This thing was designed for a party of two. I throw on the main nozzle. Reed slides his arms around me from behind, pulling me tight against him as his fingers find me again. Stroke, circle, press between my legs. His other hand cups my breast.

My consciousness feels like it's engaged in a tug-of-war between this plane and a second one where my being wants to explode into glitter and dust. His chest is an immovable wall as I go taut. His mouth is on my ear again. He kisses the hollow behind it. Tugs on the lobe.

"Reed," I breathe.

"Yes." He bites my ear as he plunges fingers back into me.

I gasp. "I want you, right the fuck now."

His arms loosen, and I grab his wrists, pulling him into the shower. The door flops shut behind us as I start to work his black T-shirt, still stuck to him like a second skin, up, off. I roll it off his abs. *Oh my god.* His pecs. He raises his arms. The shirt hits the shower floor with a splat.

"Over there." I point him to the bench about a foot off the wall with a well-placed metal handle. He obeys, padding over, watching me, rapt, as he lowers onto the marble, steam filling the glass shower, billowing around us.

I take a half second to drink him in as my body pulses. Thick-built thighs that you could crush a damn orange between. Broad shoulders, built arms, cut torso. He's *hot.* I've never been with someone so physically adept before. There's so much to explore.

But the ache in my core won't allow for that right now. The need for more of him is palpable. My heart feels like a strobe light in my chest as I move toward him again. As soon as I'm within reach, Reed snatches my waist, squeezes my ass, before sliding his hands up to the arms of my bodysuit. He tugs them down, freeing my breasts.

"Rikki. Jesus Christ."

"Condom?"

He slips his hand into the band of his underwear and pulls one out.

I take it. "I'll ask about this later."

His mouth twitches upward as I free him from his purple boxers, running my hand up and down over his soft skin a few times before sliding on the condom.

He continues staring at me, blazing into my eyes, and breathing hard as I arrange myself over him on my knees. A noise slips out of me as his erection teases the thin material at the apex of the bodysuit. He tugs it to the side as I lower myself onto him. I gasp, a beam of hot light striking up my torso as I stretch around him.

"Fuck, Rikki." He catches my mouth as we start to move. Together. Like we've done this before. Like it's a dance we've been trying to do with other partners our whole lives, but the pieces never fit. Adrenaline courses through me as we increase the tempo.

He grabs me by the creases of my hips, groaning, fingers burrowing in, slamming into me. Each time an explosion of stardust hurtles up into my body. *Why does this feel better than anything ever has?*

"Rikki."

I arch back, digging my nails into his shoulder blade, clutching at the railing above his head with my other hand for leverage. "Yes."

"Fuck me—I'm already close."

I look down into his molten-blue eyes, his abs on full display. "You are so fucking beautiful." I ride him harder. Kiss him like I'm trying to consume his final breath. "Let the fuck go."

"Christ, Romona."

His fingers find me as we kick the tempo up another notch, gasping against each other.

"Let go," I demand again, and this time he obeys, relinquishing control, eyes blowing wide. The building wave of sparkling, hot bliss crashes through me, and he closes his lips over mine, swallowing the satisfied moan rising in my throat.

When the kiss breaks, he presses his forehead against mine. "Holy shit."

"Holy shit," I breathe, clutching at his surprisingly muscular neck.

He rises from the bench, picking me up with him like I'm no heavier than a bag of groceries, still inside me, and walks us toward the showerhead. His fingers dig into my upper thighs, and my palms press into his cheeks as I demand more of his lips.

I don't want to ever separate from him. I want to be right here, fused to this man.

He pulls his mouth back a half centimeter from mine. "Rikki, you just fucked me into another dimension I didn't know existed."

I tug on his bottom lip. Kiss the shit out of him one more time. "How did you know how to do that to me so easily?"

He smiles against my mouth. "I studied that chapter, Rikki. I study you. You're my favorite subject."

He finishes me again before we even start to shower.

43 | FOOD

I've never felt like this before. I keep saying that. It keeps being true. Like I can levitate. Like a sorceress. Like I could conquer the world.

Sex has always been a thing that happened to me. That I was there for. Tonight I happened to sex. I wanted it with this man, and we made it happen. I was in full control, and he was in full control, and it was more than I could ever have imagined sex could be.

I let the sex goblin take control and *wow, that bitch is confident*. She's the coolest version of me I've ever met. I've never told anyone I wanted them. I've never wanted to.

"Two burgers, two Caesar salads, the charcuterie board, two Sprites, two bowls of uncooked rice, two waters, a banana split, and two baked potatoes, please."

My stomach grumbles excitedly as Reed talks to the hotel employee on the other end of the line. It's been way too long since we had an actual meal. We didn't get doggie bags before we left the wedding. We're famished.

I'm in underwear and his trench coat. He's in royal-blue boxers with yellow stripes, black sweats and nothing else, and I'm staring at him from my spot among the pillows on the bed closest to the window. He's pacing as he listens to the phone. I watch his stomach muscles move as his weight shifts. As he breathes.

This man is my boyfriend.

I feel his attention shift to me like static over my skin as he says goodbye and hangs up the phone.

"What are you doing?" he says playfully.

"Admiring you."

"Staring."

"I think you like it."

He drops his head back to smile at the ceiling. "I definitely do. My stomach is full of fucking butterflies. I can feel your eyes on me the whole time." He looks me up and down. "Why are you half naked in that jacket?" He crosses his arms, staring at me, hunger in his eyes. "What are you trying to do to me, Rikki, I'm fucking weak in the knees."

He picks up a T-shirt off the back of the desk chair and moves to put it on.

"Reed, put down the shirt."

He turns and cocks a brow.

"It's a crime for you to put on that shirt right now. The people want to see you."

He grins. "The people?"

"I'm the people."

His eyes flash as his mouth knots up.

"How much time before the food is here?"

"Forty minutes to an hour," he says.

"Lie down." I point to the space next to me.

He obeys, lowering down next to me on his side. I watch as his body contracts and shifts to accommodate his movements, and I climb over him. The goblin comes back full force. Desire coalescing, gaining mass and momentum as our skin makes contact because he's beautiful and considerate and kind and funny and smart and *mine*, and I'm leaving tomorrow. I need more before we part.

So much more. I feel like Bella the first time she slept with Edward and couldn't compute how on earth she could go back to a regular life when she knew there was this. *When I know there is sex with Reed.* A different dimension of solid, hot, liquid, molten bliss.

I lower over him. Trace the deep ridges of his abdomen with my tongue. Kissing. Licking. He's spectacular. Such art.

"Rikki," he breathes.

He shivers as I slowly make my way down. Knot my hands in his sweatpants, maneuver them down, and take him in my mouth.

He convulses and groans, and I bring him to the edge before he pulls me up and flips me over.

"I want to feel you," he demands, and it lights up my every cell again as he grabs a condom from a box he left on the nightstand, and he pushes into me. Stars burst for the second time in the last hour as perfect puzzle pieces snap together. As we dance against each other, letting go completely, feral, screaming for each other, as we flip into that other plane.

Our phones are in rice.

We'll see how that pans out. We've devoured our room service. *Friends* is playing on low on the TV. We're tangled up in the bed—clothed. Reed's in a Mathematics Tour Ed Sheeran T-shirt and boxers. I'm in shorts, a tank, and the trench.

"Have I told you how you smell amazing?" I inhale near Reed's neck.

I feel the vibrations off his chest as he laughs, but I can't catalog his specific facial reaction, because from this vantage point I don't get that view.

"Yes, and I now own every product that scent has to offer."

I smile. "Did I tell you you smell like the forest became a person and went to the beach with a book after like, a long day of work?"

His chest rumbles under me. I shift slightly off his chest, and he takes the opportunity to turn toward me and prop up his head. "The problem with snuggling like this is, I don't get to see your face when you talk."

It's so wild when he says things that I'm thinking like that. He's literally been doing it since the moment we met.

I prop up my head, smiling. "Reed, you have such a great face—it's so weird that you never show it on your Instagram grid."

Reed snorts.

"For real, why is there not one face in any of your pictures? Your grid looks like a hipster's account from the year 2012."

A laugh bursts out of him. "I'm fine with that. 2012 was a great year. No one wants to see pictures of a face. So mainstream."

A *pfft* sizzles out of me.

His grin kicks up sideways. "So you like my face?"

"You have a face for the mid-1800s."

He eyes me dubiously. "You have a thing for Civil War–era men?"

"I do now."

His head falls back with a laugh.

"Your face gives *I'm an 1860s war hero, there's a statue of me in the town square*. What do you think my face gives?"

He beams, shaking his head. "I don't know, I've never considered this. Early 2000s?"

"You can't pick early 2000s. That's when I'm actually from."

He snorts. "Fine, your face is giving 800 BC."

"Excuse me? BC? I give before Jesus?"

"It gives Vikings."

"I'm not even blond!"

"You look blond to me."

"My hair is bronze, Reed."

"We're talking face, not hair. You have fierce, light features. It's giving Scandinavian."

I roll my eyes. "All right. I'll take it."

"I love looking at your before-Jesus face."

I flop backward onto the bed, smiling at the ceiling. "So. Is that usually what sex is like for you?"

He leans over me, grinning. "Did you not hear me when I said you fucked me into a different dimension I didn't know existed?"

"Just making sure you weren't just being polite."

An abrupt laugh barks out of him. "In what world?" He grabs my thigh and hitches my leg over his hip. A wave of heat pours through me as I wiggle closer.

"That was the most magnificent merging I've ever experienced," he says.

"Merging?"

He arches a brow. "Just trying to be polite."

A laugh hisses out of me.

"Was it not for you?"

"Oh, it definitely was."

His lips press into a pout. "Lived up to the chapter?"

I arch a brow. "Blew the chapter out of the water. Well done."

His head lolls back. "When do you leave tomorrow? How much time do we have before you head back east?"

"Are you asking me how many times we can have sex before I leave?"

"Among other things."

"I leave tomorrow night."

"Can I drive you to the airport?"

I smile, tugging his Ed Sheeran shirt to close the distance between our faces, and kiss him deeply.

"Is that a yes?"

"Yes, Reed. I would let you drive me anywhere. You could murder me right now, and I'd be upset because there are a lot of work things I'm excited about, but also I would die happy."

He tugs me closer, pulling my leg higher over his hip. "What's your week look like?"

I swallow, my heartbeat speeding up without permission as he shifts under me. "I've got the podcast recording Monday . . . I'll be framing the picture of us with Regent Fallow and hanging it next to my bookshelf when I have a free second—please, Lord, ensure that it made it to the cloud."

Reed smirks. "We can only hope."

"I've got the monthly pitch meeting for *The Minute* on Wednesday, Etsy cards Thursday, last passes for this week's article, first draft of next week's."

He nods, his finger now drawing shapes across my thigh.

"I'll be changing my phone background to a picture of your Civil War–era face."

He chuckles.

"And then WWU Sunday at three. Favorite part of my week."

"Still waiting for the QR invite to the WWU but honored to be a part of SFAU." A smile tugs up my cheek: *Sluts for Adventure United.*

I shift, rolling over him and pushing up onto my knees. "The SFAU is quickly becoming my favorite club."

My hair falls around us in a sheet as I lean forward to meet his lips. He flips us so I'm on my back. He hovers over me, searchlights flaring in his eyes. "So when did you step off, Renee?" he asks.

I purse my lips and stare at him, feeling suddenly shy. "I don't know."

He grins, like he expected this response. "Yeah, I don't believe you."

He pushes up my shirt, exposing my stomach, and kisses over my belly button.

Between my breasts.

Over my hip.

On my underwear line, before sliding off my shorts and tossing them in the corner. He hasn't even touched me, and my heart is beating out of my chest. My body is a ticking time bomb under him. He spreads my legs, and my breathing hitches.

"This is blackmail," I bleat.

His lips land in the crease at the top of the inside of my thigh.

"Reed," I breathe.

"When?" he says. His mouth brushes against me, and I can't handle how turned on I already am.

"At the beach." The words are barely a whisper as I writhe against his static lips.

He starts moving his mouth again.

Stardust implodes, swirls, coalesces, explodes again. The process restarts, sensation growing, building.

"Which time, Renee?"

I rock into him. "Don't stop."

"When," he demands.

I exhale, exhale, exhale, trying to focus, dying for him to continue, keep going, electrifying me. "When you answered the question."

"Which question?"

"What is love to you?"

He gets back to work, and my world dissolves and explodes in bursts. Kaleidoscopes of euphoria.

When he's done, he collapses next to me. I'm a boneless pile of human, blissed out, adoration for this man filling every corner of my being.

"I stepped off when you answered the same question."

44 | SPACE

I don't ever want to leave this room.

But also I do. I know I do—there are reasons. I want to go to work. I want to see Jordyn and Micah. I have to put my address into the journal. See what kind of task lies ahead today.

We slept like two rocks, fit perfectly against each other. I woke up feeling amazing. We had sex in bed. And sex in the shower. My body is tingling just thinking about it. I love this bubble.

I've never had so much consecutive sex. I've never wanted to. I'm insatiable.

I could go again right now.

I'm so annoying.

I feel like I've morphed into a pubescent boy.

I'm gonna accidentally give myself a urinary-tract infection.

We have twenty minutes till checkout, and I'm doing my makeup in the bathroom. My eyes are bright. Lips are swollen. Skin is red and irritated from his stubble. I quietly close the door and pull out the journal.

Feedback?

I sigh.

Did you know I was gonna shit myself in my ex's office?

I flip the page.

That's neither here nor there.

"Oh my god!"

"You okay?" Reed calls from the room.

"Fine! Sorry, thought I saw a spider. It was just . . . mascara."

I turn the page again, more aggressively this time.

My intentions are pure.

Flip again.

5) Where would you like to go

X ____________________

I write out my address, holding my breath as I flip.

Confront your father about showing up unannounced.

That is all.

Have fun.

I smack the small black print, irritation hissing out of me. "*Why are you like this?* What happened to bathing in a pool of 2 percent milk? Are you trying to get me killed?"

Should I just buy a plane ticket?

That'll take the entire night and be extremely expensive in a world where I'm trying to save every penny until I have an updated salary locked in so I can afford a new, not-my-dad's apartment.

I flip to the next page, like maybe there'll be a different, less impossible thing waiting there that I can do instead.

Just trying to help you live a less fearful, fulfilling life.

I slam the journal shut and finish my makeup. I'm stiff with anxiety as I walk back into the room. Reed's waiting on the bed, looking like a hot, concerned statue in an NYU T-shirt and jeans.

"I actually have to stop in and see my dad today. Would you maybe want to come?"

◆ ◆ ◆

It's 3 p.m. on a Sunday, and we're in Pasadena, parked outside my dad's house. I don't think I can go in. But I googled plane tickets in the business lounge at our hotel, and it's currently six hundred dollars for a one-way flight to Jersey.

Our phones are still dead. So I'm already going to be at least five hundred dollars in the hole there. I can't drop six hundred dollars on a flight that I don't have to take when I have a magical, all-knowing journal that's both enhancing and ruining my life.

"May I ask the purpose of this visit?" Reed asks gently as I fiddle with my fingers. I offer a small smile. My hands are shaking.

"Remember when we were on the dock?"

The tiniest smile twitches into his lips. "That was yesterday. Yes. I remember."

I huff a nothing-laugh. "Um, when you asked me what I would tell a patient who was going through this with their dad."

He nods. "I didn't ask you that to force you into an immediate confrontation."

I press my lips together. "I think I would tell them to start small. Especially if they were in a precarious living situation. Delicate. To talk to him and gently explain how the most disruptive current behavior is hurting you, and that if it doesn't stop, it's going to hurt your relationship. All my dad supposedly wants is . . . to be a part of my life. And right now the bare minimum he could do is let me know when he's going to be stopping over—"

"And you're stopping over unannounced at his house to explain this?"

I nod, swallowing hard like a terrified cartoon character. "Sometimes it's the most effective way to explain how something simple can be emotionally deregulating, inconvenient, and disruptive. Especially with people who lack the capacity to put themselves in someone else's shoes."

Hopefully he isn't home, and I can just call him instead.

"And you're terrified."

"Well, no, I'm . . . mildly worried."

"You're literally shaking, Rick."

"It's going to be fine."

"You don't have to do this right now if you're not ready."

I close my eyes and blow out one more long breath. *Don't be a fucking coward.* It's long overdue that my father gets a lecture about boundaries. I should have done this a long time ago in regard to a million other things.

"I'm doing it. I'll be right back. Keep the engine running, just in case we need a fast getaway."

I hop out of the car with my everyday black purse slung across my chest and power walk to the yellow door of his house. I take the front steps at a run and pause, with my finger hovering over his doorbell.

Press it.

"You don't have to press it."

I jump out of my skin. Reed steadies me with hands on my shoulders before I can stumble off the steps. "What are you doing? You were supposed to wait in the car!"

"We can leave, Renee."

"No, we can't."

"Why not?"

"You should just wait in the car," I stress. "I don't know how he's going to react."

"Exactly why there's no chance in hell I'm going to wait in the car."

I stab the doorbell and cringe as an old-fashioned grandfather clock noise reverberates through the house.

Don't be home, don't be home, don't be home.

The door swings open.

45 | I LOVE YOU. IT'S RUINING MY LIFE

Dad stands behind the threshold of his home, smiling at us. "Rikki? We're just about to have Sunday dinner. Holy cow, perfect timing. Come on in!"

His hair is a deep chestnut brown. It's usually mostly gray. It was mostly gray a week and a half ago. *It's been freshly dyed.* And he's wearing reading glasses. And he's in a cream-colored sweater with leather elbow patches? Is he cosplaying as a professor?

"We're? Who's *we're*?" I ask.

"Who's this?" My father gestures to Reed and serves him a charming smile.

"Um, this is my Reed. My boyfriend. Reed. This is my boyfriend, Reed."

Reed holds out a hand, and my father shakes it. "Hi, I'm Reed, her boyfriend."

"Wow, kid, I didn't know you had a boyfriend. Come on in. We're all in the dining room."

I hesitantly follow him into the house I've been avoiding stepping into for seventeen years of my life. It's . . . really nice. Beautiful, even. We're in a foyer full of dark wood with a staircase that curves up to a second floor with a balcony.

We follow him through an archway into a cozy living room full of bookshelves that are built into the walls and brown leather furniture. He has a fire burning on his TV just like I always have going on mine.

I hate it.

The living room funnels into a wood-floor dining room with dark medieval-chandelier light fixtures that I'm immediately obsessed with. They look like they belong in a castle.

And at the table is a woman. And two kids. Two daughters. One around ten, the other probably five or six. My stomach squeegees itself.

You're not allowed to date anyone, let alone a woman with kids.

But what if he is on medication now? Maybe he is truthfully doing better. He hasn't done anything to prove otherwise yet.

But he always says shit like that when he's trying to gain a foothold back into my life.

But I haven't spent enough time with him in the last ten years to know if it's ever been true.

But nothing he ever says is true.

But he's dressed all different, and he's dyeing his hair. Is this him doing better?

He just dyed his hair in the past two weeks.

"Enora, Ellen, Erica, this is my daughter, Rikki, and her boyfriend. What's your name again, son?"

Reed clears his throat. "Reed, sir."

Enora grabs an extra chair from the corner of the dining room and shoves it next to the empty chair left at their table.

"Rikki!" she gushes. "It's so nice to finally meet you. I've heard such amazing things from your father about everything you do."

I glance at my dad. "You have?"

The girls are quiet. They stare at me wide eyed.

"Yes! *Love Today*? The column and the podcast? And a relationship counselor to boot. That's amazing. So many hats you wear."

"I, um, thank you."

"Sit down, kids, take a load off," my father says. Enora runs out of the room for a moment and returns with two extra plates and forks. There's lasagna on the table. And Italian bread. And roasted broccoli.

"We only came to have a quick word with you, Dad."

"Have the word with us at the table," he says cheerily as Enora retakes her seat. Does she live with him?

Reed shoots me a look. *Do you want to leave?*

I shake my head the slightest bit. The only way out is through. I pull out the chair across from Enora's two girls and sit down. Reed settles in the chair next to me.

"How old are you?" asks the younger girl.

"I'm thirty."

"Wow, she's old," the girl says loudly. "Why is your kid so old?" she asks my father.

My dad laughs. I would laugh, but I'm incapable.

"Are you vegan or something, Reed?"

Reed shakes his head. "No, sir."

I clear my throat. "We already ate. I just wanted to talk to you about the apartment."

"My apartment?" My father smiles at me.

"Yes, I wanted to talk about some logistics real quick."

He nods, cutting through a piece of lasagna with his fork.

"I hear the place is beautiful." Enora smiles sweetly at me.

I nod. "It is." I turn to my dad. "Um, I know you want our relationship to flourish, and I do too." I force the words out stiffly.

I just want to make it to January without an incident.

"You know how you surprised me there when the place was being painted? And then again when you were just there when I got home from work, because you got the cabinet handles replaced."

He nods. "Yes."

"I just think it would be beneficial, for both of us, if you could give me advanced notice when you plan on being in the apartment. It's, um, disconcerting as a single woman to come back to where you live and find a man there—"

"You're not single. You have a boyfriend," he says simply.

I close my eyes and nod. "Yes, but he doesn't live there with me. Sorry, I meant a woman living alone in New York."

"The apartment's in Jersey."

"Dad, you know what I mean, right outside the city. I have to be careful, and it's very scary to come home to find a man in my apartment without pretense."

"You're scared of your dad?"

I suck in a sharp breath and stare down at my empty plate as tears sting behind my eyes. *Stay calm.* I exhale and look up. "No, it's the surprise of it all. It gives me a lot of anxiety. I would really appreciate if you texted me beforehand to let me know these things are happening and you're going to be in the apartment."

Like I've gently asked both times.

"What does it matter, Rikki?"

Reed reaches for my hand and squeezes it under the table.

"It matters . . ." I inhale slowly again. "Because I'm a grown woman with multiple jobs and a tight schedule, and it's currently my place of residence. And if . . ." I cut myself off.

My father tilts his head. "If what?"

"If it keeps happening, it's going to hurt our relationship because it slowly builds resentment when a thing that bothers someone keeps happening, despite said someone voicing their concerns. And as an adult, I'll have to put up some firmer . . . boundaries to protect my peace."

My father laughs. "Firmer boundaries? You live in my apartment rent-free, sweetheart. Your generation doesn't understand how good they have it."

I close my eyes as my blood comes to a boil.

"Sir—" Reed starts, but I put a hand on his leg, stopping him.

I turn to my father. "Dad. I want to keep open lines of communication. I know you don't want me to have to resort to going no contact."

My father laughs. "Oh please, Rikki. I'm your father. Your mother and I are on good terms. There's no reason the two of us can't be as well."

A lump lodges itself between my mouth and my vocal cords. "You want me to text you when I leave the state. And that has to go both ways. You need to text me when you're in Jersey."

He smiles. "I do text you, Rikki. Both of those times I texted you."

I shake my head. "No, you didn't."

"Yes, I did. You don't check my texts often enough."

I level my gaze on him. "*Yes,* I do."

"Maybe make sure your ringer is up. I know how all you young people like to have your phones constantly on silent."

I stand up and smile tightly. "Okay. I will. And I would also love for you to stop watching me on the Ring camera. It's incredibly uncomfortable."

My father laughs. "You think I have nothing better to do than watch you on the damn Ring camera, Rikki? You think your comings and goings are ESPN? Gimme a break."

"You literally text me when I come and go all the time."

"I text you when I get a notification of concern. I don't watch the Ring. I have it for security."

I clench my teeth and glance from my father to Reed, who's now standing next to me. "O-kay. We actually have to go. Please think about how this is going to affect our relationship long term." I turn to Enora. "It was so nice meeting you. We should exchange numbers. I'd love to get to know you better."

"You're not going to have any food?" my dad laments, feigning disappointment.

Enora smiles, surprised. "Oh wow, that's very nice of you. Do you have your phone?"

No, it's currently a useless paperweight. "Do you have yours?" I ask.

She nods and pushes her phone across the table. I grab it. It's already unlocked. I shoot myself a text that says, Hi Rikki, this is Enora, and send it back across the table.

"So nice meeting you, girlies!" I wave to her kids. The smaller one waves back.

"Nice meeting all of you," Reed says politely, following my lead as I head toward the door.

Once we're in the car, I pull the journal out of my bag and check the pen. Green.

Thank god.

"Are you okay?" Reed asks as he closes the driver's side door.

I sigh. "It feels like nothing I say ever gets through to him. I'll be okay."

"You think he's going to keep dropping in on you unannounced?"

"I guess we'll see."

"Hey."

I look up from my hands into Reed's eyes.

"I know that was hard, and I don't know what prompted it right now, but I'm proud of you for saying something. And I'm glad you asked me to come."

I nod, trying to keep my cool as a river of emotions rages through me. "Thank you for coming."

"One more SFAU dinner before I bring you to the airport?" He pronounces it *sauvoo*, and it makes me laugh.

I tell Reed my flight is at eleven. We make a pit stop at Verizon to replace our phones. Neither of them made a miraculous recovery, and neither of us had insurance—so that was an expense.

After dinner, he parks us up in the Hollywood Hills at one of the many viewpoint turnoffs to watch the sunset. As we sit there in the quietly fading light, my mind winds back through the weekend. So much has changed in the last forty-eight hours.

The Wedding Garter Universe Magic has resulted in the acquisition of an incredible boyfriend.

The Rikki Curse has ensured said boyfriend lives on the opposite end of the United States.

"I already hate this part," I breathe.

"Which part?" Reed says. His hand lightly caresses my thigh, fingers dancing up and down. It's making me want to snuggle into him and fall asleep. Or cry. Or kiss him into oblivion.

"The part where I have to leave and go back to my side of the country, thousands of miles away, and remember why this is a shit idea."

He chortles. Studies me for a moment. "I don't think it's a shit idea."

I smile. "How exactly is this not a shit idea?"

"Because you bring me an exorbitant amount of joy."

I have to press my lips together to stop them from quivering.

"Are you happy?"

My smile stretches. "One could say I am full of joy."

"Does it have anything to do with me?"

"Yes."

He shifts to face me, grinning. "I think we owe it to ourselves to be happy when we're happy. That's the goal, right? Happiness? It's counterintuitive to shut out the source of the happiness in the name of protecting ourselves from potential pain."

My lips fold into a smirk. "Are you about to spew some shit about how it's better to have loved and lost than to have never loved at all?"

He smirks back. "*It is* better to have loved and lost than to never have loved at all. I thought you read my book!"

I snort and fall back against the seat as the first part of that statement settles over me like a weighted blanket. "So you don't regret your eighteen-year-old fiancée?"

He blinks at me. "How can I regret the thing that led to the most exciting moment of my professional life so far? That experience gave me the insight to write a novel that was featured in *The New York Minute* that I was really, really proud of. I sold the film rights back then too. That was so exciting. For a second I had big fat dreams of playing the lead in my own book. I learned a shitload about myself. I got into therapy. I became a better person because of it. I know I'm going to be a better partner now than I could have ever been back then, just because of everything you become aware of through the therapy process. I could never regret that."

"I always wonder if my mom regrets marrying my dad. If she regrets staying with him as long as she did." I fiddle with my shirt. "I think I'd regret it . . . I think I'd regret *me*. I chained her to him. I was an extra weight tying her to a life full of pain and anxiety."

"Rikki—"

"For so long I blamed her for staying with him." I stare at a bush out in the darkness as my eyes lose focus. "She'd never yell or scream or fight back. I didn't understand it.

"And all the while I was so confident I could fix it. I could talk sense into him. Because my dad and I were buddies. We had a book club. Surely if anyone could get through to him, it would be me."

I let go of a self-deprecating snort.

"My mom let me lecture him. For five years I looped in circles with that man while my mother lived with the consequences. And eventually it started to feel like it was my fault. I *wasn't* getting through to him. And because I couldn't teach basic decency, my mom had a broken finger. Or a bruised face, or a missing patch of hair, or couldn't breathe without pain.

"She didn't realize how much it was affecting her ability to be the mom she wanted to be. How much she was disassociating. How bad it was getting. And despite everything I've studied and know about abuse, a part of me is still in there, blaming her for everything he did. And everything he continues to do now.

"She still talks to him. They do phone calls. And coffee. And I always eventually end up accepting his empty apologies for whatever the latest fucked up thing he did was. I let it go. I continue to humor his cursory attempts to prove himself a good father, because she refuses to give up on him." My voice dips to a shameful whisper. "And it makes her happy when I forgive him, and I love her."

Reed pushes back the driver's seat, tugs my hand, and scoops me into his lap. My face is wet. I'm crying. He runs his fingers through my hair, combing it back in a soothing motion as I nuzzle into his shirt. We sit there like that for a while before I push up, off his chest. "Sorry"—I suck in a breath—"I shouldn't have said that out loud. You probably think I'm a horrible—"

Reed rests his hand against the side of my face. "Rikki. When I found out about my mom cheating on my dad, I hated her. It was like an instantaneous switch. And I hated how much I hated her. And I hated myself. When my dad died it just got so much worse. For like three years. I *hated* her. Deeply.

"And I've come so far from that moment, from that headspace. I've forgiven myself for existing. But somewhere in the depths of my mind there's still this little bit of anger that I haven't been able to let go of. Because I don't know why she did it. She still won't tell me. And it kills me, not knowing. And I know she's just another person who must have been going through a hard time. I get it."

His irises flare, catching the light in the darkness. "Having emotions doesn't make us horrible people. It just makes us people. It's what we do with them that informs who we are."

A laugh huffs out of me at this therapeutic staple statement. "Preaching to the choir with that wisdom."

"Sometimes when you're in the choir, singing the same thing every day, you lose track of what you're preaching."

I frown, trying to stop crying. "I really enjoy your brain."

He laughs. "Rikki, you dole out grace to everyone you interact with, everyone you know, but you don't give it to yourself. I can tell you right now, there's no fucking way your mom regrets loving your dad. Because loving your dad gave her you."

I shake my head. "You don't know."

"I know," he says confidently.

We peer at each other for a long, potent moment as the thread between us reinforces into something stronger. As this weekend solidifies into something ironclad. "If you reached out to your bio dad," I whisper, "maybe he could tell you why what happened, happened."

Reed leans his forehead against mine. "If you talked to your mom about this, she would tell you word for word what I just said. And if she knew how you felt, I bet she'd reexamine her relationship with your dad."

We gaze at each other for a few more seconds, before we both laugh, discharging emotional huffs of air.

"Maybe," I say quietly. "Or maybe she'd tell me I'm being dramatic and dismiss it."

He sighs. "Maybe bio dad would tell me the story, or maybe I'd work up the courage to reach out, and he'd ignore me altogether. And knowing he still doesn't want anything to do with me as an adult who doesn't need something from him would be worse than not knowing at all."

"Hey," I tell him.

"Hey," he says back.

"If we're going to do this official thing, it'd be cool to be one of those couples that challenges each other to grow and evolve and face their shit."

"I think we're already doing that, Romona."

I smile through my lingering tears. "I love that."

He swipes the wetness from my cheeks, staring into my eyes. "How did I find you?"

"I have it on good authority that the cosmos are shipping us."

He tilts forward to catch my lips in a kiss. Kisses that grow longer and deeper and more intense. Until we've relocated to the back seat. And when we're fitted together, approaching a crescendo, and I'm reveling in his scent and his lips are fit against mine, I breathe the words I haven't quite been able to articulate yet.

"See you at the airport, Derek."

His nails dig into my shoulder blades as I match his intensity. He waits till I'm on the edge before he brings his smiling mouth to my ear. "Fuck you, Renee."

I arch back, head lolling, as an entire universe shifts inside me.

46 | SYATA

At the curb of LAX, he takes my face in his hands, and we kiss again like it's our last day on earth. "I'll see you soon, Renee. It won't be more than two weeks."

I nod, dread collecting in my gut before he's even stepped away because even *two weeks* is an extremely long time at the start of a relationship.

I stand outside his car, waiting for him to drive away. He rolls down the window. "Are you going inside?"

"Are you going to leave?" I ask.

He laughs.

"Yes, I'm going to go inside. You can leave."

"I'll leave when you go inside. I want a last shot of you walking away in my mental library."

I roll my eyes and swallow. "Why does this feel so hard already?"

He grins. "Because it is."

"That doesn't make any logical sense."

"When does this shit ever make logical sense?"

"Shit like a childhood friends-to-lovers situation makes sense. We just met."

He snorts. "We met over a month ago, Renee."

"Semantics." I tip my emotional expression toward the sky. "Okay."

"Okay."

"Drive safe," I tell him.

"Fly safe."

"This is so dumb," I blurt. "Okay, I'm leaving."

"Okay."

I pivot toward the sliding doors of the United terminal.

I only make it a few steps before he catches my arm. I know it's Reed before I turn around. He must have jumped out of the car. He gives a sharp tug, and his mouth is on mine again. Tingly wisps of stardust billow in tiny spirals outward from my heart.

Then he casually lets go. Turns around without catching my eyes and throws up a hand as he walks back to his open car. "See you at the airport, Renee."

47 | NOTIFICATIONS

I land on all fours outside my apartment complex at 12:30 a.m.

My phone dings with a picture thirty seconds later. From Reed. *Us at the wedding with the bride and groom.* The Regent Fallow picture made it to the cloud!

I glance at the sky. "Thank you, genuinely. Thank you for this weekend. I'll never ever forget it."

I heart the picture. It feels too soon to say anything. We need to let that goodbye sit for a second. He's probably not even home yet. He had a thirty-minute drive, and I'm already in New Jersey.

I haven't touched this new phone yet. Not really. There were a shit ton of notifications once I booted it up because I've barely touched technology since Friday night. I have a thousand different messages across a variety of apps to sift through.

I collapse onto the ugly brown couch in my father's apartment.

That was my fifth jump. I have eight left. Four back-and-forth trips. Maybe Reed could come here a few times so I can stretch those across the rest of the year.

I unlock the new phone.

Before I can pull up Gmail, a new notification dings in.

Dad: Wow you made it back fast, you should have told us you had a flight to catch

Not watching the Ring camera, my ass.

Me: Hope you had a nice rest of your night Dad
Dad: Glad you got to meet Enora, she's wonderful. I hope you liked her too.
Me: Yeah she seems really sweet

I tap out of the thread with him and open the text I sent myself from Enora's phone. I save her contact info before shooting her a quick response.

Me: Enora, my father has anger management problems and a history of DV, please be careful.

I have a slew of missed texts from Jordyn. I told her I was flying out to be a plus-one for Reed this weekend. I thumb through the messages. They're all asking for details, updates, if I'm alive, if I'm okay, if I've been murdered, where the fuck am I: *hello Rikki??? Rikki I'm panicked. Answer me Rikki!* I tap on her contact info and call her.

She picks up on the second ring. "Rikki!"

"I'm alive!"

"What is wrong with you? Are you incapable of answering a text with five letters over the course of forty-eight hours? If you didn't get in touch with me by tomorrow morning, I was about to start phoning your entire family and then calling the police."

"Sorry! I got swept up in the moment and then I dropped my phone in the ocean, and it stopped working, I just had to put five hundred dollars down on a new one."

"I'm coming over."

"Don't you have work tomorrow?" I ask.

"Like that matters right now!"

"Doesn't pregnancy make you tired? It's past midnight."

"Pregnancy makes it possible for me to roll into work a little late. Gimme five minutes—I'm gonna make popcorn." She hangs up.

I skim through the rest of my texts. Whitney asking for updates. And multiple from my mom.

MOM [12:25 p.m.]: Sweetheart! Layla and I decided we're moving the wedding date! We think spring will be nicer—switching it to our first-date-aversary EARTH DAY! Next year!
It'll be nice for our anniversaries to line up, don't you think? Can you go through the appointments you've made thus far and update them? I've already talked to the park people!

I flop forward onto my face across the couch cushions. I've already booked flowers, a dog photographer, a regular photographer, a videographer, a caterer, a decorator, four dog trainers, a photo booth, a DJ, and a balloon arch for December 31.

Mom [6:30 p.m.]: What's this? Dad says you have a boyfriend! And you brought him to his house? When do I get to meet him? Wait till Aunt Teresa hears.

I flip through my Google calendar for Earth Day, April 22nd.

Me: Mom, Earth Day is on a Tuesday next year.
Mom: I know, isn't it great? The park is way cheaper.
Me: won't your guests have work?
Mom: it won't start till 3! They can leave early if they want to come.

There's a knock at my door. I open it as I'm pulling open my email. I have something from Maya that came in at 5:30 p.m. on Friday. I tap it open as Jordyn, who's finally starting to look pregnant, throws herself on the couch with her bowl of popcorn.

Oh Rikki. I forgot to shoot this over earlier. After lunch Ted stopped by my office. Said you two had a great talk and pitched an article to cowrite for your column: The 8 cracks that broke my last relationship. Byline being: A story with two sides, as written by both me and my ex. I think it's genius! And yes, not his place to go pitching me things, so maybe you weren't too gung-ho about it but listen—it goes so well with the other pieces you wrote earlier this year. It'll make a great follow up to investigate the opposing point of view. It's nuanced. And I have an extra twist that I think is going to make it even juicier. I want you to take Ted with you to talk to each of those other men you dated during the first half of the year (as many as you can wrangle on short notice)—interview them in person about why it didn't work out. Having him there is going to make them feel more comfortable. More likely to share an honest response. And to be frank it's going to make the inquiry feel official and less like you're looking to date them again.

Ask if you can record them for the podcast. Write down what you think went wrong, and juxtapose it with what they think. I already can't wait to read it. I'd love for this to go live the Sunday after next: It'll be a great piece to show the board during your renegotiation meeting. That gives you till next Monday to get me a draft.

I think this is going to be really good for you. I've seen you and Ted not talking for the last year and a half.

—Maya

"Oh, my god." *Fucking Ted.*

"What?" Jordyn demands.

"Email from Maya."

"Okay, pin in that. First things first: Did you two do the deed?"

I nod diplomatically. "We did it, I kid you not, like, seven times in the last twenty-four hours."

Jordyn screams. "And?"

"Best sex in the history of ever. I can't wrap my head around it. I had to scrape myself off him after. I felt like cheese melted onto a burger."

A cackle flies out of Jordyn. "What?"

"Like you can't get the cheese off once it melts on—it's stuck."

"Don't compare yourself to cheese."

"His hand is like a team of professional fire dancers doing extensive gymnastics in my abdomen."

She throws popcorn at me. "Oh my god."

"And . . . he's my boyfriend."

She screams again.

I'm lying awake in bed at 4:00 a.m., post the adrenaline rush of reliving the weekend with Jordyn, when my phone lights up with an email.

—

SUBJECT: re:re:re:re:re: RE: RE: Re: Been feeling inspired. Had some fun.

Reed Tyler <RTYLER48@gmail.com> August 31

LINK

—

TYLER-ROMONA | MESSAGE IN A BOTTLE

CHAPTER 5

Derek

She's coming. I've never been more jazzed for a wedding in my entire life.

I kick my feet, giggling. And I die a flattered, turned-on, lustful death, reading our time together from his point of view.

I've never been this optimistic about my future. Can someone be so lucky as to have their career and personal life come to a crux at the same time?

Is this really happening? I'm ecstatic and completely terrified at the same time.

September 1—TO DO

- 15 days till the Netflix pitch—get on it
- 8 days till contract renegotiation meeting: practice spiel
- 7 days to draft the breakup article with Ted
- Pilates
- Let the tiling people in at 8:00 a.m.
- Record the pod
- Scold Ted
- Call all the vendors for Mom's wedding and reschedule
- Plan out next week's pod
- Spend at least an hour on the Netflix pitch
- Grocery store
- Interview Ted about his reasons
- Contact Cedric, Rob, Ed, Sal, Neil, Jasper, Bill, and Bruce
- Call Reed

48 | THE AFTERGLOW

Nothing says Happy Monday like sprinting for your eight thirty train in a skirt and kitten heels. The tiling guys my dad scheduled didn't show up till eight fifteen. I briefly debated using the journal to get to work, but it'd be a deplorable waste of a jump that I could utilize to get across the country.

My phone vibrates in my purse as I'm clacking my way aboard New Jersey transit. I yank it out as I flop into a window seat.

Reed: Morning beautiful
Me: Morning R. Tyler slash boyfriend =) why are you always awake?
Reed: couldn't sleep. early run
Me: What a coincidence I just went for a little run myself. It was for the train but it still counts
Reed: time for a second morning shower?
Me: care to pop over and join me?
Reed: *googles flights*
Me: =P
Reed: don't tempt me Renee. If I didn't have a crazy work week ahead I would be all over that
Reed: new phone background who dis

A lock screen screenshot comes through—the picture of me in Reed's trench and sweats from the streaking night with my pinkie in my mouth. I snort.

The WWU group chat starts to ping. I tap it open.

Babe: THEY'VE FINALLY DROPPED THE CAST FOR ELIZABETH ROSS HULU ADAPTATION AND IT'S COMING OUT NEXT MONTH!
Me: AHHHHH! WHAT! WAIT WHY ARE YOU EVEN EXCITED I THOUGHT YOU DIDN'T WANT TO READ IT BECAUSE IT'S NOT FANTASY.
Babe: What?! Woman I read it like two weeks after you did, you wouldn't shut up about it.
Jordyn: UM HAVE YALL LOOKED AT THE CAST LIST YET.
Babe: Only the leads! MATTHEW TRENCH IS PLAYING RYAN!!! This woman I haven't heard of before, Eliza Trainer, is playing Elizabeth!

I stare at the names, heart suddenly pounding behind my face.

Matthew Trench? As in Regent Fallow of Yorlabala?

As in the wedding I was just at?

Eliza? It can't be Eliza as in the lady who got me water?

I frantically tap out of the chat and google the cast list. The first result is a Deadline article.

MATT TRENCH AND UNKNOWN ELIZA TRAINER SCORE LEADS IN MUCH ANTICIPATED BESTSELLER ADAPTATION: ELIZABETH ROSS FALLS FOR RYAN

Hulu is trying a new marketing approach with this drop. Nothing for two years and then an entire promotional campaign a month before release for their new thirteen-episode limited series. We finally have

the cast for our beloved post–World War I romance,
Elizabeth Ross Falls for Ryan.
Drum roll please!
Elizabeth Ross, played by Eliza Trainer
Ryan Edmunson, played by Matt Trench
Vince O'Brien, played by Rome Overland
Selena Diamond, played by Brittany Richards
Raymond Smith, played by Will Murphy

My ears are ringing as I stare at that name on the cast list. *Rome.* The group chat continues to vibrate. I ignore it.

I need to start calling you Rome *so I don't fuck it up on the press tour.*

I scroll down. There are headshots of everyone. Eliza. Matt.

And then Reed.

Reed with his mouth folded into a pout with just a hint of smirk buried behind it. The top of his auburn hair grown out longer.

I scroll down further. There's a poster. Eliza and Matt big, back-to-back in the middle, with Reed smaller along the edges with *Britt* and *Will.* I was literally sitting at the *Elizabeth Ross Falls for Ryan* cast table at the wedding.

I need to breathe. Keep breathing. Breathe.

I told him not to tell me.

I told him not to tell me.

And I forgot to google it.

And I told him not to tell me.

And I don't want to tell him about the articles I'm writing. One called "How I Thought I'd Lose the Guy in Ten Days" is supposed to go live next Sunday, and it's straight up about him.

It would make things weird. This is a good rule. And this *why all my relationships have broken* piece I've been roped into writing *for immediate release* is so, *so* not what I want to be bringing into conversation with my shiny-new relationship with Reed. I don't want anything to mess this up.

This casting is amazing for him. This is a big break. He is about to fucking shoot off into space. He's playing Vince! Ryan's roommate. He's also a World War I vet, and he channels all his PTSD into . . . dance.

He and Elizabeth have a flirtation going, which ends up complicating things with his best friend, Ryan. The love triangle aspect of it is heartbreaking and really well done. They're all just trying to help each other through hard times. Elizabeth is trying to get back to 2019, where she belongs, and all the while she's falling for the new people she's connecting with in 1919.

Rome Overland. His acting name sounds like a sci-fi character. I type Rome Overland into Google and then delete it.

Honor the pact. If you want him to honor it, you have to honor it.

I tap open my thread with Reed and heart the picture of his new background. I update mine as well, opting for the book-cover picture at Santa Monica Pier. I screenshot it and send it to him.

Me: I just saw the news!! You're fucking doing the thing. Proud of you Rome Overland.

I switch my phone to "Do Not Disturb" and drop it in my purse.

My first two hours in the office are spent recording *Love Today* with my producer, who runs our socials. The second we're done, I'm up out of my chair, storming toward Ted's office.

His door's open, so I stride right in and slam it shut behind me. Ted's sitting at his desk, in a white button-up and a skinny light-blue tie, click-clacking away at his desktop. He glances up calmly, blond curls grown out and askew.

I shove my hands onto my hips. "How dare you go to Maya behind my back and pitch a piece?"

He shrugs. "You should be thanking me. She loved it!"

"Yeah, and now I get no say in whether or not we move forward with it!"

"I want to make things better between us, Rick."

"Going behind my back is not the way to *make things better* between us, Ted."

"Going in front of your back, you would never take the time to listen to my side of the story."

I throw my hands up in the air. "Because I don't want to fucking hear it!"

"Well, we're in this now, and Maya thinks it's going to be great."

"Yeah, fantastic, I'm already working three jobs plus wedding planning for my mother. Let's add a week of interviews with eight dudes I dated briefly and my latest ex."

Ted turns back to his computer. "She wants a draft by next Monday morning, so we should get moving as soon as possible." His voice is laced with an infuriating air of enthusiasm. "We should start with our interview. When are you free? Got time during lunch?"

"No. I have to make ten calls, rescheduling shit for my mom's wedding . . . but she wants the interviews to be in person, so we should start organizing today." I press my lips together and close my eyes for a moment, groaning internally. "Okay, I can do after work. You can come over at seven. We'll schedule out the rest of the week, and we can do our interview."

Ted looks up. "Where do you live now?"

"Same building. I'll text you the address."

Ted claps his hands. "Okay, great!"

"Okay, great!" I plaster on a fake smile before throwing up the finger and walking out of his office.

I hate that I'm cleaning my apartment for a meeting with Ted. I'm putting out crackers and Costco spinach artichoke dip as a polite snack for Ted.

I've typed up my reasons for why we broke up in my Word document.

Ted

- Thought I was a freak for hosting a witch book club?

- Couldn't be with someone so fucked up they didn't even talk to their parents

- Too much of a hassle to love

- Teenage level emotional intelligence

- Wanted kids

- Just cute and never hot

He knocks at 7:10 p.m. Ted is always late.

I usher him in and show him to the kitchen table. He eats a cracker as I plop down next to my laptop. Ted sits across from me and pulls out his computer. I put our portable podcast mic on the table and press record.

"Okay, let's get this over with."

Ted rolls his eyes. "Okay," he says in a stupid sarcastic cartoon voice. "'Why do you think we broke up,' I think is a good place to start."

I rebut him with an eye roll of my own. "Well, initially I felt like it came entirely out of the blue. You had this weird tone change one morning. You were talking about having kids, even though I had told you I'm not sure I'm interested in that, and suddenly you wanted four. And then you spewed a whole slew of shit about me being unlovable because of exhibit (a) my relationship with my parents, (b) my book club, and (c) the fact that I'm 'too much.' I think you also threw in a jab about me spending an excessive amount of time working and not enough time giving you both attention and sex." I spin my Word document around and let him read it.

Ted heaves a sigh. "Okay, I have three things written down." He opens his laptop. "The first and biggest one was I felt like you didn't like me—"

I scoff. "I was dating you."

"Yeah, but you'd prioritize so many things ahead of me that I started to look for an excuse to end things because it felt like you were just too busy to end things with me."

"How did I *not like you*?" I demand.

"Well, you would never initiate sex—"

"I barely enjoyed our sex."

Hurt flashes across his face. "What?"

"Our sex was all for you! You never tried to make sure I was enjoying it. Or ask questions, or learn anything about me. What incentive was there to initiate?"

"You never mentioned that."

"Honestly, looking back," I say coolly, "I can't believe I didn't break up with you before you broke up with me. Maybe because we worked together, I wanted to keep trying. It seemed like it could be easy. Should be easy? Or convenient. But it wasn't. We're really different."

He lowers his brow. "So are you admitting right now that I was right and you didn't actually even like me?"

"I wanted to like you more than I actually did. But that doesn't excuse all the terrible shit you said to me."

He throws a hand out and lets it fall. "I'm sorry about all that shit."

It takes everything in me not to roll my entire body in response.

"I was insecure about my place in the company," he says. "You had a real job at *The Minute*, and I was working on freelance pieces and—I don't know. I was feeling emasculated. And in my defense, you clearly had this weird, heavy relationship with your parents, and you never told me anything about it. Like not one detail other than 'it's complicated,' and then I'm supposed to understand why you ignore one of them constantly and only periodically talk to the other?"

"You *wouldn't* understand. You have a perfect family life."

"You didn't even try me, Rikki. I threw all that shit at you to break this off because resentment was building, and I was stupid and didn't know what else to do! After five months I kind of still barely knew you.

Like . . . I couldn't believe you would kick me out on weekends when you had your meetings with your precious WWU."

I gawk at him. "You didn't live with me, Ted. I was allowed to kick you out."

"Yeah, but you didn't ever let me meet your friends except for Jordyn, and that's just because you lived with her. And even then, we never all hung out. I never got to meet your witch friends. I never really got to know Jordyn and Micah. You can't do that when you want to actually be someone's partner."

"You didn't actually want to be my partner!"

He slams a hand down on the tabletop. "Yes, I did, Rikki!"

I scoot back an inch. One of the things I was initially attracted to about Ted was how calm he always was. Level. He never really got mad. It felt safe at the time.

"Sorry. I didn't mean to yell. I—I tried my best, and obviously that wasn't good enough. I didn't know how to communicate with you. I was stupid, but you barely wanted to be with me and strung me along for months like a toy boyfriend who you'd take out of the box from time to time when you felt like it for specific dates and activities."

A sarcastic huff escapes my lips. "O-kay, Ted." I turn off the recorder and exhale. "That should be enough. Let's start going through these dudes I briefly went out with and get them on our schedule."

One at a time I open the contact files in my phone for the Hinge men I dated earlier this year and punch the call button. When they pick up, I put on my best corporate girlie voice and propose an anonymous in-person interview for *The Minute's* Love Today. I tell them the topic is an exposé on why we stopped dating. Around this point Ted interjects, informing them that he, too, is someone I stopped dating, and he will be joining us as a neutralizing party to help the interview along.

Eventually we figure out a day that works for the majority of them (a couple couldn't make it, or didn't pick up) and schedule the lot who are available back-to-back for this coming Sunday at my apartment.

September 7. Interview Schedule
9:00 a.m.—interview with Bruce
10:00 a.m.—interview with Sal
11:00 a.m.—interview with Ed
12:00 p.m.—lunch break
1:00 p.m.—interview with Cedric
2:00 p.m.—interview with Rob
3:00 p.m.—interview with Neil
4:00 p.m. to 9:00 p.m.—draft the article

I text the WWU and let them know we're going to have to reschedule this Sunday's meeting so I can write the first draft with Ted.

It's going to be a long fucking day.

It's 8:40 p.m. when I finally hop onto my bed and reopen my earlier message thread with Reed.

Me [8:46 a.m.]: Proud of you Rome Overland.
Reed [9:00 a.m.]: thank you <3 it was torturous keeping it from you this weekend.

I smile at his response before shooting off a new text.

Me: any chance you're near a bed?
Reed: Two minutes

49 | LONG DISTANCE

MONDAY

"Rome Overland—it's giving sci-fi character."

His laugh rumbles on the other end of the line. "We can't all have names as highbrow as Rose Thyme."

I'm curled up on my bed in pajamas with a cup of tea on the bedside table. I giggle, snuggling into my blankets. "Excuse me, while simple and food-adjacent, Rose Thyme is both unique and sophisticated."

"How'd your day go, gorgeous?"

I *pffi* over the line. "I don't think I can handle you casually calling me gorgeous."

"I'm your boyfriend, I'm not allowed to call you gorgeous?" I can hear the smile in his voice.

"It sounds like hyperbole. Like you're being slick, just to get me into bed."

He laughs again. "You've got to be kidding me, Rikki. Get the fuck over yourself. I've already gotten you into bed. Multiple times."

"Never in *your bed*."

"I hope to soon."

I bite back my smile as that statement zings through me. A slight ache wanes across my chest. *When will that be?*

"What if I called you gorgeous?" I pose.

"I'd be flattered."

"Well, you are."

"Well, I'm fucking flattered, thank you. I'm blushing—see how easy that is?"

I roll my eyes, still smiling. "How was your day, Rome? Insane, I'm betting?"

"How was *your* day, Rose? I bet it was insane as well."

"Why would my day be insane?"

"Because you're a superstar that works a million jobs and kills them all every day."

I snort. "My day's been a lot, but it wasn't anything special like yours. Tell me about your launch into society. This is amazing! I can't believe you're playing Vince in the *Elizabeth Ross* adaptation! Your dreams are *coming true* as we speak."

He laughs. "It's been a wild day, and I'm very grateful for the positive response we've all been getting."

I beam at my ceiling, thinking of the conversation during our first date while he was helping me unlace the corset. I'm overjoyed, listening as he gives me a play-by-play of his day full of press interviews in a Four Seasons down in Beverly Hills.

Once his stories wrap, we devolve into random nonsense banter. Talking about our childhood screen names. Our favorite board games. Cartoons. Movies we used to rewatch a thousand times. Me: *The Dark Knight Rises*. Him: *When Harry Met Sally*.

He tells me he'll be traveling to Europe on Wednesday for more show promotional interviews and videos overseas. They have him scheduled for two weeks of nonstop marketing gigs before he gets a four-day break.

I sigh as we hang up, already missing him more than I did before the phone call. His upcoming month of launch promo and all its subsequent travel is about to make this relationship even more complicated.

TUESDAY

Reed [5:03 p.m.]: Hope the day went well, gorgeous. Mine was jam packed and now I'm in the car with Eliza and Matt on the way to the airport. We're heading to France first and then London. Can I call you? =P

Me [5:05 p.m.]: Really, we're sticking with gorgeous? That's amazing! Travel safe! I'm cooking dinner so I'm not on a mattress either. We'll talk next time we're both feat. bed? =P Can't wait to hear about all your adventures! Miss your 1860s face.

Reed [5:10 p.m.]: Missing that before-Christ complexion. The second my ass hits a mattress I'm FaceTiming you.

WEDNESDAY

Me [6:33 p.m.]: thinking of you!! hope all's going well in France!

Reed [6:35 p.m.]: been thinking out loud about you all day

Me [6:37 p.m.]: Is that an Ed Sheeran pun XD

Reed [6:38 p.m.]: it's accurate ;) I have to be up at five for a shoot, so I'm about to go to sleep. Everything's going well, just super chaotic. How are you? How was work?

Me [6:40 p.m.]: I'm good! don't let me keep you up! I know you have a crazy schedule. I'll talk to you tomorrow. Night R. Tyler!

Reed [6:41 p.m.]: The schedule they have set for us tomorrow is insane too, so if by chance I miss you with the time difference, I will most definitely talk to you on Friday <3 How's your schedule for the weekend looking?

Me [6:42 p.m.]: I'm around Friday night and Saturday. Sunday will be a little busy, but we can catch up in the evening!

THURSDAY

Mom [3:00 p.m.]: HONEY! what do you think about Vegas for the bachelorette? Do you have a theme in mind? You, me, Aunt Teresa and Whitney? Maybe we can get concert tickets! Can you design us matching shirts? With the kind of doodles you do on your Etsy shop? That would be so cute! Let me know when we can have a planning meeting!

Me [3:14 p.m.]: Hey Mom, I have a session with Whitney and Glenn at 6:30 my time. I'll call you after that.

It's only 9 p.m., but Reed's already asleep in France. I've been debating using the journal all day. I know what hotel he's in.

But he's working. And I have work. And a jump that far would constitute a sizable task both ways. And take a significant toll on my body.

And he's asleep. What would I do when he woke? Follow him around like a groupie through his interview circuit? Would we even have time together? And how would I explain myself? I just dropped, what, a thousand dollars on a Thursday evening to maybe hang out with him halfway across the world while he's working? One week into our relationship?

FRIDAY

I cry on the train home. I stare unseeing out the window as tears well over, down my cheeks. I barely know why. Because I haven't spoken to Reed since Wednesday?

Because I'm growing increasingly anxious about this weekend's ex-interview-pocalypse?

I have no idea how that's going to go. All these men gradually stopped speaking to me after I told them I work for Love Today. Will they apologize? Seeing them again is going to be incredibly uncomfortable, and all these confrontations are going to take place in front of fucking Ted.

Ted thought I didn't even like him.

I liked Ted. Didn't I? He was nice. He was attractive. We had similar interests. I made him laugh. He made me feel . . . wanted.

But being with him was constant work with very little payoff. I spent all my spare time planning dates. Organizing quality time. Trying to get him to commit to a schedule. I was living off love kernels. Tiny things he would say that somehow proved that he cared about me and I should continue trying to make it work.

The way Ted frames our story is so skewed. He *says* he wanted to be with me, but his actions never reflected that. He never tried to enjoy things I was passionate about like I tried to enjoy soccer. I watched every game with him, and the man wouldn't read one book with me. Wouldn't even listen to me gush about them after I finished one. *Babe, I didn't read it because I wasn't interested in it. That hasn't changed.* Why the fuck would I invite him to meet my book club after that?

I feel like I got more from Reed in two dates than I did my entire relationship with Ted. Everything decent Ted ever did was me directing him to be kind. To return the care and consideration I was doling out constantly.

He didn't yell at me. He didn't hit me. He didn't break my stuff. He didn't threaten me. He would cook with me when I asked. He was the bare minimum.

Did I string him along like a toy? Not consciously. But I never had strong feelings. I never felt like I feel right now about Reed.

When I think about how much I like Reed, I feel like I'm folding in on myself. I picture my body shrinking into a dense marble lost in a heap of clothes on my seat as I clutch my legs to my chest, watching the darkness rush by.

He lives thousands of miles away. I have my eight jumps left on the journal, but what happens after that? How will this ever work?

What if we never puzzle out how to be short distance? I already have such big feelings for him, and it's all happened so fast.

My twenties lasted a hundred years, but a month into thirty, and I feel like I'm hurtling toward old age. How long will it be before we can be a *sees each other casually throughout the week* couple?

I want to be with someone I can come home to. That I can smile at from the stove while I'm cooking. That I can pore over a recipe with. That I can read next to in bed at night.

I want what he said *he wanted.* To go to bed at this same time, together. I want to rearrange my schedule for someone and make that a reality.

And there's a very high probability that we'll never get to that point.

What if I never find someone I like this much who I can actually *be* with?

It was a new sort of strange back in July at Whitney's wedding, noticing that my aunts and uncles had aged. It happened in the blink of an eye. For so many years they all looked the same: Frozen in middle age as all of us youths rapidly morphed from kids to teens to young adults. Now my cousins are popping out kids. Those aunts and uncles are grandparents. They're all building out separate new families that I'm not a part of.

Whitney's married. My mom's getting remarried. Micah and Jordyn are gonna have a baby. They're probably going to move to a house soon after that.

I'm quickly becoming a party of one.

Everyone's moving forward, and I'm at the starting line, incessantly revving my engine, getting absolutely nowhere.

I want to build a life with someone before I've crossed over into grandparent age. I want the option of starting a family with someone if I ever decide I want to. I want the stupid traditional things that I've been ingrained to believe are a guarantee, and I might never get them.

I'm having a mild panic attack against the train window.

I close my eyes and slow my breathing. Counting as I inhale and exhale.

Jordyn holds a fork in the air over her empty plate like a teacher's pointer. She jabs it in my general direction. "I think that's just what being in a long-distance relationship is."

"What do you mean?"

We just finished having dinner together. Micah's on the couch, working, but Jordyn and I have lingered at the table.

"I think a known side effect of being in a long-distance relationship is living on an emotional precipice in a perpetual state of existential crisis and second-guessing all your life decisions. Crying on trains, planes . . . automobiles."

"I'm sorry, what?" I say flatly.

"Long-distance relationships drive people insane."

"Jordyn, you encouraged me to get into this long-distance relationship."

"Yeah, and you're wildly happy now that you did."

"And apparently wildly unstable," I yelp.

She lifts a shoulder and drops it. "The lows are worth it for the highs. And I have faith you'll figure it out."

"I'm five days in, and I've already had an existential breakdown."

"Long-distance love is like a muscle, though. You have to build it up. Gradually you'll get better at it. It won't be as hard once you've developed tricks and tips and all that shit. You need to learn how to be together when you're not together."

"I've never ever heard anyone I know who's actually been in a long-distance relationship say something even vaguely to that effect."

She nods. "Yeah, I made it up just now, but I think it's true."

I frame my empty plate with my elbows, pressing my fingers into my temples, tears pricking at my eyes again.

Feedback?

I stare at the blank space in the journal for five minutes before twisting on the pen.

Why did you seek me out if this relationship is doomed

to blow up in my face? Is it? Is it going to work out? Eight jumps is only four trips. Are you helping me find a happy ending, or are you teaching me some other hard earned lesson that I've yet to understand?

I am so tired of not having a mutual number one. Do you ever think about things like that? Like if you were dangling over the edge of a building, and someone else that your number one knows was also dangling, and they could only save one of you, you know they'd always choose you, no questions asked. And you'd always choose them. That's a number one. And there's nothing in the world like the bond between mutual number ones. I don't care how stupid that sounds. It's true. The loyalty. The safety you feel with them. It's rare. And precious. And I miss it with every fiber of my fucking soul.

Jordyn was mine until she and Micah got married. And I was Whitney's before Glenn came along.

It takes a lot of reframing to accept that being a single adult with all married friends means by default you're never anyone's first priority. But a lot of people are yours. And we just have to be okay with it. And I try really hard to be.

I love my freedom. But then there are days like this where I feel like I'm falling without a safety net, and there's no one to catch me. I just tumble through the darkness until I regain the strength to pull myself out.

Reed said he wants to take care of me. I want to do that for him, and I want to learn to let him do that for me. But how can I? How can he? How can I be there for him when I can't be there for him? How can we be each other's number ones without destroying the careers we've been busting our asses to build over the last decade? Every day that we continue to live on different coasts, we choose work over each other.

Why is it like this? Why do these two areas of life always present as warring parties? How do you choose both?

I heave in a breath and flip the page.

<3

I snort.

Wow that's the nicest thing you've ever said to me.

Flip.

No, I think you miss understood, that was a manipulative heart.

A maniacal cackle bubbles up from my throat.

Did we just become best friends?

Flip.

Don't get too excited. If you're dangling off the edge of a building the best I can do is appear on the ledge.

Me [7:30 p.m.]: Can we nail down a day on the calendar when we'll for sure be able to see each other? =) The control freak in me is losing her mind. Maybe we could make that a rule? Before we say IRL goodbye we put a date on the calendar for the next IRL hello?

Reed [7:38 p.m.]: Big yes to etching that law into our constitution. I had a conversation with my agent earlier—I'll be solidly back in LA Saturday, September 14. There's a beginner West Coast swing class on Saturdays. Do you think you could maybe make it out for that weekend?
Me [7:40 p.m.]: It's a date!!!
Reed [7:40 p.m.]: Any chance you're on a bed?

"Do you think doing long distance is basically synonymous with voluntarily living on an emotionally unstable precipice at all times?" I wasn't planning to bring this up. I told myself not to. But here we are. "How do we be each other's rocks," I continue, "if we're not physically in each other's orbits, to ground each other?"

Reed takes a deep breath on the line. "I think when we're not close physically, we have to make ourselves more available emotionally."

"You sound like an LMFT."

"You sound like a layman," he says playfully.

I laugh, well aware. "When it comes to my own life, I have trouble thinking like a therapist. I'm too close to it."

"That makes sense."

"Is there any part of you that regrets making this something real?" I say quietly.

"Are *you* regretting it?" he says carefully.

"I guess I'm just feeling like you're spreading your wings, setting flight for your big pie-in-the-sky dream life and . . . I don't want to hold you back."

"Renee, I have another big pie-in-the-sky goal that I didn't share with you that night 'cause it's cheesy and embarrassing."

"You, the theater kid who loves Ed Sheeran, harboring a cheesy, embarrassing dream? Do tell."

He looses a quiet laugh. "To fall in love with my soulmate. Build a life together. Share our successes and failures. Maybe get a dog."

I'm quiet for a moment. "I like that one."

"I don't regret it."

I clear my throat. "If you want, we could revert back to Pact Level One: dating while we're in the same state, friends when we're not."

"But alas. I do not want." I can sense him smiling into the phone.

I chortle. "Okay. Good. I don't regret it either."

"Good. Romona?"

"Reed."

"I feel really lucky to have met you."

"Likewise."

50 | INTERVIEW-POCALYPSE

Ted shows up at my apartment at 8:00 a.m. to help me set up. He brings me a bagel and a coffee as a peace offering. He's still never apologized for pitching this article behind my back, but I guess I appreciate the gesture.

My father's kitchen is doubling as our makeshift studio. I set up mics as Ted organizes our notes and laptops, getting everything plugged in and sorted. I'm dreading editing whatever this audio becomes. There's no way these men are going to remember to refer to me as Rose Thyme. It's going to require a lot of clever chopping, and I don't trust our in-house editor with this personal a topic.

At 9:00 a.m. my first pseudo-ex, Bruce, of five-dates fame, arrives at the apartment. I let Ted get the door and usher him in.

Bruce's an attractive medium-height guy with brown skin and dark, slicked-back hair. My stomach knots up as he walks toward our setup.

I hate this. I hate everything about this.

I press record on the mics, heave in a hefty breath, and exhale. Bruce was the first guy I dated this year. It was during date four that I told him about my job at Love Today. He got so frazzled. Then he started taking twelve-plus hours to respond to texts. I scheduled us for a fifth date to feel out what the fuck was going on. The fifth date was incredibly awkward. He wouldn't make any conversation. I threw questions at him like the Riddler all night, and he answered with one-to-four-word sentences. Neither of us texted each other after that.

I jotted little breakup recaps down for Ted next to every dude's name in my notebook. He's glancing at it now as Bruce gets settled in the hot seat (the chair across the table from us).

Ted puts down the notebook. "Thanks for doing this, Bruce. It should only take about twenty minutes."

Bruce glances at me, and I give him a small nod.

"So, we just want you to be totally honest today," Ted says. "Don't worry about hurting any feelings."

I put my hands up in surrender. "Yeah, I'm good. Speak your truth."

This is such an invasion of my privacy. But my contract renegotiation is tomorrow afternoon. This is not the time to look like I'm not a team player. If having this on deck impresses the higher-ups, like Maya thinks it will, it can only work in my favor.

Bruce fixes his gaze on Ted. "Well, she straight-up lied to me for four weeks, and I didn't want to date a liar."

A *pfft* of disdain flies out of me. Bruce's eyes dart to mine.

"Lied to you?" I blurt. "What are you talking about?"

"You told me you made greeting cards for a living."

My mouth flops open. "I *do* make greeting cards."

Bruce shakes his head. "You have an Etsy shop that you fulfill once a week. Four weeks into dating, you drop that you're the Love Today columnist at the biggest paper in the tristate area and their podcast host? It made me feel like our entire month of dating was a story device. Like you were seeing me so you could talk about it on your various outlets. You're not a greeting card writer, *Rose Thyme*."

An offended noise scrapes up my throat. "I do write greeting cards!"

Ted shoots me a look. "Let him *speak his truth*."

"I'm letting him. I'm just clarifying that I do make greeting cards every week. It's a side hustle, but it's real."

"Rikki, I train dogs. It's my main grind, but I also teach kids about the Bible once a week on Sundays. If I told you I was a Bible studies professor, that would be a lie."

My brows pull together. "I didn't say I had a doctorate in greeting cards!"

Bruce rolls his eyes and shifts toward Ted. "Anyway, that's what turned me off. I felt used."

"If I would have told you from the get-go that I wrote about relationships, you wouldn't have even responded to my Hinge message!"

"We'll never know, because you didn't."

I bulge my eyes at him. "I do know because it happened many, *many* times."

"So Sal, you and Rikki went on five dates together. It seemed to be going all right, and then out of the blue, you ghosted? Tell us what happened."

"On our first date, she told me she had a dog at home with separation anxiety and that she might have to leave early. I spent five minutes asking her questions about him, and she answered them all quickly before changing the subject."

I drop my head in my hand.

"Fast-forward to five dates later, I come to pick her up at her apartment—by the way, she wouldn't tell me where she lived until that point. I got there all excited, looking for the damn dog she hadn't mentioned in two weeks, and there was no dog living in that apartment."

I sigh, already feeling exhausted. "Sal, I just said that on our first date to give myself an out if it was bad."

Sal throws up his palm and lets it flutter to the table. "I love dogs, Rikki. I was so thrilled I had met a fellow single dog parent! Why would you make up an animal? That's fucked up. Just get a fake phone call or say you have to leave like a normal person."

"Rikki told me she owned a little greeting card shop," Ed says flatly as he stares at me.

Ted cuts me a surprised look, and I roll my eyes, leaning back in my chair.

"And on our fifth date," Ed continues, "she divulged she was actually a relationship writer and wrote a column in *The Minute* about her dating experiences under a pseudonym. I asked her if she had talked about our dates. She said *yes*. I felt violated, you know? Like I thought I was getting to know this woman in private, but she'd been filming me the whole time, you know?"

Ted nods like he does know. I swallow back a groan.

"So, question," Ted says. "If you had known this from the start about her job, would it have been different?"

Ed widens his eyes. "Of course."

"Ofcoursemyass," I mumble.

Ed's gaze flits to mine. "I'm sorry, what?"

Ted turns to me as well. "Yeah, Rikki, what? You mumbled a little bit over there."

Cedric shrugs. "Well, she lied about what she does for a living for an entire month, man. It was wild. She said she had a greeting card shop."

Ted starts laughing.

Rob shakes his head. "Date one she told me she was a relationship therapist, and then on date four, she said she technically doesn't practice and didn't have *any* patients. She apparently works for *The Minute*."

"I do, but I am also a licensed relationship therapist."

"Who doesn't practice."

"That doesn't make it not true."

Rob ignores me, talking only to Ted. "And she revealed this new tidbit like she was unveiling a government secret. Like she was in the CIA or the Witness Protection Program or something. Like lying about her job wasn't an insane thing to do, but like, a sacrifice she made for the greater good."

Dad [2:01 p.m.]: What in the hell is going on over there why are there so many guys coming and leaving the apartment?
Dad [2:18 p.m.]: Hello? Answer me.
Dad [2:20 p.m.]: So help me god Rikki, you tell me what's going on right now.
Dad [2:25 p.m.]: HELLLOOO??!

I throw my phone down on the table, switch it back to "Do Not Disturb." "I texted Neil not to come."

"Why?" Ted says cheerily. "Let's just see this through."

I glare at him, tilting backward in my chair at a precarious angle while my insides churn in a pit of undiluted rage. "Because we don't need to, Ted. It's not interesting anymore. It's repetitive."

"It's almost quarter to three—it's rude to cancel on him now."

"Well, maybe he'll miss the text and show up anyway, and you'll get to revel some more in this little game you're enjoying so much: *Shit the fuck all over Rikki.*" I let the chair slam back to the floor.

"It's actually hilarious. You thought everyone didn't want you to write about them, when in reality they thought you were an unhinged con artist."

"I don't want to talk about this with you. There's obviously more to it than what they're saying."

Ted laughs. "We have to talk about this! That's the assignment. That's why I'm here!" He flops onto my dad's couch with his open laptop. "I'm sending you a Google doc with the transcripts so far and notes I've been taking as we go," he says. "I'm thinking, you open on how your longest relationship ended a year and five months ago, and six short dating escapades this year all ended within five dates. You thought they ended because of *a*, *b*, and *c*—"

"Ted, I know how to do my job. I'm actually pretty good at it," I snap as I open my laptop and click the link to his fucking Google doc.

This piece we're doing feels *wildly* one sided. We haven't talked to *any* of Ted's recent relationship failures. As far as I know, he's single. How have we managed to avoid that discussion?

Out of the corner of my eye, I watch Ted close his computer. He leans forward on the couch, resting his elbows on his knees. "Rikki, I know you're good at your job. Believe it or not, I am too. And I still really care about you. And I don't know, I think we kinda work well together." He shrugs innocently. "Maybe after this we could try again with all the new information we've learned about each other."

I slam my laptop closed and blink at him before standing abruptly. "Are you kidding me right now, Ted? I can't even fucking tell." I hightail it to the bathroom and lock the door.

I glare at myself in the mirror, willing the tsunami of emotions rising in my chest to recede. Pressure mounts behind my eyes, in my chest, at the top of my throat. I feel like an overinflated balloon.

This is too much. I should have said no to Maya. *Even with the renegotiation meeting coming up, this isn't worth it.*

I startle as the doorbell goes off and glance at my watch.

3 p.m. Neil still came. Fucking *great.*

I hear Ted get the door.

I slap my cheeks in the mirror.

Pull it together. One more. You can handle one more.

Neil is the most recent of my date-scapades; the scientist I was banking on bringing to Whitney's wedding. We stopped seeing each other because he told me he was moving to Washington DC.

Can't wait to discuss that.

I exhale a gust of anxiety and head back into the living room. Someone with white hair is standing in the doorway. Neil had curly dark hair. Ted's body is blocking the majority of the guy as he chats with them. I maneuver closer to see around his curly blond head.

It's a guy dressed . . . as the Witcher. That video game character Henry Cavill plays in the Netflix show. My eyes pop out of my skull as the newcomer's gaze slices to mine. No, not Neil. It's Reed.

FIFTH ENCOUNTER

51 | I SEE FIRE

My mouth moves to say his name, and nothing comes out. Fear clutches at my throat like a vise. He's looking at me like . . . I stabbed him in the face. *Why is he looking at me like that?*

"I'm here for book club. Did I get the wrong address?" Reed's voice comes out flat, like he's being strangled. *Oh god.*

Ted nods. "She canceled this week because we're on deadline for a Love Today piece about our relationship."

Reed's eyes slide back to me. I watch as they glaze over. Shut down. Go dark.

My vocal cords are held momentarily hostage as the crux of *Broken and Bruised* streams in HD across my mind.

"Your relationship?" Reed asks, monotone.

"About how it ended!" I blurt. "How our relationship *ended*!"

He blinks. "You're doing a piece for Love Today with your ex-boyfriend? In your apartment on a Sunday afternoon?"

"No, he also writes at *The Minute*. It's a long story—we haven't talked in like, a year, but I ran into him last Friday and—"

Reed shakes his head, blinking rapidly. He pivots and disappears from the doorway.

"Reed! Where are you going?" I breeze by Ted, into the hallway. "Please come back!"

He's already halfway to the elevator.

"Wait! We're just working, Reed!" I catch his arm, and he flinches away. "Reed. I'm so happy you're here. I can't believe you're here! You look amazing. This is perfect for WWU. I—I can get Jordyn over here. We can have a makeshift book club. I rescheduled because we had a draft due but, but I'll kick Ted out—"

Reed's expression smooths into an emotionless slate. "You work with your ex?" He won't look directly at me. The small shift makes me feel invisible.

"I—I work adjacent to him."

"You didn't think that was relevant to mention in passing in any one of our conversations? Even after I shoveled out all my shit about my ex-fiancée?"

"We don't work *together* together," I babble. "We're only doing this one piece. We barely even see each other."

"How long have you been working on this piece?"

"Just this week!"

"This week?" He blinks at a spot to the left of my face. "And you didn't mention it at all? We've talked almost every day."

"I didn't because—church and state!" I bleat. "It's in our contract! Just like you didn't tell me about *Elizabeth Ross*."

His eyes are steel-blue doors bolted shut. "I was under an NDA for *Elizabeth Ross*, Rikki. I had an actual contract. I couldn't wait to tell you. When you sent that text recommending the book back in July, my heart fucking stopped."

"I'm not with him!" I wave my arms around like a crazed bird. "I'm not the barest bit with him or interested. I'm so uninterested! He went behind my back and convinced my boss that I needed to do this piece, and she wants it on her desk by tomorrow!"

He finally meets my eyes. His expression is hard and pleading like I'm a stranger trying to mug him on the street.

I hold his gaze, willing it to soften. "Reed. Please come back to the apartment with me. Ted is going to leave."

He is a drop-dead gorgeous Witcher. It hurts, how gorgeous he looks. *This is the sweetest thing.*

"I need a second." He turns, continuing toward the elevator.

"Okay, and you'll come back?" When he doesn't respond, my throat goes dry. "Reed, you're gonna come back, right? We have to talk this through."

He taps the down button, and the elevator doors slide open. I sprint the last few steps to slip into the car next to him before the doors rumble closed. He keeps his eyes fixed straight ahead.

"Reed. Please just tell me you'll come back."

He doesn't respond.

"I'm going to give you a second. Just tell me we'll be able to talk after?" I say quietly.

The elevator dings again. We're at the lobby. Reed silently steps out and starts toward the street.

"Reed, this is ridiculous. You just got here, and there's nothing happening, and I'm so happy to see you! I'm so confused!"

He pivots, his hardened gaze falling somewhere to the right of my face. "Can you step into my perspective for a second?"

I mash my lips together. "Okay?"

"Today I got on a plane, and I flew across the Atlantic Ocean to surprise my girlfriend and join her for her *favorite part of the week*. I spent the plane ride trying to speed finish *Throne of Glass* on my Kindle so I'd at least have basic knowledge of the characters at play. I landed, changed into my full Witcher cosplay, and hopped in a car. I texted my girlfriend—three times in the past thirty minutes—she didn't respond."

"Oh my god. I didn't see—" My voice cracks.

"I went up to her apartment and rang the bell only to find another guy there answering the door. We texted yesterday. She said nothing about a guy coming over on Sunday or a change of plans or an article she was working on.

"This guy who answered the door is about thirty. He's not her dad—I've met him. I thought the book club was four women, but maybe this guy's in the book club. But there are no women to be seen in the living room, and this guy's dressed in jeans and a blue T-shirt. The apartment doesn't seem to be decorated for WWU.

"The guy certainly doesn't seem to have any inkling of who I might be, so I have to assume Rikki hasn't told him she's in a relationship.

"Then Rikki walks into the room. I'm simultaneously relieved and gutted. She's wearing a white shirt and jeans. Not the getup she so excitedly described to me. And she doesn't look happy."

"I *am* happy—"

"I'm still dressed up in the doorway in full Witcher cosplay. I bought the hard copy of *Throne of Glass* at an indie shop I found five blocks from here. The man in her apartment says she and he are working together on a piece about their *relationship*. Rikki just stands there, doesn't introduce me, doesn't try to explain anything further. I am a sad fucking jackass from every angle.

"She hasn't deemed me worthy of one drop of actual information about her week. I babbled on and on about the shit I've been doing every day, and she reacted and shared selfies but really said nothing of note about her day-to-day. She didn't elaborate that she had an irritating writing piece she was roped into doing. Didn't vent that she had to cancel book club. Didn't *really* share anything. And in actuality she was hanging out with her ex?" He bounces his glassy eyes to mine for a millisecond before returning them to the spot above my head. "Does that all check out with you? Is that sound?"

I blink at him, a numbness crawling up my legs as he stands there, waiting for me to respond. "Reed—I didn't do anything wrong. It was work."

He nods once, lips pressed into a flat line, accentuating the hard angles of his face. "Yeah, I guess I'm fucking delusional." He reaches into his bag and pulls out a book. "I don't want to keep this."

He holds a jacketless hardcover out like he's going to throw it to me. Instinctively I put out my hands, and he softballs it. I catch the book as he shoves open the door to the street.

◆ ◆ ◆

"Who was that? Another guy you're dating? Does he work in Times Square?" Ted laughs from the couch as I stumble back into the apartment and drop the book on the kitchen counter.

"You need to get the fuck out of my apartment, Ted."

"Another breakup?"

"We didn't break up. We're just having a disagreement. He's taking a second, and he'll be back, and you have to leave."

"What about the article?"

I throw my hands up. "I can write the article myself. I have your notes, I have your quotes. I'm good, Ted. Bye."

Ted puts his laptop in his bag and stands awkwardly near the door. "You sure you don't want to talk about it? It could be good for the piece."

"Get the fuck out, Ted!"

He puts his hands up. "Jesus, okay." He rolls his eyes, pulls open the door, and strides out. I lock it behind him, snatch my phone off the coffee table, beeline for the bedroom, and throw myself onto the mattress. I flip off "Do Not Disturb," and the phone floods with notifications. Four missed calls from my dad. Five more missed texts from my dad. I tap open the thread.

Dad [3:03 p.m.]: ANOTHER ONE, WHAT THE HELL IS HE WEARING
Dad [3:17 p.m.]: WHAT'S GOING ON OVER THERE RIKKI!
Dad [3:19 p.m.]: PICK UP THE GODDAMN PHONE
Dad [3:23 p.m.]: THE BLATANT DISRESPECT FOR YOUR FATHER IS DEAFENING
Dad [3:24 p.m.]: ??!!!!

The phone starts ringing in my hand. My fingers tighten around the screen.

Dad.

Anger, untamed and seething, scorches down my spine.

I leap off the bed, a woman possessed as I stride into the living room and toss open the coat closet I never use. There's a yellow toolbox up on the shelf. A replica of the one we had in our house when I was growing up. I tug it down, open the cold metal top, grab the hammer, fling open the door, and swing. And swing. And swing again. "Fuck this fucking camera, you fucking liar!"

Twenty seconds later the thing hangs in pieces off its mount.

A door flies open down the hall. "Rikki?"

"I'm fine, Micah!" I yell.

He closes the door.

I slam mine and lock it. Lean against it, breathing hard. "Fuck."

I pull up Chrome and get the number for a locksmith. I call and book a time slot before pulling open my text thread with Reed.

Reed [2:37 p.m.]: Getting ready for the WWU?

Reed [2:44 p.m.]: I think there's a new guy coming to join today.

Reed [2:50 p.m.]: made a pit stop on my way back to LA

Me [3:49 p.m.]: Reed! Where are you? How are you doing? When's your flight to LA? Can I meet you somewhere?

Me [3:50 p.m.]: I'm so sorry I had my phone on do not disturb because we were doing interviews! I didn't see these!

Me [3:55 p.m.]: Please please please come back. Please let's talk this through.

Me [4:00 p.m.]: I know that must have activated some really bad memories and emotions and I'm so sorry! But this isn't that! Ted is just some asshole who also works at the Minute.

Mom [5:45 p.m.]: Hon, you still have that big renegotiation thing tomorrow? I tried to call you but I guess you're working. I wanted to wish you good luck!

And also run some more ideas about the bachelorette by you! What do you think of pop girlie theme? We could try to get

tickets to Chappell Roan! She's probably not in Vegas but we could just create the party around where she's playing!
Mom [5:46 p.m.]: I guess I'll talk to you tomorrow, let me know how it goes! Layla says good luck too!

Jordyn [6:30 p.m.]: Should I come over? Micah says you destroyed the Ring camera?
Me [6:31 p.m.]: I just want to be alone right now but thanks. I'll fill you in tomorrow.

Micah [6:31 p.m.]: Meeting's at noon tomorrow, correct?
Me [6:33 p.m.]: Yep
Micah [6:34 p.m.]: GO GET'EM

It's midnight, and I'm on my side, puffy, and dehydrated when I remember Reed's book.

I push myself up for the first time in hours and hop off the bed to the kitchen. Reed's hard copy of *Throne of Glass* is on the table, abandoned in the sensory overload that was this afternoon.

I bring it back to my room and open the cover.

> 9/7/2024
> Little City Books, Hoboken NJ
> I'm taking a leap today. Surprising the woman I'm seeing by showing up at her apartment unannounced to join her book club.
> She's dropped in on me unannounced a couple of times

now, and I think it's high time I return the favor.

I haven't felt like this since I was 16.

My 16-year-old relationship was built on shared experiences and firsts.

This is more. It's based off a shared understanding of each other.

Shared passions. Flaws. Humor. Life goals. Ambitions. Attraction.

We slot together like we were built to collide.

She's invaded my every thought and dream this past week.

I've been really intentional about opening up. Letting her know me.

And I think for once I'm doing an okay job with it.

She doesn't think we're going to see each other till the 14th.

Thought it'd be more fun this way. X

September 8—TO DO

- 8 days till the Netflix pitch (all I've done is write out character profiles)
- 0 days till my Love Today contract renegotiation meeting (fml)
- Record the pod
- Get new salary sorted
- Get ahold of Reed

52 | DISTRACTED

This sex therapist could moonlight as a stand-up comic.

Lucky for me because I haven't managed to focus on our conversation for more than thirty seconds at a time. She barely needs my prompts to keep the discussion going.

I didn't draft the article last night. I emailed Maya and told her I'm going to need another week. Reed hasn't gotten back to me. I muted my father's text stream. He's since texted ten more times. I need to get out of his apartment stat. Like after this meeting, I need to go home and pack a bag.

I broke the Ring camera. *What the hell was I thinking? Why didn't I try to disconnect it like a normal person?*

When we're done recording, I pull up the Canva presentation I started putting together months ago: an easily digestible comprehensive breakdown of *Love Today*'s podcast accolades, the stats we've acquired over the past year, and how much growth it's brought to the Love Today column and the overall paper.

I'm about to run through my spiel for the fifth time when there's a knock on the frame of my open office door. I look up to find Ted lounging in the doorway.

I drop my eyes back to my screen. "What do you want, Ted?"

He pads right on in and sits across from my desk. "How'd it go with the Witcher? You make up?"

I cut him a searing look. "You know what I should do, Ted? Get in contact with your exes. Who have you dated since me?"

"It doesn't matter who I dated. This is your column. It's about your life, and you're getting dual perspective, not me. Your audience doesn't care about my backstory. They just know of me via the shitty things you've written about our relationship."

My brows slant downward. "Did you pitch this article to clear your pseudonym name in front of my readership?"

He rolls his eyes, leaning back in my guest chair. "Rikki, I pitched this because you were so upset about all the shit I said when we broke up, and so oblivious to the fact that you, too, played a big part in the downfall of our relationship. You're not perfect! It wasn't all me."

I set my jaw, pressing my palms into the desk. "How sweet of you! What a noble fucking cause!" I take a slug of my water bottle. "You think *I think* I'm perfect, Ted?"

"You think you're cursed, Rikki! I've heard the monologue! *Wake up!* The universe isn't in your way, you are!"

"Are you referring to me not sharing my job right off the bat with these Hinge men? You write about *sports*, Ted, whoop-de-fucking-do. The most universally cared about and accepted conversation topic among general society. You have no idea how quickly people dip out when they hear I write about romantic relationships. I couldn't even get to the part where we agree to meet in person. I'm not pulling this out of my ass! It's been my actual lived experience."

"Rikki, this isn't just about you lying to people you date about your job. It's about how you keep every area of your life separate—in sealed-up Rubbermaid containers. When you let people into your life, you can't just show them one room in your house and keep all the others locked! If you want to have a meaningful relationship, you have to let them walk around. Open the doors. Get to know all your different corners. It's not that you're too much of a hassle to love! You literally don't let people love you."

I stand, willing my jaw to stop quivering as renewed pressure mounts behind my eyes. "The absolute audacity you have to talk to my boss behind my back, take over my column for the week, and then try to lecture me about the way I live my life is fucking bananas."

"I bet you did the same thing with this poor schmuck."

"I didn't!" I screech, eyes bulging out of my skull. "He knows what I do!"

Ted shrugs. "He didn't know me."

My eyes drop to the desk as my phone alarm starts going off. Two minutes till the meeting. Shit.

I'm unraveling.

I scoop up my laptop and grab my phone. "Fuck you, Ted."

He holds up a hand as I stride out of the room. "So glad we're talking again."

My opening slide is on the conference-room screen: a before and after chart of the paper's numbers in print and online in relation to Love Today.

I just finished greeting the board. Three men and one woman. Maya's here as well. She shoots me a reassuring smile as I distribute little printed cheat sheets with the same info in a fun flowchart I designed.

"All right!" I clap, moving back to the front of the room. "I'm so thrilled to be talking to you about the progress we've made this year utilizing the podcast as a way to reach an entirely new branch of readership!" I carefully curate my gaze, attempting to make eye contact with each of the board members. "This past year and a half has been a whirlwind! The work and care myself and my producer have put into the content we're making has proven both . . ." I trail off as I realize not one of them is paying attention. "Sorry, we're—are we not ready to start?"

Maya lifts a discreet finger, pointing to the door behind me.

I spin around. My soul leaves my body as I set eyes on the distraction.

Dressed in a black suit, standing in the doorway, is my father.

He's my father. And not my father. It's the man I'm careful never to be within reach of. His eyes are saucer wide. Face flushed. Mouth set in what I can only describe as a subtle scowl. I know it well. I could clock it across a football field.

I glance around the conference room, trying to gauge the exits. Escape routes. And peer back at him like a caged animal.

"Um," I fumble shakily. "Hi, Richard, would you mind waiting for me in my office? I'm in an important meeting."

His brows rise. "Richard?" He says it like it's funny, but his voice is too loud. The delivery is warped. "Are we on a first-name basis now?"

I laugh weakly. "Dad, it's so nice of you to visit me at work. Sorry. I'll be done in here in about half an hour. If you could just take a seat in my office, I'll be there as soon as I can."

His impossibly wide eyes, somehow manage to expand. "No, I got my ass on a plane last minute and flew five hours to New York. I think we need to talk right now."

I swallow, glancing at my boss and my boss's bosses, who are eyeing my father with thinly veiled impatience.

"Um," I say quietly. "Is it an emergency?"

He shrugs cartoonishly and takes a step into the room. "I don't know, is it? You thought you could destroy property, change my locks, and just go on about your day, Rikki? Is this you setting a boundary? Acting like a petulant child? Smashing my expensive camera and locking me out of the apartment that I've let you live in? What are you, fifteen?"

No. *I'm eight, shivering on the steps with hands shoved against my ears, and I'm ten, sprinting to the kitchen for paper towels and ice, and I'm thirteen, glancing over my shoulder as I sling clothes into a bag.* I'm thirty, and I'm scared to move.

"Are you the people who pay her?" He takes another step. I take a step farther away as he fixes his manic gaze on the people who control my job. Points a finger at them. "You should all be ashamed of yourselves! She's working two full-time jobs here, and a card shop, and she still can't afford a damn studio apartment."

I clear my throat. "Dad, please stop."

He paces around the board table like a shark. "You know what I caught her doing yesterday? On a Sunday afternoon? The Lord's day?"

Oh god oh god oh god.

"Trying to pull in cash as a sex worker. *My daughter!*" He aggressively points to me from behind the far end of the table like they don't know who he's talking about.

"Dad, no, that's—"

"Keep your mouth shut, Rikki. I know about OnlyFans—I've seen it on the news. I'm not a goddamn idiot." I cringe as he raps his knuckles against the table. "She's so desperate to make extra cash, you've made her into a whore! She turned my apartment into a fucking brothel! *Seven guys went in and out of there yesterday!*"

"That is not what was happening!" I bleat.

He stalks toward me at the front of the room, reaches out his arm, and casually knocks my laptop off the table.

I dive to catch it before it crashes to the carpeted floor. I land on my ass with the computer in my hands, breathless as I struggle to push an explanation from my lungs. "I was interviewing them for an article!" I glance blindly from Maya to the board members. "I'm so sorry! I have to reschedule our meeting, please excuse me." I fold the laptop, grab my phone, dart for the door, and burst into the main area of the office.

I'm thirty, and I'm being chased from my conference room.

"How does it feel, Rikki?" my dad says loudly.

Fear plinks through me as I slow to a stop in the no-man's-land, among the cubicles at the center of the floor.

"To have someone try to break your expensive things?"

I spin to face him as tears spill their way down my cheeks. He's standing in the conference-room doorframe. "Dad. This is my place of work. You just derailed a meeting I've been preparing for since July."

His jaw doesn't unclench.

"Don't think I didn't hear about your little text to Enora too," he snarls. "You've more than overstepped."

I glance around at my coworkers in the cubicles. Every head is turned in our direction. Some people are gathered in the doorways of their offices.

All of them are frozen. Unmoving. Unsure. Like I'm a show to observe. I glance over at Ted, who's looking on, aghast and still, in his own doorway.

No one's coming to help me.

I watch my father's fingers stretch and curl in on themselves at his sides. "Rikki, I'm gonna need that key to my apartment."

I'm ten feet from my office.

"Security has been called," someone says.

Richard's head turns and I use the momentary distraction to dash for my office. Grab my messenger bag from my chair. My father walks in as I'm shoving my laptop in.

"You have this huge office, and you still can't afford rent? Have you been lying to me?"

He wanders over to the studio side of the room, where we record the pod. "Look at all this state-of-the-art equipment. Is this all yours?" He runs a finger over one of the stands housing our personalized top-of-the-line *Love Today* mics.

"Please don't—"

He pushes it over. The wire rips out the back as it smashes into our second mic, and they both fall to the floor.

"What the fuck, Dad?"

"This is the only way to get through to you, Rikki." He glares from the other side of the room. "You don't pick up my calls. You don't answer texts. You lock the apartment. What was I supposed to do?"

"What did you think this was going to accomplish?" I exhale the words through the small pond's worth of snot and liquid currently running down my face.

"I'm your father. You have to respect me."

"I'm a grown woman. I don't have to do anything." I stride out of the office.

"Gimmie the key, Rikki!"

Where the fuck is security?

I sprint back across the no-man's-land of cubicles, ducking and weaving toward the bathrooms, heart pounding in my ears. The stairwell is two feet from the second bathroom. I chuck it open and hightail it down the steps, whirling around the first landing as the door explodes open at the top of the flight and my sixty-two-year-old father starts hurtling down the steps after me.

I burst out of the building on the bottom floor, heaving as I sprint to the Jersey Mike's one door down and disappear inside before my father appears on the sidewalk. It's lunch hour, and the place is swarmed. There's a huge line, and I push all the way to the back of the slim rectangular-shaped mob until I'm heaving and shaking against the wall next to the restrooms as all matters of liquid run down my face. I lower into a squat.

I need napkins. And a water.

I have to get to the apartment and get my stuff. I have to move. I have to—I don't know. I have to call my mom. I whip out my phone and switch off "Do Not Disturb."

The first notification that comes in is Reed. *Thank the Disney gods!* I stumble to my feet and tap it open.

Reed: the sunrise away bag is lost

I fall into the nearest table as a wave of nausea roils through my gut. There are four businessmen there who holler at me as I push back up, until they realize I'm having an emotional breakdown. To my left someone emerges from the key-padded bathroom. I grab the handle before it locks, and catapult myself in, slamming the door behind me. I bumble around the small space, hyperventilating as I stare at the text.

The Sunrise Away Bag is lost? Why?

What did I do to deserve this text? We just have to talk! He can't give up without talking to me face-to-face. This is absurd!

We *need* to talk! And *I need to be not here.*

I shove my hand into my messenger bag, blindly searching until my fingers close around the journal. I slide the garter off and rip it open.

> 6) Where would you like to go
> X ______________________

I scribble down Reed's address. And flip.

> Write the pilot episode of *Love Today.*
> That is all.
> Have fun.

I heave in a sob. "You know I don't have time for that!"

My phone pings. An email from Maya?

> Rikki,
> I don't know what happened in there. I'm so sorry. The board has unfortunately temporarily flagged you as an "unstable individual" arguing that you're a potential liability to the corporation. You've been suspended from the premises, pending an evaluation at the end of September.
> I'm on your side, and I'm going to do everything I can to fix this.
> —Maya

The nausea is back. *End of September?* This can't be fucking happening.

That's—that's after the Netflix pitch has come and gone. They can't do that. They can't do that, can they? *What does this mean for my job?* I need this contract renegotiation meeting to secure my raise, and I need my raise to get out of my Dad's apartment. I want to throw up the last twenty-four hours and extract them from my existence. *[RIKKI ROMONA: Newly single. Newly fired. Newly homeless. New record for world's shortest-ever adult relationship. Exploded in bathroom of Jersey Mike's.]*

I grab the red-topped pen from the back of the journal and shove it in my bra.

There was an emergency loophole in the original teleportation directions. I flip to the front of the book.

> In event of emergency, if you cannot complete the allotted task, destroying the base (this journal) will allow you a final vault.

Destroy?

"Can you change the task?"

I aggressively flip to the task page.

> Write the pilot episode of *Love Today.*
> That is all.
> Have fun.

Flip again.

Blank.

I flip five more pages, rage pummeling my chest. After the sixth flip, the task appears again.

> Write the pilot episode of *Love Today.* x
> That is all.
> Have fun.

A livid calm steals over me as I slam the leather shut.

If this thing and Reed are dangling off a building, and I can only save one, I'm lunging for him.

I shove my way out of the sandwich shop, averting my gaze as I bluster my way to the bodega at the end of the street. I buy a lighter, slip into the alley along the side of my building, and set the journal on the garbage barge. I light it up.

Four minutes later the pen turns green.

I clutch my clothes and bags in my fists and click.

53 | DETERMINED

I've assumed the position.

All fours in the street, slacks and blouse clinging to my skin with sweat. I look like I fell into a koi pond at a press conference.

I scurry to Reed's gate, hunched in on myself, clutching my bags to my chest. There's a call button, and I press it, looking into the Ring camera. It's barely late morning here.

"Reed? Please let me in! I'm not leaving until I talk to you!"

When nothing happens, I lift a hand and rap on the gate.

I'm bowed in despair for thirty seconds before the electric gate shudders into movement. Hope butterflies though my torso, swooping in arcs around my swollen heart.

The garage is closed, so I wander to the side of the house where there are a few steps and an actual door. It swings open before I can even raise my hand to knock.

Reed's brother stands in the doorway. A more slight, pointier version of the man I'm looking for. Oliver.

"What happened?" he breathes nervously as I walk into the house. We're in a kitchen with lots of windows and a cozy red booth-nook-table to sit around.

I'm at . . . the other end of the hall Reed led me down the first time I was in here.

"Where's Reed?"

Oliver blinks at me. "Reed's not here. Did you . . . fall in a lake?"

"Will he be back soon? Or is he out for the day?" I collapse onto the edge of the red bench, dropping my elbows on the table and dragging my fingers through my disheveled hair.

Oliver fills a glass with water and sets it in front of me. I drink it eagerly as he slides into the opposite side of the booth.

"Rikki, he's in New York doing a slew of auditions that he organized to justify being on the East Coast for a few days before he needs to be back for more promo."

My eyes slide shut.

I place my glass onto the table and flop sideways so I'm lying on the bench, parallel with the table.

Oliver lowers himself across the other side and briefly studies me. "What are you doing?"

"Can you refill my water?" I mumble as a new round of upset sleuths through me.

Oliver sets my refilled water on the table.

"What did you do?" he asks quietly.

I push myself up, dig my emergency electrolyte packet from my purse, and dump it into the water. Oliver grabs me a spoon. I mix my drink and chug it. He settles back in across from me as I put the glass down, half empty.

"Why do you assume I did something?"

"Because I know that look."

I frown, wishing there was a mirror.

"What look?" I ask.

"Self-loathing."

"Excuse me?" I snap.

He shrugs, unmoved by my tone. "Your body language is tense, upset, buttoned up. Your eyes are screaming for help. What did you do?" he asks again.

I flinch as Ted's scathing little love monologue zings through me like a shock. "I hurt Reed. Unintentionally."

I stare at the table.

Was Ted . . . right?

Do I not let people know me?

Reed said something to the same effect. *You're afraid to be known.*

But I have friends who know me.

Well, Jordyn's been in my life since I was five, and Whitney has too. Babe is my friend . . . through Jordyn. I guess we're not "besties." We only talk about books.

But I didn't do that with Reed. I told him whatever he asked. I was open! I let go. I didn't lie about my job or avoid topics—

Dread slithers across my collarbone, an icy snake, slowly encroaching on my windpipe.

But I did.

I avoided like a master.

I compartmentalized up the ass.

I built guardrails into our discussions. I made calling difficult. I made a rule to avoid ever discussing work. I took texting off the table for three weeks.

I am a fucking basket case.

The breath whooshes out of me.

Reed thought the guardrails would disappear last weekend.

He tried to call me when I clearly wasn't in bed, and I deflected.

He told me about work all week.

He told me about his relationship history on our second date, and I never reciprocated.

How can Ted be right?

How did I misconstrue this so thoroughly?

Every guy we interviewed thinks I'm a fucking liar.

Am I?

I didn't even tell Reed about my job. It was Micah and Jordyn. I didn't tell him about Ted. Or Netflix.

I told him *not to* read my work.

How can two people be a team when there's a plexiglass wall between them? When one of them is urging the other to keep half of their life a secret?

A fresh tear rolls down my cheek as my eyes travel up to the art piece hung behind Oliver's head. A bottle-cap version of the solar system.

"He really cares about you." Oliver's voice.

I blow out a watery laugh. "I think he now associates me with the worst night of his life. I basically recreated it."

Oliver squints. "What do you mean?"

I shrug. "I—he showed up on Sunday at my apartment to surprise me and come to the book club I do, but I hadn't told him that I had to reschedule it this week. And I hadn't told him I unfortunately work with my ex-boyfriend, and we were on deadline for a piece we had to write together for Monday, and he knocked on the door, and my ex opened it and said the wrong thing. And I said all the wrong things, and he left.

"I've never seen him that way. Barred off. His eyes were frozen over. The warmth that usually fills his features when he talks was just gone."

Oliver runs a hand down his face. "I know the look. I've been on the receiving end many times." I study Oliver, watching as his own trauma with Reed washes through his expression.

"What did you do?" I say.

There's a long pause before he sighs, dropping his eyes. "It was me."

"What was you?"

"It was me with his fiancée," he tells the table. "Freshman year. On Halloween. I was the lowest I'd ever been after our dad died. I was desperate to feel something. She and I were friends. I was visiting her at college from the get-go behind Reed's back. I crossed every line, and she let me do it."

I suck in a sharp breath.

"Yeah. I was a piece of shit, and somehow he forgave me. But he hasn't gotten close to anyone new in his life since. I broke the part of him that trusts people."

Christ. And he spent years in therapy, trying to fix it. And he did, just for me to fuck him up again.

We sit in silence for a full sixty seconds before I grab my shit from where I dropped it in the booth. "I have to go. I have to get home."

"All the way to New York? You need a ride to the airport?"

I shake my head, stumbling to the door as awareness breaks against me in waves.

I'm the fucking walking, talking oxymoron.

I'm the doctor that smokes.

I'm the neurosurgeon that moonlights as an Olympic diver.

What good is a relationship therapist who can't cultivate a healthy relationship?

An LMFT in an abuse cycle with her own fucking father?

I dig out my phone and dial Whitney.

"Rikki? It's so early. What's up?"

"I need you."

"You?" Her voice falters. "You—you never—where are you? What's wrong? I'm coming."

54 | NOT THAT BAD?

Whitney thinks *this isn't that bad.*

She picked me up outside Reed's. And after word vomiting my last forty-eight hours, her first sentence was *this isn't that bad.*

She went on to say I'm the *most capable person she knows*, and everything in my life that's now *royally fucked* can be fixed.

I asked her who the fuck is gonna fix it?

And she promptly responded: *You are a dumbass.* Followed by: *You're a fixer. It's what you do.*

Then she dropped me off at the airport. Not exactly the comforting rescue I was hoping for.

Now I'm at a gate for the next flight to Newark. Stuck. Sitting with my thoughts. Waiting, like a teleportation-less peasant.

I don't feel like a fixer. I feel like a rampant, oblivious ruiner of all good things. An incessant determined trier and depressingly consistent fail-er.

I sacrificed the journal for *nothing*. I exhale a breath, dropping my head in my hands.

That task was a message in itself.

Write the pilot to Love Today*?* Translation: Sit and calm the fuck down for a few hours before you do something stupid.

◆ ◆ ◆

A story is pulling together as I board my flight.

Of course it is. The second the pitch is off the table, the characters I've been fleshing out on paper over the past month come to life. They're talking. Making decisions. Moving through their world in my mind with specific mannerisms and tics. Arcs are taking shape.

When my ass hits middle seat of row twenty-three, I shove in my AirPods and pull out my laptop.

The script pours out of me unprompted. And it just keeps coming. I let it flow into the keyboard until my computer dies. Then I whip out a notebook and continue via pen.

When I land in Newark, I have a pilot script on my computer, and I'm staring at a handwritten outline of season one.

The lead will be a relationship therapist who's never managed to procure a successful relationship herself. Each episode we'll focus on her trying to help one of her patients. The patient's issue will be prevalent to something our relationship therapist is dealing with in her personal life. She won't see the parallels, of course, but we do once she leaves the office. She's great at her job. But she doesn't practice what she preaches. Her mental health is in flux, but she's not acknowledging it.

She'll get too invested in her patients' lives. She'll befriend some of them. Connect some of them with her friends. We'll see the topics running through our most viral *Love Today* podcast episodes mirrored in the lives of her weekly regulars.

As season one progresses, little by little we learn that our relationship therapist hasn't quite cracked how to fully give herself to another person romantically. To fully merge her life with another's feels dangerous. She's independent to a degree that's inhibiting her ability to love, preventing her from reaching the goal of finding a life partner. We witness her journey as she becomes cognizant of this. As she struggles to figure out what she's doing wrong. Which of her habits are hurting her quest to find a romantic soulmate?

We'll see her trying to fall in love with lots of slightly wrong people along the way. It'll be funny and relatable. We'll enjoy some of them, but we'll know it's not going to work out. We'll start to recognize her patterns.

Eventually she'll meet the right person in a difficult circumstance. We'll root for her as she trips up and down to figure out how to navigate their connection. As she wrestles with the idea of how logistically complicated it is to try to be with this person. With whether it's worth the heartache it'll take to make it work long term. As she ignores her own advice along the way. As she figures out she's not quite the person she's aspiring to be and grapples with the changes she has to make to become her best self.

The show will have a happy ending.

The jury's out on me.

55 | EXILE

i fucked up. im so sorry. please call me so i can apologize <3

It's been an hour since I landed and sent that message to Reed. I haven't heard back.

I stop a few steps from the elevator as I exit onto the fifth floor. It's 10:00 p.m. Right around my apartment door, the hallway is clogged with shit.

As I'm walking, Micah appears, grabs a box of the shit, and moves it into their apartment. Once I'm closer, I confirm that yes, it's my shit.

Framed art and photos are just propped up against the walls. Clothes thrown into untaped boxes. Drawers' worth of my things tossed haphazardly on top of them. Books in piles on the floor.

Jordyn appears out of nowhere and pulls me into a hug.

I start crying again.

By 11:30 we've managed to get everything out of the hallway and into Micah and Jordyn's apartment. They've started nesting, but they pushed their baby things to one side of the second room and blew up one of those nifty tall air mattresses for me. My mattress and bedroom furniture are in storage from when I moved into my dad's place. His apartment was already furnished and had no room for big-ticket items.

The three of us collapse onto their sectional with fresh cups of tea.

"Can I ask you guys something?" I open.

"Obviously you can always ask us anything," Jordyn says.

"Do you think I'm a liar?"

"With me, never," she says.

I take a sip of my tea. "What do you mean, with you?"

"Sometimes you lie to people because you're a private person and you don't want to share your real life. But most of the time you just don't volunteer information when said people are around."

"What people?"

"Like book club Adrienne . . . she opened up a couple weeks ago about how she was going through a hard time financially, and you didn't share anything about being in your dad's apartment."

"Why would I? I barely know her."

Jordyn levels her gaze at me. "Come on, Rikki, you have a master's in psychology. Sharing your shit with people is how you would become better friends."

"With men, would you say I'm a liar?"

"Yes," Micah says. "You hate them."

I widen my eyes. "I do not hate them."

He cocks his head. "Rick, it took me an entire year to win you over."

I smile. "Yeah, but you did."

"Yeah, but for a long time when I was around, you only looked at Jordyn when you talked, even when we were having a group conversation."

I frown as the statement drops like a rock through my subconscious.

"You would rarely ever look me in the eye, and you wouldn't talk about anything personal when I was in the room."

Snapshots from that era of our lives flash through me. *He's . . . right.* "Wow, Micah. I'm so . . . sorry."

Jordyn reaches out and squeezes my shoulder. "It's okay. You needed time to get to know him so you wouldn't be afraid of him."

I flinch.

"Afraid of him?" I repeat it quietly, but the truth of her words clangs through me.

"Rick, you're afraid of most men. You've been the same around everyone I've ever dated."

My chin wobbles as I crash backward through hundreds of different moments that verify her claim. *"Oh my god."*

Micah raises his mug. "We've met your dad. We get it."

"You two . . . have just known this about me and never told me?" I whisper.

Jordyn's forehead scrunches in disbelief. "Rikki, we thought it was obvious."

I put down the mug and shove my palms up into my eyes, because that somehow makes this all so much worse. *It is obvious. It's all so fucking obvious.*

"That's why we jumped in with Reed and told him what you do," Micah says pointedly.

Jordyn straightens on the couch. "Oh yeah! That was fun. We were helping you out."

I de-palm my eyeballs to look at them. "What?"

"We just thought if Reed knew what you really did from the beginning, you two would have better odds. We know you're trying to protect yourself, but if you don't tell a dude real things about yourself on a first date, how are they supposed to build a real relationship with you? You can't build a sturdy foundation around a lie."

My ears start to ring. "You knew me not telling guys about my real job was messing up my dating escapades and didn't tell me?"

"We didn't know for sure. We were just going off what you would tell us about your first dates and theorizing," Jordyn says.

"Theorizing behind my back?"

"We weren't being malicious about it, Rick," Micah adds.

We sit in painful silence for thirty seconds.

"I wrote the pilot," I mumble.

"What! That's amazing! Can I read it?" Jordyn asks.

I nod, sucking in gasps of air as I try to quell my fucking parade of unending tears. "I'm not even going to get to pitch it, though, because Maya let me go today."

Jordyn slams down her mug. "What the fuck? Because of what happened with your dad? Whitney did not tell me that part! Micah, are they allowed to do that?"

Micah frowns, staring into his teacup. "They can suspend you temporarily, pending an eval, but they can't just fire you." He looks up at me. "Definitely keep prepping the pitch."

I huff a sopping breath and stare into my own teacup. "They"—inhale—"set the eval date for end of September, and Netflix is September 16. We're only a week out."

"Rikki," he says calmly.

I'm drowning.

"Rikki, look at me," Micah says.

I raise my head, swiping my sweatshirt arm across my face to remove some of the wreckage.

"You're forgetting that I'm your lawyer. Work on the pitch."

56 | PITCH

It's been seven days.

I've sent out eight apologies to Hinge men I dated.

I saw my therapist for the first time in six months.

I went to five Pilates classes.

I sent my father to voicemail twenty-seven times.

I wrote a chapter for Reed.

And I obsessively worked on my pitch.

The chapter picks up the day after we became "something real," filling in all the Ted-ridden gaps in our communication and covering all the existential long-distance relationship crises. It explains everything, up to the moment he appeared at my door. I popped it into an email with the word *link*.

I have not received a response.

And I *have not* been given permission to come back to work.

But it's 10:30 a.m. exactly as I stroll out of the elevator, head held high, onto the fourth floor of *The Minute* building in pink heels and my best black business suit, clutching my laptop and a folder full of materials against my torso. My heart feels like a Ping-Pong ball, bopping between my chest and my shoulder blades in rhythm with my steps across the floor. Micah walks two feet behind me, with his briefcase.

The meeting *starts* at 10:30. Micah said it would be better this way—less time for someone to throw up an inane roadblock on our way in.

Time slows as I make my way to the conference room. My coworkers bug their eyes as I stride by, leaning toward their neighbors to whisper whatever they feel they need to say at the sight of me back in the office.

Maya's standing at the back of the conference room, at the head of the table, when I push open the door.

"Our *Love Today* rep is unfortunately out today, but we have her assistant Victor, who—"

"Actually I'm here!" I raise my hand by the door.

Victor whips his head in my direction and exhales, falling back against his chair. He texted me three days ago to let me know that Maya had pulled him aside. The higher-ups intended to have him take this meeting and pitch in my place. *They didn't want to lose the opportunity.* I told Victor that I'd be coming in, so he must have been sweating bullets when I didn't pop up earlier.

I recognize three of the board members from my renegotiation meeting sitting at the table, plus a twenty-something, pretty Southeast Asian woman and a middle-aged blond woman in a blue blazer and white blouse. *The producer.*

I googled her the second I got her name from Maya, weeks ago. Florence Leighton. She has two hit shows already: an action thriller on Amazon, and a dramatic romance on Hulu. She's hoping this can shape up to be a heartfelt rom-com for Netflix.

Maya smiles, eyes flashing with surprise as I move to the front of the room.

"Miss Romona, you are currently suspended from the premises," one of the board members says as the other two stiffen. "Alan, call security."

Micah steps up and places his briefcase on the table. "Actually, Matthew, Ms. Romona owns the film rights and copyright to the *Love Today* podcast, a project that she herself started and fostered into the burgeoning hit it is for this establishment. As you know, prior to her involvement, Love Today was just a small column, and that column had nothing near the publicity you're seeing it get today due to the draw of Ms. Romona's articles and successful podcast."

"Excuse me—" Matthew protests.

"Being that the podcast is the property Ms. Leighton is looking to acquire and adapt," Micah continues, "Rikki has the explicit right to pitch to her as an independent contractor, rather than an extension of *The Minute*." Micah turns an apologetic look toward Florence. "Ms. Leighton, we're very sorry for the confusion today. The board is attempting to execute a tried-and-true corporate tactic to devalue Ms. Romona's worth in lieu of her contract renegotiation and what should be a considerable salary bump. Her suspension was and remains entirely unethical and was in response to a security breach that was entirely out of her control." Micah shoots Matthew a saccharine smile. "You'll all be hearing more from me about that at a later time."

"I'm sorry—who the hell are you?" Matthew snaps.

"Oh, we've met via email. During her initial contract negotiations. I'm Micah Tang, Rikki's lawyer."

"Her—I. Mmm." Matthew glances at me, and then at his coworker Alan, who's holding his phone aloft.

"Am I calling security or not calling security?" he asks.

Micah serves Matthew a hard look. "I wouldn't call them if I were you."

Matthew grips the bridge of his nose. "I"—he glances down at his lap—"don't call them."

Matthew's eyes slice back to me. I cut him an enthusiastic nod before walking over to where Florence sits and holding out a hand. "Florence, it's so nice to meet you. Thank you for coming all the way out here today. Again, so sorry for the commotion."

She grins at me, with wide *I'm sorry for whatever all of that is* eyes and shakes my hand. "Rikki, I'm so thrilled to meet you! I'm a huge fan. I was about to be so bummed when Maya started explaining that you weren't here to do the pitch. I'm excited to see what you have for us today. This is my coproducer, Dawn, who will be working on this project with me. She's also a huge fan."

I blink at the younger woman sitting next to her and shake her hand as well. "Thank you both so much for being here."

"Thank you for having us!" Dawn beams.

Florence and Dawn smile at me with kind, welcoming eyes and expectant expressions that light a warm, calming fire in my chest. I glance over to find Maya grinning as well.

Micah's whisper-arguing with Matthew at the back of the room.

He shoots me a thumbs-up.

I heave in a deep breath and walk back to the front of the table. "Okay, let's jump in." I pull out two copies of the pilot script, and the synopsis of season one, and pass them to Florence and Dawn.

"I am überpassionate about the *Love Today* podcast. It's my baby, and I have dreamed about working with a team on a creative effort like this for years. If we move forward, I would love to take on the role of showrunner for this project." I swallow at the nerves in my throat. "As far as comps go, it's giving *Fleabag* meets *Couples Therapy* meets *Shrinking*. I've written the first four episodes of a thirteen-episode season. I have a treatment for season one and then outlines of the major beats for seasons two through five."

I open my laptop, and it connects to conference-room TV. My newest Canva presentation pops onto the screen.

"Let me introduce you to our protagonist."

I am breathless, grinning at my little audience.

I don't think I've ever explained something so smoothly in my entire life. I practiced this four times yesterday, and none of those four times were as engaging and stumble-free as this one right now.

They laughed with me and got somber during the sad bits and beamed during the parts with character growth.

My insides are glowing with pride. "So, that's what I'm visualizing. I know you probably want to read through everything, look at the scripts for the next couple episodes. Do you have any questions? Concerns? I'm happy to address any and all of them. I really hope we get to collaborate on this."

"Rikki." Florence grins. "I love this so much."

"For real. It's exactly what we're looking for," Dawn adds.

I laugh, clapping my hands by accident due to overwhelming excitement. "Thank you! I'm so happy to hear that!"

"Are you available to start immediately?"

I blink at Florence. "Um, start . . . what?"

"Start work on the show? I came in here already 90 percent sold on you. I've been listening to the podcast since you started last year and reading your column religiously, and this just sealed the deal. You've got the job."

I blink at her and shake my head. "I'm sorry, what?"

"I've already been putting together a team of writers—Dawn is one of them." She gestures to her coproducer. Dawn smiles at me. "Can we set you up to come out to LA for the next sixteen weeks? We've got a soft green light from Netflix, and we're hoping to start shooting by end of March."

Dawn laughs at the expression of pure, undiluted shock that must be on my face right now. "This feels like fate. We've obviously been amping up to this for a few weeks and discussing what we wanted it to be—we're totally vibing, like it's literally exactly what we were looking for."

Florence laughs. "I'm glad your lawyer is here. Ours is too. We can jump right in."

I glance from Florence to Dawn to Maya to Micah. He's sitting at the back of the table. He nods at me.

"Work as in . . ." I clear my throat. "Come on as a showrunner? Even though I've never worked that before."

Florence nods. "Showrunner slash head writer. I'll mentor you on the showrunner front. Ideally you can come out and meet the writing team by the end of the week, and then we can get the writers' room rocking by Monday. I'll start working with our casting team. We've already got a pilot script. This is fantastic."

"Shows don't usually work like this, right?" I blurt.

She laughs. "No. It helps that your podcast is a wildly successful hit, and I've got two shows doing pretty well right now. I've been itching to make a rom-com my whole career, and I'm so thrilled you were game to adapt *Love Today* because it's the highlight of my week, and I can't wait to bring it to a visual medium. Sometimes you just know."

I glance up at the ceiling. *Universe?*

I drop my gaze to Maya. "What do you think?"

"I think the idea's fabulous. I can't wait to watch. You're gonna smash it."

"I know you're based out here," Florence says. "We'll get you set up with an apartment close to the offices to make the transition as quick and smooth as possible."

Set me up with an apartment?

Out there?

As quick as possible?

I'm internally vibrating at a frequency so high, I wouldn't be surprised if I spontaneously evaporated. This is . . . huge. This is a huge, dream-making, exciting, life-changing, unbelievable doesn't-seem-real career moment and—

I'm going to live in the same place as Reed. I'm going to be able to fix things with Reed. I can do short-distance dating with Reed. I can't wait to tell Reed. Get out there, set up my apartment, and invite him over.

What does it say about me that the most exciting part of this win is him?

I think of my neon-green binder. Pushing it on every adult I came into contact with. The day I moved to New York. Graduating from Columbia. Getting my masters. Earning my LMFT license after 4,500 hours of supervised counseling alongside doing reviews for Books Today. The day I snagged the Love Today column with my piece about my breakup with Ted. The morning I pitched the *Love Today* podcast to Maya, and three days later when she called me to say it had been approved by the board. Prepping for the first episode. Interviewing potential assistants. The day one of our historic worst-dates episodes went viral. I know this day, this exact second, will cement itself as a paramount moment in the timeline of my life.

But Reed feels just as big.

Meeting him was a shift that feels just as important.

"What about the column and our podcast?" Matthew says from the corner.

I blink at him. "I thought you found me to be an unstable employee."

"We're open to renegotiating your contract."

"That seems a little different from what you were saying thirty minutes ago. Maybe you can schedule a meeting with my lawyer."

57 | LOS ANGELES

What exactly happens to a teleportation journal after it's sacrificed? Is she born again from the ashes? Does she commence stalking someone new? Should I be jealous? Is there a secret underground club of ex-teleporters grieving her omniscient presence?

These are the questions that plague me during my five-and-a-half-hour airborne odyssey to California. I also spend an excessive amount of time dwelling on the conundrum of *what the hell is going on with Reed.*

It's been two weeks.

I know I was an asshole, but I'm trying to apologize. I texted. I spilled my heart out via book chapter. It's gotten to the point where I think I'm allowed to spin this back around on him.

I'm annoyed. Thrilled that work has brought me to Los Angeles because, don't get me wrong, I want a future with that man more than anything I've ever wanted in my life, and right now, I'm a thousand percent confident that we can work this out. But *we will* be having words. We both need to work on being more forthcoming with our communication.

Reed said he "needed a second" when he left my apartment building two weeks ago.

It's been many, many seconds!

I know he sent the breakup text, but he didn't send the forever-breakup text!

I can't fathom a reality where we don't talk this through. I refuse to be a miscommunication trope. So whatever the case may be, I'm done waiting. I'm calling him once I'm settled in my LA apartment. Not once I'm all unpacked and the place is pretty. Settled, as in, I've received my key, and my suitcases are in the unit. Tonight.

Micah negotiated his ass off for me this week.

Love Today season one will be thirteen episodes. As far as *The Minute*, I'll continue to cover the Love Today column through December, after which I'll pass the torch. I'm going to finish out the year, hosting *The Minute* podcast remote, and come January, the podcast will be mine pending a slight name change. If *The Minute* wants to relaunch their version of a *Love Today* podcast, they will have to relaunch with a slightly rebranded name as well.

I jolt to attention, smiling like a goof, as the plane touches down on the tarmac at LAX.

An intoxicating cocktail of hope and excitement pounds through me as I hobble up the center of the seat numbers with my carry-on.

A driver's going to pick me up at baggage claim! I'm going to be driven and shown around to my new (provided-by-work) prefurnished apartment!

And I'm going to reach out to Reed. I could see him *tonight.* There's a chance that *today* we finally hash out this lingering bullshit.

I'm smiling as I cross the threshold into the airport.

I beam at the exhausted people waiting to get on the plane I just vacated. I beam at the people in the queue for Habit Burger and Starbucks. I grin at the people sitting at Gates 85, 84, the people boarding their flight at 83. I'm about to move on to Gate 82 when my eyes snag. My heart stumbles over itself as I latch onto a familiar turquoise–neon green.

I reverse a few steps. Searching the crowd of travelers. My eyes home in on the WordArt gradient moving through the herd. The Sunrise Away bag.

I crane my neck and rise onto my tiptoes, tracing it up to the back of a man's head. A man in line for group three of the United flight boarding for . . . I glance at the digital sign: **Newark.**

No. *It can't—*

He steps into full view to scan his ticket. My heartbeat is in my eyeballs as he strides on toward the jetway.

What in the actual—

"Reed!" It comes out as a full-on frantic scream. A few people in my vicinity startle before they continue on.

Reed stops short at the mouth of the jetway, looking over his shoulder for the source. I awkwardly throw up my arm to wave.

His eyes widen as they cut to mine. We're a good sixty feet apart, but he sees me. He holds my gaze in shock for three eternal seconds. I feel his attention all the way in my fucking toes.

Then someone bumps his shoulder. He rocks sideways, realizing he's blocking the flow of traffic onto the plane. He walks backward a few steps before swiveling his head as he bumbles into the jetway. Swept up with the mounting horde of people trying to get to their seats.

I swallow, panic constricting in the back of my throat as I watch, hoping he'll swim upstream and come back out here so we can talk.

I'm rooted to the spot, outside the gate where the carpet meets the tile, staring at the jetway.

Five minutes pass.

Ten minutes pass. He doesn't appear.

What the fuck.

Ten more minutes, and they're sealing the door.

I'm still here, frozen, because something in me has cracked, and if I move, I'll fall apart.

He saw me, right? Maybe he didn't see me?

Was he going to Newark to visit me?

But he ignored me.

Maybe he didn't see me?

But *he saw me.*

Maybe it wasn't him?

But it was.

I'm locked in a dissociative haze as I'm given the keys to my new apartment. As I unpack and unload my things. Run errands for the items I couldn't fit in a suitcase. I'm in HomeGoods hunting for a comforter when my phone pings.

58 | ALAS

SUBJECT: RE: RE: RE: RE: RE: RE: RE: RE: RE: Been feeling inspired. Had some fun.
Reed Tyler <RTYLER48@gmail.com> September 21
LINK

—

CHAPTER 7

Derek

There's no delicate way to say this: long-distance blows. And long distance without a light at the end of the tunnel? A slow form of torture.

But when you've found a connection this potent—and the alternative is goodbye—what other option is there? It's taken me thirty-two years to stumble into something like this.

That's a long fucking time. I'm gonna figure this out.

She doesn't know I've been incessantly working on a solution.

I have a plan. I haven't shared it yet, but I'm going to tonight. I'm surprising her.

I've been talking with my agent. There are tons of big projects—movies and TV being shot in New York all the time. He's been lining up auditions for this coming week, and I'm going to book one. I can feel it in my bones.

We're gonna make this work.

It's not going to be a case of flying across the country for a three-day weekend every other weekend. I'm gonna be set up here for at least three months. And we'll take it from there.

Renee's only twenty minutes from my mom's house, so I stop in there first to drop off my luggage and change into my book club cosplay.

I texted her, but she must be running around prepping for WWU.

I'm wincing as Fiction Reed approaches my apartment.

But in his chapter, instead of finding Ted at the door, *I answer it.* In my witch gear. And I'm so excited to have him join us for WWU. He meets everyone, and we have a great time, trying to talk about what happened in book four without spoiling him.

Afterward, we have *hot Witcher / witch*-themed sexy times. He tells me about his plan and the auditions. He stays over, and the next morning we take the train together into the city. We make plans to meet up for dinner after work. He goes on three different auditions, and they all go well. He's feeling more confident in his abilities now that *Elizabeth Ross* has been announced. Now that some outlets have received early screeners and they're getting great feedback.

I didn't know that was happening! A thrill charges down my spine.

The chapter ends right before the two of us meet for dinner.

Did he get a job in New York?

"Ma'am, are you okay?" A HomeGoods employee is staring at me from above.

I'm . . . I'm crying. Sitting on the floor of the linens aisle. My cart haphazardly askew blocking foot traffic.

SUBJECT: RE:RE: RE: RE:RE: RE: RE: Been feeling inspired. Had some fun.
Rikki Romona <rikkirolling28@gmail.com> September 21
In true control freak fashion we seem to have our wires crossed. Does this mean you got a job? Because I secretly had the same plan and got a job in LA.
We seem to really enjoy talking to each other. You'd think we'd have shared these thoughts.
—

SUBJECT: we really need a new subject
Reed Tyler <RTYLER48@gmail.com> September 22
Ahh but Rikki, how could we ever share those thoughts? It goes against all our dating programming. It's like totally way too embarrassing to openly admit to trying to move across the country for someone.
Where do you live now, Romona?
—

SUBJECT: new subject
Rikki Romona <rikkirolling28@gmail.com> September 24
They've got me in Burbank.
—

SUBJECT: . . .
Reed Tyler <RTYLER48@gmail.com> September 25
Yeah I'm looking for more of an exact address Renee. I'm gonna be in state on October 1, any interest in going somewhere?
—

SUBJECT: oh like a stalk me address?
Rikki Romona <rikkirolling28@gmail.com> September 26
44815 Groundwork Ave #20, Burbank CA
—

SUBJECT: re: oh like a stalk me address?
Reed Tyler <RTYLER48@gmail.com> September 26
10/1 6:30 p.m.
—

SUBJECT: re: re: oh like a stalk me address?
Rikki Romona <rikkirolling28@gmail.com> September 26
Clothes or no clothes?
—

SUBJECT: re: re: re: oh like a stalk me address?
Reed Tyler <RTYLER48@gmail.com> September 26
Eat before. Formal attire.

59 | LOS ANGELES

Despite the naked man I saw crouched in the giant bushes outside my complex this morning (I emailed the HOA), my first week back in LA has been chaotic in the dreamiest way. I've been able to meet with my mom about wedding prep in person over dinner. I went to a movie with Whitney. I went shopping for more apartment things with my Aunt Teresa on Sunday during her day off. It's been . . . nice. Cozy even.

Jordyn and I have been talking every day via text or phone call when she's heading to bed and I'm heading home from work. I miss her, but so far I think we're rocking the long-distance friendship thing.

Everything with *Love Today* thus far has been challenging and overwhelming but wonderful. I love the work, and I love the people I'm working with. They've been kind, helpful, and encouraging, and it's made the transition into this job feel so *right*. When I walk into that writers' room every morning, I'm part of something that's bigger than me, and it fills me with a sense of purpose I've found hard to come by, working on projects alone.

LA itself already feels like mine. Muscle memory kicked in, and I've slipped back into its rhythm. But the apartment is finally starting to look like *mine*. I had Jordyn ship out a box of my books and the things I hang on the walls after I left last week. There's a bookshelf in my new bedroom. (Three shelves drilled over a desk.) It's hard to articulate how big of a difference it makes to be able to look over at those shelves and see my favorite books. They make this place feel like home.

Tonight I get to see Reed, and I don't know what to think.

Should I still be upset with him for not responding to me for fourteen days? For leaving me hanging at the airport? For having the same secret plan that I had?

It's been three weeks.

I am upset with him. But I've also been looking forward to this for the last six days with every jostled, confused, lovesick piece of my heart. I don't know how I *should* feel, but what I do feel is ravenous. For his presence. His laugh. His understanding. His jokes. His empathy. His compliments. His curiosity. Passion. Conversation. Wit. Warmth. Mouth. Body. Strength. Unpredictability. His quirks. Emotional depth. Proactive nature. His energy. How observant he is. How playful he is. I could keep going. Reed scratches so many itches.

The email said formal wear.

I found a blood-red gown. It's corseted with pointed edges at the top left and right. It cinches in a downward *V* as it approaches my hips and flows out to a full skirt with a slit over my right leg. It's covered in lines of red beading, so it glitters in the light. I'm wearing a matching blood-red beaded choker and gloves that go up to my biceps. I debate fifty different hairstyles, only to eventually land on curling it and leaving it down.

The apartment's clean. My mind is open.

It's 6:30 p.m. on the dot when there's a knock at my door.

I suck in a steadying breath and pull it open.

Reed's in a full black tux. His auburn hair is a smidgen longer, carefully tousled back. There's a light layer of stubble on his face. His gaze drops as he takes in my outfit.

"Ho-ly shit."

"You said wear clothes."

He meets my eyes, mouth slanted up the side of his cheek. "You went above and beyond there." We stare at each other for a beat, scanning, inspecting, analyzing for any subtle changes since the last time we were together in person. There's something a little different about him tonight. More guarded. There's a protective edge of mischief carved into his expression.

"Hi," he says.

"Hi."

"You ready?"

I nod, sliding my new beaded, red purse off the marble countertop. I pluck my keys from their hook and pull the door shut behind me.

"So, you broke up with me." I shoot a smirk in his direction before bolting the door.

Reed smirks back, offering the crook of his elbow. "*Broke up* is a strong word."

I loop my arm through his. "You sent the phrase."

"And you apologized."

My heels clack along the tiled hallway. "You ignored it for thirteen days."

"But then I didn't."

We make our way down the stairs. "You wrote a chapter."

"Still a response."

"It was a great chapter," I concede.

A warm rumble vibrates through him. "Thank you."

"You blew me off at the airport." We stride out from the building and into the night.

He purses his lips. "Does catching your eye while boarding a flight qualify as blowing you off?"

"I felt blown."

He smothers a laugh. "You caught me off guard, Renee. I was heading out to a job."

I sigh as he drops a hand against the small of my back, directing me toward a black SUV. "What are we doing, Reed?"

"We're going to the *Elizabeth Ross* premiere."

I shoot him a grin. "That was one of my theories, considering the release date's a week out." He opens the door to the SUV, and I step in. "But it's not what I meant."

Inside there are two benches situated across from each other about two feet apart and closed off from the driver like a carriage from the 1800s. I wait for Reed to situate himself on one and then I situate myself across from him on the other.

"Your hair's longer," he comments.

"That's what happens to hair. Your eyes are still scary blue."

"That's what happens to eyes."

He tilts his head, studying me.

"So what's this new job?"

"Supporting role in a new John Krasinski film shooting in New York."

I lean forward, a gush of enthusiasm lurching through me. "Whoa, congrats, Reed."

He bobs his head to the side. "Thanks. What's yours?"

I purse my lips. "Hold up, you deflected my original question."

He cocks a brow.

"Are you dating anyone right now?" I ask.

"Do you count?"

"No."

He shakes his head. "Then no."

I close my eyes, bracing against the seat as the car starts to move. "I'm really sorry." I exhale and meet his unflappable gaze. "Turns out my fatal relationship flaw isn't control freak-ing . . . It's an indomitable urge to compartmentalize my life so if a relationship implodes, I don't have to feel it everywhere." My voice drops to a whisper. "Which is a fucking stupid tactic because it doesn't work."

He nods, lips pressing into a sad line.

"I almost threw up when you sent that text. I guess . . . I guess I thought we were past the phrase."

"I guess I thought we were past the rules," he says softly.

"I really thought you'd come back and talk it through."

He leans forward, resting his elbows on his knees. His woodsy-ocean scent washes over me. I dig my fingers into the edge of the bench. "I was drunk when I sent it."

"It was 12:30 in the afternoon."

"I was still drunk from the night before."

I swallow. "Because I made you relive one of the worst nights of your life?"

"Because I care about you more than you care about me."

I shake my head, tilting closer, resting my gloved elbows on my skirt-covered legs as I search his eyes. The impish edge I noticed earlier has already melted out. They're open again. Vulnerable. "I'm sorry I put you in a situation that threw you back to that day with your brother."

He nods. "I know. I'm sorry I didn't come back."

My heart somersaults across my chest as his eyes pierce me in that debilitating x-ray fashion that electrifies all logical thoughts into clear panes of glass.

"Why didn't you just come back?" I croak.

"I fucked up. I was in pain. And then I saw you on the Ring at my house. I knew you must have gone inside to my brother." He shakes his head. "I was already so anxious. It threw me into another spiral."

"We only talked about you."

"I know. He told me."

I hang my head, a hopeless feeling coiling around my chest. "I miss you. A lot. Like all the time."

"If I could go back to that moment and try it again, I wouldn't leave the building. I'd pace it out for five minutes in the hall, come back, and talk it through."

I close my eyes. "Yeah well . . . if you didn't leave, maybe I'd never realize what I was doing with all the stupid fucking rules I was throwing at you."

"I would have brought them up, Rikki. I realized."

"I still had my pitch coming up. I would have still ended up heading to LA."

He arches a brow, the hint of a smile on his lips. "What was the pitch? You deflected."

I huff a laugh. "A producer, um, maybe you know her, Florence Leighton—"

Recognition flashes in his eyes. "*Fire on the Lake* on Amazon?"

"Yeah!"

"And *College Girls After a Murder*?"

"Yes!" I smile at him. "Turns out she's a huge fan of the *Love Today* podcast. She wanted to adapt it into a rom-com series."

Reed's jaw falls into an open grin. "Rikki! That's amazing!"

"Yeah, it doesn't feel real. She loved my pitch, and this still sounds *ridiculous* to say out loud: She hired me as head writer and showrunner. It's all happened so fast, my head is still spinning."

"What do you mean, ridiculous? That's fucking fantastic, Rikki! I'm so happy for you! This is your *Kelly Clarkson Show*!"

I snort. "That's what I said!"

We smile at each other across the shrinking chasm between us.

Reed shakes his head. "You would have told me about the pitch if I brought your attention to deleting our rules. And I wouldn't have taken any job in New York."

"But I didn't know I was going to get pulled out here like that. I had no idea."

"If you told me the situation with Florence, Rikki, I would have known."

I heave in a deep breath, fighting the urge to cry.

I shrug instead. "I don't know if I would have had the whole self-realization epiphany I did, if I didn't go to your house and talk to your brother the day you sent the breakup text.

"That series of unfortunate events sent me into a creative tailspin that ended in me vomiting up the script for the *Love Today* pilot."

Reed frowns at me, a deep sadness growing in his eyes. "What realization epiphany?"

"That I don't know how to be a good partner. I keep things from people and gaslight myself into thinking it's okay. I'm a relationship therapist who can't hold on to relationships. I would have found some way to fuck this up if I wasn't pummeled into looking in the mirror and reflecting on my own shit at the end of that day."

Reed narrows his eyes. "Rikki. You know exactly how to be an amazing partner. I think deep down you just don't believe you deserve someone good. And that's bullshit."

My skin bristles as part of me curls in on itself in recognition. I feel naked. So known. Seen. It scares the shit out of me.

"We're here!"

The first episode of *Elizabeth Ross Falls for Ryan* is phenomenal. Rome Overland is excellent. He skillfully showcases the nuances of the lovable, protective Vince, and he has great chemistry with Elizabeth. In my humble opinion, it's perfection. I whisper this to Reed as the credits roll, and he smiles and shakes his head.

I shake mine right back. "Nah, you can't tell me I can't take a compliment and then respond to yours with a headshake. I'm so proud for you."

His smile splits open. He reaches out to catch a rogue tear rolling down my cheek before sliding his hand into my curled hair, pulling me to his mouth, and kissing me in the semidark of the theater. His lips are slow and intentional. Passionate and steady. Laced with emotion. Words and feelings that have floated by unsaid between the two of us for weeks on end. Slowly, one by one, the lights flip on in my chest. I knot my hands up in the front of his tux. His fingers tighten around a fistful of my hair, and I physically restrain myself from climbing into his lap. I want to curl up in him and stay here in the dark together, huddled just outside of reality for as long as the night will allow. Reed pulls back with bright eyes and lipstick on his mouth. The light of the screen is reflected in his gaze. "There's an after-party I have to be at," he breathes.

I'm quiet as we maneuver around the party on the roof of the building. I smile and say hi to about twenty different people who go on to praise Reed's performance. I stand by his side, frustration a knot in my gut as I examine and reexamine our current situation, trying to land on a viable solution.

How did this happen?

The universe trolled me into a false sense of security with its stupid blessing just to disappear and pull this bullshit. To tell me in the most irritating, roundabout way what I already know: It doesn't matter how much fate or whimsy or magic you have on your side, relationships are still complicated as fuck. They require a strict diet: constant communication, openness, generosity, compromise, courage, and *presence*. And those are things two commitment rookies with deep-seated trust issues—in their early thirties, with full, well-rounded, established lives—can't do from across the country. Even if they're both willing, capable, intelligent people who care about each other an incredibly inappropriate amount in proportion to how long they've been together.

When we disengage from Reed's latest admirer, he pulls me into one of three different vintage photo booths they have along the perimeter of the roof. I scoot in with him and tug the curtain shut. He taps the red "Go" button inside and pulls me into a kiss that sends my head spinning. The flash goes off.

We smile before the next flash. He gathers me by his side before the last one.

"Reed," I say softly. "We have to talk about what we're doing."

He angles himself toward me in the small space. "I'll be done with this movie by the end of January."

"It's October."

He tucks a loose strand of my hair back behind my ear. "New pact?"

I shake my head the tiniest bit to the right, staring at the place where our strip of pictures will appear. "I can't do another pact. I've caught feelings."

Reed tips up my chin to peer into my glassy eyes.

"Rikki!" He blows out a sad laugh. "I don't want a pact either. I want to be with you. I love you."

My mouth quivers as his confident words rocket through me, searing hot and joyous as they wind around my heart.

That's the first time anyone I've dated has ever said them to me. Emotion wells in my throat. "Reed, we haven't even figured out how to fight."

"Fight with me then. Let's figure it out."

"But there's no figuring it out. We . . . fucked ourselves." I drop my eyes as my voice cracks. "We worked separately on the group project."

Reed tangles our hands together, gripping mine tight. "Rikki."

I stare at his bow tie. "I don't want to do this half ass, and I know you don't either." I squeeze his hands. "We . . . can't be a team. We can't go to bed together. *We can't do any of the things we define love to be!*

"I want to pick you up at the fucking airport, Reed. We can't be a safe place to land for each other from three thousand miles away, in different time zones. And *you know it.*"

Reed's eyes plead with mine. It sends a web of cracks running through my heart. "Rikki, I love you."

". . . I love you too." It comes out on an exhale. Low and breathy. Like it could have just been the wind.

"What if I can make it out here, though," Reed says, "Whenever I can. What if I can make that happen once a week for a couple months."

I shake my head, squeezing my eyes at the ache in my chest. "Love doesn't grow right like this. It's going to be jagged and cracked. Crooked and stiff. Like a limb that was never properly set after it broke. Our jobs are too irregular and all-consuming. More miscommunications would be imminent. Pain and anxiety would be unavoidable." I pause, sliding my hands up the front of his tux. "Even people who live in the same city have to *live together* to really know if they're compatible long term. We can't even get close. What we have are fun trips, excursions, three-day adventures. Love isn't just the happy-go-lucky shit."

He looks at me hard, his face war-hero somber. "You *want* this to be over?"

"I don't want it to be over," I mumble. "I want it to be real."

He drops his forehead against my chest. "It *is* real."

But we live in two separate universes.

I wish I could slice them open and sew them back together as one.

I run my fingers through his hair. Down his neck. He shivers against me.

"I think . . ." I suck in a slow, arduous breath. "I think the healthiest thing we can do right now is let go. And if we're ever single, living in the same state, we ask each other out."

He lifts his head to search my eyes. He looks miserable.

I hate this.

"How will we know when we're living in the same state if we're not talking?"

"Post about it on your hipster Instagram."

He huffs. "What, and you'll post every time you move home base on yours?"

I nod.

"In the main feed?"

The ghost of a laugh escapes my lips. "Yes."

He frowns. "I haven't told someone I love them since I was eighteen."

"I've never said it to someone until today."

60 | NEW YEAR'S EVE

"Why did we go to Vegas to get drunk at dinner and go back to the room to play cards? It's only nine o'clock!" Whitney complains.

"Because our room is amazing!" Mom squeals.

Someone on the writing team knew someone who could get us upgraded to a suite full of windows at the Venetian, and I have to agree, the view up here is kind of worth the hang.

"And because we're old," Aunt Teresa snarks. "We already went to a day club and Cirque du Soleil—what else do you want from us? We need sleep."

The four of us are in matching sparkly sequined dresses, and we've all got dog doodles on our faces. I did them with waterproof eyeliner before we went out to dinner: An ode to our mutual love of the *Friends* episode where Ross and Rachel get married, and also dogs. It's been a fun, exhausting day of bachelorette-ing my mother.

"You know what we should all go do right now?" Whitney says as my aunt doles out a new round of cards. "The SkyJump off the Stratosphere!"

Oh god. "That's not on the itinerary," I tell her. "You know how I feel about jumping off shit on a rope."

"Is it a bungee jump?" Mom asks.

"No thank you!" Aunt Teresa comments.

"It's not a bungee jump. It's just a vertical zipline!"

I eye her flatly. "Is there a difference?"

"Of course there's a difference. Come on, this trip is supposed to be spicy!"

"I'm listening," my mother says.

I throw out my arms. "How about we do something 'spicy,' here in the room, *group of drunk people I'm caring for*. What about truth or dare?"

"Oh, I like that better! I vote truth or dare," my aunt says.

Whitney grabs the wine from the little kitchenette. "Fine! But only if we make it a drinking game." She drops four glasses on our table and fills them all with wine before flinging herself back into a chair. "Rules are you drink when you're truthed or dared."

"That's not a game," I argue.

"That's the game. Live with it, Rick."

"I'll go first!" my mom exclaims, throwing back half her wine. "Teresa! Are you and Dr. Flanagan heading down a marriage path? Should Rikki quit her job and start a wedding planning business already?" She giggles.

"Mom, that's not how you play truth or dare. You have to ask 'truth or dare?'"

My aunt puts up her hand. "It's fine. I'll go." She takes a chug. "I think we might be." We all whoop. "But don't worry, Rikki, I won't be enlisting you. I know it's burning you out."

I shoot her a grateful look.

"What are you talking about?" My mom smiles. "Rikki loves doing this stuff! You should get her ideas. She thinks of everything!"

Teresa sighs. "No, she doesn't, Kelli. She's good at it, but she doesn't enjoy it. She's working at all hours, and you're adding a lot of stress on her day-to-day."

An awkward silence settles over us as I stare into my drink.

"Rikki, is that true?" Mom asks.

She's not going to hate you for telling the truth. So says my therapist. "I mean . . ."

"You mean what?" Mom prods emotionally.

"I mean, Aunt Teresa's right. I'm happy to help you with some wedding things, but I wish you'd hire someone instead of leaning on me for everything."

"I thought you loved weddings!"

An irritated noise drawls out of me. "I do love weddings. I just don't have time for another job on top of the ones I already have. And I don't love planning them. I love witnessing them."

My aunt nods. "She went from Whitney to you with like a week's break in between."

My mother's mouth falls open. "Rikki, why didn't you tell Layla and me when we asked you?"

"Because I couldn't disappoint you. You and Aunt Teresa and Whit are the only family I talk to, and I don't want to lose you."

I haven't spoken to my father since the incident, but I still get texts every day apologizing, telling me I need to get over this, asking me to come to his house, taking back his apologies, apologizing again. Multiple voicemails when I ignore his calls. Each one hits like a pinprick, a shallow needle sliding under my skin, making me feel like a terrible daughter.

To top it all off, every couple weeks my mom shoots me a text urging me to hear him out. Telling me how sorry he is about the apartment.

I never told her my side of that story.

Aunt Teresa reaches out and grabs my wrist. "You're never going to lose us, Rikki. You can tell us anything. Our love isn't conditional. If you murdered someone, we'd help you bury the body."

"I've told her that a thousand times!" Whitney drawls. "My turn." She chugs some wine. "Okay, Rikki, truth or dare."

I sigh. "Truth."

"When are you going to get back on the dating scene? You've been in a mood for months. You need to get laid and stop wearing that creepy coat."

"Can we not, in front of our parents? The coat is not creepy. It's comfortable. And I have not been in a mood. I'm very happy. I love my job."

Whitney's trying not to laugh as she exchanges a look with my aunt.

"It's called truth for a reason, honey. You gotta be honest," Aunt Teresa says.

"You've been so fucking mean the last two months," Whitney says.

I scoff. "I've been mean because I'm tired and overworked! I can't believe I'm still giving you free couples therapy, *five months later*. I'm out of bandwidth, Whitney. I can't perpetually do endless favors for you."

Whitney bulges her eyes. "Rick, again, what the fuck? Why didn't you tell me you felt like that?"

"Because I love you, and I want to help you out. I thought when you said a couple sessions you meant two to three sessions! A couple means two!"

"Wow, this is not as lighthearted as I was expecting it to be." My aunt throws back the rest of her wine.

My mom snorts. "I dare you to lower your voice, Rikki."

I bark a humorless laugh. "I dare *you* to stop fucking talking to Dad."

"Whoaaaa." Whitney grabs her wine. "This is why I don't like hanging out with sober people at a party."

"Shut up, Whitney," I mumble, exhausted.

"He's you're father, Rikki, he loves you. He's just trying to make things right, *he's family*," my mom pleads.

I drop against the chair, banging my torso against the wooden backrest. "Mom! He never makes things right! He only makes it worse! When are you gonna see that? When are you going to stop choosing him over me? He's not any better! He's not changing!"

My mom gasps. "Rikki!"

I snicker. "You know he evicted me, right?"

"He said you had a disagreement—"

"No, let me clear this up, because we've been politely skirting around it for the last three and a half months. He had someone come and toss all my shit from his apartment into the hallway. He came to my office and verbally assaulted my superiors. He told them I was moonlighting as a sex worker because he saw me bringing men into the apartment, over his fucking Ring camera—I was conducting interviews for a Love Today piece! He destroyed property in *The Minute* office and almost got me fired. He called me a whore . . . Oh, and he would show up out of nowhere like a scary overlord in the one-bedroom apartment and decide he was sleeping over."

Whitney and my aunt exchange a look.

My mom blinks at me, lips wobbling. "Rikki, I didn't—"

"Yeah, I didn't want to upset you. But I guess I'm finally moving past that hurdle! He still texts me every day. Every. Day. And I haven't been able to press the block button because I know it would disappoint you. Because you so badly want him to be someone else. You act like he's never crossed the line into irredeemable! *When he's crossed it a hundred thousand times.* He continues to be toxic in every way that counts. You choose him over me, and you choose him over yourself. Over and over again.

"I want to stop letting him back in. But I need your support on that, Mom. I need *you* to acknowledge that my life would be better if I stopped inviting him into it."

My mom looks away as her brows pull together.

Aunt Teresa reaches across the table and grabs my wrist again. "Hon, block him. You have my full blessing. Please do it. Do it now."

Whitney pumps her wine in the air. "I thought you already blocked him! Block that fucker."

My mom's lips are quivering now. "Rikki, I know he's troubled, but there are such wonderful pockets of him too. You know. I've tried so hard for so long to remember those. I . . ."

"You're allowed to let him go," Teresa says to her firmly. "I've been trying to tell you this same shit your daughter's saying for years. You don't owe him anything. You're moving on with Layla. Why do you still tolerate him?"

My mom blinks slowly, tears gathering in her eyes. "I don't know. A part of me has trouble accepting that I chose so poorly. It's hard to live in that reality. I hate feeling like . . . a failure."

"Mom." Tears bloom in my own eyes. "You're not a failure. You've rebuilt yourself a beautiful life. And I think you did pretty okay with me."

A wet laugh blows out of her. "Are you kidding? You are my biggest triumph. I would choose it all again for you."

I wipe at my eyes. "Then why do you talk to him?"

"I . . . I don't know. I felt like I made my bed, you know."

"Fuck the bed!" Aunt Teresa roars. "You left the bed. It's gone. You have a new one!"

"Yeah, fuck the bed!" Whitney roars drunkenly.

Mom turns her watery gaze on me. "I'm so sorry. I wasn't thinking of it the way you described. Like I was choosing. Rikki, I choose you always." Something hardens in her eyes. She pulls out her phone. "Okay."

"Okay?" I repeat, confused.

She sucks a tooth. "Yeah. Okay. Yeah. Let's block him."

"Fuck yeah!" Whitney encourages.

I blink at her in disbelief. "What? You're—you're going to block him too?"

My mom smiles, nodding now. "Yeah. Fuck yeah," she says, parroting Whitney.

"Just like that?" I squeak.

Mom peers into my eyes, her gray ones bright with resolve. "Just like that," she says simply.

Tears spill down my cheeks.

"Block him. Block him. Block him!" Whitney's chanting. My (now-emotional) aunt joins in.

I tap open the text thread with my father. There are hundreds of unanswered messages. I open his contact info. My mom hands me her phone. I pull up the same window and hand it back to her.

"Ready?" she says.

I nod.

"One," she starts.

"Two."

"Three."

We press the block button. Whitney and my aunt scream like Taylor Swift just walked into the room.

My mom grins, pushing her chair out, swiping at her eyes. "Honesty is hard, and we should all do it more! It's only 9:20—we should go do the Stratosphere jump! Let's start off the New Year fearlessly, bitches!"

I snort. "Mom, you did not just call us bitches."

◆ ◆ ◆

By 10:30 we're all decked out in green jumpsuits and a plethora of different harnesses to jump off the top of the tallest hotel in Vegas. I'm sweating in a way that can only be described as profusely.

Whitney goes first. Then my aunt. While my aunt is going, my mom pulls me into a tight hug. She tells me she'll love me no matter how mean I am to her, and that no matter how uncomfortable or upset she gets when I tell her things she doesn't want to hear, she still wants to hear them. I laugh and tell her I love her too. And apologize for being moody tonight.

I'm not usually a moody person.

I'm not usually one to snap at people I love.

I'm not *usually* one to wear a trench coat around the house.

When it's my turn to jump, I step out onto the ledge and pause, taking a second to acknowledge the incredible view of the strip 835 feet up.

I'm not afraid of views. I'm simply afraid of jumping from them. I'm afraid of the integrity of the ropes. Ropes aren't people. *They don't care about saving us.*

I wonder where Reed is right now. Probably at a supercool party full of celebrities with hit movies and shows. I haven't heard from him since the night of his premiere. Not an email. A double tap on the 'gram. Nothing.

All thirteen episodes of *Elizabeth Ross* were spectacular. It's got a lot of award buzz. Rome Overland's been on every damn talk show (I've watched them all). He's been seen around a lot with his costar

Eliza (the beautiful, super nice woman I met at the wedding, who plays Elizabeth). Paparazzi photos of them pop up in my fucking "Suggested" on Instagram.

Sometimes I imagine I can smell him when I walk into the office in LA, and then I wander around, sniffing like a deranged human bloodhound.

And then I remind myself what we could have right now *was not what I wanted.* What we could have was making me perpetually sad. I *told him* to let us go.

I don't want to let go.

But I *can* stop moping. I can stop being mad at myself for doing the healthy thing. I can give myself a fresh start. A fresh chance to be happy.

I close my eyes as the wind tousles my hair.

Universe, you were really generous with me this year. Thank you for the good times.

I learned a lot of shit. I teleported. I confronted people. I fell in love. I sold a show. I'm running a show.

I'm sorry I ever doubted you. Here's to more in the new year. Here's to being ridiculously honest with everyone I care about. Or might end up caring about.

Dating's always going to be scary. There's no controlling that. So what do I really have to lose? Here's to being fucking fearless.

My own frenzied heartbeat fills my ears. I open my eyes, step off the platform, and scream.

At 11:59 p.m. the four of us are back in the hotel room, gathered around the TV to watch the ball drop. At 12:01 a.m. my phone pings with an email.

61 | CORRESPONDENCE

SUBJECT: feeling inspired the sequel

Reed Tyler <RTYLER48@gmail.com> January 1

I finished a book!

Thought you should be the first one to read it since you're the coauthor. Feel free to make any edits or changes you see fit.

x Derek

Message in a Bottle. D1 Full Manuscript.docx

—

Effervescent delight fizzles through me as I stare at my phone screen. I feel like a Nintendo character who just swallowed a star. My family doesn't register the change, so I must not be a fluorescent flashing blob.

I tilt my head back toward the celling of our hotel room.

I'm up all night reading Reed's book.

Our book.

He's gone over the front half, smoothing it out, fitting it into a more classic story structure. A month into his version of the story, while the couple temporarily both live in New York, Renee is called to her new job in LA. They break up, and it's gut wrenching. But in time, they go on to date other people, and the two of them fall in love with two *separate* people who aren't each other.

We jump five years, and they're both married—to those people they fell in love with. Derek's on Broadway. He's been in a slew of extremely successful movies, but his true love is theater, and he's playing Hamilton.

Renee has spearheaded four successful three-plus season shows. She's still in LA. When she travels to New York for work, Renee goes to see Derek in *Hamilton.* She imagines that he can see her from the stage. It feels like he's looking right at her, but she doesn't text him, and he doesn't get in contact with her.

She goes to see the show three more times before flying back to LA.

Derek religiously watches everything Renee makes.

I'm sobbing.

We jump another five years. Renee's divorced. She's forty. She's alone in a beautiful house with her dog, making dinner when her phone pings.

It's Derek Roosevelt out of the blue . . . sharing his location.

We jump to Derek. He's on a plane. He's been divorced for a year and a half, and he's decided that the joys of Broadway are no longer a good enough reason to keep him in New York. He's moving back to California. When he's an hour out from LAX, he shares his location with Renee.

It's stupid. He doesn't know what the fuck he's doing, but he's doing it because what does he have to lose?

Renee hasn't heard from Derek in ten years. But his location reads that he's in Vegas? She realizes his dot is moving. *He's on a plane.*

Renee doesn't think. She just grabs her jacket. From experience, she knows he flies United. Only Alaska and United fly direct out of EWR, and that's his airport of choice. She googles the flights out of EWR to LAX from the two airlines and confirms that a United flight is landing in an hour at LAX.

Renee's at baggage claim when the flight lands. She's waiting at the foot of the escalator when Derek comes down. Their eyes meet, and they smile at each other. It's been ten years, but at the same time, it's *only been ten years*. They have so much to catch up on. So much that they've missed. They've led so many different lives since they last spoke, but there's still so much life they could do together.

They start dating again.

They fall in love like they never fell out of it.

Because maybe they never did.

I finish at noon on January 1. Whitney is still asleep, and my mom is just getting up to shower. I feel like I just lived a whole microcosm life in between last night and today.

I spend three weeks editing the book after work hours. We're outlining the last two episodes for season one of *Love Today*, and the writing room's been extra chaotic. I'm preparing to launch my spin-off of the *Love Today* podcast: *Chaotic, Stupid, Love with Rose Thyme*. The name's still a pop-culture reference: *Crazy, Stupid, Love* is a rom-com classic. I've spent the last three months prepping the *Love Today* listeners for the shift. The empty *Chaotic, Stupid, Love* feed already has fifty thousand subscribers, and our socials have been growing steadily since my announcement.

I'm bringing Victor with me, which is fantastic, so the show will basically be the same, operating under a different name, free of the strings that came along with corporate management. Victor's been prepping the back end of things, creating a new website, a blog to be our version of the Love Today column, and hiring a team for our socials.

The relationship therapist on the *Love Today* TV adaptation has an LMFT podcast that's also called *Chaotic, Stupid, Love*, so the two will feed in and out of each other nicely once the show eventually comes out (fingers crossed) over Christmas.

All that to say.

It takes me a while to get back to Reed. But I do.

—

SUBJECT: Re: feeling inspired the sequel

Rikki Romona <rikkirolling28@gmail.com> January 22

This is so beautiful. Congratulations, Reed, I have no words.

Well, I did an editing pass of the manuscript and it's attached here. But I have no words for the way you shaped our nonsense into art. *I love it.*

Thank you for sharing with me. I'm so proud of you. Please don't worry about giving me an author credit. This is your baby! Air quotes author my ass.

I feel like I see you all over the place these days. You're killing it. I hope all is well!

x Renee

—

SUBJECT: re: re: feeling inspired the sequel

Reed Tyler <RTYLER48@gmail.com> February 5

Your edits were inspired. Thank you so much for taking the time to read it. I'm doing one more pass, and I'll be going on submission with it in March.

x Derek

—

SUBJECT: Re: re: re: re: feeling inspired the sequel

Rikki Romona <rikkirolling28@gmail.com> February 18

That's so exciting! Good luck! I know it's going to get snatched up. Who will you submit as? Derek? Rome? New pen name for this one?

x Renee

—

SUBJECT: re: re: re: re: re: re: feeling inspired the sequel

Reed Tyler <RTYLER48@gmail.com> February 19

I'm thinking Reed Tyler.

—

SUBJECT: Re: re: re: re: feeling inspired the sequel

Rikki Romona <rikkirolling28@gmail.com> February 19

It's a great name for a writer.

62 | DOG WEDDING

Earth Day crept up on me.

We're getting ready to move into filming for *Love Today*. I'm prepping to be uprooted again so I can be present on set. But first things first: My mom is getting married. Yes, I told her wedding prep was burning me out, but let's be real, I was in too deep by New Year's to let go of the reins. This dog wedding is my weird, quirky child.

I have my handy clipboard clutched against my chest as I watch Mom and Layla from the edge of the lavish white tent we put up in the park. They're doing a couple's version of the "willow" choreography from Taylor Swift's Eras Tour, and it's the best first dance I've ever seen. They're wearing green capes and clutching glowing orbs as they prance around each other, lip-synching, posing to all the sharp accents in the music. A good half of the guests are watching from their seats with their dogs, but the youths present are sitting at the edge of the portable wooden dance floor, cheering Mom and Layla on.

Micah and Jordyn are at a table toward the front of the tent, near the dance floor. They have a brand-new baby girl named Celaena back in New Jersey (currently staying with Micah's parents). I made it to the hospital about eight hours after she was born.

Jordyn insisted on flying out here for my mother's second wedding despite my many assurances that it would be fine if she missed it. She gave birth two months ago!

Whitney and Glenn are here too (obviously). I've stopped giving them couples sessions. Whitney assured me that they'd find a new therapist. I don't know if she has, and it's taken everything in me not to ask. But I haven't. I have to trust that she'll be able to do what's best for her and her husband.

I've been working hard at being a better version of myself. I've been engaging with the people I work with. Opening up about my personal life in the writers' room. Hanging out with them *outside of work*. I never did that at *The Minute*. I had work acquaintances that I knew nothing about. It changes the game, having real friends at work.

I've been spending more time with my mom. Telling her when things annoy me. And I've been making an effort to accept compliments when they're given rather than chucking them off as fake or insincere. I've been doing CBT (cognitive behavioral therapy) paired with EMDR (eye movement desensitization and reprocessing) to dig into that.

Being on the therapist side of EMDR feels like being the "guy in the chair," directing your top agent to reach their objective and take down their demons in the process.

Being on the patient side of EMDR is like lying awake on an operating table, glowering at your own insides. Not quite as fun or rewarding; but hell, if we didn't uncover and work through some shit, that should have been glaringly obvious.

I'm bad at compliments because I don't think I deserve good things. And I think I don't deserve good things because eight-year-old Rikki thinks she's a failure. She failed her mother when she failed to successfully reform her father, and she's still in here with me.

Once I pulled that wound out from the depths of my chest, we were able to start reframing her narrative, and, in turn, start to reframe the way I walk through the world.

I've been stuck on that mental loop my entire life. I couldn't outrun it. I couldn't outsmart it with my degrees. I had to face it like everyone else. And if I'd never met Reed, and my fucking magic journal, I don't know how long it would have taken me to look it in the eye. To admit to myself that I have issues that I need help to conquer. And for that I will always be grateful.

The guests and I cheer as the "willow" dance finishes, and the DJ opens up the floor. I grin as people swarm around my mom and stepmom. The two of them are in gold to honor their favorites—golden retrievers (you can't make this shit up). I'm wearing a white vintage swing dress with black polka dots (in honor of dalmatians) that my mom picked out. Layla's sister and maid of honor, Melody, is in a white poodle skirt with her hair in tight curls (poodles). There's a whole slew of people lined up along the right side of the tent with their pups for our dog photographer. Everyone looks so happy. *I think I did good.*

We're about thirty-five minutes into the dance party portion of this wedding when my mom gets up on stage with her bouquet and exchanges words with the DJ. I squint at her from my seat next to Jordyn. We've been catching up on her new life as a mom.

"What is she doing?" I mumble. "There's nothing on the schedule until after dinner when we do the cake cutting and karaoke hour."

The DJ picks up the mic. "All right, folks, time for the bouquet toss."

I snort, shooting Jordyn a look. "Is she kidding? This is a queer wedding. Why are we engaging in this hetero nonsense?"

Jordyn shrugs. "It's your mom's wedding. She gets to do what she wants!"

"HOT TO GO!" blasts from the speakers. "Single ladies! You're up! Get out here on the dance floor!"

I sigh and wander onto the floor. There's a few uncomfortable late-teenage, maybe early twenties women out here with me (my mom's friends' kids), but no *adult* adults. My mom waves to me as I shuffle to the right edge of the floor. She spins around, and I groan as her pink bouquet spirals right for me. All I have to do is extend my arms, and it lands in my hands without any effort. *Oh boy.*

Does she have a plant she's trying to set me up with?

To her dismay, I haven't been dating. I haven't wanted to, and I've been so busy anyway. I pad over to the front of the floor next to the DJ. Layla walks onto the faux wood with a chair and gestures to my mom with a flourish to sit. Our guests get out of their seats, closing in around the perimeter to watch the theatrics. They're all giggles and cheers as Layla makes a show of getting under my mother's gold dress and removes a shiny pink garter with her teeth. I chuckle as Layla does a little victory dance.

"All right, we have our bouquet girl!" the DJ chimes in. "Our maid of honor! I believe her mother told me she's straight! So, let's get all the single guys who date women up here!"

I pull the bouquet up to block my face as a blush creeps up my chest. I'm scared of the sheer number of divorced sixty-plus men present that could wander out onto the floor. Behind me, Layla climbs onto the stage with the sequined pink garter. She puts a hand on my shoulder. "Rikki, are you okay? No pressure here. Your mom thought this would be fun."

I look up at her and laugh awkwardly. "I'm okay. It's fine. I'll just tell whoever gets it to put it on my wrist." Layla squeezes my arm and stands up as "Shake It Off" bursts from the speakers.

I swallow and peek out at the suitors. I scan past three late-teen, early twenties youths too. And, oof, two sixty-plus fellows. I take an alarmed step back, ramming into the stage and falling on my ass along the edge as my eyes latch onto Reed, standing behind them all. Shock spears through me. Chills race down my limbs as his cyber gaze locks with mine. He's in a black fitted suit. Clean shaven. The sides of his thick auburn hair are buzzed, and the top is long. My heart twists as his lips press into his adorable, dimpled, closed-mouth smile.

When Layla tosses the garter in Reed's direction, I know this has been fucking rigged. He catches it easily. Reaching an arm up and snatching it out of the air, without even breaking eye contact. Warmth blooms across my chest.

"Legend has it!" The DJ comes back on. "The couple who completes the garter cycle are blessed with romantic luck for the next year. You two up for this?"

I think I've seen this film before. Someone's brought the chair back to center stage. I throw up my thumb without looking away from Reed, and he does the same. Jet's "Are You Gonna Be My Girl" erupts from the speakers as we meet in the center of the floor.

My mouth splits into a smile. "What the hell are you doing here?"

His lips tilt up. "I'm your plus-one."

I laugh, sitting back into the chair as he lowers onto his knee with the garter.

"You comfortable with this?"

"Just keep the show PG, sailor. The sun's out."

He picks up my foot and slips off my red heel. Tingling threads of heat dance up my leg from where his fingers brush my skin. Reed tastefully slips the garter up over my toes, arch, and heel as the photographer's camera flashes. Then his hands disappear under my swing dress. He carefully leads it up, over my knee. I press my smile into a purse as his fingers caress my upper thigh under the cover of my skirt. Hot sparks tornado around my abdomen. He winks as he releases the garter, and I gasp in a shallow breath as he drags his nails down the inside of my thigh, over the length of my leg, before extracting his arm from my dress.

Reed stands to an abundance of cheers around the room and innocently offers me his hand. "Are You Gonna Be My Girl" is still blaring from the speakers as he tugs me off the chair, and we explode into movement with the beat. Twisting and turning across the floor as the song crescendos, and the other guests converge around the DJ. It feels like we're out there lip-synching and giggling at each other for an eternity. But eventually the song ends and shifts to "Lover." We naturally slow our roll to a snail-paced mosey.

I smile at him. I haven't stopped smiling. I don't think I physically could right now.

Nope, just tried. Can't.

I have no idea what this visit is about, but it's absolutely wonderful to see him in person after all this time spent watching him from afar. Seven months. It's been almost seven months.

"It's nice to see you IRL."

He smiles freely back. "Likewise, Renee."

"You look great."

"You look gorgeous."

I laugh through my 100-watt smile. "Thanks. I'm gonna circle back to *what in the hell are you doing here, Reed Tyler*? You get lost on your way to a meeting?"

He leads me into a slow twirl and catches my hand. "I was invited."

I arch a brow. "Unlikely."

"I'm Rose Thyme's plus-one?"

"Rose Thyme? Is she a girl or a bread?"

"Am I sensing some jealousy?"

"Depends. You like her?"

"Oh yeah, she planned this whole thing."

"Event planner?"

"Nah, writer. She's got a show coming out on Netflix, top of next year, starts shooting in May. She just went independent with her very popular relationship podcast. Haven't pitched her on my company yet, but I think we could really help her out."

I snort. "Are you here to launch a business proposal?"

"Oh no, I'm here because I'm in love with her."

My heart glows white in my chest, and *the* smile—oh god, it threatens to overtake my entire face. At this point I'm basically just teeth and eyes. "I thought we talked about this whole love thing."

He grins, twirling me again as the music shifts to a Frankie Valli classic. "Oh, we did." My dress flowers out and falls back to my legs.

"So—"

"I'm back," Reed finishes.

I huff a hesitant laugh. "What do you mean?"

"I'm done shooting in New York. I'm moving back into my house. I'd like to ask you out."

He grabs my hands, moving us into a rhythmic side-to-side shuffle, expanding our arms and bringing them back together with the music, as my heart loses its shit in my chest.

"Reed . . ." I stare into his twinkling eyes. "I leave for Atlanta to shoot the show in two weeks."

The amused knot rolls up his cheek. "Move in with me."

I choke on a laugh. "Did you not just hear me about Atlanta?"

"Apparently the only way we can test for long-term compatibility is by living together? I believe someone told me that over and over and over again last year?"

I loll my head. "Yeah, but not for two weeks, and you don't even know if I'm dating someone."

"Oh, I wasn't assuming anything. I have a reputable source."

"Who?"

"Jordyn . . . and Whitney."

I swivel around, looking for either of them, and find them both on the floor in different spots with their significant others, staring at us. Whitney quickly looks away, but Jordyn grins and Micah shoots me a thumbs-up.

I turn back to Reed's laser beams. "You're not dating anyone?"

"Do you count?"

"No."

"Then no."

"Not Eliza?"

He laughs. "We're friends. She dates women, Rick. She has a very public girlfriend. I guess you're not following her on socials."

My mouth pops open. "Oh."

He nods. "Yeah." He double-twirls me and catches my hip.

"So what, you show up here out of nowhere, and you're expecting to just pick up where we left off. Pretty bold."

"We've been through this." He pulls me tight against his torso, one hand firm against my lower back, and hovers his mouth over my ear. "I'm obnoxiously confident." He coaxes us side to side, in beat with the song. "Will you go out with me? We're overdue for an official fourth date."

A disbelieving laugh flies out of me.

I want to say yes. I want to say yes with every fiber of my being, but we're just going to end up doing long distance *again.*

He arches a brow. "What would you say if you weren't leaving for Atlanta in two weeks?"

Heat winds up my spine. "I'd say fuck yes, Reed, I've missed you every goddamn day. I feel like you're mine, and I know that's not true, and it's bad to say, but I hate thinking about anyone else with you." His hands slip down to the grooves of my hips, and his fingers tighten possessively.

"I am yours," he says.

I swallow hard as my body lights in response. Our lips are an inch apart, and it's taking all my willpower to hold the space.

"What's next right now for you?" I ask, desperate for a less depressing topic.

"Well, the book just sold—"

I pull back, beaming at him. "Oh my god, Reed! Congratulations!"

"—and I'm going to Atlanta in two weeks."

I blink, processing that. "Wait, what?"

"I got a job there."

I stop dancing as my heart rate picks up, thumping against my chest so hard it's all I can hear for a good five seconds. "What . . . what job?"

"You remember how I was on that improv team back in the day with the host of *Attached at the Hip* and now Oh Brother Audio produces their podcast?"

"Uh . . . yeah?"

"The cohost of the podcast—do you remember her name is Dawn?"

My jaw unhinges as I work to connect the dots. *Dawn cohosts the* Attached at the Hip *podcast?*

"She was also in that improv group. We're also friends."

I bulge my eyes as he tugs me back into motion, and we start our millionth circle around the floor. "Are you talking about my Dawn? Coproducer and writer Dawn on *Love Today*?"

"That Dawn."

"What?"

"She thought I'd be great in one of the parts on the new show she was looking to cast."

I grip his wrists. "You're shitting me."

"I auditioned two months ago at the office."

"No you didn't! Why didn't you tell me? Why haven't I seen your name?"

"I asked if she could do me a favor and use a pseudonym on the audition sheets for now."

"A pseudonym for your fucking pseudonym?"

He grins. "Exactly. We had lunch. I told her what was going on with us. She said it'd be her pleasure to help me out, so I could tell you myself."

I am in shock. My jaw is on the floor. I feel like I just got hit by a truck. But like in a good way. Where I didn't die or get hurt. I am shook to my very core.

"What are you telling me? Are you in the main cast, and I don't fucking know about it?"

"I'm playing the show equivalent of Micah."

I gasp, yanking my hands up to my face to cover my open mouth as tears flood my eyes.

"No, you're not," I blurt.

"Yes, I am."

"You're coming to Atlanta with me for the next . . . five months?"

He shrugs, smiling. "If you'll have me."

My body is shuddering. This is too much. This is not real. This is too good. I glance up at the tent. Do I really get to have this?

Reed pulls me back to him and holds me against his chest. "I thought you were doing movies now?" I croak.

"Rikki, I've spent the last six months rearranging my life because I want to walk it in lockstep with you, even if it means taking a longer route to wherever we're going."

I'm high. Floating. Levitating as we speak. "And what if it doesn't work out?" I say it with a huge smile because something in me knows it will. I've never had a gut feeling as strong as I do in this moment, contradicting the words coming out of my mouth.

He smirks, pulling back so he can look me in the face. "It's gonna work out."

"Confident, bordering on cocky."

"The universe is on our side."

I try to purse my lips. It's borderline painful with the smile situation I'm dealing with. "What makes you say that?"

"I've been being stalked by a journal that says it knows you, since September?" My eyes bulge. "Looks a lot like the one you got in the goody bag at Willem's wedding. Ring a bell?"

I gawk at him. "No shit." Shake my head. "No. *Way.* You're in the creepy journal club?"

He bites his smile down. "Oh, so you do know it?"

We've stopped moving, mid-dance floor, standing together, in hold. "Oh yeah, that thing's been helping us out for a while. Have you used it?"

"I have."

"Nasty side effects."

"Nakedness was a surprise. You really were thinking on your feet when that happened."

I snort. "I really was. Where'd you go that first time?"

"To you." He tugs us back into the music, twirling me into a quick burst of pirouettes as I gape some more.

"What! When?" I bleat mid-spin. I stop myself with a hand on his chest. "How could you deny me the satisfaction of making fun of you for also being an accidental streaker!"

"The morning of the *Elizabeth Ross* premiere. I was flying out that day anyway—"

"Oh my god."

"What?"

"That morning there was a naked guy! Were you the creepy naked guy in our bushes?"

He *pffts*.

"I couldn't see any details, just the outline of a naked guy! I emailed the HOA about you."

Laughter rumbles through him. "A good Samaritan in your parking lot lent me their cell, and I got Oliver to pick me up."

"I'm so sad you didn't come to me."

He renders his expression back to a chill grin. (He's so talented.) "We were still in our awkward gray breakup era. I needed to show up looking impressive, not huddling naked in a bush."

I shake my head. "Reed, I'm sure you're already aware of this, but you look very impressive naked."

He rolls his eyes back into his head, before abruptly twirling me twice, catching me over his arm, and whipping me back up to his chest.

"I used it to come out here and audition three times for the *Love Today* role. And once to see my brother. I knew I couldn't come to you until I had a solid plan in place. But good news: All-knowing stalker journal says we can use the last four jumps together."

A bordering manic laugh spills out of me. "This is *wild*. What is happening!"

Reed tips his forehead to mine as he sways us side to side. "What do you say, Romona? Are you in?"

"In, as in moving in?"

He chuckles. "In, as in moving in."

I wind my arms around his neck. "If we do this, we do it full force. No secrets. No rules. No compartmentalizing."

"Renee." Reed's voice dips low as his fingers slide back into my hip bones and squeeze. "I'm so excited for full force."

"You're going to have to meet all my people."

He's grinning harder than I've ever seen him grin. "I so look forward to it."

"I'm going to introduce you as my boyfriend."

"Thrilled to have my title back."

I slide my nose over his. "You're going to have to join the WWU."

"That's all I've wanted this whole time. I've been playing the long con."

I chuckle a centimeter from his mouth as "Good Luck, Babe!" comes over the speakers. "And you're coming back to my place tonight."

He tugs me flush against his torso, smiling as he moves our hips slowly from left to right. "So, I'm hearing a *yes* on the moving in?"

I micronod, dipping my forehead into his. "R. Tyler. I am so obnoxiously in love with you."

He sucks in a sharp breath. "Thank the fucking Disney gods, you finally said it."

I explode into a cloud of gold confetti as our mouths collide.

[Rikki Romona: Thirty-plus, almost not single, dies of happiness dancing to Chappell Roan at dog wedding dressed as dalmatian when man she hasn't seen in seven months asks her to move in with him with zero pretense. Swept off feet. Not at all creeped out.]

63 | EPILOGUE

17 MONTHS LATER

"Can we wear our trenches to the first event?"

I laugh from the walk-in closet. Reed comes up behind me, twists his arms around my torso, and nips my ear. "Only if we wear cute outfits underneath them. We can't walk into the Union Square Barnes & Noble as a flasher couple."

He presses his lips into my neck. "It's in the book."

I let go of the hanger I'm examining to lean into his chest. "Yeah, but stop one, no one's going to have read the book."

His chest rumbles against my back. "Mm, good point."

Message in a Bottle by Reed Tyler and Rose Thyme (we needed at least one of our known names in there for brand recognition) comes out in three days. We have an eleven-stop book tour over the next two weeks, and then we come back to our place in Atlanta to start shooting season two of *Love Today*. Season one was kind of a Netflix rom-com phenomenon? The internet was a tither with excitement and memes. It was such a trip. And Reed has joined the *Love Today* writers' room for season two.

"Should we bring the journal?" Reed murmurs, lips pressed to the slope of my shoulder. I stifle a shiver. "One jump left. Maybe we use it at the end of the tour, before we come back?"

I glance up at the leather notebook on the top shelf of our closet that now has both of our names carved into the back. Our trips with it *together* have been some of the most magical days of my life. Saying goodbye, in tandem with the release of our book about a long-distance relationship feels pretty poetic. "That sounds perfect," I say quietly.

Reed nods behind me, before scraping his teeth up the slope of my neck. "I thought so too."

I exhale a breathy laugh. "Are we going to leave packing to the very last minute?"

"Yes?" He kisses my cheek, and my chin, all the while directing us back out toward our bedroom. I swivel my head to the right and catch his full mouth. Glittering heat dances up my torso.

Ed Sheeran's playing lightly from Reed's Spotify.

When we step out into our blue-walled room, I stop short. There's a long, flat, rectangular package wrapped in brown paper propped up against the shams on our blue-and-gold comforter.

I laugh. He's made a habit of bestowing random, extremely thoughtful gifts on me this past year, and they always bring me so much joy. "What'd you do now?"

He casts his eyes skyward for a moment before pulling me tight against his chest again.

"We've had a good year—would you agree?" he says over my ear. I nod, closing my eyes as his voice rumbles through me. "The show got picked up for a second season after a week on the air. We wrote a book. I feel like living together's going pretty well."

I spin to face him, slipping my hands into his back pockets. "Agreed. We're surprisingly good at this."

He raises his brow. "I never doubted us."

I scoff.

"Renee Granger. I know you stressed, I know you tired, I know you hangry, I know you happy, I know you sad. I love every iteration of you."

"You can't love me hangry. I'm so mean."

"Hangry Rikki is sexy."

I laugh.

"She loves to roast the shit out of me."

"She's cutting."

"She's hot and quick on her feet."

"My favorite Reed is post shower. He's cuddly and vulnerable and sexy all at the same time."

"All right, we're losing the plot here—I like this thing we've got going. And I think it's worth celebrating. Do you agree?"

I nod. "Yeah."

"Okay, go unwrap it."

I walk over to the bed and start to tear the paper off.

"Oh! Is it a bottle-cap art?" The little triangle of paper I ripped from the middle has revealed a palette of gold, deep-metallic blue, and silver that matches our bedroom aesthetic. I stuff my hand through the hole and rip it in both ways. It's words—It's—

In giant metallic gold script against a backdrop that's been painted to look like the universe . . . it says *something real.* The stars in the background behind the words form an infinity sign.

Emotion pricks at my eyes. "Reed, it's perfect."

I glance back at him. He's sitting on the edge of the bed now, holding an early copy of *Message in a Bottle*, mouth rolled up the side of his face.

I narrow my eyes. "What? What's happening?"

He slides off the bed, onto one knee, and holds out the book. "Rikki Romona. I know you're convinced you've been cursed to be forever alone, but if you let me do the honor, I'd love to prove you very, very wrong."

I laugh and hop off the bed, heart thrashing in my chest. I take the book from him. "What now?"

He snorts. "I'm thinking you open it."

I inhale a stilted breath. "Are you sure?"

His mouth curls at the edges. "Don't fucking play with me, Romona. Open the goddamn book."

I pull open the hardcover to find that he's carved up the entire inside and painted it white. He's created a sort of circular word-spattered dais out of the pages to hold the coolest ring I've ever seen.

The gemstones are yellow and orange. They're cut like a sun, glittering in the light with tiny white diamonds laced between. The dark-gold band is made of delicate twisting pieces that rotate over and around themselves. My hand's shaking as I pick it up. Engraved on the inside in delicate script, it says **SEE YOU AT THE AIRPORT.**

That phrase is about to become our readers'.

But right now, in this moment, it's still just ours.

It will always be ours. I clear my throat. "What if I said no?"

Whip-fast, Reed snags me up by my thighs. I'm laughing maniacally as we fall onto the bed. He hovers over me, smiling as I catch my breath.

I sober quickly, soaking in the adoration beaming out of his eyes. "I love you so much."

He leans in closer, pushing a lock of hair off my face. "Is that a yes?"

I lock my legs around his torso, flip him onto his back. "Okay, yeah, but if we get married, like . . . what are the rules? Are we only married when we're in the same state? And like friends when we're not?"

ACKNOWLEDGMENTS

Dude. Book Four. This was a humdinger. What a time. I've written an adult novel! Who am I? Like a full-blown adult or something? I wrote spice? What a milestone. I'm proud. This idea came to me at the airport after losing hope in humanity via yet another wave on the dating apps, and I had so much fun crafting these characters and dreaming up very intensely themed weddings. Huge thank you to my agent, Suzie, who gave me the most encouraging feedback ever when I sent her the first chunk of words and, of course, to the fabulous Olivia Coleman! Thank you to the team at New Leaf!

Thank you to my editors Maria Gomez and Mackenzie Walton!

Huge thank you to Kat O'Keefe, my critique partner extraordinaire, who helped me talk through so many aspects of this novel. She is a writing wizard, and I'm so grateful to have her in my life.

Thank you, Katie McCormick-Huhn, for your endless support and enthusiasm for this idea! Thank you for reading it in its early, wild form, and giving me such wonderful feedback.

Thank you, Natasha Polis, for listening to me play-by-play a million different parts of this book over the phone and reading an early draft when I was desperate for your thoughts!

Thank you, Cynthia Ye, for listening to me babble incoherently about every random stage of this novel creation on our dog walks every day, and inspiring me to write a neighbor bestie for Rikki!

Thank you, Jenna Presto, Kristina Marjieh, and Julia Friley, for listening to me pitch this book back in 2023 and sharing my enthusiasm. Thank you, Chloe Laverson, Holly Springhorn, Caroline Springhorn, and Allison Gottlieb for being so supportive and enthusiastic about the things I make!

Thank you everyone in "women's group" I haven't mentioned yet: Danielle, Kayla, Taylor, Natalee, Taya, and Becca, for being such strong, kick-ass, empowering female presences in my life. Y'all inspire me so much.

Thank you, Tessa Netting, for inviting me to your spectacular, beautiful wedding—literally the coolest thing I've ever seen!

Mom and Nana, as always, thank you for being my unending cheerleaders and support team. Love you!

Siblings! Olivia and Paul, thanks for proudly talking about my books to the people in your lives. It means a lot. Love yous.

To my plethora of fabulous cousins, one of y'all has gotten married almost every year from 2001 on. Thank you for inviting me to your gorgeous tristate area style weddings, all of which were magical and informed the backdrop of various moments in this book. Love y'all!

To everyone in the Those Forking Fangirls fam, thank you so much for lighting up my life every week with your hilarious commentary and unending support. I love y'all so much.

To my YouTube fam and all the OG PolandbananasBOOKS watchers out there, thank you for sticking with me for all these years. I love you. You're the reason I'm able to do the things I love. I will forever be grateful that you decided I was worth paying attention to.

To the book-interest girlies who have shared any of my books on socials, TikTok, or YouTube over the years. Thank you! Your support means the world to me. Thank you for helping me share my book children with the world.

To all the readers who found me through the book world, oh my gosh, hi! Thank you for reading my work. I hope it made you happy and feel seen or heard in some way that brightened your day. I hope you laughed. I'm so grateful that you're here. Thank you for picking up my first full adult romance! My first three rom-com novels are considered crossover—they follow women in their early twenties! I can't believe I'm thirty-four, y'all; what a trip. If you want to find me on the interwebs, I'm always around to chat (@xtinemay on socials), and I host a podcast called *Those Forking Fangirls*.

To all the single thirty-somethings out there still scouring the earth for their soulmate, the struggle is real—I feel you. I am with you. I hope you found some solace and hope via Rikki's journey.

You are not alone. <3

xoxo
2025 Christine

About the Author

Photo © 2022 Jenna Clare

Christine Riccio is an author, YouTuber, and all-around book guru with a degree in film and television from Boston University. She's the *New York Times* bestselling author of *Again, but Better*, *Attached at the Hip*, and *Better Together*. Christine started making videos about books on YouTube in 2010, and now her channel, PolandbananasBOOKS, has over 450,000 book-loving subscribers. For thirteen years and counting, she has been making comedic book reviews, vlogs, and sketches, as well as writing videos to chronicle the creation of her novels. She also cohosts the weekly podcast *Those Forking Fangirls*, where she talks all things nerdy in books, TV, movies, and pop culture. Although originally from New Jersey, she now lives in Los Angeles.